Carol Rivers

Eve of the Isle

POCKET
BOOKS

LONDON • NEW YORK • TORONTO • SYDNEY

First published in Great Britain by Simon & Schuster, 2009
This edition first published by Pocket Books, 2009
An imprint of Simon & Schuster UK Ltd
A CBS COMPANY

1 3 5 7 9 10 8 6 4 2

Simon & Schuster UK Ltd
1st Floor
222 Gray's Inn Road
London WC1X 8HB

www.simonandschuster.co.uk

Simon & Schuster Australia
Sydney

A CIP catalogue record for this book is available from the British Library

ISBN: 978-1-84739-361-6

Typeset in Bembo by Ellipsis Books Limited, Glasgow
Printed and bound in Great Britain by
Cox & Wyman Ltd, Reading, Berkshire

Eve is dedicated to the Columbia Road days

Acknowledgements

I would like to thank those kind people who have shared their intimate memories and colourful descriptions of the East End lascars with me. And again, thanks to the libraries who made the research of London's first mobile police force and the poignant plight of the capital's early twentieth-century flower-sellers such a rich and rewarding experience.

Chapter One

Isle of Dogs, East London.
Friday 6th January 1928

It was late at night and the cobbled streets of London's East End were awash with rain. Eve listened to the swirling, gurgling and churning of the river close by and was reminded of the legend of Old Father Thames, the spirit god of England's most noble river. Regarded as a genial and protective deity, capable of curing all kinds of ailments, the giant slumbered peacefully on the river bed. But if prematurely woken, he could rise up from his watery grave and tower menacingly over the city. The myths of her childhood, ones that she had passed down to her own twin sons, Samuel and Albert, now came back to mind as she huddled her boys close. Wet and shivering in the dark and threatening night, it seemed as though there might be substance to the old myths after all.

Eve had never seen the like of it before, though it brought back to mind the events that had led to the

Great Stink of the last century. It was said that Old Father Thames had been furious at the pollution of his beloved river by London's antiquated sewerage system. In his disgust he had consulted his brother gods on the matter. As punishment, they had unleashed the dreaded water-borne disease cholera to teach humanity the error of its ways. Many a night as a child, Eve had gone to bed in terror of the stories embellished upon by each generation. Now as the Thames crashed and crackled over the wharf edges, clawing away at the cobbles, it was seven-year-old Samuel who spoke her thoughts.

'It's Old Father Thames, ain't it, Mum? He's wakin' up.'

Eve pulled the boy closer, attempting to shelter both her sons under the drenched wool of her old coat. But the eaves of the bargee's wooden hut were no protection against wind and rain. Why had she insisted they go out tonight? Who would want posies of snowdrops in this weather?

'He's not woken, love. It'd take more than a bit of a winter's blow to wake him up.'

'He's angry, ain't he?' This from Albert who, like his twin, knew every word of the old stories by heart. ''E's gonna swallow us to def!'

'He won't do that, Albert,' Eve tried to reassure, though there was no denying the elements were in unusual turmoil.

'Looks like he will,' Albert persisted, clutching her tightly as a great wave crashed against the broken pier that rattled and creaked on its mossy stilts. 'Peg said 'er rheumatics was achin', and that always means bad weather. She said we should've stayed in wiv her.'

'Well, we didn't,' replied Eve dismissively, nevertheless recalling the warning Peg Riggs had given her only hours before the storm. For all the years they had lodged with Peg in her dilapidated cottage on Isle Street, she had never been far wrong when predicting the weather. Her aches and pains gained momentum when bad weather was brewing. Eve was also aware that Albert would exploit any opportunity to avoid helping her sell the flowers and watercress that was the family's hard-earned living. 'Now, best foot forward,' urged Eve tugging him along.

But just as they rounded the corner, another spray gusted against them. Eve could hardly believe the conditions could have deteriorated so swiftly. Not half an hour ago, they had been forced to halt on their journey from Aldgate to the Isle of Dogs and abandon the flower basket; in the driving wind and rain it had become a heavy burden. It was only just possible to manage the lamp and when Eve had been forced to leave her profits behind, she'd had her first misgivings at ignoring Peg's warning.

As they hurried on the river continued its relentless battle with the land. If Old Father Thames had really woken, then Mother Nature was providing a full orchestra for his watery resurrection, thought Eve as she pulled a reluctant Albert alongside her.

'The river's gonna drown us! The monster's coming up!' he puffed, slowing their progress.

'There's no monster, Albert, only the river.'

'He's got all that 'air made of seaweed and a long, drippy beard. I don't want him to get me.'

'Stop it, now, love,' Eve spluttered, 'no one's going to get you. The faster we run, the sooner we'll be home.'

Albert halted and stamped his foot. 'Can't! Me legs ache from all that walkin' and standin' we done up Aldgate.'

Just then an icy spray drenched them and Albert began to wail. Eve clutched the two little bodies against her. 'Listen, we'll go another way,' she decided, grateful at least for the lamp strung over her arm, miraculously still alight. 'And take the lane, away from the river.'

Eve thought longingly of the dock cottage they shared with Peg and her other lodger, Jimmy Jones, a young runner for the paint factory. Despite its worm-eaten timbers and crumbling walls, home now seemed like heaven. She promised herself that never again would she risk putting her boys into such discomfort and danger. Not that Isle Street was too distant now. But in January, when the recent falls of snow had left the streets wet and icy, the return journey from Aldgate had seemed endless.

Eve raised the Tilley and they hurried on once more. But when eerie shadows cast themselves across the unlit streets, her heart sank. The gas lamps were all extinguished! Now they were at the night's mercy with only the glow of the lamp to guide them.

Albert screamed, terrified of the dark, forcing Eve to halt. 'Hush there now, boy. Climb on my back and I'll give you a ride.' She passed the lamp to Samuel.

'Can you manage this for me, son?'

He nodded and slipped the loop over his arm. 'It ain't far now, Albert,' he encouraged his brother. 'And Peg'll be waitin' for us.'

Eve smiled gratefully at Samuel. For an instant she saw her dead husband, Raj, reflected in Samuel's rain-soaked face. There were his sparkling dark eyes and ebony skin illuminated perfectly in the light. Despite being twins, the boys were not identical. Albert had inherited her deep brown curls and rounded proportions whilst Samuel's hair grew straight and black, his long, slender limbs a mirror to his father's. For a moment Eve felt a deep longing for her dead husband. If only he were here now to help them! He would have lifted his sons easily in his arms and carried them home safely.

Resolutely, Eve pushed back her wet hair flattened against the delicate curve of her face and set off again. With the extra weight she carried, her steps were slower. Every now and then she would halt beside Samuel, and pat him encouragingly on the back.

As they went, they saw men erecting barriers at front doors and windows. Eve could hear panic in their voices. What force of nature had caused the river to rise so threateningly?

But when Samuel fell, it was with a dreadful shattering. Eve rushed to his aid. 'Samuel, did you hurt yourself?'

He climbed shakily to his feet. 'No,' he replied bravely. 'But the Tilley's broke!'

Eve drew him to her. 'Never mind, love, we'll manage.'

'There's a gap through the houses somewhere round here,' he said as they peered into the darkness. 'Me and Albert found it once.'

'Where does it lead to?'

'Down by the dock wall.'

Eve didn't reply that she disliked her sons to play anywhere near the high walls of the docks. On one side of them were deep basins of water traversed by a lifting bridge. The ships passed under when entering and it was a busy thoroughfare.

Just then Eve felt Albert shudder violently. 'Not far to go now, Albert,' she threw over her shoulder, the guilt assailing her once more. If only she had allowed them to remain with Peg! But she quickly shrugged off the emotion. The traders with whom she dealt were a hard bunch, and Albert and Samuel would grow up in their midst, having to fight if necessary, for survival. Things might have been different if their father had survived and their dreams of travelling across the sea to the golden Indian sands of Raj's homeland had matured. But now, after the passing of five long years, Eve had only the memories of those dreams to console her.

'Here's the gap, Mum! I've found it!' Samuel's small hand closed tightly over hers as he urged her to follow him. 'Step careful like over the bricks and slide down.'

Eve dropped to her knees. 'Albert, you go first.'

'Can't,' refused Albert stubbornly.

'Come on, I'll catch you,' shouted Samuel already through.

'Can't,' protested Albert again. 'Me legs won't work.'

Eve's answer this time came less gently. 'Son, if you choose to come this way to the dock walls, knowing full well I frown on that little adventure, then you can manage the effort now with my full consent. And I can tell you this, Albert Kumar, my patience is wearing thin!'

There was no hesitation now as he scrambled through and stood beside Samuel. Eve joined them and grasping hands, all three set off again.

At last they arrived at the top of Isle Street. Number three stood by itself in a deep dip. It was one of eight remaining dock cottages of an original ten; two had been reduced to rubble over the years, crumbling into the soft, unstable earth beneath. Their damp and decay was fed by a trickle of a stream that ran under their foundations, nuzzling its way to the docks beyond. Here it was occasionally blocked by a stone and then would turn in on itself and penetrate the cottage floors. To solve this problem, the leaking quarry tiles were covered in permanent layers of duckboards. It was rumoured that a big river flood would wash away Isle Street entirely – certainly number three, Peg's cottage, that nestled in its own little valley.

Lamps bobbed in the darkness. There were voices, and Eve recognized one of them. As they hurried down the slope, there came the heart-warming cussing of Peg.

Eve was not surprised to feel Albert break free of her grasp and run towards the familiar echo.

'Lordy, just look at the state of you! Get yerselves in!' commanded Peg, clad in her ancient fisherman's cape and rope threaded hood. Hoisting a lamp above their heads, she peered closely at their wet faces. 'I've been marching up and down the isle for the past three hours looking for you. A palace guard ain't had as much exercise as I've had t'night.'

'Sorry Peg, but the river's up,' Eve gasped as they hurried towards the cottage. 'I'm surprised it ain't followed us home.'

Peg put her shoulder to the wooden front door. 'I'd send it back with a slap if it did!' She pushed them inside.

Albert clung to her in the dim passage. 'Old Father Thames was gonna gobble us up.'

She cackled loudly. 'He'd spit you out, chic. The likes of you is too small to fill his plate.'

Samuel looked hopeful at the mention of food. 'What's to eat, Peg?'

'First, get them wet clothes off, lads. The stove won't light as the coke got rained on in the yard. But I put a nice bread and cheese supper upstairs for you.'

Eve began to strip off the boys' wet clothes, leaving them in only their pants and vests.

They couldn't wait to find their food.

'Go on you two, get up them stairs and under the

bedclothes to warm yourselves.' Peg's bush of frizzy grey hair sprang forth as she removed her hood and two gnarled brown fingers cuffed a drip from her long, crooked nose.

The boys ran up the stairs and Peg nodded to Eve. 'Go on, you too, my girl. Hope to Gawd yer don't get pneumonia. I knew you should have stayed with me t'night. Me rheumatics were playing me up terrible.'

Eve accepted the gentle rebuke for she knew it was warranted. It had been foolhardy to take the boys with her, but she had only meant to walk as far as Aldgate. A shower of rain was nothing to a flower-seller. It was her streak of stubborn determination that made her blind to the dangers and in losing her basket and nearly drowning her children she had paid a heavy price for not listening.

At the top of the stairs, Eve stood in the glow of the two Tilley lamps that Peg had lit, listening to the beat of the rain on the leaking roof. She could hear but not see the many drips that bounced mysteriously from the worm-eaten architraves to the bare boards below.

'Hurry up, you two and into bed,' she called as she passed the first room to her left, and entered the second.

'Jimmy ain't home, I tried his door,' said Samuel, his teeth chattering as he hurried to pull on the cut downs, second-hand men's combinations, he wore as pyjamas.

'He might be sheltering from the storm. Them deliveries he makes for the paint factory take him all over the city.' Eve knew how fond the boys were of

9

Jimmy. He was a brother to them, with no family of his own, a waif from the streets. He regarded Peg as dearly as he would a mother for without her and the shelter and love she had given him over the years, he would, he maintained, have come to no good.

'I'm going to buy meself a bicycle like Jimmy's one day,' Samuel grinned as he rolled back the warm woollen sleeves that overlapped his arms. 'Ride it all the way up to the North Pole and back again.'

'You'll need a stronger pair of legs first, my lad,' Eve smiled. 'And a smart bicycle like Jimmy's, needs saving up for.'

'It's cold at the North Pole,' commented Albert dourly, securing the baggy cloth at his waist with a large button and frowning at his brother. 'Wish I could sit by the stove. It's freezing in here.'

'You heard Peg, son,' replied his mother. 'The stove's out.'

'I bet it'll be hot still, though.'

She patted his round bottom. 'You'll be just as warm in bed.'

Eve tucked her sons beneath the worn and well-darned bedclothes draped over the two small horsehair mattresses positioned side by side on the floor. A long chintz curtain divided the room. In the second space was Eve's own brass bed. Its austerity was softened by a blanket embroidered with rainbow coloured silks. Next to this was a chest on which stood a white china jug and bowl. Four shelves overhead were filled with bottles;

Eve's own homemade remedies for ills and agues. A black framed photograph of Eve's parents, a tall young man and dark haired girl, hung on the wall, illuminated in the lamp's light.

'Peg said I ain't gonna die from being gobbled up,' Albert chattered, drawing his eiderdown up to his nose. 'I'm gonna die from nomonia instead. I just 'ope that sort of dying ain't as horrible as it would've been drownin'.'

'You're not about to die of anything.' Eve hid a rueful smile at her son's unintended humour. 'Unless it's the complaints-ague. And even then, it won't kill you, though you could be in mortal danger of getting jaw-ache.'

Samuel burst into laughter. Eve began to laugh too, and Albert finally joined in, pleased to be the centre of attention.

'Can we eat our suppers now?' Both boys eyed the two enamel plates overflowing with bread and cheese.

'Yes, but chew slowly and don't get crumbs in your beds.'

As they ate, Eve untied the tassel of the curtain, drawing it across the width of the room affording her a modicum of privacy. She was soaked to the skin and beginning to shiver uncontrollably. The noise of the rain on the roof was loud and threatening. How long would the storm last?

Taking a set of clean smalls from the bottom drawer of the chest, a warm jumper and skirt, she dried herself and dressed quickly. Her boots were ruined and wouldn't be wearable for days. Slipping her feet into her only other pair, ones that were held together by a length of coarse string, she was suddenly filled with exhaustion. From early light this morning she had been collecting and preparing the winter flowers she bought from market. The early snowdrops sold well at the picture houses and theatres alike. But she had lost all her stock tonight! It was a calamity and she cringed to think of the loss.

As she sat wearily on her bed, her eyes closed and Raj's dear face came to mind; her sailor husband who had lived here with her for three short years before his death. Somehow they had always made ends meet. Those years had been the happiest of her life.

'Mum, I've finished me supper!'

'So've I.'

Her sons' voices brought her back to reality. Drawing back the curtain, she turned down the lamp, leaving a soft glow in the room.

'Tell us a story. A river one,' said Albert, as she placed the plates to one side and sat on his mattress. 'About Old Father Thames and the Stink.'

Eve chuckled. 'After tonight I don't think I'll tell you them stories again.'

'I was only joking,' yawned Albert. 'I wasn't really afraid. There ain't no monster is there?'

'Not if you don't tempt him,' said Eve warningly. 'But if you play on the barges and fall in, you'll soon find out what Old Father Thames looks like.'

'Samuel makes me do it.' Albert peeped accusingly at his brother from behind the sheet.

'We only watch the other boys,' Samuel said hurriedly. 'We don't jump the barges.'

'I should hope not,' said Eve firmly. 'You know what happened to Tommy Higgins.'

Some years ago there had been a river fatality in Isle Street. Maude Higgins' youngest son of fifteen had missed his footing whilst thieving from one of the barges. His body was swept away by the current and gruesomely retrieved weeks later. The Higgins' six sons were rough diamonds, but they were salt of the earth and the loss of their brother had affected them deeply.

Eve indicated the bucket. 'Do you want a wee?'

'No, we done one whilst you was changing,' giggled Samuel. 'The bucket's half full already from the leak in the roof.'

'It came down on me head as I was doing one,' chuckled Albert.

They all laughed and when Eve had kissed them both, she made the sign of the cross, saying one Our Father and One Hail Mary as was their usual night-time prayer. 'Goodnight and God Bless,' she ended, 'see you in the morning, by God's good grace, Amen.'

'Amen,' replied the boys sleepily.

Tiptoeing to her small space, she took a tartan shawl from the chest. Though old and worn from its many flower-selling days, the shawl had been her mother's and gave Eve great comfort. Pinning up her long hair, she glanced in the small mirror nailed on the wall. Her large amber eyes were heavy with tiredness, shielded by the flutter of her thick brown lashes. She knew from the photograph that her dark hair and delicate bone structure were inherited from her mother. Peg always maintained that if Sarah Flynn had survived the flu epidemic of 1918, she would have preserved her Irish good looks to this day, despite the hard work and worry that had had turned her hair prematurely grey. It was down to Sarah, she insisted, that Eve was possessed of the timeless beauty of her forefathers.

Another wave of tiredness crept over her as the noise of the rain on the roof seemed to increase. She turned and trod softly over to gaze at her sleeping children. Two little boys, both beautiful in their own way. A hard life awaited them. No amount of wishing otherwise could change the fact. But she had built up many contacts over the years and preserved a good reputation. The watercress would always sell well. The posies and buttonholes too, if you knew how to present them. These gifts from the earth were bread and butter to them. At least Albert and Samuel would inherit the knowledge.

Once more she leaned to kiss them lightly, then pulling her shawl round her, made her way downstairs.

In the kitchen, she found Peg cursing loudly. A pool of dirty brown water funnelled up through the kitchen duckboards making little whirlpools and sucking noises.

'Isn't there something we can do?' Eve stood still,

her eyes wide with concern.

Peg turned round slowly, a look of resignation on her lined, worn face. She snatched the dog end from her lips and cast it into the muddy puddle. 'Watch this,' she croaked.

Eve waited as the bobbing article made its way with speed to the feet of the stove. It swirled there and Eve held her breath, praying the level would drop. But then the dog end was sucked down between the two submerged clawed black feet of the stove.

'It's risin',' said Peg. 'And fast.'

'The stream must be blocked.'

The enormity of the problem suddenly struck Eve. Once the kitchen and scullery were flooded, what would happen? Would it flow over the kitchen step?

Peg muttered under her breath, shaking her head. 'This is different, girl. We ain't had nothing like this 'afore.'

Eve nodded in agreement. It was true, the stream had never raised the duckboards to make a lake of its own. Then Peg gave a hoarse gasp. Lifting a shaking finger she pointed along the passage.

Eve blinked and blinked again. It couldn't be! A glistening tongue was creeping slowly but surely under the front door and moving towards them.

Chapter Two

Soon the water was running over the cracked linoleum and up to the stairs.

'We need to build a barricade,' said Eve, knowing as she spoke it was a ridiculous idea. The force outside the door was building, even the hinges were creaking.

'It'd have to be a big one,' sighed Peg, shaking her head. 'No, there's only one thing we can do and that's to take shelter upstairs.'

Eve knew it was the only answer, even though she didn't want to accept the fact.

'Come on,' said Peg, clutching Eve's arm. 'We've got to work fast. We'll take the stuff what's movable from me room up to safety. You get the food from the larder. Put it in the wicker basket hanging on the door. We don't know how long this is going to last.'

Whilst Peg began to collect her things together, Eve returned to the kitchen. The water level had risen to ankle depth. She undid the string round her boots and removed them then, gritting her teeth against the cold, waded barefoot to the larder. Placing the cheese, bread and dripping she found there in the wicker basket, she hitched up her skirt and returned to the passage.

'I took all me papers and bedclothes upstairs,' said Peg breathlessly. 'This here is me clothes. The furniture will have to look after itself. There ain't much anyway. Just a few nice ornaments and I put them on the mantel.' Peg paused, then said regretfully, 'I don't like to say it, ducks, but them little cress seedlings of yours will already be under water.'

Eve shrugged. 'There's nothing to be done about that.' Her small patch of cress by the stream would be lost to the main thrust of water from the docks.

'I'm sorry for you,' said Peg heavily. 'You've brought that little piece of land into life over the past few years.'

'I'm not going to think about that now, Peg. We need to save all we can in the house. Don't know how deep it's going to get.'

Peg went back to her room and Eve took the food upstairs relived to find the boys still fast asleep. The creaks and gurgles of the cottage hadn't woken them.

'Blimey, look at your feet girl, they're turning blue,' Peg said when Eve returned to help her.

Until that moment Eve hadn't felt her feet; the cold water had numbed them.

'I took me boots off. They're me only dry pair.'

'Well, bloody well put them on then again. You won't be no use to God nor man if your feet are frozen off.'

When Eve had put on her boots she lifted the two hooded capes from the nail on the wall.

'Yeah, better take them,' nodded Peg. 'If the roof falls in we might need 'em.' Despite the severity of the situation, she gave a chuckle. 'Run them upstairs then come and help me with the mattress. I've cleared a space on top of the sideboard where it could balance.'

Eve was soon helping Peg to lift the sagging mattress on top of the wooden cabinet. It took them several attempts but finally it was in place.

'It'd have to come waist high to reach this.'

Eve nodded. 'Let's roll up the rugs and put them high too.'

When all was complete, Peg pushed back her bush of hair. Wiping her hands down her thin face, she frowned. 'We'd better turn off the lamp for safety's sake.'

Eve did so, leaving the room in darkness. Only the lamps upstairs reflected a glow as they paddled through the wet passage and ascended the stairs.

'Oh, me flamin' rheumatics!' exclaimed Peg as she paused half way. 'Me pins are creaking like trees.'

'Give me your hand,' Eve extended her arm, 'and I'll help you up.'

'The bugger you will!' exclaimed Peg, waving her off. 'I might be old and slow, but I ain't dead yet.'

As Peg shuffled one stair at a time, Eve heard more gurgling outside. Was it about to force open the door?

'I never thought this could happen,' she said as Peg joined her on the landing.

'Me neither,' agreed Peg wearily, wiping the back of her hand across her forehead. 'We've had a bit of spillage from the docks over the years, but nothing we can't manage. Are the boys still kipping?'

Eve nodded. 'They were a minute ago.'

'Where the bloody 'ell has Jimmy got to?' demanded Peg, frowning at the closed door to their left. 'He should be here now, helping us out.'

'P'raps he got cut off by the river,' shrugged Eve. 'Or the paint factory needs help.'

'More like he's onto a fiddle,' grumbled Peg irritably.

Jimmy's no angel, but it's unusual for him to be absent this late at night, thought Eve worriedly. Or was it now the early hours of the morning?

A resounding crack came from downstairs. They both jumped as the cottage seemed to shudder.

'The front door's gone!' whispered Peg. 'Gawd help us.'

It was as they stood waiting for the next eruption that Eve realized the next few hours were going to be crucial. The cottage was old and already in a state of disrepair. Would it simply fall apart at its seams? Just how high would the river rise? What would they do if it came up the stairs?

It was dark; the lamps had finally burned out and the four small bodies were huddled together on the mattresses for warmth. They had drawn Peg's eiderdown over them, unable to sleep as they listened to the sucking and swirling noises below.

'Will Old Father Thames come in?' said Albert in a small, frightened voice.

'No, chic,' Peg assured him. 'Not whilst me and your mum have a say in it.'

'Morning ain't long now.' Samuel's little croak was a brave one. Eve knew he was frightened like his brother, but wouldn't show it.

'Yes, the daylight will cheer us up.' Peg's husky voice was coarse and deep, and she coughed and cursed herself for leaving her tobacco on the scullery windowsill.

'But the water could come upstairs,' persisted Albert. 'And wash us away.'

Peg chuckled. 'No chance of that love, 'cos Peg Riggs would tell it to sling its 'ook.'

Eve and the boys laughed, despite or perhaps because of their fear. Peg's light-hearted defiance throughout the night had kept them going but when would the morning come? How high was the water? No one knew.

'Is it going to be like the Great Stink again?' asked Samuel, touching on Eve's own concerns. 'Has everyone's lavs gone in the river?'

'I ain't done a poo in our lav today,' giggled Albert. 'But I done one at school.'

'It don't matter what goes down a lav, son,' replied Peg with a chuckle, 'it's what's comes up that's the problem. And it won't be just us, but every other poor sod who gets flooded out.'

'Wonder what's happened to the Higgins?' Eve's thoughts were with their rough and ready neighbours.

'And what about Mr Petrovsky at number seven?' said Samuel.

'The authorities will send out the fire engines no doubt,' suggested Eve. 'With their pumps and long hoses.'

'Yeah, but unless it's the ones with horses, none of them motorized vehicles could get near us,' Peg reflected.

'They might send a ship,' said Albert, 'like our Dad's, the *Star of Bengal*. It sailed all the way from India across seven seas. Tell us about it, Mum.'

Eve smiled in the darkness; the boys loved to hear the stories of their father over and over again.

'Your dad was born in India,' Eve's voice was filled with a soft longing. 'A beautiful paradise.'

'Where the palm trees sway on the sand,' Albert prompted, eager for her to continue.

'Yes, and where it's always hot even in the monsoon.'

'That's the big rains, ain't it?' Samuel said.

'It rains for months solid,' nodded Eve, 'as I've described to you hundreds of times.'

'We was going there,' Samuel continued, taking up the story. 'To meet our grandparents who was still alive when we was born.'

'Was they all black?' This interruption from Albert, his favourite question.

'Your granddad was Indian, your grandma, Portuguese.'

'What's that then?'

'A mixture. A bit like we are on the Isle of Dogs. People settle on the island from all over the world, since Queen Elizabeth's time when the Mudchute was used as a hunting ground for her dogs. Your father came here not to live, but work for a big shipping company. They employ men from all over the world, called lascars. As I've told you many times, he started as a just "boy" but soon became "topman". And you both know what "topman" means in English, don't you?'

'Able Seaman,' shouted Samuel and Albert together.

'Very good. And, of course, you know it was your father who brought us the watercress seeds and gave us our livelihood. You were only babies when we planted them in the stream and from that day forward they've grown there in abundance.' She didn't add that by now the delicate plants might have perished.

'Tell us about our other granny,' went on Samuel, eager not to fall asleep, but yawning loudly.

'Aren't you tired yet?'

'No,' said both boys sleepily.

Eve smiled. 'Your other granny – the one called Sarah Flynn – was my mother and came from Ireland and sold flowers like us.'

'She's gone to heaven, ain't she?'

'Yes,' replied Eve wistfully. 'She died in the flu epidemic of 1918, just after the war.'

'And Granddad is dead too, ain't he?'

Before Eve could reply Albert interrupted. 'Yeah, but he didn't get the flu. He died from bein' coloured yellow in the war.'

'Will we get the flu or the yellow?' asked Samuel knowing the answer already.

'No and you're not likely to,' interrupted Peg with

a nod to the shelf. 'What with all your mother's medicines up there.'

Silence descended at last as Albert snuggled down on the pillow. 'Tell us about our granny, Peg. How she was your best friend.'

Peg gave a deep sigh. 'Well, your gran was one in a million and I was proud to call her me best pal. She was the prettiest flower-seller in all of London and to be honest we had the time of our lives. Selling at all the theatre doors, we'd meet lots of 'andsome gents, who'd give us the eye and pay us a pretty penny for our posies. Like your mum, your granny had long brown hair when she was a girl and eyes of sparkling amber. But no man matched up to your granddad, of Irish descent too, but a true Cockney at heart. 'Course, like a prince and princess, they fell in love and got married. They had your mum, followed by a little boy but he didn't survive, sad to say. Soon after, came the war. Now, you know all about that from school, how all the blokes were 'eroes and your granddad went off to fight for king and country. But he got the yella', a bugger it was an' all. They sent him 'ome on one of them 'ospital ships, but it was too late.' Peg sighed again, her eyes sad and far away. 'And as if the war weren't enough with all its dead, then came the flu. I done all I could for your gran when she caught it, but she had no resistance. I reckon she missed your granddad so much that she decided to walk up heaven's stairs to join him.'

'The same stairs we'll walk up one day,' said Samuel as he too wriggled down into the warmth.

'Yes, ducks, the same stairs.'

'And we'll see Tommy Higgins too. We can ask him what Old Father Thames looks like layin' under all that water.'

Albert was silent. Eve knew he had fallen asleep. Within minutes Samuel also began to snore.

In the quietness, Eve felt a pang of deep regret for her sons. They had stories instead of real people to remember. The other kids at school took for granted their aunts and uncles, cousins and grandparents. Even their fathers and mothers. But there was no family left for Albert and Samuel, only her and Peg. And Peg wasn't even blood related, although they considered her and Jimmy family, nonetheless. Eve had brought her boys up to believe in the hereafter, where one day they would join their father, family and friends again.

A slow, coarse chuckle came from Peg. 'These kids don't need no telling, they could repeat their family 'istory word for word. And heaven's stairs – I ask you! It's as real to them as Piccadilly Circus is to us. Though to tell you the truth, last night when I saw that water coming in, I would have gladly climbed up them stairs meself!'

'Don't say that Peg.'

'Oh, I'm only having a laugh, gel. We've all got to go one day, and it don't worry me in the least.'

Eve didn't like to joke about losing Peg. She was all

the family they had and the mainstay of their lives, the cog around which the family wheel turned. She had welcomed Raj into the household and loved him like a son.

Resting her head on the thin pillow, Eve thought of Raj, the tall, willowy young man she had met at the market whilst he was on shore leave from the *Star of Bengal*. Wearing a brightly coloured tarboosh on his head, pyjama like trousers on his long legs and heelless flat sandals, he had made a dashing and elegant figure. It was just after her mother's death and to make her smile, he had bought her a bunch of carnations, coals to Newcastle was Peg's expression. The handsome young sailor with skin the colour of dark gold had visited her again on his next leave. They had fallen in love and married, despite the prejudice against Asiatic seamen. Ten months later, their twins had been born. Eve knew that if Raj hadn't fallen overboard, they would have been blissfully happy. Raj was the light of her life and she had their two beautiful boys to prove it.

Eve woke with a start. A grey light was streaming through the large holes in the lace curtains. There was an eerie silence, no dripping or gurgling or creaking. But the silence seemed worse.

Samuel and Albert lay fast asleep, but the space beyond them was empty. Peg was nowhere to be seen. Aware of a thumping headache that was beating inside her skull, Eve gently rolled back the covers. Easing herself from the mattress, she put on her boots and shawl, careful not to make a noise. The cottage was freezing, the door to their room closed. Opening it a fraction, Eve peered along the landing. Peg was sitting on the top stair. She was dressed in her heavy coat, her arms wrapped round herself against the cold.

She glanced up as Eve approached. 'Hello, gel. I had to do a pee but didn't want to disturb you. There was no point. See?' She lifted a crooked finger to indicate downstairs.

Eve rubbed the tiredness from her eyes, pulling her shawl close round her shoulders. She gasped.

'High, ain't it?'

They gazed down at the filthy water that had covered the bottom stairs. 'We're marooned!'

'That's about the size of it.'

Eve rushed to the bedroom window as though it would present her with another picture. But as she moved the lace to one side, all she could see in the grim light of dawn was muddy brown water. A movement came from where the road used to be. A dog was swimming along. It only just kept its head above water. Soon it was out of sight. Eve pressed her nose against the glass.

To the right she could see nothing, only water, though numbers two and four opposite were visible, their derelict remains now deluged by water. It was such an incredible sight that Eve stood motionless.

Peg touched her shoulder. 'At least the rain's eased.'

'How long has it been like this?'

Peg nodded to the black and blue sky. 'Gawd only knows.'

'No sign of the Higgins.'

'They'd be luckier than us. They're all sitting high.'

Eve turned to Peg and shook her head. 'How are we going to get out?'

'Dunno, ducks. We'll have to wait and see.'

'I can't believe we're surrounded. Do you think the walls will hold?'

Peg shrugged. 'They did a fair bit of complaining last night.'

'The noises have stopped now.'

'Yeah and it's this silence I don't like. Feels like there's no other bugger left on earth.' Peg coughed and looked round the small room filled with their salvaged belongings. Her lined face broke into a thousand creases as she smiled at the sight of the sleeping children. 'Bless 'em. We'll let them kip until it's really light. Then we'll have something to eat. See what to do afterwards.'

'Someone will help, won't they?'

Again Peg smiled. ''Course they will. The king's sent out the royal yacht for us. It'll be sailing up Isle Street in just a minute or two.'

The irony of Peg's words was not lost on Eve. She couldn't imagine the king having to retreat upstairs in Buckingham Palace as all the posh furniture and carpets were ruined below. The Palace Guard would be out in their dozens blocking up every inch of space. She sighed as she reflected on the two derelict cottages across the road. Families had lived there once, before the walls crumbled. Who were they and what were they like? Would someone one day ask that question of number three?

Time wore on and the rain continued to fall. Eve had no idea what time it was; no one had a watch and Peg's clock was downstairs on the mantel.

As the hours passed all they could do was sit and wait. Eve had talked to Peg about the big clear up that was sure to take place when the water went down, but their conversation was short. A house flooded to this degree might stay partially flooded for weeks. And even if the water went down, there would be an unmentionable mess to remove. It was too big to consider and their spirits sank. The food was the only distraction and it would not last for ever. The water was rationed, the bucket was filling – and not just with rain. Their circumstances were dire.

Every so often a noise outside could be heard and they'd rush to the window, but it seemed as if everyone had forgotten Isle Street. The house in the dip in particular.

'Why don't someone help us?' said Eve impatiently, going to the window again. 'Someone must.'

'Is it raining again?' asked Samuel, standing beside her and peering over the edge of the sill.

'No, it's stopped for a while.'

Just then they heard an echo. It was tiny at first, a lonely wail in the distance. And then it got louder.

Eve gasped. 'Look, it's a boat!'

They stared in wonder as a small clinker rowing boat appeared. 'It's Jimmy!' they shouted as Peg and Albert joined them at the window.

Everyone jumped up and down. 'It's Jimmy, and he's come to save us!'

Eve hoped that was true. But the boat was small and a bit lopsided. Eve pushed up the sash and a cold wind blew in their faces, but they didn't care. Jimmy had come to their rescue!

''Ang on a sec, I'll have to tie up somewhere.' Jimmy stood gingerly up in the boat. It banged against the wall of the cottage and he sat down again. Catching hold of the oars he slid them safely to the bottom of the boat.

'Jimmy! Jimmy!' cried Samuel and Albert.

''Ello, everyone.'

'Where the bleeding 'ell, have you been,' Peg called down.

'Finding meself a decent boat,' cried Jimmy as he gazed up. 'They're all out, rescuing people.'

Eve calculated the height from the top window where they were all gathered down to the boat. It was too much of a drop to jump.

'How deep is it?' she called as Jimmy caught hold of the submerged lamppost.

30

'About three feet I should think. Too deep to walk in, it would come up to your waist. And anyway, it's filthy.'

'Oh, gawd,' sighed Peg, beside Eve. 'The drains must have gone.'

'Is it the Big Stink again?' cried Albert.

'Dunno. But it won't do us no good swimming in it.'

Eve leaned forward. 'Can you see in through the door, Jimmy, to the stairs? Could we jump from them to the boat?'

'You'd never get across. Tell you what, I'll row round the side of the cottage, see if I can get up on the khazi roof below my window. Maybe there's room for me to tie up and you could climb down.'

Before Eve could reply, Jimmy had pushed off.

'I'm too old for all this,' said Peg suddenly. 'How am I going to shin down a roof at my age?'

'We'll help you, Peg.' The boys regarded her with concern.

'Sit down a minute on me bed,' said Eve gently. 'Me and the boys will go into Jimmy's room first, see what the lookout is.'

With shoulders hunched, Peg pulled her coat round her and disappeared behind the curtain. Eve knew that it would not be easy for Peg to negotiate the corrugated iron roof, much less jump from the wall into Jimmy's boat.

Eve and the twins found Jimmy's small room cold

and damp. A hole in the rafters had grown larger and the permanent pail on the floor beneath was over-flowing. The surrounding boards were wet, as was the blanket on top of the bed. The only thing that seemed dry was a chest in the corner, hiding the neglected, exposed brickwork.

'Lift the sash with me boys.' They all pushed up the wooden frame of the window. It was stiff, swollen by the rain.

Outside in the yard the water resembled a brown sea with odd looking icebergs. Buckets, boxes, bales of straw, barrels and papers bobbed up and down. There was even a dead chicken which gave Eve the shivers but fascinated the twins. She tried not to look at it.

The boat came slowly into view. Jimmy almost lost an oar, but then caught it.

'I'll tie me bit of rope to the top of the wall,' he shouted, pushing back his spiky brown hair from his face as the boat rocked dangerously. In his belted donkey jacket and trousers encircled at the ankles he looked not much older than the twins.

'Do you think it's safe on the lav roof?' Eve called.

'I slid down it lots of times,' said Samuel. 'It's easy.'

'Me too,' agreed Albert. 'We jump all the lav roofs to climb up to the ships' bowsprits.'

'I hope the neighbours don't catch you,' said Eve worriedly, ''specially Mr Petrovsky. He's not keen on little boys ever since they broke his window playing football.'

'It wasn't us.' Samuel grinned at his brother. 'And we wasn't even playing football.'

'Look, Jimmy's climbing up.' Samuel pointed to the small, agile figure of Jimmy Jones balancing his way along the top of the wall.

''Ello mateys, Jimmy at your service.' He shinned up the roof like a monkey.

'We thought rescue would never come!' Eve exclaimed. 'What's happening? Is all London flooded?'

'Yeah,' nodded Jimmy, his big eyes wide. 'The Chelsea Embankment's collapsed and even the House of Commons is under water. Not to mention the Underground and the Blackwall and Rotherhithe tunnels. Someone said the moat at the Tower has filled up and that's been empty for nearly an 'undred years.'

'What about the Higgins?' asked Eve. 'And Mr Petrovsky?'

'The Higgins are away. And the old boy at number seven wasn't touched as he's higher up. When I row you back to Westferry Road, the Sally Army are waiting to take you to the nearest church hall with hot food and beds for the night.'

'Thank the Lord for that,' sighed Eve.

'What's going on?' Peg shuffled her way towards them.

'Jimmy's rescuing us,' shouted the boys. 'Then we're going for a dinner up the Sally Army.'

'Can you take us all?' asked Eve, doubtful that the small craft could fit in all four.

'Yeah, dead easy,' Jimmy assured them. 'I'm a first class rower.'

But Eve wasn't so certain. Jimmy might be able to ride a bicycle like the wind, but he hadn't seemed proficient with the oars. What would happen if the boat capsized?

Chapter Three

After some debate, they decided the two boys should go first. Jimmy held the boat steady with the rope as, clad in caps, scarves and raincoats, they slipped down the closet roof to the yard wall. A gust of wind made the little boat sway and Eve held her breath as she watched Jimmy help first Albert and then Samuel aboard.

'I'll be back before you can blink,' Jimmy called as he untied.

'You keep my babies safe, or else, Jimmy Jones!' Eve wagged her finger as she watched her boys being rowed away, her emotions torn. She prayed the boat wouldn't sink. It didn't look safe and the rain had started again and was falling steadily into it. But who else would rescue them?

'Suppose we'd better get out there ourselves,' said Peg when the boat had gone. 'Be ready for the wanderer's return.'

They dressed in the capes and after climbing carefully

out of the window herself, Eve reached back in to help Peg.

'This is a right caper, girl,' said Peg, falling back in again. 'I'll skid down that roof like a roller skate in all this wet.'

Eve shook her head. 'No you won't. Hold on to me.'

'Oh, all right,' sighed Peg, grabbing her hand. 'I'm all yours.'

Eve put one hand around Peg's waist as she sat on the window ledge, then pulled.

'Blimey, you're only small, but you've got the strength of 'ercules,' gasped Peg as she tumbled down on to the roof.

'Are you all in one piece?' Eve helped her up.

'I dunno. But me mouth is still working.'

They stood like two full-blown sails on the unstable roof, clinging to the sill.

'Right, off you go,' said Peg. 'Slide down and I'll join you.'

Lowering herself and, reluctantly leaving Peg, Eve slid down to the wall.

A few seconds later, the sight of a large green cape billowing above her, made Eve gulp.

'Go steady, Peg.'

'I can't do nothing else!'

With a whoosh, Peg let go of the sill and somehow ended up beside Eve. They put their arms round each other, half laughing, half crying in the wind and rain.

'An acrobat at my age!' exclaimed Peg with a throaty

chuckle. 'Now, I just hope that Jimmy don't lose his way back to us and end up down Greenwich Reach.'

Eve smiled, but it soon faded as the rain soaked them once more. They clung together, waiting for rescue.

At first Eve didn't hear the shouts. She was too busy burying her head into Peg's neck, holding on for dear life as the rain tried to wash them off their precarious perch.

'Ahoy there!' A deep voice came over the drum of the rain.

Eve looked up. Squinting against the waterfall that seemed to be over them, she saw it wasn't Jimmy but another boat. Steering with a long, thin pole, aiming towards her, was a tall figure dressed in navy blue. Another man, clad in a blue cape and hood sat at the helm. On the side of the boat was a sign that read, 'Property of the Port of London'.

'It's the police,' said Eve, surprised at their appearance. There was no love lost between the law and islanders. To see them attempting to help ordinary folk was a rarity.

'Take hold of the pole,' the young man shouted. 'And step towards me.'

'You took your time!' cried Peg as Eve helped her forward. 'You better catch me laddo! I ain't no spring chicken and I'd sink like a stone if I fell in.'

'Just catch the pole,' said the calm voice. 'I'll do the rest.'

Peg gave him a grimace then grabbed the pole. The boat banged against the side of the wall. Before Peg could cry out, the young man had swung her down in the boat.

Eve could hardly see through the fine, watery mist that seemed to be rising up from the flood. 'Hold on, miss.' The boat rocked as he positioned the pole for Eve to hold. Her clothes felt heavy and seemed to weigh her down as she stepped forward. If she fell, swimming would be out of the question. How fast would she sink?

'You're safe now.' In the blink of an eye she was caught by the waist and transferred to the boat.

'You all right, gel?' croaked Peg as they sat, shivering together, and the policeman pushed off from the wall.

Eve nodded. She was aware of the brilliant blue gaze of their rescuer as he gave them a smile, something that was rarely seen on the face of the enemy.

Despite Peg's glare, Eve was almost tempted to return it.

That night the boys lay fast asleep on the rush mats provided by the Salvation Army. After a meal of hot soup, bread and cheese, they had all been provided with a blanket and pillow. The chapel hall used for the emergency was crowded with victims of the storm. A dozen red-ribboned bonnets bobbed here and there, tending to the needy. The pungent aroma of soup from the kitchens mingled with the humid smell of wet bodies and clothes as they dried out in the crowded hall.

'Well, it could be worse,' said Peg, draining the last dregs of tea from her mug. 'We've filled our stomachs and got a dry roof over our heads.'

Eve was sitting with a blanket around her shoulders on the hard bench next to Peg. Their wet clothes had dried on them, and she was trying hard not to worry about the cottage. How bad was the damage? Would they ever be able to live there again? Certainly it would be contaminated. All Peg's furniture must be soaked through, the couch and chairs especially. Had the mattress on the sideboard fared better?

But for all their problems they were luckier than some.

'Poor buggers,' said Peg, shaking her head. 'Wonder if the rest of the country suffered too?'

Eve shuddered. 'We'll know soon enough. Look, the captain is going to speak to us.'

A large, portly man in uniform cleared his throat, waving a sheaf of papers in front of him. 'I'm sure you are all curious to know what's happened to the city. Well, I can tell you. Everywhere has suffered. Even the Tate Gallery was flooded and some of the valuable exhibits were lost.'

Eve glanced round. There was surprise on people's faces, but not alarm. The Tate could be a million miles away from their world of poverty and deprivation. The exhibits were only relics of history, not real life. They wanted to know about their homes.

'And worst of all,' continued the captain, 'lives have been lost.'

A loud 'Oh!' went up, a distinct reaction and the captain nodded gravely.

'Very sad indeed. We are given to understand that the worst affected areas are as follows: Millbank has suffered greatly, with many of its old buildings and warehouses swept away. There is flooding at Charing Cross and Waterloo Bridge and roads all over the city have been lost to several inches of water. Tramcars have been abandoned and the public subway at Westminster Bridge is flooded to a depth of four feet. Now, about the island . . .'

There was absolute silence. Everyone was holding their breath as they waited for news of their own homes.

'Unfortunately we haven't any detailed information.'

A collective groan filled the room.

The captain raised his hand. 'Be patient, as now the rain has eased, we hope that the water will recede. For tonight, try to sleep well and with luck you will all be home tomorrow.'

Before anyone could stop him to ask questions, he made a swift exit.

'He don't want to tell us the worst,' said Peg. 'Maybe tomorrow we'll find out from his 'oppos.'

Eve nodded thoughtfully. She was longing for a good wash. Her hair, hanging in tangled tails, needed a brush, but she didn't have one. No one had anything. Like her and Peg, they had left most of it behind. Everyone was down to the bare minimum.

'I'm all done in, gel. Don't fancy kipping on them

rush mats, but it's better than nothing. Reckon I'd kip on a bed of nails tonight.'

Eve suppressed a yawn. 'Do you think Jimmy is all right? He disappeared after rowing the boys to safety.'

'You can understand why. He probably spotted them grasshoppers.'

'Hope he's not up to mischief.'

'No more than anyone else in this day and age,' replied Peg. 'And a blue uniform is enough to send chills down anyone's spine.'

'At least they rescued us.'

'Took their time, though.'

Eve knew that Peg distrusted the police as did most of the islanders. Old Bill was not well regarded in the East End. Tradesmen and flower-sellers were often targets, moved on from corner to corner by an unsympathetic constable. If there was a problem to sort, it was kept amongst the community where rough justice was preferred to the long arm of the law.

Peg gave a loud cough and her hair shivered like a windblown bush. 'Right, let's get our heads down,' she sighed. Reaching under her skirt she began to loosen her stockings. 'What you lot looking at?' she growled to the family next to them who were all eyes.

'Thought you was gonna produce a golden egg,' laughed a man in a woollen hat and overcoat.

'Wish I could, mate,' responded Peg good-naturedly. 'I'd flap me arms and cluck like a chicken all night long if gold was the prize.'

Everyone joined in the joke; they were the lucky ones and they knew it. The atmosphere in the church hall was one of relief and hope, despite the incoming bad news.

Soon Peg was snoring loudly on her mat, but Eve couldn't sleep. Her mind was full of the events of the last two days. First the storm and then the flood. And finally the rescue by a smiling policeman who had courteously helped them on to dry land at Westferry Road.

Just as Eve's eyes began to close she heard Albert cough. Sitting bolt upright, she looked across at him. He turned over, snuffling under his blanket. She hoped this wasn't the start of a cold.

She lay down again listening to the coughs and sneezes filling the hall. The germs would be having a field day in the damp and confined space. Eve sighed, what would tomorrow bring?

Breakfast consisted of porridge and a slice of dry bread with a mug of weak tea. The windows of the hall were no longer streaked with rain but condensation; a grey but dry morning had dawned. Everyone was waiting for news of their homes as the Army members came round.

A young girl dressed in uniform, but with her bonnet tied rather crookedly, approached. She carried a notebook and pencil.

'I'm Clara,' she told them hesitantly. 'Have you eaten breakfast?'

Eve, Peg and the two boys nodded. They had been told that there was to be a service for flood victims in the room next door. The congregation was going to pray for all the casualties of the storm. But no one paid attention. There were more important things to get on with, like going home.

'Where is it you live?' Clara sat down by the boys who shuffled up to make space for her.

'Isle Street,' Eve replied.

'Oh, dear.' Clara's pale cheeks flushed. She glanced down at the notebook.

'Go on then, gel,' said Peg sharply. 'Spit it out. What's the damage?'

'The captain's made a list of the streets that are still flooded. I'm sorry to say that Isle Street is one of them.'

'Bugger,' muttered Peg, then sniffed. 'Sorry.'

'How bad is it?' asked Eve.

'I don't know. But it won't be possible for you to return yet. And even when you do – well, there will be a lot of clearing up.'

'You mean the lavs overflowed?'

Clara blushed again. 'It was unavoidable, I'm afraid. In such a storm.'

'So is it gonna be like the Great Stink?' Albert looked shyly up at the pretty young girl beside him.

She smiled gently. 'No, not as bad. London's got a better drainage system now. But the water rose so high, no one could have anticipated the damage that we're hearing about.'

'Is it true people have died?' asked Eve.

'Yes, I'm afraid so.'

'Was it just the storm that done it?' Peg wrinkled her brow.

'The newspapers say it was a sudden thaw after Christmas and the heavy falls of snow at the river's source, in the Cotswold Hills, combined with the storm.'

'That don't help us, much,' said Peg crossly. 'What are we going to do now?'

Clara shifted uneasily. 'We're trying to re-house the most needy first. That is, the children and the aged—' Clara stopped and went scarlet as she glanced at Peg.

'You're calling me old and decrepit?'

'I didn't mean to offend you.'

But Peg only laughed. 'I'm only 'avin an 'at and scarf, love.' She looked the young girl in the eyes, 'But I can tell you this for nothing, your superiors have dropped you in at the deep end with this lot. Bet you ain't been round the pubs yet?'

Clara shook her head.

'They'll soon toughen you up. You're good sorts, the Sally Army. But don't you go trying not to hurt people's feelings. Just say it like it is.'

Clara gave a hesitant smile. 'I'll try to remember that.'

'And don't go judging a book by its cover. I still got me wits about me even though me body works a bit slower these days. I may look past me prime, but me noddle is in full possession of its faculties.'

'The Army is only trying to prioritize the situation.'

'Well, you don't have to worry about me, I ain't claiming priority attention.'

Clara looked hopeful. 'In that case, I'm sure we can find the two boys a bed for the night.'

But now it was Eve who objected. 'We're not splitting up, we're a family and staying together.' She wouldn't be parted from her boys, no matter what.

Clara looked confused. 'But I've got no one on my list that would take all four of you.'

'Why can't we stay here?' demanded Peg.

'The chapel is already refuge to the homeless. We have little space now.'

'That's what we are,' pointed out Eve, 'homeless.'

'Yes – temporarily, but you see, even when the water goes down—'

'It will mean a lot of clearing up, yes, we know,' said Eve, nodding vigorously. 'And we're not asking for any help, just somewhere to stay until we return.'

Clara looked at the two boys. She frowned. 'Do you have any relatives you could call upon – temporarily?'

'No,' said Eve. 'None.'

Peg grimaced, then looked at Clara. 'Me sister lives up Blackwall in Bambury Street. Council tenement it is. I ain't seen our Joan in years, nor her old man.'

Eve knew that Joan Slygo and her husband were estranged from Peg. She didn't know why, Peg never spoke of it.

'Well, perhaps this is the answer for a joyful reunion,' said Clara, her eyes wide. 'The Lord, you know, works in mysterious ways. In your case, this storm and its ravages could have been sent for a purpose.'

Peg stared in surprise at the young woman, then threw back her head and laughed riotously. 'Well, dearie, if the Lord gets me and mine a bed to kip on under me sister's roof tonight, I'll bloody well go round sellin' the *War Cry* meself.'

Eve couldn't hide her amusement and the boys began to giggle. She knew they didn't understand what was going on, but even Clara began to smile.

'There's always hope,' she said quietly. 'All the churches on the island are making a valiant effort to help the flood victims. Perhaps I could come with you? Sometimes the sight of our uniform and all that it stands for, helps to pave the way.'

Peg, who had just managed to control her laughter, began to laugh once more. 'You're a card you are my girl! To tell you the truth, I ain't had such a good laugh in years. And if I have another good chuckle standing outside Joan's door, when she hears those pearls of wisdom, then it'll be worth the fag of going over.'

Eve saw the mischievous light in Peg's eyes and prepared herself for another eventful day.

Joan Slygo cautiously opened the door of her fourth floor tenement rooms accessed only by flights of narrow stone steps and peeling iron railings and frowned at the little group assembled on the grime-ridden balcony in front of her.

'No thank you, don't want none of your handouts, I'm devout C of E.'

'My name is Clara Wilkins,' said the young Salvationist. 'I'm—'

'I can see who you are and I said no. We go regular to church and are God-fearing Christians, so save your breath for the sinners.' The brown painted door with a small opaque glass window began to close.

'It's me, you silly moo,' said Peg stepping forward. 'Your long lost skin and blister.'

The door stopped. The woman peered out suspiciously. 'Christ Almighty, it's you, Peg!'

'Been a long time, ain't it, Joan?'

'What do you want?'

'A good turn,' interrupted Clara sweetly, also stepping up to the door.

Eve watched the expressions that passed over Joan Slygo's face. After the first shock, it was fear. She was certain the door would soon close, but then Peg took hold of Albert's shoulder and pulled him forward. 'Say hello to your Aunty Joan, love.'

'Hello, Aunty Joan,' said Albert timidly.

'Why the bloody hell did you tell him to say that?' Joan glared at Peg who merely shrugged.

'Thought it would break the ice.'

'The ice is thick round this way,' replied Joan sourly. 'It don't melt easy.'

Eve watched Peg's sister visibly bristle. Her frizzy hair, identical to Peg's, was coloured red. The close-set eyes and thin faces of the two sisters were alike, but there the resemblance ended. Joan was plump and dressed in a smart green tailored suit. 'So what do you and them kids want?' she demanded, ignoring Eve and scowling at the boys.

'Mrs Slygo,' interrupted Clara once more, 'as members of the Church of England we are hoping that you might consider helping your sister. She and Mrs Kumar and her two sons are victims of the recent flood. They need shelter – as did the good Lord himself – just for a night or two, until the water recedes.'

'You mean they *all* want to stay *here*?' croaked Joan, clutching her chest. 'And where am I supposed to put 'em? Hang them all from me ceiling?'

'As I said, it's quite a temporary arrangement. A space on the floor would be sufficient. And surely at times like this we are all members of God's family?'

Eve saw Peg smile wickedly as Joan Slygo stumbled back as though someone had physically hit her.

'Joan? What is it?' A portly man came to the door. He was of average height and wore a Sunday suit, stiff collar and tie. 'No thank you,' he said to Clara. 'We don't want converting round here.'

'I told her we're C of E,' said Joan flatly.

'Indeed we are,' he agreed, 'and proud of it.'

'Hello, Harold,' said Peg with a chuckle.

'Good Lord!' he gasped. 'Joan, it's your sister!'

'I ain't blind, Harold,' Joan snapped as she folded her arms across her chest.

'But we've not seen you in years!'

'Just after the war to be precise,' said Peg tartly. 'Give or take a month or two.'

Harold Slygo stretched his neck in his tight collar. 'If I remember correctly, there was an epidemic at the time. We all had to be careful of our health, didn't we Joan?'

His wife sneered, looking her sister up and down. 'You ain't changed a bit, Peggy.'

'Nor have you by the looks of it. Older and fatter, but then you was always prone to a belly.'

Eve closed her eyes in dismay. When she opened them, Joan was mouthing a reply that seemed stuck in her throat.

Quickly Eve stepped forward. They had to have a place to sleep for the night and this was their only hope. 'Perhaps I'd better introduce myself,' she began in a friendly manner. 'I'm Eve and lodge with Peg. These are my boys, Samuel and Albert.' She added politely, 'We're sorry to put on you, but the Salvation Army have no room for us and we've no one else to ask . . .' She looked hopefully into Harold's eyes.

'Come on now Harold,' said Peg suddenly drawing everyone's attention. Eve saw a curious light in her eyes. 'Your wife might not have no Christian charity, but if me memory serves me right, you was always a champion of the poor and needy. Church warden, wasn't it? Still doing all them good deeds and serving the community are you?'

For a moment all was silent. Then to Eve's surprise, Harold smiled, his fat hands clasped together in a pious gesture. 'Well,' he mumbled vaguely, 'yes, yes . . . I see you've not forgotten that er . . . me and Joan are always to be relied upon in an emergency. And, of course, this terrible disaster does throw a different light on things, doesn't it Joan?'

'No it flamin' doesn't,' answered his wife angrily.

'We can't refuse our Christian duty.'

'You must be joking, Harold.'

'It's only for one night.'

'One night!' Joan shrieked. 'Where would we put them?'

Harold smiled again at Eve, giving her a cold shiver. 'In mother's room dear. We could move the furniture around.'

Joan glared at him. 'Well, be it on your own head, because I ain't going in there and breaking me back, I can tell you that for a start.' She turned and walked away.

There was a long silence before Clara Wilkins began to thank Harold. Eve noted that she was soon dismissed as they entered the dark hall of number thirty-three Bambury Buildings.

Chapter Four

They stood in the front room of the tenement flat and gazed at the faded rose-patterned wallpaper, the ugly wooden dresser adorned with Sunday best china and a draw-leaf table under which stood two wooden straight-backed chairs. A pair of elderly upholstered armchairs were positioned either side of a hearth filled by an iron fireguard. The brown linoleum floor was covered by a thin, multicoloured carpet and the room smelt of mothballs and stale food.

Joan stood stiffly, staring at her husband. Eve knew she was annoyed with him and that they weren't welcome, but Joan was not prepared for a public showdown. Eve hoped Peg wouldn't try to start a row, as she wrinkled her nose visibly at the surroundings.

'Not good enough for your ladyship?' demanded Joan unable to disguise her displeasure at their arrival.

Eve was relieved when Peg merely shrugged. 'It's all right,' she murmured. 'Where you gonna put us?'

'Out on the balcony if I have my way. There's no

room in this place. You must be mad, Harold, agreeing to that woman.'

'They can have the spare room, dear. It's only one night.'

'It's full up with our valuables!' Joan glared at her husband. 'There ain't room to swing a cat.'

'Perhaps we can put some of it to one side.'

'Not so much of the "we", Harold. You offered, you do it.' Joan went to one of the fireside chairs, sat down with a huff and picked up the Sunday newspaper.

'Yes, Joan, go on, ignore us and have a good butcher's at the paper,' said Peg provokingly, 'and whilst you're about it, have a nice cup of tea and rest your weary legs. 'Spect you've been cooped up in church today praying hard for the sinners like us.'

Eve gripped Peg's arm warningly. The tension in the room was palpable as the two sisters glared at one another.

'You'd better follow me.' Harold hurriedly pushed them all into the dark hall again. 'It's er, the next door on the right. He bustled ahead of them, clearly agitated and Eve felt a moment's pity for him. At least he had offered them shelter. 'In you come.'

They all squeezed in to a freezing cold room half the size of the previous one and twice as cluttered. The light from the small square window was obscured by a wall of furniture. Amongst other things, Eve could discern two large armchairs, a bureau, a large brown oak cupboard and a single brass bedstead turned on its side.

'These things were my mother's,' said Harold, pushing back the door as far as it would go. 'She lived with us until she died three months ago. Joan is selling the furniture. It was never to her taste.'

'Nothing wrong with this,' said Peg examining the polished cupboard. 'It's maple, ain't it? If you ask me your old girl had an eye for good quality.'

'Oh, well, er, thank you. Mother had her likes, but they weren't Joan's.'

'So me sister decided to cash in on—'

'It's good of you to put us up,' Eve interrupted, casting a warning look at Peg. 'We shan't be no trouble.'

Harold tore his gaze away from Peg who was now inspecting the contents of the bureau. His plump face, moustache and slicked down fingers of thin hair across his bald pate added to the stiff Sunday collar under his chin gave him an upright air. He turned to Eve. 'I don't know about blankets and so forth, I will have to ask Joan if she has any to spare. It is rather cold in here.'

Eve feared a request such as this would only make the situation worse. 'Oh, I shouldn't trouble her again.'

'Perhaps you're right,' Harold said quickly. 'If you look in the wardrobe you'll find Mother's clothes. I think her bed linen must be in there too. There's no mattress for the bed though. We had to dispose of it after her death.'

Samuel tugged Eve's arm and whispered, 'What about the lav, Mum?'

Harold overheard. 'The toilet at the end of the balcony

is used by the residents of this floor, six flats in all. I would suggest you er . . . pay a call before retiring.'

'Do we have to walk out there in the dark?' Albert glanced into the hall.

'Yes, but I'll come with you,' Eve assured him.

'My wife sleeps lightly,' Harold said hurriedly.

'Don't worry,' Eve nodded, 'you won't hear a murmur from us.'

He gave Eve a long, interested look. She felt uncomfortable under his stare and wondered why he had done them this favour. She guessed the moment he returned to his wife there would be hell to pay.

''Ere, Harold, you got something for these kids to eat?' Peg asked as she shuffled across the floor. 'Don't mind about us, but these boys only had a bit of porridge and bread this morning at the Sally Army.'

Harold visibly jumped as he stared into Peg's close, beady eyes. 'Uh, oh, yes, yes of course. I'll see what I can find.'

'We won't come snooping after you,' Peg added, giving him a gentle push to the door. 'Don't want to upset the apple cart do we?'

'No – no, quite,' agreed Harold. 'Stay here and er . . . make yourselves at home.'

The door closed and Peg stared at it. She turned slowly to Eve, raised her eyebrows and smiled. 'Reckon he's gonna get a strip torn off him by old Joan.'

'Do we call him "Uncle"?' said Samuel looking from Peg to Eve. 'We ain't got one of them.'

'Yeah, why not?' said Peg a little maliciously.

'Do they have any kids?' asked Eve curiously.

'They only had one, a girl gone to Australia.'

'It's good of them to put us up,' said Eve, genuinely grateful.

'Yeah, ain't it?' Peg made her way to the end of the bed. 'Come on boys, give me a hand. Let's dig out this bed and some of them clothes from the wardrobe. Make ourselves comfortable.'

When the bed was lowered to the floor, the boys bounced on the squeaky round springs. 'Did someone die on this bed?' asked Albert.

'Yeah,' nodded Samuel, 'she was Uncle Harold's mother, so she might be a ghost.'

Peg laughed. 'No chance of that, Samuel. The poor old girl wouldn't haunt here. Bet she was glad to be shot of this place.'

'At least Mrs Slygo was looked after,' commented Eve, as she opened the wardrobe door.

'You can bet me sister would have done it only if she was on a promise from the old girl.' Peg pulled out a long brown fox fur from a small round box. 'Blimey, does this bite?' Dangling it in front of Albert she gave a raucous laugh as he squealed. They were all too busy laughing to notice the door opening. Joan Slygo stood there, with a face as black as thunder.

That night, Eve lay awake listening to the strange sounds of the tenement building. The pitter-patter of tiny feet was incessant. She guessed it was the pigeons who took shelter in the roof above the top floor rooms. And perhaps other kinds of furry animals that came out to scavenge at night. Before twelve there had been the usual drunken cussing and cursing from outside the window. Men returning from the pubs and attempting to find their way up the echoing stairs. At least she was warm, if not comfortable. The two boys and Peg had crammed into the bed, the springs well padded by the entire collection of Mrs Slygo senior's voluminous coats. The fox fur acted as pillow for the twins, whilst Peg's small body curled at the other end, her head buried in one of two feather pillows that reeked of Sloan's liniment. The strong substance used as a muscular rub was no stranger to Peg who inhaled it with relish and fell asleep instantly.

Eve had tried to make herself comfortable in one of the ancient armchairs. An army of moths escaped from the worn fabric but Eve wouldn't have minded if it was a nest of snakes. She was too tired to care and wrapping her tartan shawl about her, she used an embroidered antimacassar to cover her legs. The cold seemed to penetrate her frozen limbs, despite this.

She wondered what Harold's mother had been like. And how had Joan coped with an invalid? She didn't seem the nursing type. And what was the bone of contention between Peg and Joan? Peg never talked of her sister. What had happened to make them such enemies?

Just then a small figure crawled into Eve's lap. 'I had a bad dream,' complained Albert sleepily. 'Old Father Thames was chasing me.'

Eve hugged him tight. 'It was just a dream, love. You're safe here with me.'

'Why don't Aunty Joan want us?'

Eve reflected on the moment when Joan had entered the bedroom and found them playing with the old fur. Peg had laughed at her sister's infuriated expression. Joan had demanded they keep the noise down and banged the door behind her. Peg had made a face and set the boys off again. Once more, Eve had felt a pang of sympathy for Joan. Her home was not her own any longer. They were strangers to her. And now they were here, Peg seemed determined to settle old scores.

Eve stroked Albert's curly head and kissed his brow. 'Aunty Joan doesn't really know us.'

'Will she like us better when she does?'

Eve hoped they wouldn't be here long enough to find out. 'Who couldn't love two adorable little scamps like you?'

Albert snuggled closer. 'Uncle Harold ain't bad,' he murmured, yawning loudly. 'He gave us a nice bit of bread pudding.'

The carefully quartered cubes of bread pudding had vanished along with the tea. But Eve had hoped for a hot meal for the twins, if not herself and Peg. She guessed that Harold hadn't the courage to give them more.

What would happen in the morning? It was Monday, and Harold would probably be going to work. Would Joan chuck them out on the street as soon as he left?

Eve woke with a start. There was no familiar chintz curtain beside her and she was curled in an armchair. Where was she? Rivulets of moisture ran down the unfamiliar window, pooling on the sill. Then she remembered. Pushing herself from the chair she glanced at the bed where three small bodies were top and tailed. Eve recalled stumbling there in the middle of the night, lowering Albert from her arms into the warmth of the coats. She had tucked him in and he hadn't woken. Now they all slept soundly.

Eve pulled her shawl around her and replaced the antimacassar in the wardrobe. She listened for sounds and heard a faint shuffling. Opening the door quietly she peered into the dark passage. A door opened and Harold emerged. He saw her and turned to close the bedroom door quietly behind him. Treading lightly towards her, he whispered, 'This way to the kitchen.'

Eve followed. The kitchen was small, without table or chairs. To the right was a larder, a wooden drainer and sink. The stove stood beside a workmanlike mangle under the window. The dirty glass let in the dawn's light, showing railings beyond that skirted all the outside balconies. There was washing already out on some of the lines strung in succession from door to door. Against the whiteness, the smoky black brick of the tenement looked grimy and depressing.

'Joan sleeps late,' Harold warned her with a nervous smile. 'I'm off to work.'

'Where's that?' enquired Eve.

'The Commercial Road,' replied Harold, pulling himself up another inch. 'Gentlemen's good quality attire, you know, a professional establishment of widespread repute.'

'Oh,' Eve nodded. 'Very nice.'

'By the way, I heard on the radio this morning that much of the city has been flooded. Over your way most of the streets have been affected.'

'But we must go home.' Eve shivered as they stood in the cold kitchen.

'I know, my dear.' Harold moved closer. Eve could smell the grease he used on his thin, flattened hair and bristly moustache. 'My sympathies are with you. But I fear you may have to wait.'

'Joan won't like that,' said Eve worriedly.

Harold smiled thoughtfully, showing browned, uneven teeth under the abundance of facial hair. 'I could put a good word in for you.'

Eve pulled her shawl tighter around her. She didn't like the look in Harold's puffy eyes.

'I'll speak to her tonight.' Harold lay his damp, plump hand on her arm as he put his face close. 'I have no objection to you being here . . . none at all, in fact it's . . . refreshing to have such pleasant company . . .' His thin eyebrows rose above a sickly smile and Eve wanted to recoil as he breathed over her. He gripped her tighter. 'I'm sure if you tried, you could win my wife over. A cup of tea in bed and a little breakfast? A few kind words?' His hand ran up and down her arm. His eyes shone as he pushed against her.

Eve turned her face, the hairs on her neck standing up. She wanted to run out of the kitchen, but he was holding on to her. His other hand rose. 'You have such pretty hair . . .'

Before Eve could react, a little voice made them both jump. 'Mum, I want a wee.'

Eve said a prayer of thanks as she moved quickly to Albert, pulling him into her arms. 'Let's go and wake Samuel, then all go together.'

Harold reached for his coat and said briefly, 'Good day to you.'

They watched him bustle along the passage and out the front door. She dreaded to think what would have happened if Albert hadn't appeared. She couldn't have cried out. Joan might have heard. The atmosphere was bad enough between the two sisters without making it worse.

Eve woke Samuel, leaving Peg to sleep. In the grey light of dawn she could see the lavatory was filthy. The roaches were busy scuttling around the walls and the smell of urine was overpowering. At least at home, Eve thought, they had a decent toilet. But in Bambury

Buildings, no one troubled to clean up or leave squares of newspaper on the string.

'I don't like it here,' said Albert as they returned along the balcony.

'When can we go home?' asked Samuel.

'Soon,' said Eve, and knowing what she did about Harold now, she couldn't wait for the time to come.

When they returned to the passage, Eve stood in silence with the boys. They looked up at her.

'Aunty Joan ain't awake yet.'

'Uncle Harold said we should make her a nice cup of tea.' She would take Harold's advice about making herself useful.

'Is there anything to eat?' asked Albert.

Eve squeezed his hand in hers and nodded. 'We'll have a look.'

But the truth was, Eve was reluctant to wake Joan as she was certain to be told to clear off.

Eve slowly pushed open the door of the room Harold had come out of. She had left the two boys in the kitchen with Peg, drinking weak tea and eating bread and dripping. She couldn't let them go hungry and had helped herself to the bread and dripping in the larder which had been surprisingly well stocked. There had been a shin bone with beef on it, probably left from yesterday's dinner, a wedge of cheese under a gauze cover, several eggs, a large loaf and a china pot

of dripping. There was a shelf overflowing with vegetables and the rest of the bread pudding in an enamel
baking tin. But she had not touched any of this; she
hoped Joan would understand how hungry the boys
were.

Eve pulled the curtains. The room smelt musty and
sweet. She made her way to one of the twin beds positioned far apart. Harold's bed was neatly made, but Joan
was fast asleep in hers. Eve lowered the cup and saucer
to the bedside cabinet.

The snoring was loud. Eve stood back, unwilling to
wake her. Then suddenly Joan started. She threw back
the clothes.

'What are *you* doing in me bedroom?'

Eve pointed to the cup. 'I've made you tea.'

Joan leaned up on one elbow, pushing back her frizzy
hair from her face. She looked tired and worn without
make-up. 'I thought you'd be gone.'

'It's early yet.'

'Well, you know where the front door is.'

Eve felt a lurch of her stomach. 'Joan, Harold said he
heard our roads are still flooded.'

'Well, you ain't staying here. Now bugger off, I've
got a flaming great headache and want to sleep.'

Eve stood there, uncertain what to do. When Joan
pulled the sheet over her head, she quietly left. Harold
had said it was possible to influence his wife but Eve
was doubtful.

She just wished she knew what was going on in the

outside world, so at least she'd know how long they'd have to stay here.

Suddenly there was a hammering on the front door. Eve jumped and Peg, Samuel and Albert all rushed from the kitchen.

'Who is it?' demanded Peg, squinting through the small pane of opaque glass.

'Officers of the law,' came the reply.

'They might have come to tell us we can go home!' Eve opened the door immediately. Two policemen stood there.

'You're the bottle and stopper from yesterday!' exclaimed Peg to the younger man.

'Mrs Kumar?'

Eve nodded.

'I am Sergeant Moody and this is P.C. Merritt. I understand from a Miss Wilkins at the Salvation Army that you was brought here from Isle Street?'

'Yes, that's right.'

'I would like you to accompany us to Wapping police station in order to assist us with our enquiries.'

Eve was startled. 'What enquiries? I thought you'd come to tell us about our cottage.'

'I don't know nothing about that,' barked the policeman. 'Our records show that a man named Raj Kumar disappeared aboard the *Star of Bengal* five years ago.'

Eve's stomach tightened. 'Yes . . . yes, he was my husband.'

The policeman looked her up and down. 'A body

was washed up in the flood yesterday. A lascar, with evidence on him to show he crewed for the same ship.'

Eve felt sick, and as the policeman opened his mouth to continue, she slowly buckled at the knees.

'What's going on?'

Through the fogginess in her head Eve heard the sound of Joan's angry demand.

'Mum nearly fainted, Aunty Joan.' Samuel held Eve's hand tightly. 'It's about our dad.'

Eve struggled to stand straight assisted by the young policeman who seemed to be holding her up.

'What time of day do you call this, waking people up at the crack of dawn?' Joan continued relentlessly as she glared at the policemen.

'We are here on official business, madam. I am Sergeant Moody—'

'I don't care who you are,' interrupted Joan, holding her head and groaning. 'I want you out right this moment. Tongues will never stop wagging if they see you lot. Coppers ain't welcome round this way, so 'oppit.'

Sergeant Moody pulled back his shoulders. 'A death has to be investigated, madam.'

'Are you telling me you think this person is my husband?' Eve interrupted hastily.

'We don't know who it is,' said P.C. Merritt, speaking for the first time. 'It's unlikely that you will be able to help us, but since the case has been left open we are obliged to follow it up.'

'You'd better go, girl,' said Peg, placing her hands on the boys' shoulders. 'I'll look after the nippers for you.'

'This ain't a nursery!' spluttered Joan going red in the face.

'I'm sorry, I'll try not to be long,' Eve apologized.

Sergeant Moody laid a heavy hand on Eve's shoulder. 'The car is downstairs.'

Before Eve could say more, she was being marched down the four flights of stone steps by her escort. The Blakeys on the policemen's boots echoed into the air as they hurried to the waiting car. It was a sound she would never forget.

Eve sat in the rear of the vehicle, her mind in turmoil. This dead person couldn't be Raj; it was impossible. After five years she had accepted that he was dead even though no authority had ever told her for certain.

Despite her thoughts, she was suddenly aware of all the storm damage. Gutters were blocked and over-flowing; rotting fruit and vegetables, bricks and glass had been washed up in the road and people were chucking water out of their front doors.

It was much worse than she had imagined. She wanted to ask about it, but the two policemen were silent. Sergeant Moody drove fast through the puddles and splashed the pedestrians. A few fists went up and Eve could understand why the police were disliked in the East End. If they called at your house it was either to bring bad news or arrest you. They were always on the side of justice, supposedly, but the ordinary man didn't experience much of that. But P.C. Merritt hadn't seemed so bad. He was young though, and hadn't yet become hard-bitten like many of his profession.

When they arrived at Wapping morgue, the two policemen climbed out.

P.C. Merritt opened her door. 'This way, Mrs Kumar,' he said in a polite voice.

She felt her legs tremble as they walked inside.

'I'll complete the paperwork,' said Sergeant Moody, nodding to the office. 'P.C. Merritt will accompany you to the identification room.'

P.C. Merritt looked down at Eve. 'It's just along here.'

She felt a wave of nausea as they walked down a long corridor smelling unpleasantly of disinfectant and another underlying smell that she knew was death.

'Would you like to sit down for a moment?' he asked as they came to a halt.

'No I'd prefer to get it over.'

They walked into a long, cold room. Eve's head swam. What if it was Raj?

A man in overalls was mopping the stone floor. He quickly disappeared and an attendant came to stand by a table with a white sheet draped across it.

P.C. Merritt removed his helmet. He said softly, 'Are you ready?'

Eve nodded.

'You can pull it back now,' instructed the policeman. She felt a dropping sensation as she gazed upon the face of a young black man. The water had swollen his body and bloated his features. He had close-cropped hair and a large nose, but in no way did he resemble her beautiful Raj. Eve couldn't stop herself from sinking against the young constable.

He supported her gently. 'Is it your husband?'

'No,' she mumbled.

The sheet was replaced and he led her away.

'I'm sorry you had to go through that,' said P.C. Merritt, seating her on a hard chair in the corridor. 'I'll get you some water.'

Eve hadn't been prepared for this, and she wasn't sure which was worse; thinking the dead man may have been Raj or that Raj may have been alive all this time and she hadn't known it. But he would have contacted her if he was alive. Of course he was dead. Nothing else would stop Raj from returning to his family.

'Here, sip this.' P.C. Merritt returned and held a glass to her lips. 'Looking at the dead is not a pleasant duty.'

Eve drank slowly then returned the glass. 'Thank you.'

'I'll go and tell my superior the outcome.'

When she was alone, Eve sat quietly as if in a trance. That poor man was not Raj but he was someone's son, husband or brother. He had once been in the prime of life. It seemed such a waste.

'How are you feeling?'

Eve jumped as she realized the constable had returned and was sitting beside her.

'Better now.'

'From the records I see your husband was lost overboard and his body never recovered.'

'Yes.'

'And there's been no news in five years?'

Eve shook her head. 'I tried to find out from the port authorities exactly what happened, but they didn't know. They seemed to think it wasn't their job, but that of the shipping company or the Indian police.'

'So no one ever followed it up?'

'Raj wasn't British,' Eve said as she gazed into the direct stare of the young man. 'It might have been different if he was. But he was born in Goa, India and half Portuguese.'

P.C. Merritt frowned. 'Did he have any friends who sailed with him that you knew? Someone you could ask about the accident?'

Eve shrugged. 'We were married at St Francis of Assisi on Grove Road where a lot of lascars worship. I went with the boys to Mass there hoping to recognize someone that knew Raj. But I didn't see anyone. When the ship sailed out of port, there was nothing more I could do.' She frowned. 'Do you think I will ever find out what really happened to my husband?'

'I wish I could say it was likely, but after all this time . . .' He lifted his shoulders in a shrug. 'And it's very distressing for you to have to perform this duty.'

Eve looked down. 'How did you know this poor man was on the *Star*?'

'We don't for certain. But he was wearing an ensign

that denoted the owners of the *Star* though the ship has been out of commission for some time. This man may never have sailed on her, of course, he may have purchased the jacket or been given it.'

Eve shivered. She wanted to leave this place now and try to forget the sight of that poor young sailor.

'I'll drive you home,' said P.C. Merritt as she stood up. 'Although I'm not an official police car driver, my sergeant has given me permission to take you.'

Eve took in a deep breath of fresh air as they left the morgue. The constable opened the door. 'If you sit up front, you'll be able to see the scenery. This vehicle is on loan from the city, whilst the emergency is on. It's a rare occurrence, as it's only Scotland Yard that has the transport section.'

As she took her seat, Eve thought he wasn't like an ordinary policeman, but then, he was new to the profession and had plenty of time to become like Sergeant Moody.

Unlike his colleague he was considerate of pedestrians and steered clear of the puddles when possible.

'Everyone seems to have suffered,' said Eve as she took in the flooded basements of the buildings all being mopped up and cleaned by every conceivable method.

'Yes, it was certainly a shock to the city,' he nodded. 'An untold amount of merchandise on the wharfs and quays is ruined and even the electricity sub-station at Poplar was put out of action.'

'Is it true people have died?'

'At the last count, fourteen.'

'Do you know what's happened at Isle Street?'

'Still underwater I'm afraid.'

Eve sighed. 'Harold was right then.'

'Harold?'

'He's Peg's brother-in-law, Joan's husband, the lady we are staying with. They've agreed to put us up for one night, but we was hoping to get back to the cottage today. The boys should be at school while I go selling. At this time of the year, every penny counts.'

'What do you sell?'

'Flowers and cress. Even fruit in winter to get by.'

'It will take a while to return to normal. Perhaps it's a good thing you're with relatives for the time being.'

'I don't know about that,' said Eve doubtfully.

'I'm a Stepney lad myself,' said the young man breezily. 'Still live with Mum and Dad. We were lucky as we only had the outside lav to worry about. The sewers took a pounding and consequently so did our WCs.'

Eve smiled. 'The boys were asking about the Great Stink. Looks like they're going to find out for themselves when we get home.'

P.C. Merritt frowned. 'Lots of people are in the same boat, I'm afraid.'

Eve turned in time to catch the twinkle in his blue eyes. They both laughed at the unintended pun.

Quickly she looked away. Without a doubt, he was definitely not a run of the mill copper.

Chapter Five

P.C. Merritt brought the car to a halt outside Bambury Buildings. 'Thank you, Mrs Kumar, that wasn't a pleasant duty to perform.'

'What will happen to him – the dead man?' Eve asked as they stood on the pavement in the cold January air.

'There'll be a post mortem to decide the cause of death.'

'I hope you find his relatives. I know how it feels to lose someone and not know what happened to them. Not to be able to bury them or bring your grief to a close.'

The young constable looked at the run-down tenement. 'I wish there was more we could do for you.'

Eve didn't know whether to believe him. He seemed too considerate and polite to be a policeman. She turned away.

'Mrs Kumar, I was wondering . . .'

Eve looked over her shoulder.

'I could look in on your cottage, assess the damage?'

'Why would you do that?' She was suspicious of his motives. Did he want to know what they had, to poke around inside and see what he could find out like all policemen?

'The Force is doing its best to help islanders.' He looked a little uncomfortable under his helmet. 'It's just an offer of help, that's all.'

Eve smiled ruefully. 'We don't usually get many of them.'

'Well, you've got one now.'

Just then the twins rushed out to greet her. 'Mum! Mum!'

Eve scooped them into her arms. 'What's the matter?'

'Aunty Joan's fell over.'

'Is she hurt?'

'Dunno. Come and see.' They grabbed her hands and Eve was hurried up the stone steps where a small crowd had gathered on the top floor. 'Silly cow,' one of them said as she approached. 'One day she'll do herself a real damage.'

'Serve her right if she never walks again,' remarked an elderly lady wearing an apron. 'Mind, she weren't one for walking, not in a straight line, anyway.'

Eve pushed her way through to where Peg was standing over Joan who was lying on her back.

'What happened?'

'The first thing I heard,' said Peg, 'was the two boys calling out. They found Joan, collapsed out here.'

'Oh, me back.' Joan lifted her head as she stared at the crowd. 'What are you lot gawping at?'

'Is there anything I can do?' P.C. Merritt's voice made everyone jump and quickly the neighbours disappeared.

'Looks like you've done it,' Peg scowled. 'You might as well have shouted the black plague, the way that lot buggered off when they saw you.'

Ignoring the insult, the young man went down on his haunches. 'Are you hurt? Can you move?'

'Haven't tried.' Joan looked vague. 'What's going on?'

'You ain't with it, gel,' said Peg loudly. 'You fell arse over tit, Joan. Don't you remember?'

P.C. Merritt smiled uncertainly at the twins. 'Do you know what happened, lads?'

'We found her on the stairs,' said Samuel in a rush, 'just as we was going along to the lav.'

They all peered into Joan's glassy eyes and were assaulted with a strong whiff of gin.

'Well, one thing's for sure, if she's broken anything at all, she can't feel it. Not yet anyway, not until the old thick and thin wears off,' Peg remarked as the policeman took Joan's arm.

'Shall I fetch the doctor?' P.C. Merritt enquired as he slowly lowered Joan to the bed.

'No.' Eve pulled across the covers. 'She'll be all right.'

'A good kip will do the trick,' agreed the constable. 'From my observations, anyway.'

'You mind your own flaming business, copper!' Joan

tried to raise herself from the bed, but relapsed with a groan.

'Lay still, Joan. You're lucky the policeman was here to help you in.' Eve steered P.C. Merritt to the door. 'Thank you for helping.'

'All in the line of duty.'

'Your duty seems to cover a lot of things. Are you new to the job?'

He went red under his helmet. 'Yes, does it show?'

'Only a bit.'

He grinned. 'I hope to be back with some news on your cottage.'

Eve watched him leave then hurried back to the bedroom. The twins were all eyes, watching a prostrate Joan as Peg held up an empty bottle. 'Didn't know you was on the jollop, gel.'

'I'm not. That bottle's been in the cupboard years.'

'And I'm the pope,' laughed Peg.

'Get your face out of me private things, you nosy cow,' screamed Joan, flinging back the bedclothes and giving a wail of agony.

'Oh, stop moaning,' said Peg unsympathetically, throwing them back. 'The truth is you're just coming to after all the booze. You fell and hurt your back, which ain't a life-threatening condition at all. Mind, it might have been if you'd gone over the railings.'

Joan whimpered pitifully. 'Ain't you got no sympathy at all?'

'As much sympathy as you had when we turned up on your doorstep last night,' retaliated Peg.

'Oh, get out the lot of you. I don't want you in me place. Bugger off to somewhere else.'

Eve grasped Peg's arm. 'Come on, let's do as she says. I'm tired of feeling unwanted. We'll go back to the Sally Army, find that young Clara again and ask her to help us.'

As they all began to file from the room, Joan called out, 'Wait!'

Eve returned to the bed. 'What do you want, Joan?'

'I'm in pain. I need a wee and can't move.'

Eve turned to Peg and the boys. 'Wait for me by the front door. I'll help her on the po before we leave.'

As Eve helped Joan out of bed, the grunting and groaning was excessive. After sliding down Joan's drawers and supporting her on the po, Eve got her back into bed.

'You'll have to ask Harold to help you tonight.'

Joan closed her eyes and sobbed. 'He'll chew me off something rotten.'

'Why? Doesn't he know you enjoy a tipple?'

'He's dead against it,' Joan lifted a shaky hand to wipe away a tear.

'Well, that's your problem, Joan.'

'You could tell him it was just a trip.'

'But we won't be here.'

Joan sniffed and gulped at the same time. 'You can stay a bit longer if you like.'

75

'I don't know about that now. I'd rather my boys be put up at the Sally Army than stay here where we're not wanted.'

'It ain't them I don't want, it's *her*.'

'How can you say that about your own sister?'

'You don't know the past,' Joan whimpered. 'Oh, me back!'

Eve pushed one of the pillows under her hip. 'Is that easier?'

'Yes, a bit.' Joan looked up under her puffy lids. 'Just keep her out of me way, that's all.'

Eve was greatly relieved but wasn't going to show it. Clara Wilkins was kind, but only a young girl without much authority. Eve didn't fancy sleeping on the street in some doorway just because her pride wouldn't let her stay under Joan's roof.

'And remember, I don't want Harold knowing,' Joan mumbled looking slyly up. 'Get rid of that.'

Eve glanced at the empty bottle that Peg had left on the cupboard. 'All right.'

'What about *her*, old loose lips?'

Eve sighed. 'Look, Joan, I don't know what's gone on in the past, that's yours and Peg's business. But she's your sister and your blood. She's not going to say anything to drop you in it.'

For the first time, Joan hesitated. Then after a while she shrugged. 'You can help yourself to a bit of food, I suppose. Harold will want his meal at half past six, and don't forget, keep that so-called sister of mine away from the room as she does me head in.'

Eve didn't respond but left the room quickly before Joan changed her mind.

That evening, Harold returned to a meal of cold beef, cabbage and mashed potatoes followed by oven-browned rice pudding. Eve had taken care to feed them all before he arrived home. She had managed a miracle and eked out enough without making the larder look empty, intending to replace the food as soon as she could. She didn't want Joan's charity or to be obliged any more than she already was. She would repay the debt as there was two pounds in coins in one of her bottles at home. It was kept aside for an emergency but in the rush to leave she had forgotten to bring it with her.

'Very nice, my dear, you're an excellent cook,' said Harold after he had eaten. His small, alert eyes were watching her as she washed up at the sink. Standing close to her, he placed his plate on the draining board. 'My wife could take a tip or two from you. I'm relieved she saw the sense in having you here. At least whilst she's incapacitated.'

Eve kept her concentration on the dirty dishes, scrubbing them thoroughly. She could hear Peg and the boys in the other room but Harold's manner made her feel uneasy. The smell of his hair and moustache dressing made her wince.

'You say she fell on the steps outside?' Harold asked again.

'Yes. As I told you, the policeman helped us to bring her in.'

'I hope we shan't be seeing too much of the law,' Harold mumbled. 'It doesn't do round here to have them knocking at your front door. People get the wrong idea.'

Eve had explained all about the dead man and having to identify a corpse but Harold wasn't bothered about the fact that it might have been her husband.

He pressed against her. 'A young woman like you should have a real man to look after her.'

Eve turned slowly. 'My Raj was a real man.'

'Of course.' He put his hand on her waist. 'But you must get lonely on your own.'

Eve froze. 'I don't have time to get lonely. I've got a family to provide for.'

'All work and no play, you know the old saying.' His grasp tightened as he tried to pull her towards him.

'Don't!'

'Come now, my dear. I'm being reasonable in allowing you to stay here.'

Eve felt like slapping his face, but instead said sharply, 'You'd better go to your wife. She's the one who's lonely.'

He looked annoyed. 'So that's the thanks I get for doing a good deed.'

Eve's cheeks were hot with anger. Harold was a dirty old man and she would like to tell him so. The only reason he let them stay was in his own interest and they both knew it.

He wiped his sweating forehead with a handkerchief. 'We'll resume this conversation later when you're in a more – friendly mood.'

Eve was about to say that he would have a long wait, when Joan's voice echoed along the passage.

'Your wife is calling.'

He lifted his chin and fussily tightened his tie. Tugging irritably at the bottom of his jacket, he left the room.

Eve gripped the edge of the draining board and closed her eyes. The smell of him was still in the air and made her feel sick.

'Mum, you going to come in and play with us?' She swung round. Samuel was standing at the door. 'We found a box of dominoes in the cupboard.'

'Yes, love.' She gave him a big smile.

'What was Uncle Harold doing?'

Eve's heart raced. 'Nothing, why?'

'He had his arm round you.'

'He was just being friendly, that's all. Now, come on, let's go and play.'

Eve took his hand and they went into the other room. Samuel was too young to guess what had been going on. But she would have to be careful in future. Her sons were growing up fast.

The next morning, Eve listened at the door until Harold left for work. When she heard the front door close, she waited ten minutes before going to the kitchen. He'd left his shaving soap and brush on the windowsill beside the comb that was glistening with grease. Eve felt her stomach heave. Then quickly looking away, she made a mug of tea and bowl of porridge for Joan.

'What time do you call this?' groaned Joan when Eve woke her. 'Go away.'

'I've brought you breakfast. Something to start the day on.'

Joan sat up grumpily. 'Did you see Harold?'

'No.' Eve placed the tray in front of her.

'You didn't tell him anything?'

'Only that you had a fall.' Eve nodded to the breakfast. 'When you've finished, I'll help you on the po.'

'I'll need a bucket after this lot.' Joan indicated the steaming bowl of porridge. 'I just have a fag, usually, out on the balcony. Harold don't approve of me smoking. I dunno where I put me fags either. You'll have to get me some when you do me shopping.'

Eve realized that Joan was going to make use of her whilst they stayed. But she didn't mind. Just as long as she didn't bump into Harold.

Joan tasted the porridge. 'Not bad. And that plate of cold beef and potato you gave me last night was all right. Where did you learn to cook like this?'

'My husband was a cook on board ship.'

Joan put down the spoon. 'Was it him yesterday?' She didn't seem a bit interested.

'No.'

'Not a bad cup of tea either.' She drained the cup then took a hand mirror from the bedside table. 'I look a bleeding wreck.'

'I'll help you to wash and brush up if you like.'

'Don't like water on me face. You can bring over me make-up though. It's in a bag in the drawer there.'

Eve found the bag and handed it to Joan, then helped her to the po. When she was finished, she took the pot to the lavatory and emptied it. No one was about but the toilet stank as usual.

When she returned, Joan was fully made-up. Her eyes still looked puffy but were alert and her lips painted a bright red.

'I'll have another cup of tea. And when you come back I want you to do me hair. Then I'll tell you what chores need to be done. Oh, and I know you'll be feeding your hungry gannets at my expense. So don't try to pull the wool over my eyes as I know exactly what I've got in me cupboard. I'll want every penny back.'

'You needn't worry about that.'

'Oh, but I do.' Joan glanced up suspiciously.

Eve was furious, but managed not to show it. Until she discovered how soon they could go home, she would have to hold the candle to the devil, that being the devoted couple, Joan and Harold Slygo.

Eve had finished all the jobs and was cooking the boys their tea when a knock came at the front door.

P.C. Merritt was dressed in a light grey overcoat, grey flannels and a loose striped scarf. He had combed his thick, dark brown hair neatly to one side making a perfect parting across his well-shaped head. Without his helmet he looked almost human, thought Eve.

'You're not on duty, then? Or are you doing a stint in plain clothes.'

'No, this is me day off. And I've some news for you, Mrs Kumar.'

She took a deep breath. Was this the light at the end of a long, dark tunnel? 'You'd better come in.'

Samuel and Albert came running up.

'Hello lads.'

The twins gazed at him curiously. 'You ain't got your uniform on.'

'Not today. It had to go to a meeting with all the other uniforms. Get its buttons shined up all sparkly.'

The boys laughed and he winked at them.

Eve led the way down to the kitchen where Peg was stirring the saucepan of steaming potatoes.

'So you turned up, after all.' Peg took the cigarette from her mouth and balanced it on a saucer. She narrowed her eyes at the young man. 'So what's the news then?'

The policeman straightened his back. 'The water's gone down but it's left a lot of waste behind.'

'We expected that,' nodded Eve, excited at the prospect of going home. She couldn't wait to leave Bambury Buildings and Harold's fat, grasping hands and stomach-turning smell. Even if the cottage was a bit damp and dirty it didn't matter. It was home.

'It might be a bit more than you think.' He scratched his head and frowned. 'Put it like this, the mud's every-where, but there's other stuff too. A spade and shovel won't go amiss and a wheelbarrow to cart it all in.'

Eve gasped. 'You're joking!'

'Just don't get your hopes up too high.'

Peg patted her arm. 'Never mind, gel. It's not that bad here. And we don't want to go back to a sewer.'

Eve didn't want to let on about Harold, but how was she going to avoid him?

Peg pushed her hair from her face and cuffed the drip from her nose. 'Are the schools open?'

The policeman nodded.

'Right, the boys can go to school in the morning, then we can start the cleaning.'

'We'll help,' chorused the twins who had been listening at the door. 'We don't want to go to school.'

'On second thoughts,' nodded Peg thoughtfully, 'the more hands the better. Though where we'll get a wheel-barrow from is anyone's guess.'

'I can solve that problem for you,' said P.C. Merritt looking a little hesitant as all eyes fell on him. 'My dad's got a barrow. I could bring it over.'

Peg and Eve stared in surprise at the young constable. The fact that he offered more help had momentarily struck everyone dumb. The police never did anything like this for the public. It was unheard of.

'Anyway, I'll bid you all good evening,' said the young man hurriedly as the silence deepened. 'I'll see myself out.'

'Blimey!' gasped Peg when he'd gone. 'That's a turn up for the books.' She snatched her cigarette and puffed at it fiercely. 'What do you suppose he's up to?'

Eve shrugged as she looked at the twins. 'Time for tea you two. Amuse yourselves in the other room whilst we cook it.'

When alone with Peg, Eve lowered her voice. 'You don't think Jimmy's in trouble do you? That the police are interested in him.'

Peg creased her brow. 'I was wondering the same.'

'I suppose he could really be genuine.'

But Peg shook her head. 'Coppers just ain't like that. He's got a motive for wanting to help. Young Jimmy is a bit iffy, ain't he? Perhaps he's being watched.'

Eve sighed. 'What shall we do?'

'We'll have to put the copper off.' Peg sucked in the smoke until she coughed. Clearing her throat, she nodded. 'Wonder if he nosed round the cottage in order to find incriminating evidence?'

'We've got nothing to hide,' Eve shrugged. 'But there is that big chest up in Jimmy's room.'

'He keeps it well and truly locked.'

Eve looked sharply at Peg. 'How do you know?'

'I've tried it, gel.'

'But it's private.'

Peg laughed. 'Look, ducks, I regard Jimmy as I would

a son, but that roof over our heads is the only one we've got. If the council got to hear of anything dodgy, they'd have us out quicker than you could say swag. So all I do is keep an eye on our boy. He knows full well I'm broad minded, but there is a limit.'

Eve sighed. 'We're assuming it's Jimmy they're after but we don't really know.'

'We'll have to play a bit canny with this one,' said Peg, to which Eve gave a hearty nod.

'Anyway, it's first things first. We'll get an early start in the morning, get back into our home,' suggested Peg, grasping the saucepan and draining the potatoes with a plate. 'Now, let's slice that bit of bacon I found in the larder and we'll feed the kids before his nibs arrives home.'

Eve shuddered as she set to work, dreading the sound of Harold's key in the lock.

Much to Joan's annoyance, Eve was up at the crack of dawn. She took in porridge and tea as usual, but was greeted with complaints.

'I won't manage on me own.'

'Yes, you will. You've got your legs back again.'

'They're not like they were.'

'I'll be home in time to cook dinner. Meanwhile I'll bring in a tray to tide you over. Now let me help you on the po.'

'I wouldn't mind a drop of mother's ruin for medicinal purposes,' Joan murmured as she leaned on Eve. 'It would do me the world of good. You could buy some. I'll give you the money. The pub at the end of the road has an offie.'

Eve helped Joan back into bed. 'You don't want another accident.'

Tears of self-pity filled Joan's eyes. 'No one understands. I could do away with meself.'

'Don't say that.'

'It's true.'

Eve relented a little. 'We'll see. In the morning if you still feel a bit down, I'll buy some. But it will be on ration.'

'Who are you to tell me how much to drink?' Joan's meekness turned swiftly to anger. 'I'm only having you here out the goodness of me heart.'

'Oh, rubbish, Joan. You know as well as I do that without us, Harold would have to look after you.'

Joan tightened her lips, giving Eve a scowl. 'All right, you've made yer point.'

'Here's your cigarettes.'

Joan grabbed them and taking one from the packet with shaking hands, pushed it between her quivering lips. Eve lit it for her with a match. Looking down into Joan's grey, lined face and swollen eyes, she saw an unhappy woman.

'Oh, gel, I can't believe it.' Peg stared at the sad sight before them. 'That used to be our home.'

Eve fought back the tears as she gazed at the filth-ridden passage, the thick, brown sludge that clung to the walls and the remnants of other people's lives and their own, washed into piles on the unrecognizable ground floor of the cottage. No wonder P.C. Merritt had said not to get their hopes up. The urge to turn round and pretend it wasn't real almost overcame her, but she knew she had to face reality.

Samuel and Albert stood at the front door where there was now a gaping hole. 'It's like the Great Stink!' Albert yelled over his shoulder. 'There's a big poo over there, look!'

Samuel dug his brother in the ribs, glancing back at his mother. 'It might just be mud.'

'And there's a dead fish. That's what stinks.'

'Don't go in,' Eve told them firmly. She had too many memories of the old cholera stories in her mind to think of stepping over the threshold.

'How are we going to clean it?' Albert's warm breath wove up into the cold January air. 'We ain't got no boots, nor nothing.'

'It's only gone up four stairs.' It was the only positive comment Eve could think of. The brown band that went round the walls was about three feet high. Below it was badly discoloured and bricks were exposed through gaping holes. The smell was overpowering. Eve could see through to the kitchen, and she wondered what had happened to the larder and stove. It was an impossible job; they had no boots, no spade or pan to clear the mud with. No disinfectant or masks to use against the germs. Outside on the pavement the rain had washed the mud into the gutters and drains, but the cottage had served as a reservoir in the dip, retaining all the muck and mess.

Peg pulled her coat round her and shivered. 'What we going to do?'

'I don't know.' Eve searched her brain for an answer. They needed help, but from whom would they get it? The town hall was the only place to try. But she had seen as they travelled in the police car that ordinary people were doing what they could to help themselves. The fire engines and officials were attending to the important places in the city. As usual, the East End would have to look after itself.

Just then, Eve heard shouting. They turned to see Jimmy Jones riding down the slope. He was carrying something in his basket on the front of the bicycle.

'Jimmy, Jimmy!' The boys ran to him.

He pulled on his brakes, his nose and cheeks red with the cold. 'Hello, mateys!'

Eve hurried up. 'Jimmy, where have you been?'

'Couldn't hang around the other day. Saw the blue-bottles coming for you in their boat. Knew you'd be OK. I went over to me mate's place at Shoreditch. He give me a bed for the time being.'

'Well talk of the devil,' puffed Peg, joining them as they stared at the overloaded bicycle. 'Where did you bugger off to?'

Jimmy tapped the side of his nose. 'Had to see a man

about a dog. Look what I got.' He untied the corners of a dirty cloth covering the basket. 'These are from the rubber factory down the road. Half a dozen pairs of rubber boots and some empty paint pots. We can shovel the muck into these and I'll dump it down at the docks. There's big piles there that people are leaving.'

'Jimmy, they aren't knocked off, are they?' Eve gazed at the boots.

Jimmy's eyes were wide. ''Course not. I paid for 'em fair and square.'

'Do they fit us?' The boys pulled out the boots and tried them on. They fell about laughing at their big feet.

'How much did they cost?' Eve asked.

'Nothing. They was surplus to requirements.' He pointed over her shoulder. 'Look. Here's Eric coming down the hill.'

The broad-shouldered figure of their neighbour, Eric Higgins, came hurrying down the incline. He was carrying a spade, fork and large sack. 'Maude's coming soon with some disinfectant gel,' he shouted. 'Got a few pans and brushes in here.'

Soon they were joined by Eric's plump, bustling wife who brought a mop and broom and Joseph Petrovsky who supported a long hose wound over his arm. 'My dears, my dears, we'll soon wash away all that filth.'

Eve was clasped tightly in Maude Higgins' buxom embrace. 'We was just waiting for you to come back so we could muck in. Our lads are coming to help too.

Apologies for not showing up sooner. We was away till yesterday at a family reunion.' She winked. 'The sort that takes a few days if you know what I mean. We came back to find this lot and you gone.'

'We're with Peg's sister Joan.'

'Didn't know she had one.'

'It's over Blackwall.'

'Oh. Well, we'll have you ship shape in no time.'

Eve's eyes filled with tears of gratitude. All their neighbours had rallied round. But even with their help, how soon would it be before they could live at the cottage again?

Chapter Six

It was as Eve was standing with Joseph Petrovsky at the edge of a dark and foul-smelling hole in the road, searching for the sight of the water main, that a vehicle came into sight. It was a motor van with 'Merritt's Bakery & Provisions' written in big letters on its side. A tall figure climbed out.

'Hello there,' called P.C. Merritt, hurrying up to where they stood. Unlike the day before he was dressed in corduroy working trousers and a thick winter jumper. 'Sorry I'm late. I've had to wait till me dad got back from his deliveries to borrow the van.' He rubbed his cold hands together and smiled.

'Is your dad a baker?' Eve was curious.

'He runs a baker's and provisions shop off the Commercial Road. We've lived over the top of it for years.'

'Is that where you learned to drive?'

'Yes. Me dad got rid of his cart and invested in one of the newfangled motor vans. Lucky for me, it was handy to know how to drive in my line of work. Now, I'll get the barrow.'

Eve glanced quickly at Joseph Petrovsky. She didn't want to say this was a policeman. The mention of the law would have the street deserted in seconds. But she couldn't introduce him by his first name as she didn't know it.

'A nice young fellow, my dear,' said the old man when they were alone. 'A friend of yours?'

Eve felt flustered. 'Not really.' Eve reached out to assist him with the hose. 'Let me help you with that.'

'This is not a woman's job. The sewer is unhealthy.'

'Quite right,' called P.C. Merritt as he returned with the wheelbarrow. 'Leave it to us.' He grinned at Joseph.

The clatter of the wheelbarrow drew Maude and Eric's attention. Soon everyone had gathered round, expecting her to introduce the tall young man. Eve tucked a stray lock of hair under her turban trying to think what to say. But the newcomer's hand was firmly shaken as he told them all to call him Charlie.

'Righto,' he grinned when the meeting was over. 'Let's see what we can find in this hole, Joseph. I'm sure we'll be up and running in no time.'

'I'm sure we will, young man. Are you from the fire brigade?' asked Joseph.

'I had a bit of training in that direction.'

'I also, in my native Russia many years ago. As a boy I helped in the water works of our village.'

'You never did!' Charlie handed Joseph a spanner from a tool box at his side. 'Hang on to this then. We may need it.'

'My boy, you have made my day.'

Eve saw Joseph's face brighten. He was an elderly man who had fled Russia in his youth. He had married but never spoke of his wife and it was not unusual to see a strange face or two turn up at his home. They were said to be visitors from Russia and sometimes they stayed for weeks, even months. Eric Higgins had told Peg he suspected they were downtrodden and persecuted and often in fear of their lives. Joseph gave them shelter until they were ready to set off again.

Eve knew that Isle Street was regarded as a slum but, she was proud to say, in this road it was live and let live. People might look down on this place: the cottages were condemned and the council ignored the crumbling walls and penetrating damp, but Isle Street residents never complained. They were happy to be left alone and live their lives without interference. They didn't care if they were classed as misfits, even though the label was unjustified. Gazing around her Eve felt only gratitude to the people who lived here; her neighbours had hearts of gold, they were salt of the earth, and she would never forget their loyalty and friendship.

Peg's dirty furniture and her waterlogged possessions were carried out by the Higgins' strong sons in order to be cleaned by Peg and Maude. Jimmy and Eric piled muck into paint pots and the wheelbarrow. Maude was also wearing a turban and had set about scrubbing the leather sofa. Eve could hear the twins' laughter. She knew they would be round the back looking for the dead chicken.

'What are you two up to?' she asked as she looked over the wall at the rear of the cottage.

'Nothing,' said Albert, looking guilty.

'I don't want you touching nothing dead.'

'It ain't got no feathers,' spluttered Samuel, pushing his boot against a lump on the ground. 'We was going to bury it.'

Eve pointed to the cress patch by the underground stream. 'Make yourselves useful and tell me if you can see the cress.'

Both boys ran over. They trod around in their big boots. 'Can't see,' shouted Samuel, 'it's all muddy.'

Eve sighed. She knew that in winter the little shoots were delicate and struggling for life. How could they have survived under all that?

Suddenly there were shouts from the front of the house. Eve ran back to see the long hose coming to life.

'The pump is working!' cried Joseph as Charlie sprang to his feet from the hole in the road. He was only just in time to catch the nozzle. There were cheers and laughter as the water burst up like a fountain.

'What time do you call this?' yelled Joan as Eve, Peg and the twins entered the dark hall. Joan was wearing her dressing gown and standing in the kitchen. She had an empty bottle in her hand. 'It's half past seven. You might as well not have bothered to come back!'

'Oh, shut your gob, you old soak,' retaliated Peg as she pushed her way forward, causing Eve's spirits to plummet. 'Are you on the gin again?'

'No.' Joan slipped the bottle in her pocket. 'I could hardly walk with the pain I'm in.'

'Pain? You don't know what pain is! We've been up to our eyeballs in muck all day and all you can do is complain.' Peg shook off Eve's restraining hand and lunged towards her sister. 'What stopped you from cooking Harold a meal?'

'You uncaring bitch!' screamed Joan, waving a wooden spoon in Peg's face. 'Get away from me. You stink.'

'And you would too, if you'd had to go through what we did today. You should see me home, or what's left of it. Ruined it is, most of it.'

'That's your bloody problem,' cried Joan retreating to the passage. She glared at Eve. 'I warned you to keep her away from me!'

Eve placed herself between the two angry women. 'Stop it both of you. We're home now, Joan. I'll cook you your tea.'

'No bloody point. Harold's been in and gone out again as there was nothing for him. Nothing. Not even a cup of tea on the go.'

'I'm sorry.'

'Don't apologize to her,' cried Peg, trying to push Eve to one side. 'She should be ashamed of herself. What's wrong with her getting off her fat arse and cooking for us?'

Eve took hold of Peg's shoulders and guided her into their room. 'Peg, calm down now. You and the boys stay in here. I'll bring some hot water so you can all wash.'

Samuel took Peg's hand. 'We can play dominoes after.'

'Yeah,' agreed Albert, looking anxious.

Eve quickly returned to Joan. 'Your sister has had a bad shock.'

'So have I. Harold was upset.'

'Where's he gone?'

'How would I know?'

'He'll be back.'

'There will be hell to pay when he comes in. If it's one thing that annoys him, it's his grub. He likes it on the table when he comes in. And that was all I asked of you in return for keeping you and your brats and her – *her* – that cow of a sister of mine has the cheek to accuse me of being an old soak.' Joan moved towards the bedroom, holding her hand over her chest. 'I can't take it no more. You've had out of me all you're going to get. Push off, the lot of you. Go on. And I mean it this time.' The door slammed.

Eve stood in her filthy clothes. It wasn't fair. They had worked so hard all day and wouldn't be home even now had not Charlie, formerly known as P.C. Merritt, given them a lift in his van. Eve slumped against the wall, as weariness overcame her. At least Harold was out. But if Joan meant what she said, was she expecting them to leave now? And where would they go?

Going to the kitchen, Eve boiled a large pan of water. Being as quiet as she could she poured it into two enamel bowls. If they had to leave tonight, they would be clean at least. She found Peg laughing and playing with the boys.

'Play with us, Mum.' The boys had forgotten how hungry they were.

'First, have a good wash.'

Three dirty faces gazed up at her. They were still able to laugh after all that had happened. She couldn't make them go out into the cold night. There was something she could do, although she resented doing it. But once again, there was no choice.

'I'll just be a minute.'

'Where are you going?'

'To the pub at the end of the road.' Eve knew that if she bought Joan what she wanted, then she might let them stay. She had her savings in her pocket, the two shillings from the cottage. It was a waste to spend it on gin. But it was the only way of keeping a roof over their heads.

Eve listened to the raised voices in the early hours of the morning. She guessed that Harold must have come home and a fight ensued. Joan had said he would be in a bad mood. And all because of a missed dinner! Would Harold come into their room? And if Joan was tipsy would it make matters worse? Eve felt responsible.

She listened, holding her breath and staring at the

door in the dark, fearing that either Joan or Harold might burst through it. It seemed like hours before the voices subsided and peace reigned. Well, it wasn't quite peace as she could hear muffled noises coming from the tenement block. Some were children crying, others were distant but with the same note of aggression as the Slygos'. Doors banged and thumps echoed along the balcony. Fortunately there was no one above them to bang on the ceiling, only the birds and the mice.

Eve felt dirty and her hair and skin still reeked of the sewers. After today it was a smell ingrained in her nose. She could now imagine what the Great Stink had been like and her sympathies went to the victims, even though they were all now relegated to history.

They had all washed tonight but their clothes were contaminated. The clean ones they had managed to salvage from upstairs were almost as bad as their dirty ones. The stink had got into them. Even though they had managed to shovel and sweep the worst of the mud and debris out into the gutters and down the drains, there was still a lot left. The clean water from the hose hadn't cleared it away. As many times as the floors were washed down, the filth seemed to return through the nooks and crannies.

Her dreams were filled with water. It was rising up to the windows of the tenement. She was trying to wake the twins and Peg, but they were fast asleep. Then she was being chased along the dark streets. Harold's sweating face was close and he pulled her down. Once more she was in water. Filthy water, with the smell of death in her nostrils. She was sinking below the surface and lay on the bottom of the river. Her hair had turned into long green ribbons of seaweed and the body next to her was the man she had seen in the morgue.

'Eve, Eve, wake up.'

She sat up, the slip she was wearing soaked through. Her shawl had fallen away and she was shivering in the cold night air.

'You were dreaming, ducks.'

'I was drowning.' She shuddered as Peg pulled the shawl round her. 'And I saw that dead man again. He was lying beside me on the riverbed.'

'It was only a dream, a nightmare. Gawd love you, gel, no wonder, after all you've been through.'

Eve looked round the dark room. There was no light creeping through the window. 'Is it morning?'

'No.' Peg sat on the end of the squeaky bed. A glowing red end denoted a cigarette. Soon after the smell of tobacco filled the room.

'Did I wake you?' Eve asked in concern.

'No, I wasn't asleep.'

'Did you hear Joan and Harold?'

'Yes, they were going hammer and tongs.'

'She said he would be angry.'

Peg inhaled throatily and coughed. 'Do you reckon she was drunk?'

Eve sighed. 'I hope not. She said she would only have a nightcap.'

'Bet she wanted us gone. You bought it to keep her happy, didn't you?'

'I thought it was the only way. Now I'm not so sure.'

'Oh, stop worrying, girl. She ain't worth the effort.'

But Eve had decided that at whatever cost, she had to keep Joan happy. 'Tomorrow we'll be back for six. We can do a lot at the cottage before then.'

She knew it was more important than ever that they keep a roof over their heads. From what she had seen at the cottage today, there would be no early return; the cottage was uninhabitable. As much as she disliked the Slygos, where would they be without them?

'I must go back to work,' Eve said anxiously. 'I don't want to live off their charity.'

'Couldn't give a fig meself,' said Peg and the red tip extinguished. 'Anyway, I think I'll get me head down now all the shouting's over.'

'I wish we had a clock.'

'I'll bring mine back from the cottage tomorrow.'

Eve lay back and listened to Peg climbing on the springy bed. 'Your copper coming again, is he?' Peg asked as she made herself comfortable.

'If you mean P.C. Merritt, no, he's back on duty tomorrow. But he's left the wheelbarrow for us to use. His dad says there's no hurry to return it.'

'He didn't tell no one he was a copper, then.'

'No. And I told the boys not to say.'

'Good. If I was you I'd tell him to keep his profession under his helmet, or else we won't have no friends or neighbours to help us out. They'll think we've gone ruddy barmy involving Mr Plod.'

Eve gazed into the darkness. She didn't know whether she was relieved or disappointed that Charlie had said goodbye when he brought them home and wished her good luck. Good luck sounded rather final, but surely she didn't expect anything else?

'Thought he might have offered to help us,' yawned Peg.

'No.'

'Can't fathom him out. Didn't see him after Jimmy, or snooping around. All he did was work like a bloody beaver. Still, that could be a front. Them coppers are as crafty as a barge load of monkeys.'

Eve wanted to believe that Charlie's efforts to help were genuine, that there was no ulterior motive. But was she being naïve? Anyway, that was the last they could expect to see of him. It was probably all for the best.

Even so, she lay awake thinking of the young policeman. She must just have started to doze when she heard Harold's movements in the hall. She sat up quickly, immediately alert. It was the first alarm call of the day.

P.C. Charlie Merritt went on duty with a spring in his step. He had stowed his football kit in the changing room at the station and couldn't wait to knock the socks off the opposing team, West Ham Waterworks, at the game tonight. When he'd worked in the docks for the PLA football had been a dream. He'd lived and breathed for the game and at twenty-four had high hopes of being signed on to a professional team. The docks were only a means to an end, a job that he'd gone in to for the money. Crane driving paid well and he liked sitting up high in the goose-necks with a bird's-eye view of London. But his aim was to play for Walthamstow Avenue, a team that by his reckoning was the best in the country. Maybe not first division, not yet, it was early days. But then some bright spark had kicked his cartilage into goal instead of the ball and he'd wound up in hospital with a season's lay-off. What a gut-wrencher that had been. The next year he was twenty-five and with his dodgy knee still giving him gyp, he lost out to Kenny Marchmant, who at three years his junior had signed for Walthamstow and was on the reserves.

'All right, Charlie?' His chum, Robbie Lawrence, a new recruit to the Force last year and also a bit of a sportsman, nudged his arm as they left Stepney station.

'Fit as a flea, Robbie.'

'Nice day for a foot soldier.'

'We're the king's men all right.' Charlie grinned. He didn't take their banter seriously, for they were green behind their ears and they knew it. But walking the streets in a uniform was a pleasure to him. He would smile and nod when he could, though he received little response in return. But he'd promised himself that if he stuck his training, he'd try to make a good copper.

It was a bit of an uphill struggle, mind, especially with Sergeant Moody in tow. Now past his prime, Moody had missed out on the promotions, and had taken root behind the station desk. It was only six months ago that the powers that be had decided he needed an airing. He had a real sour puss on him, not a shred of humour. He liked to give the rookies a verbalizing, a kick up the arse and a dressing down before they'd even set foot on the beat. If he'd had them sprinting round the yard with packs on their backs, none of them would have been surprised. It would have been acceptable if there was an up-side, a twinkle in his eye when the punishment was over. But the man was made of stone.

'What time will you get to the ground?' Robbie asked, breaking into Charlie's distracted thoughts.

'About half six, kick off is seven. I can't make it earlier as it'll take me twenty minutes after work to get there.' As Robbie was goalie and Charlie right wing, they liked to get in a warm-up.

'I'm on duty till three. So I'll be there early.'

'Lucky sod.'

'Yeah, but I've got Moody with me all day tomorrow. Takes the shine off a bit.'

Charlie grinned. 'Not so lucky, eh?'

Rob removed his helmet and stroked his corn-coloured hair, snapping the strap back under his chin. His dark eyes sparkled handsomely and at six foot, the same height as Charlie, they made a striking pair.

'Eyes left,' whispered Robbie from the corner of his mouth, 'now that's what I call tasty.'

Charlie glanced in the direction of the two young girls walking arm in arm towards the Isle of Dogs. They wore white turbans on their heads, overalls under their coats and clogs on their feet. Both were laughing and glancing in their direction, which was about as much female attention as they would draw today. The girls were young, fifteen or sixteen, too young to have developed a dislike of the law. Charlie smiled, but was nudged hard by Robbie, who said under his breath, 'I didn't mean give them your name and address, mate.'

'It was only a smile.'

'Moody would have you in the cells for that.'

'Moody ain't here.' If it was one thing that dismayed Charlie about the Force it was public relations. Or rather the lack of it. The general attitude was them and us. Well, he wanted to make a difference to this community. If you couldn't give a smile to the public now and then, what was the world coming to?

'Incidentally,' said Robbie as they stopped at a jeweller's and he tried the door. 'What happened at the morgue?'

Charlie was startled at the question. He had no idea that anyone knew of the incident other than Moody. 'We took a widow to identify a corpse to see if it was her sailor husband,' he said briefly.

'Was she young?'

'Who?'

'The widow, of course.'

Charlie went on the defensive. 'What's all this about? It was just an ordinary identification process.'

'Which means she was a bit of all right.'

Charlie looked into his friend's eyes. 'I don't know what you're talking about, Robbie. And how come you know about it anyway?'

'From old Moody. I was on the desk when he came back.'

Charlie felt his heart beat hard against his ribs. 'What did he say?'

'He was in a right strop, said he was late because the paperwork he'd had to do at the morgue had taken him all day. Said the case should have been chucked in the bin five years ago. That it was all a load of red tape that cost the tax payer a fortune. A bloody foreigner, were his words. And why should half of Stepney manpower still be called out on the job?'

Charlie's pleasant start to the day suddenly evaporated. Who did Moody think he was, talking about Eve's husband like that? He may have been born abroad but he lived here, didn't he? Worked bloody hard for his living and supported a family. Since meeting Eve he'd done a bit of enquiring into the lascars. He'd seen them about often enough, slender figures dressed in flimsy cotton coats and trousers, summer and winter alike. But he'd never had anything to do with them, just accepted them as part of the landscape. Now he'd turned up a few facts he hadn't known before. These Asiatic seamen were officially defined as natives of the British Empire and were highly regarded in their trade. Conscientious and loyal to the line that employed them, they were, however, a sitting target for the keepers of lodging houses and opium dens who preyed on the innocent. In fact, though they could be seen on leave, trailing round the docks and markets in their fascination for all things English, their sobriety, patience and obedience to their employers were exemplary. For Moody to denigrate the dead man like that was a sin to Charlie.

'You shouldn't take notice of Moody,' he replied as his friend looked at him curiously. 'You know what he's like, a right ignoramus at times.'

Robbie frowned, his fair eyebrows coming low over his eyes. 'So why don't you enlighten me, chum?'

Charlie shrugged. 'For a start, half of the Force ain't on the case.'

'Well, you and him were.'

'The truth is the sailor, this Raj Kumar, died in mysterious circumstances. He was lost from a ship run by a British company.'

'And?'

'Well, ask yourself this. The master reports his disappearance. Kumar wasn't a novice, but a sailor who'd gone up through the lascar ranks. There was no enquiry, no investigation in London and none that came to light from abroad. The case surfaced again when this body turned up in the flood. The ensign on the dead man's jacket denoted the same company as Kumar's and Mrs Kumar was brought in to see the body.'

Charlie was pleased to see that he had given Robbie something to think about. Had Eve's husband been a member of an English crew would there have been an enquiry? The two policemen began to walk on. Their steps were in unison, but Charlie could feel a certain unrest between them.

'Anyway Moody says the case is closed,' said Robbie after a while. 'You should think yourself lucky not having to follow it up.'

'I reckon there's more to it than meets the eye. I did a bit of checking up and Oriental seamen are protected by the Indian Merchant Shipping Acts. So why wasn't they involved?'

'But this isn't your concern, Charlie.'

'It's our job to seek justice and uphold it, isn't it?'

'You're sure it's not because you fancy the widow?'

'Hey watch it,' Charlie returned sharply. 'She's not that sort. She's a decent woman.'

'You're sure of that, are you?'

This time, Charlie caught his arm hard. 'Look, Robbie, I might only be a copper on the beat but I do know something about human nature.'

His friend gave him an even stare. 'Charlie, it's only ever a woman that makes a man talk like you're talking. Don't get involved. Moody would call it fraternizing with the enemy. You've got a good career in front of you. You'll go far one day if you don't confuse your high and mighty ideals with the way the law works.'

'I thought the law was an ideal.'

'To you, my friend, perhaps.'

'And you?'

'All I'm saying is beware of the wrong women.'

'And look who's talking, Casanova himself!' exclaimed Charlie in a gasp.

'Yeah, well take a tip from a bloke that's not always been led by his brains,' Robbie answered dryly. 'I learned a valuable lesson last year. The little hiccup I had over Diana Thomas was too close for comfort even though she was a real stunner and absolutely up for anything. But she was also married – and to another copper. I was only bedding her for the hell of it anyway. If it wasn't for my CO pulling a few strings, I'd have been out on my backside with a DD.' Robbie grinned gently. 'So concentrate on your job and grow a tough skin. And remember, you're my pal, I'm looking out for you.'

Charlie couldn't believe he'd just received a lecture from someone whom he'd heard boast that he'd only joined the Force for the uniform and the power it gave a man over females. Not that Robbie wasn't his best chum and a damn fine footballer, but Charlie had heard rumours that he was still playing the field, and again, with married women.

Charlie knew that if he opened his mouth now, he'd end up saying something he'd regret. So he shut it firmly and without saying more, they walked on.

By the end of their beat, they had returned to the subject of football and the match that night. But Charlie was still ruminating on what his friend had said about the Kumar case. He wondered now if Moody had mentioned something else – hinted in some way about Eve – that had Robbie pressing all the wrong buttons today. Well, he would take what his friend had said into account, but the truth was he didn't regret the help he had given Eve and her boys. They'd had a rough time of it and he'd tried to do his best to help. But what irked Charlie the most was the casual dispatch of the circumstances surrounding Eve's husband's death. Both Moody and Robbie had been of the same mind; Raj Kumar warranted no interest.

But why?

Charlie felt the sting of the winter wind on his cheeks and pulled back his shoulders. Maybe he'd done all he could in this case and now should leave it alone. He certainly had no power to investigate a case that was closed.

He tried to propel his mind forward to the match at Locke Lancaster's ground. It would be exciting, challenging. He needed a shot of adrenaline that would put an end to the disturbed feeling inside him.

A solid career was what he was after. It wasn't the docks, it wasn't in professional football; it was the Force. But with this admission came certain responsibilities. Should he stick to the letter of the law and put the unresolved death of a lascar behind him? Or should he follow his instincts and delve deeper?

Chapter Seven

The next morning Eve took breakfast to Joan as usual. But she was shooed away by a bad tempered grunt. Leaving the tray on the bedside table she paused at the door.

'I'll be home in time to cook Harold's dinner and do the chores,' she promised but received no response.

All day at the cottage, she was thinking about money. Her patch of watercress had been destroyed. In winter there was practically no cress sold on the streets but each spring she would harvest from her crop and sell it to shops and factories. When she had none she would sell posies of flowers that she bought from Covent Garden, rising early to ride on the back of a coster's cart. But now she had no basket or money for stock.

As she worked, piling the mud and dirt in the wheelbarrow, she decided the boys must return to school. St Saviour's was a highly respected Catholic school and Eve encouraged the twins to observe their religion. But the nuns insisted they learn their catechism and the Latin responses to Mass. Samuel and Albert were not star pupils, and frequently they missed confession on Saturday morning because Eve allowed them to sleep in after their late Friday nights.

This sin, especially, went against being a good Catholic and Eve didn't want the boys to be ridiculed or singled out at school. So on Monday she would hang her head and apologize to Sister Mary for their extended absence.

As Eve watched them from the kitchen window, her eyes lingered on their two small figures. In their too-big boots, warm scarves and peaked caps, Samuel and Albert looked the picture of health. They gazed up admiringly at the Higgins' sons as they flexed their muscles under their rolled-up shirt sleeves.

Suddenly there was a loud yell, and Jimmy opened the closet door. Eve stepped back from the window. She didn't want to see what horrible surprise was in there.

The day wore on and Eve was with Peg in the kitchen. Although Jimmy had shovelled away the top layer in the wheelbarrow, the drying mud clung to every surface. Eve knew it was a health hazard. She found a large drowned rat in the larder and shrieked. The men came running in and disposed of it.

A little later it was Peg's turn. 'Oh my Gawd!' screamed Peg as she jumped back from the stove. An army of black shiny roaches poured out of the oven.

'Oh, Peg, what next?'

'They took refuge from the water I suppose. Bugs can't swim.'

Eric Higgins rushed in, a look of alarm on his face. 'What's up now?'

Peg and Eve pointed to the oven. Eric aimed his broom at the interior, but it was useless. The roaches, beetles and insects flopped out onto the dirty floor and scuttled away. Even the heavy sole of Eric's boot didn't deter them.

'Sorry girls, what you have here is an infestation. Rats, mice, bugs, you name it, they're here.'

Eve knew this warranted a visit from the council. It was the one thing they couldn't remedy themselves. A fumigation had to take place. If the bugs weren't killed by a naphtha disinfectant spray, they would multiply.

'We'll put in a request at the town hall,' sighed Peg, wiping her thin face with the bottom of her apron. 'Next week when I pay the rent.'

Eve knew she hadn't got the two shillings to give to Peg towards the rent. It had been spent on gin.

Peg slammed the oven door shut. 'Well, we ain't gonna be cooking no dinners in that for a while.'

Maude entered, slapping her hand over her mouth as she saw the trail of little black bodies. Some flopped on their backs in the still wet patches. Others sped up the walls.

'Oh, you poor loves.' Maude's buxom breasts heaved under her brightly coloured jacket. Her black hair was scraped back from her rosy face in a bun and her gold hoop earrings dangled, banging against her face as she shook her head sadly.

'And whilst you're at it, you'll need old Slippery and his dog,' added Eric with a wink. 'There's rats all over the yard. The boys and me have hit a few on the head with the spade, but the khazi is alive with the buggers. They're coming up the hole underneath.'

'Oh, no.' Eve wanted to cry. 'I didn't think it would be so bad.'

'We'll come again tomorrow to help you,' said Maude gently, patting her hand. 'But the following day we're off to our relatives in Kent.'

Eve nodded gratefully. 'You've done enough already.'

'Will your friend help again?'

Eve blushed. 'No he's—' She was about to say on duty but stopped in time. 'At work.'

'Well, the wheelbarrow has been useful.'

Eve stepped back to avoid something larger and hairier that sped across the tiles. Peg and Maude shrieked and hurried off. Eve was left with Eric. He put his arm round her. 'Sorry, lovely, but you gotta accept this place ain't gonna be 'abitable for some time.'

Eve suppressed a sob and nodded.

'At least you've got a roof over your heads for now.'

Again Eve nodded. But for how long? What would happen tonight when she went back to face the Slygos?

To Eve's dismay, Harold had arrived home. He was sitting in the parlour reading a newspaper.

'Hello, Uncle Harold,' the boys chorused, hiding their dirty hands behind their backs.

He gazed at the four of them standing in the hall. They were all in their smelly clothes and Peg and Eve still wore turbans.

'What is that dreadful smell?'

Eve glanced warningly at Peg who was about to respond, the look on her face telling Eve that Harold was about to receive sharp words.

'We're going to wash.'

'You'd better all go to the communal wash house downstairs.'

Eve had looked in on the tin-roofed hut that housed a water pump, two brown-rimmed china basins and a long trough. It didn't smell as bad as the lavatories on each floor, but it was freezing cold and the water was liquid ice. She would prefer to boil up a saucepan or two and wash in the privacy of their room, but she didn't want to upset Harold.

'Then when you're done, I should like my dinner. I don't want a repeat of yesterday. Joan is still upset that you let us down so badly. My wife deserves more consideration after all she's been through.'

Eve was seething. After all Joan had been through! She had only tripped over because she was tipsy and her bad back was not so bad that she couldn't get out of bed and search for her gin. If Joan was upset, it was because of Harold and the row they'd had last night. 'You'll have it on the table for six,' Eve said coldly.

In their room, Peg was red in the face with anger. 'The bare-faced cheek of it! I could strangle the pair of them.' She wagged a finger at the door. 'No wonder I kept me distance from the pair of bloody hypocrites. C of E they call themselves. I'll bet Lucifer himself would turn them away from his fire.'

'Calm down, Peg. Let's wash.'

But Peg sat on the bed and folded her arms. 'You won't catch me down in that dump.'

'It's only to keep him happy.'

'I'd like to land him one. And her too.'

'Well, don't just yet. We need this room.'

But Peg threw back her head and snorted. 'Tell you what, girl, I've just about had enough of this.'

Eve sighed deeply. She had too, but there was nowhere else to go. 'Come on, boys, we'll brave the elements for a wash. Now bring that towel and bar of Sunlight.'

The boys nodded obediently and followed her, shoulders sloping and heads bowed. Eve could see that even their young spirits were being crushed.

'I'm hungry,' complained Albert as they slowly filed down the cold and draughty stairs. A wind rattled through the open spaces and shadows were hiding in the corners.

'I'll cook dinner soon.'

'Will Uncle Harold get his first?'

'Of course.'

Eve pushed Albert and Samuel through the creaking door of the hut.

116

'It's dark in here,' Albert cried. 'Can't see nothing.'

'And freezing,' said Samuel, shivering.

'We can see by the moonshine through the window. Strip to your waists, boys. The quicker you get your shirts and vests off the sooner they'll be back on. I'll test the water first.'

Eve turned on the tap and put her hands and face under. She tried to stifle a gasp. Washing as best she could, anger and rebellion ignited inside her as her children were made to suffer the indignities of Bambury Buildings.

She could never live in a place like this. No wonder all the residents quarrelled and looked depressed and unhappy. Isle Street might be classed as a slum, but it was heaven compared to this.

The boys' teeth rattled as they dressed again. Eve made a promise to herself; she would find the money from somewhere to rent lodgings. But first she had to go back to work.

That night, when Harold had finished his dinner, Eve attempted to create a miracle from what was left in the larder. Dividing the two sausages and vegetables amongst the four of them it was a meagre offering. But she didn't dare tell Joan the larder was empty.

Approaching Harold was even worse. She didn't want to speak to him. So far she had managed to keep one of the boys or Peg with her, so that she was never alone with him. Now she was quickly washing up, keeping alert for his footsteps yet again.

She had just put away the final plate when he appeared. Her heart raced so fast, she felt dizzy. Trying to side-step him, she was stopped by his plump body as it moved faster than she expected across her path.

'Eve, I'd like to speak to you.'

Eve shrank back. Her eyes darted around the small space searching for escape. But Harold had positioned himself strategically, blocking the doorway. The smell of him drifted towards her, as he stroked his moustache thoughtfully.

'I'd like you to come into the parlour.'

Eve stiffened. 'We can talk here.'

'No, the parlour if you please.'

She was frightened. Would he trap her in there, try something on? She tried to reassure herself that Peg and the boys were in calling distance. But how could she expose Harold without causing trouble?

'I can't be long.'

'What is there to rush for?'

'I say prayers with the boys before they go to sleep.'

Harold smirked. 'Oh, yes, you're RC.' He said it sarcastically, a nasty look in his watery eyes.

He stood back and extended his arm for Eve to pass by. She almost ran into the parlour and searched quickly for an escape route, but there was only the door. Harold followed her and closed it.

'Please sit down.'

'No thanks, I'd rather stand.'

Harold took the settee by the table on which the

radio stood. He made himself comfortable, patting the seat beside him. 'Sit down, Eve.' He took out a hand-kerchief and wiped his forehead. 'Let's try to be friends. You may need a shoulder to cry on from what I've heard.'

'What do you mean?' Eve felt sick with apprehension.

'Your cottage is ruined.'

'That's not true.'

'I heard it from an official source.'

Eve swallowed. 'What source?'

'The police. I went to the station at Stepney today and spoke to the desk sergeant.'

Eve gasped. 'But why?'

'I wanted to find out the true position of your circumstances. After all, you've been with us a week and last night Joan was upset about your behaviour towards her.'

'I only tried to help,' Eve spluttered. She felt like she was on trial. And what right did he have to check on her?

'You leave her alone too much. The point of you being here was to be with her, provide a bit of company and to help with the chores in return for our hospi-tality. I told you she gets lonely and needs cheering up. Last night she had sunk into one of her depressions. I couldn't console her.'

'Perhaps that was because you were shouting too loud,' Eve said before she could stop herself.

Harold's smug smile disappeared. 'I wasn't shouting.' For a portly man, he rose quickly. 'How dare you speak to me like that? I'm your host.'

Eve took a step back as he moved towards her.

'When will you see reason?' He stopped and put out his hand. 'I only want to help you.'

'Then leave me alone.'

'But I want to comfort you.'

'I don't need comforting.' Eve couldn't move either way.

'Of course you do. I could give you so much, my dear. Look, here, this is for your boys.' He dug in his pocket and brought out a handful of silver coins. 'You can buy them some new clothes and whatever you want for yourself. A nice dress instead of that dreadful shawl. Take it off, it spoils your lovely figure.'

Eve was insulted. 'This was my mother's. I don't want your money.'

'Everyone has a price.'

'Get away from me or I'll scream.'

'This is your home now and you'll do as I say. Take this and enjoy it. All I ask is that you allow me to be your friend.'

Eve pushed him away and the coins fell on the floor. She let out a scream as he fell on her, covering her mouth with his hand. She fought to push him off but he was strong. She tried to drag away his arm; he was suffocating her. His eyes were glazed and unfocused as he mumbled, the smell of him making her want to retch.

'Just one kiss, Eve, just one and I'll let you go . . .' He moved his hand away from her mouth. She was about to scream when his lips closed over hers. His tongue forced its way into her mouth. Eve closed her eyes in terror. She couldn't move as he was leaning hard on her. It took all her willpower to go limp and quiet, as though she would allow him to do what he wanted. She kept her eyes closed, as he tore off her shawl and found her breast. His tongue drove into her mouth again. When he pulled up her skirt she offered no resistance. 'Good girl,' he whispered, 'this won't take long.'

Eve opened her eyes slowly. She looked into his face contorted with lust. How could Joan ever let this man touch her?

'You have a beautiful body. It should not go to waste.'

As he fumbled to unzip his trousers, Eve brought up her knee. The last thing she saw before she fled the room was the strands of thin hair across his bald pate as he choked and fell to the floor.

'You bitch! You cow!' screamed Joan as she faced Eve in the hall. 'Try it on with my husband would you? Then run away?'

'It wasn't me who tried it on.'

'Liar!'

Eve stared at the woman who half an hour ago had been suffering such a severe depression she was unable to get out of bed. She was now on her feet, yelling at the top of her voice as Eve gathered the boys together whilst Peg packed their bags. Thank goodness they didn't have much, Eve thought as she pushed Samuel and Albert towards the front door and opened it. After Harold's attack Eve knew they had come to the end of their time here. When she'd run back to their room, she had told the boys they were about to leave. Peg knew there was something wrong, but asked no questions, telling the boys to do as their mother asked.

'You tart!' exclaimed Joan, flying at Eve, her arms outstretched.

But Peg caught hold of her sister. 'Listen, you dozy mare, for once in your life open your eyes. Why would a good-looking girl like Eve want to be bothered with an old coot like Harold?'

'Don't you speak about my husband like that!'

'I don't know what went on,' Peg answered as she stood with a bag under each arm, 'but I know who I'd rather believe and it ain't your old man.'

Eve led the boys out into the frosty night air. She didn't want to confront Joan in their presence and Harold was too much of a coward to come out from the parlour. She hoped he was suffering after what he had done.

'You eat us out of house and home and take advantage of our hospitality,' cried Joan following them to the front door. 'And then you accuse my poor Harold of . . . of . . .'

'Being a dirty old man,' yelled Peg as she hurried to join Eve. When she had caught her breath she looked back at her sister. 'It's a bit like 'istory repeating itself ain't it, Joan? Only I was prepared to give the old lecher the benefit of the doubt when we came here a week ago. I thought, seeing as he's now a pillar of the Christian community, he might have changed his ways, become the loving husband you always professed he was. You certainly told me a few home truths all those years ago, and accused me of what you accused Eve of tonight. But if you've got any sense, you'll take a good long look at the saint you live with and ask yourself a few questions. Or do you know the truth and drown it in gin?'

Eve watched Joan's expression change: her eyes filled with tears and her body seemed to shake, until, reaching out to the wall, she steadied herself. 'Get out,' she whispered hoarsely. 'Get out and don't ever come back. I don't want to set eyes on you again. To me, you are dead.'

The slam of the door made Eve jump. She looked at Peg whose face in the darkness was white.

'Peg, you all right?' Eve asked gently.

'Yeah, gel, it'll take more than her to get me down.'

'Why was she shouting?' asked Albert, sniffing loudly as he took Eve's hand. 'We ain't done nothing wrong.'

'Oh, take no notice of her, chic,' Peg dismissed, waving her hand. 'You two have seen a bit of the grown-up world tonight, but don't let it worry you. It's what happens in families, a tiff or two never hurt anyone.

123

Come on, let's get down those stairs and find ourselves a bed for the night. We'll try the old Sally again, they won't turn us away.' She winked quickly at Eve.

'What did Uncle Harold do?' persisted Albert, as they went down the dark stairs.

'He put his arm round Mummy,' answered Samuel before Peg or Eve could reply.

'When?' his brother asked curiously.

'The other night. It was in the kitchen when you was playing dominoes with Peg. He jumped away when he saw me.'

There was silence as they all stood outside in the light of the lamp that reflected dully on Bambury Buildings. Albert looked up at Peg. 'Did he put his arm round you too, Peg?'

She threw back her head and laughed. 'Yes, chic, he tried to once, but it was a long time ago.'

'I don't want to cuddle no girls,' said Albert, wrinkling his nose in disgust. 'That Bernadette Flanagan at school is always trying to kiss me. And she stinks worse than our lav!'

Everyone laughed, dispelling the tension. Eve smiled to herself. Kids had a wonderful way of making light of things. At least she didn't have to convince Peg that she was innocent of leading Harold on; it seemed that Peg knew only too well for herself.

Once more they were sleeping on the mats in the church hall, though none of the Sally Army members they had met before were there. Another captain had allowed them a corner as there were no free beds. The number of homeless had expanded; they were mostly men now who snored and coughed in their sleep or shuffled out noisily to the lavatory. Eve thought longingly of their cottage, but now it was infested with rats, mice and bugs it was too unsanitary to inhabit – she still had images in her mind of the cholera stories. Once more she tossed and turned on the hard mats.

'You asleep, gel?' Peg's coarse whisper came from over the heads of the two sleeping boys.

'No. Me mind won't stop working.'

Peg gave a cough. 'I could do with a fag. Jimmy's promised to get me a bit of cheap baccy, seeing as how there was plenty ditched at the docks in the flood.'

'Won't it be ruined?'

'There was plenty that wasn't. It was first come first served to those who were in the know.'

Eve sat up. 'I hope he knows what he's doing. Is Jimmy still with his mate at Shoreditch?'

'So he says.'

'When do you think we can go back to the cottage?'

'Dunno, love.'

'Peg, why didn't you warn me about Harold?'

Her friend was silent for a while, then gave a deep sigh. 'It was a long time ago. I thought he might have turned over a new leaf. And if you remember we was desperate.'

Eve thought about this. They had been desperate. She could understand Peg not saying. 'Well, he ain't changed.'

'What happened?'

'He said he wanted to talk to me in the parlour. I shouldn't have gone in there. I had to put me knee in his privates.'

Peg snorted. 'Good for you, girl.'

'Joan don't know what he's like. I feel sorry for her.'

'Reckon they deserve each other.'

'Is Harold the reason you broke up with her? Harold hinted it was the flu epidemic.'

'Huh! He would say that, wouldn't he?' Peg gave a grunt of unpleasant remembrance. 'She thought I was trying to take him off her. 'Course, she wouldn't listen to me, her own sister. Thought I was lying through me teeth, just as she said to you today. So now you know why we got such a warm welcome on our arrival there.'

'I wouldn't have gone if I'd known that's what happened to you.'

'Oh, well, let's try to kip. Me bones are achin' something rotten. I reckon we'll have rain tomorrow.'

'I hope not. We've got to find somewhere to stay.'

'Something will turn up,' Peg yawned. 'Now, get some sleep, love.'

But sleep wouldn't come and once more Eve found herself awake, wondering what tomorrow would bring.

Chapter Eight

Peg was right about the rain. The morning began with drizzle falling from skies that were gloomy and grey. Eve asked the captain if they could stay another night, but like last time, the answer was no.

'Our Poplar mission will help,' he told her. 'Certainly your boys will be found places to stay.'

But Eve shook her head. She had heard stories of children disappearing or put into homes. The Welfare was classed as the Worker's Bogeyman and according to rumour it lost no opportunity to send children to institutions. Neglect was easy to prove as there was no money coming in to the poverty-stricken homes of the East End. The Depression had spread its shadow over every family; stories abounded of children whisked away to be supplied as cheap labour in other parts of the country or even abroad. Eve had heard several terrify-ing accounts from her co-workers and the public at large. She didn't trust the authorities and nor did anyone else who had been robbed of their livelihoods by an uncaring government.

'We'll find somewhere,' she told the captain as they packed up their few belongings and, after a breakfast consisting of hot tea and porridge, they stood undecided on the pavement outside.

'I want to go home,' said Albert stubbornly. He was shivering in the cold breeze that now added a winter chill to the air.

'I can kill the rats,' nodded Samuel. 'Duggie Higgins showed me how. You clock them with the back of a spade.'

'I don't want you near them,' said Eve, shuddering at the thought. 'It's a job for the council.'

'They ain't open on Saturdays,' said Peg, as they hoisted their bundles and began to walk down the street.

'We'll go to the ladies at Hailing House,' Eve decided as they hurried along. 'They might know of some-where.' The big manor house on the island was run by an aristocratic family for the poor and needy. The Hailings were well known for their charitable works and as a last resort for the destitute.

'Doubt it,' muttered Peg. 'If the Sally can't have us, no one will. We can't sleep rough, not with the boys.'

Eve kept walking, her chin stuck out and her steps fast. They might have to walk the length and breadth of the island and even sleep illegally aboard a barge under the tarpaulin covers, but it would be better than being separated.

The ladies of Hailing House were away for the weekend at their country seat, they were told by a stiff-backed retainer, who barely opened the big front door to their knock. Call again on Monday.

They set off once more, walking the long way back to Isle Street. As they stood at the open gap of the front door, they were met by an evil smell.

Even the two boys were reluctant to go in. 'Let's go and look in the yard,' said Samuel. 'Duggie might have killed all the rats.'

'Upstairs won't be so bad,' said Peg when the two boys had gone. 'Might be able to sleep on your bed. And there's my mattress too.'

They went in slowly and looked in the front room. Just then a large black rat wriggled out of a hole in Peg's mattress. All the stuffing was on the floor. Eve closed her eyes. It was worse than she thought.

What were they to do? Could they exist even for one night amidst the rats, roaches, lice and beetles that infested the rooms?

The two boys returned from the backyard.

'What did you find?' asked Eve.

'The lav is boarded up. Duggie must've done it.'

Eve looked crestfallen.

'We could clean the yard up a bit with the wheel-barrow,' said Samuel enthusiastically. 'Charlie ain't come back for it.'

But Eve shook her head. 'It's nearly dark.'

Peg pushed her hands over her face. 'I reckon we've got no choice. It's upstairs or nothing.'

Albert began to cry. 'I want to go back to Aunty Joan's.'

Eve knew they couldn't. But what were they going to do?

They were standing outside the cottage when Eve heard a call.

'My dears, my dears!'

They looked round. Joseph Petrovsky was coming down the slope. He wore an overcoat and a peaked cap hid his silver hair.

'Hello, Mr Petrovsky.' Eve managed to smile.

'What are you doing so late in the day?'

'We ain't got nowhere to go,' wailed Albert, bursting into tears once more.

'Is that true?' The old man gazed at Eve from under his silvery eyebrows. 'I thought you were in the care of relatives.'

'Not no more we ain't,' said Peg, pulling her collar up to her ears.

'You are entertaining living once more here?'

'We would but for the rats and bugs,' said Eve.

'I saw them,' nodded Joseph, 'you cannot stay under this roof.'

'It's the only roof we have.' Eve held out her arms. 'We tried the Salvation Army, but they give you one night's shelter then split you up. I couldn't agree to that.'

Joseph smiled. 'And so you shouldn't.' He took Samuel and Albert's hands. 'Come with me. My home is yours, my friends.'

'But Joseph, there are four of us,' Eve protested.

'And what does that matter?'

Eve and Peg turned to each other. They didn't know whether to laugh or cry with relief. The boys began to lead the way, the old man between them.

Everyone laughed when they heard Albert's next comment. 'We never meant to break your window, Mr Petrovsky. It wasn't us. And we ain't never played football up your end any more. Only down in the dip where there ain't no windows to break, only ours.'

Eve looked round the upstairs room of number seven Isle Street, at the three single beds squeezed into the same space as they had occupied at Peg's cottage. Each brass bed boasted a thin pillow and grey blanket and the walls were hung with photographs of men, women and children wearing what looked like Russian clothes. The children wore heavy cloth hats and bulbous trousers and the women had long skirts and wide-sleeved blouses. The military men carried sabres and looked fierce. There were one or two photographs of men with long black beards and penetrating dark eyes.

'My antecedents,' announced Joseph proudly. 'Though I left Russia many years ago, this is my heritage. Many of these died in the revolution. It was a painful time.'

Eve saw sadness in his eyes.

Peg was the last to climb the stairs and enter the room. She gazed around. 'Blimey, rogues gallery.'

Eve was afraid Joseph would take this as an insult

but he smiled. 'There is a smaller room at the rear,' he said quietly. 'I sleep there but you ladies are welcome to occupy it. I have a comfortable settee downstairs that I often sleep on when guests are here.'

'No thank you,' Eve said immediately, not wishing to outwear their welcome. 'We don't want to put you to any trouble.' She paused. 'This is a nice room.'

'Just the job,' said Peg, dropping one of their two bundles on the floor. 'We've got a curtain back at the cottage. We can hang it across the middle.'

Eve nodded. 'The boys can sleep top and tail in one bed.'

'If you are certain?'

'I don't know what we would have done if you hadn't come along,' Eve said gratefully.

'The room is cold and, like all the cottages, rather damp. But I have a stove in the scullery. Come down when you are ready and warm yourselves.'

'Can we go with Mr Petrovsky?' the twins asked Eve.

'No. You must stay out of the way.'

The elderly man frowned at them from under his silver hair. 'Do you have your football?'

Both looked startled. 'No, Mr Petrovsky.'

'In that case, I shall still have my windows in one piece when you leave.'

Seeing the stern look on his face, they glanced at Eve. But she was already smiling at his joke and soon everyone was laughing again.

★

Joseph Petrovsky's cottage was arranged, like Peg's, with two rooms upstairs and two down, a kitchen and scullery at the rear. The parlour, Eve discovered, was furnished with a settee, two fireside chairs and a large wooden dresser filled with ornate pieces of china. The fireplace was surrounded by a mantel, intricately carved in dark wood, and a large firescreen which looked very old.

The kitchen and scullery had no duckboards to spoil the polished red warmth of the tiles, although there were big patches of damp on the walls. This cottage was built on the hill and was not at risk of flooding. The yard was small and over it hung the bowsprit of a tall ship at rest in the dry dock behind. Its mermaid figurehead was impressive and could be viewed from the kitchen window. The closet, unfortunately, was positioned below. Eve knew the boys of the neighbourhood often climbed the wall and stood on the closet roof where they could lasso the bowsprit. Mr Petrovsky was always driving them away. She would have to tell Samuel and Albert that however much of a temptation this would be, they were to avoid it.

'What's this?' Albert hurriedly spooned the broth into his mouth as they all ate at the small wooden table by the stove.

Joseph raised his bushy eyebrows. 'Do you like it?'

Both boys nodded.

'In Russia we call it borsch.'

'What's in it?' asked Peg.

'Cabbage, potato and plenty of beets,' replied the old man, providing them all with a second helping.

'We ain't had beet before.'

Joseph smiled. 'It's good for you. Excellent for the bowels.'

'You mean it will make us go to the lav,' said Albert with a giggle.

Everyone laughed and soon their dishes were empty. Joseph poured them all tea from a strange-looking urn on the dresser. The rich brown liquid was prepared in what they learned was a samovar; a barrel-like container with a large tap at the bottom used as a tea-making system in Russia.

'It was presented to me by . . .' Joseph hesitated as he gave a wistful smile, '. . . my friends from the old country. They brought it in many pieces, giving me a section or two each time they visited. The exterior is crafted from copper and bronze. The teapot on top is used to brew the zavarka, the tea you are now drinking.'

'It's strong enough to grow hairs on me chest,' Peg laughed, as she smacked her lips. 'Now this is what I call real tea, not like the dishwater you get served up these days.'

Joseph nodded. 'The samovar is a symbol of leisure, Peg. Russians take care to sit and enjoy the moment whilst tea drinking, much like our Japanese brothers and sisters.'

'What's that big pipe running through the middle?' Eve asked.

'The samovar has its own independent heating system,' Joseph explained proudly as he showed Eve a small basket full of tiny objects. 'I fill the pipe with these small shards of coke or coal, even fragments of wood. In Russia we use the fir cones from the trees. After the burning is over, we place the teapot on the very top to simmer on the passing hot air. It also keeps this room very warm and enjoyable.'

'Why ain't the British ever thought of this?' demanded Peg, finishing her tea with a satisfied gulp. 'We're s'posed to be tea drinkers and yet we can't hold a candle to what you got here.'

Joseph only smiled faintly. 'Russia is full of nostalgia, my friends. And once upon a time it was thought that the samovar seemed to contain all of our memories, hopes and unfulfilled dreams that would come flowing out into the air as we sat round drinking . . . much like the lamp of the incredible Aladdin.'

There were a few moments of silence then as the old man's words seemed to create the perfect picture as they sat in the warm, sweet-scented kitchen that now also seemed full of nostalgia.

'Joseph, we're so grateful for all you've done for us,' said Eve as she too finished her tea.

But Joseph dismissed this quickly. 'I am honoured to have you as guests.'

'I wish I could pay you something towards our keep. And you have my word that I will.'

'Don't upset yourself, my dear.' Joseph patted her

shoulder. 'You will be in a better position soon. Until then, accept my small offerings. This has been a difficult time for you. But you are young and have your health. The situation will soon improve.'

'We can do jobs for you,' said Samuel brightly. 'We're good at cleaning things or polishin' boots.'

Joseph nodded, wagging a stern finger. 'Is that so? Well, I have forty pairs of boots upstairs and I would like them all clean for tomorrow.'

This time the boys knew he was joking. They laughed as they drank from clean white china cups on undamaged saucers. Eve was relieved to see that Peg also looked happy. She had given the seal of approval to their room and was examining the contours of a small china bowl, no doubt assessing the value.

Thanks to this kindly neighbour they now had shelter and full stomachs. Tonight they would sleep in real beds under warm blankets. Eve could hardly wait to lay her head on the pillow.

On Sunday they set about cleaning the cottage again. But the rats seemed to have increased overnight. By the afternoon, Eve was eager to return to number seven. The fear of the vermin had got the better of them, even the boys refused to venture inside.

When they arrived back at Joseph's, Eve was surprised by a large tin bath in the scullery.

'I have boiled water and prepared you the bath,' Joseph said as the boys gazed at the clean water, towels and large bar of Sunlight soap. 'Fill it up as you please. Boys, come into the parlour with me whilst the ladies bathe first.'

'This is luxury!' exclaimed Peg as they undressed by the warmth of the stove. 'You go first, gel. I'll keep me drawers and vest on for a bit.'

Eve removed her underclothes quickly. The steaming water looked enticing. She sat in it as Peg poured a saucepan of warm water over her.

'Peg, I'm in heaven.'

'I'll scrub your head. Reckon we've got nits, don't you?'

'We need the disinfectant to get rid of them.'

'Next week we'll go to the council.'

Lulled by the warmth, soap and cleanliness, Eve slid down. As Peg rubbed the Sunlight soap into her scalp, Eve thought about her cress patch at the cottage. It had vanished under the sewage and now only a brown stain remained. The water from the stream had resumed its gentle trickle, seeping under the wall and back to the docks, but all the carefully positioned stones and moss that Eve had arranged over the years to encourage the seedlings were gone.

'Peg, I ain't got no rent money,' she burst out.

'Nor me, gel. But don't worry. We'll tell them we'll owe it, pay two bob a week off the arrears when we're solvent. What can they do? Come and turn us out of a rat-infested cottage that should be pulled down anyway?'

Eve sat up quickly, spilling the water. 'They wouldn't do that, would they?'

'Over my dead body.'

'Tomorrow I'll go up Covent Garden early. See what work's around. The boys will be at school.'

'Do you want me to see them nuns for you at St Saviour's?'

'No, I'll speak to Sister Mary later.' Eve winced under the fierce scrubbing of her head. She didn't want to get on the wrong side of the nuns. 'Hope there's something up the market.'

'You'll have to smile nicely at the old boys.'

'At least I'll smell nice.'

'If you get anything, I'll help you sell it. We'll go up Pall Mall and the Strand, like the old days. Me and your mum used to wink at all the gents. They'd buy a dead flower if you looked at them the right way.'

Eve wasn't so sure about winking at the men. Peg was out of touch as she didn't sell on the streets much these days. Now it was the merchandise that counted with customers. The buttonholes had to be manipulated to keep the flowers fresh. The competition was fierce and Eve took a pride in her stock. But would she be able to start again without a basket?

Eve set off. It was dark and cold in the early hours of the morning, but the streets were busy with horse-drawn traffic. She was offered a ride by a costermonger and sat on the back of the cart, watching the city wake up. Less than an hour later, the lights of the busiest market in London were upon them.

They parted, each to their own entrances, the clip clop of the old horse ringing out on the cobbles. Eve made her way through the busy arcade under the imposing cast iron structure. Looking round the lofty naves and glass fanlights, Eve inhaled the familiar scents of flowers and ripe vegetables and she remembered her lessons at school. Covent Garden had been designed by Inigo Jones in 1632 and had survived the test of time. Already the traders and porters were hard at work.

'And the best of mornings to you,' cried one Irish man whom Eve knew well. His flowers had often filled her basket. His ruddy face under his cap was welcoming and Eve's spirits rose.

She began to explain that she had lost her basket on the night of the storm. Busy with his customers, he pointed her in the direction of the next trader. Eve hurried through the gathering crowds, waiting patiently as the workers heaved large baskets of cabbage, carrots, potatoes, oranges, apples and bananas over their heads to pile onto the back of carts and motor vehicles waiting outside. For a moment, she paused to watch and enjoy the sights and sounds surrounding her. The reds, blues and yellows of the flowers, even in winter, the ripe and healthy fruit and vegetables and the shouting and jostling of the men, women and children on the perimeters, waiting for the discarded bargains of the morning to fill their empty barrows.

Eve repeated her story to the trader as he worked swiftly to replenish his stand, but he had no basket free to offer her. As soon as one was empty it was immediately refilled.

'Come and see me at the end of the day,' he shouted as he heaved a large sack of potatoes on his shoulders.

Eve thanked him and moved on, her eyes searching for empty baskets in which she could carry her wares. But there were many like her, desperate for an opportunity.

By midday, Eve's hopes were fading. She had been offered one large basket but even empty it was too heavy for her to carry. It was quickly snapped up. If the twins had been with her, they could have carried it.

She stood in the piazza, tugging the collar of her coat up to her ears to keep out the winter breeze. It was whistling through the beautiful stone and glass architecture, causing her to lower her head against its force. Even if she had found a basket, she had nothing to put in it.

What was she to do now?

Joseph Petrovsky shovelled a little coke into the stove and turned to study the young woman at his table. She was eating the last of the borsch, but her pale face and weary expression told him that her day had been long and exhausting. Her long brown hair was dressed in a plait and she wore clothes that were old and darned. His heart went out to her. A young woman, in the prime of her life, with two young boys to support. He knew she worked hard as a flower-seller and that she had lost her livelihood in the flood. He knew what it was to lose everything. To have no identity and beg on the streets. His youth had been a mountain of worry and fear. Until he had come to this country, he had not known freedom in the true sense of the word. And he owed his existence to strangers, good people who had welcomed him into the community, given him work and the opportunity to make a new life for himself.

He poured tea from the samovar and sat beside her at the table. She smiled, but he could see the fear in her eyes. Beautiful eyes, he noted, golden eyes, that were honest and good.

'Your journey was not productive?' he asked gently.

She nodded and put down her spoon. 'Good working baskets with handles are in short supply.'

'Can you not buy one?'

'I bought me last basket years ago. It was a good one, not too big and lasted a long time.' She sighed. 'If only I hadn't gone out the night of the flood.'

'Let me give you a few shillings for the investment.'

She shook her head firmly. 'No, thanks all the same.'

'It's merely a loan.'

'I'll find one tomorrow.'

He sat back on the hard chair. 'You are a stubborn young woman.'

She laughed. 'That's what Peg says.'

He understood her pride and respected it. He had known Eve Kumar for many years but in Isle Street people kept themselves to themselves, their secrets were important to them. He had seen many things, but one of the most pleasant was the sight of a young couple, a black-haired lascar and a pretty young flower-seller, walking hand in hand, the light of love in their eyes. It had reminded him of Gilda, the woman he had loved and who had not survived the flight from their homeland. Suddenly the pain went through him as he thought of her. The ache was still there in his heart after all these years. In many ways, Eve reminded him of her. And the young sailor who had married her could well have been him.

'Now, you must drink your tea.' He pushed the cup towards her.

'I hope me boys have behaved themselves.'

'They are good boys. But they told me the Sister Mary was unhappy.'

She nodded. 'The nuns are strict.'

He paused. 'A good education will benefit them. If I have any regrets it was that I had so little. The Zemstvo, the council of men who provided the schools, were removed from the needs of the peasants. I was only a little older than Samuel and Albert when I was sent to the water company to dig holes and mend drains.'

'That must have been hard.'

'But I was alive. Many of my countrymen died or were robbed of their education. Eventually the Jews were blamed for the assassination of our Czar, Alexander. Thousands of our towns were destroyed. Russia was an imprisonment but it was also home. Yet even this was to be taken away from us.'

'What about your family?'

At her enquiry Joseph felt the old memories stirring inside him and the longing for physical contact from the long-dead. 'They perished.' He shook his head slightly and straightened his bent back. 'But that was many years ago.'

'I ain't ever going to complain after what you just told me,' she said quietly.

Joseph stood up. 'My dear, say your *tefilla*, your prayers of thanks, and God will look kindly on your face.'

'I hope so.' She rose and carried her plate to the sink, glancing over her shoulder with a smile. 'Though according to Sister Superior at St Saviour's she says she has a lot of work to do on us sinners.'

'Oh yes? And why is that?'

'The boys ain't been to Mass or confession in weeks.'

'The Sister Superior lives in a nice dry house and is safely under the care of Rome,' he was swift to point out. 'It is easy to be saintly in those conditions. Has she ever had to accommodate, I wonder, such things as those unwelcome guests that frequent your cottage? Or scrape the mud from the church walls? Or stand on a cold corner selling from a basket in order to forge a living.'

'And I bet she wouldn't get much custom in that black rig-out,' she laughed as she washed the dishes.

Joseph was glad to put a smile on her lips. In the face of adversity it was always humour that got you through.

★

'Goodnight and God bless.' Eve kissed the boys good-night. 'See you in the morning, by God's good grace, Amen.'

'Amen,' they replied sleepily.

'And say a prayer for our cottage.'

'We have.'

'And for Mr Petrovsky too.'

'It ain't bad here,' said Albert from under the covers. 'We've got a real china po under the bed.'

'And when we got home from school,' said Samuel eagerly, 'Mr Petrovsky cooked us more borsch.'

'And let us sit near the stove. Me feet was as warm as toast.'

'You're lucky,' nodded Eve.

'And tomorrow we're having somethin' else nice. I forgot what he said as it's got a funny name.'

'*Todah rabah* means thank you,' said Samuel quietly. 'Mr Petrovsky learned it to us.'

'He taught it to you.'

'I'm gonna say it to Sister Mary,' said Albert, laughing.

Eve smiled. Her boys were full of mischief. She wondered what Sister Mary's answer would be.

Eve pulled the curtain across. Peg was already in bed. Dressed in a thick woollen jumper over her nightdress, she was smoking a roll-up. A saucer was perched precariously on the bedclothes. 'Don't worry, I won't set the place alight.'

'You'd better not. We're running out of places to stay.'

'The old boy ain't half bad. Never had much to do

with him, even though he's lived here since before the war. Always said hello mind, and passed the time of day. Even bought a few of me flowers once or twice. I seen a few odd bods visiting him, the type that keep their caps on and collars turned up. Mind up here on the hill you can't see much more than from where we are. But I tell you this, I never thought I'd be living under me sister's roof and an old Russian bloke's, all in the same month. If anyone had told me that before Christmas, I would have said they was barmy.'

'You never know what's round the corner.' Eve undressed and climbed into bed. She shivered even though Joseph had given them two blankets each to add to their outdoor coats and the musty eiderdowns they had rescued from the cottage.

'And he ain't bad with the lads,' Peg continued, coughing as she inhaled. 'Whilst I was up the council he fed them when they got home from school. I reckon we fell on our feet coming here.'

'But I don't want him to think we would take advantage,' said Eve as she snuggled down.

'Why would he think that?' shrugged Peg, blowing out a cloud of smoke.

'Because he feels sorry for us. He even offered to buy me a basket,' Eve whispered so the boys wouldn't hear.

'Blimey, that solves a big problem!'

'Of course I refused.'

'What!' Peg's bushy grey head whipped round.

'He's an old man and hasn't got much himself.'

'How do you know that? He might be loaded.'

'Even if he was, I wouldn't accept. I'll find a basket tomorrow if I set off earlier.'

'Well, I think you're daft,' muttered Peg flattening the dog-end in the saucer.

But Eve had her pride. 'Did you speak to the council about the rats?'

Peg shrugged as she crushed the dog-end. 'They won't do nothing till we pay our rent.'

'Did you tell them we would?'

''Course I did.'

'What did they say?'

Peg was silent then yawned loudly. 'I told this stuffed shirt he should come round and see what seven and six a week buys. More ruddy rats than in an African jungle.'

Eve groaned. 'They'll never come round now.'

'Well, this time they can sing for their supper.'

'What do you mean?'

'Look, I've lived in that cottage years, long before you was born, ducks. And in all that time, I've paid me way, not missing a week and the bleeding council have sat on their fat arses, never lifting a finger to help. The walls are wet and the floors even wetter. The roof is leaking and if it wasn't for Jimmy, the slates he's nailed back would've stayed where they were, in the gutter. Now, I reckon it's about time the government wallahs held out the olive branch to Isle Street, came along and did their duty before I pay them a penny more. Right, now I'm off to get me beauty sleep.'

Eve closed her eyes. What was she going to do? Peg was at loggerheads with the council and they wouldn't come to fumigate if the rent wasn't paid.

She had to make some money. But how?

Chapter Nine

Eve rose early and hailed a ride on a milk cart. Covent Garden market was already busy, the traders and porters attending their stands. It was as the dawn's rays broke through the glass fanlights that she met a costermonger trying to sell off his old stock. He took her out to his cart.

'How much do you want for it?' Eve asked.

'How much do you offer?'

'I could pay you when I've sold it.'

He grinned. 'So I'd have to trust you, would I?'

'I'm known to some of the traders here.'

'Yeah, your face is familiar. Are you the flower-and cress-seller from up Aldgate High Street on Friday nights? The one with two teapot lids?'

Eve smiled. 'My boys, Samuel and Albert. But we lost our basket the night of the flood.'

He pushed his cap back from his sweating face. 'So how do you propose to flog this stuff?'

'I could do it easy if I had a basket,' said Eve, though

she didn't like the look of some of the crushed apples and oranges.

'How much business have you been doing up Aldgate?' he asked curiously.

'Brisk,' said Eve.

'Well, how is this for a deal, young woman. You take me leftovers each day, early mind, so I can load up me cart without the stuff rotting underneath. I've got two baskets so you can borrow one of 'em and at the end of the week, return me five bob.'

'Five bob is a lot of money.'

'You said you could sell it easy!' exclaimed the coster-monger.

Eve looked him in the eye. 'You drive a hard bargain.'

'Are we on?'

'Four bob and we'll shake hands.'

He threw back his head and laughed. 'It ain't me who drives a hard bargain, lass. But I like the look of you, so the deal's on.'

He stretched out his hand and she shook it.

'Me name's Archie Fuller. What's yours?'

'Eve.'

He gave her a wink. 'Get cracking then, lass. I'm going in to buy meself fresh stock. When I come out in an hour I want to see me cart empty.'

As Eve rummaged through the fruit and vegetables, an idea came to her. She worked swiftly to retrieve only the fruit and vegetables that she could make present-able to the public. When the basket was full, she called to two Irish families whom she recognized from yesterday. The women and children had been standing on the sides, waiting to carry baskets for purchasers.

'Do you want what's in here, all free?' she asked pointing to the cart.

They nodded eagerly.

'You can have it if you help me out to the street with my basket.'

Ten minutes later Eve was standing on the corner of a road close by. She had told her new employees that if they wanted a repeat performance they were to meet her early the next day. The offer was accepted immediately.

Eve looked down at her laden basket. Discreetly she shined the top layer of fruit with her cuff. Soon she began to call out to the passers-by. 'Oranges, apples and pears. Cheaper than the market.'

By two o'clock she had sold out to the city folk. With the money she had made she returned to the stands where some of the traders were packing up. She offered to buy their unsold stock and at once struck a deal.

Once more she asked the Irish family for their help and by tea time she had sold everything. Eve counted her takings of five shillings and six pence. She had made enough money for the rent and enough left to give some to Joseph.

She couldn't wait to tell everyone that Eve Kumar was back in business!

★

Archie Fuller was a man of his word. He met Eve each morning and out of her earnings she bought herself two strong baskets which he agreed to stow on the cart. Over the following weeks, she returned him four shillings every Tuesday, whilst her profits increased by the day.

One Sunday morning in February, Eve woke with a start. A strong wind was whistling through the gaps in the window. It was still dark outside and she got up, careful not to disturb Peg or the boys. Dressing quickly she went downstairs.

A light was on in the scullery. Joseph was already up. 'Just listen to the wind,' he said as they stood by the draughty door.

'I'm glad I'm not out selling today,' said Eve, pulling her shawl around her shoulders. The wind seemed to be getting stronger.

'Come along, I've made tea.'

Eve thought how cosy it was in Joseph's house as they sat together at the table. They were happy here. And she felt better about them staying now she could pay her way. 'It's Sunday so I'm going to the cottage,' she told him as she sipped the warm brew. 'I bought a strong disinfectant to deter the rats.'

'Will it work do you think?'

'I don't know but anything's worth a try. I don't like going inside but if I wait for the council to come, I could wait forever.'

'I shall come with you and whilst you work, chase the devils off with a broom.'

Eve smiled. She had been hoping he would offer as she knew the boys and Peg would only stand at the door or in the yard. After living in Joseph's clean and comfortable house, they were as reluctant as she was to go inside their old home.

Just then the wind blew the back door open. A gale blew round the kitchen, sweeping up the cloths and curtains with an invisible hand. Eve rushed to close it.

Joseph looked out of the window. 'A most unusual turn of events indeed. First the flood and now this.'

After breakfast they all sat in the parlour.

'Can we go out to play in the street?' asked Samuel and Albert.

Before Eve could answer there was a rushing noise in the chimney. Suddenly a cloud of black soot swept into the hearth. They all jumped up.

'It's Old Father Thames again,' cried Albert as a dusty fog enveloped them.

'Oy vay!' Joseph flung his arms up in distress. 'What evil *dybbuk* is this?'

'We'll soon clear it up,' said Eve, rushing out to find the brush and pan. But when she returned, Peg and Joseph were trying to stop another avalanche.

Their faces were black and the room was filled with soot.

Joseph placed a heavy board across the hearth to prevent any more catastrophes. The soot and dust covered everything, turning the room a gloomy grey.

They spent the morning cleaning, sweeping and washing. Outside the wind was turning into a hurricane blowing things along the street.

'Why can't we go out in it?' The boys wanted some excitement.

But when they saw Duggie Higgins in distress, they knew going out was too dangerous. All six feet two of Duggie was thrown back the way he had come.

'He's hanging on to the lamppost,' gasped Eve as they craned their necks to watch for the next development.

Duggie was losing his battle despite his great strength. He let go and toppled back. When he fell on his backside everyone laughed. But Eve was thinking about the cottage. If the wind was able to blow human bodies about like rag dolls would the cottage be able to withstand its force?

That afternoon they played dominoes. Peg smoked nervously, getting up to look out of the window now and then. When a dustbin clattered by they all rushed to see what it was. Followed by a chair with a broken leg, Eve knew that this was no ordinary wind. The country was experiencing another storm. She said a silent prayer, that no matter how much it blew, it wouldn't rain.

That night, the wind still hadn't given up. It rattled around the house, under the doors, through the windows and into every room.

'Do you reckon the cottage is still standing?' whispered Peg as they sat in their beds that night talking in whispers so as not to disturb the boys.

'A wind couldn't knock it down, could it?'

'Don't think so. A few slates or bricks could come loose. And we've got the copper's barrow to clear up the mess.'

Eve hadn't forgotten Charlie Merritt. Why had he never reclaimed the wheelbarrow? Perhaps he didn't want to be seen with the likes of them again. Had Harold spoken badly of them when he went to the station?

'Funny he ain't come for it,' said Peg voicing Eve's thoughts.

'Perhaps he couldn't borrow his dad's van.'

'Or perhaps he didn't find anything when he nosed around.'

'I didn't see him snooping,' replied Eve defensively. 'All he did was help us.'

'So why's he left that barrow?' persisted Peg irritatingly. 'Is it an excuse to have a butcher's when he feels like it?'

Eve sighed. 'What's he going to find? An old tumbled down cottage full of rats. I can't believe the police are interested in us.'

Peg sniffed. 'Never trust a copper that's what I say.'

Eve didn't reply as although she agreed with Peg about not trusting the police, Charlie Merritt seemed different. He had worked hard that day and cleared some of the mud. But his enthusiasm must have faded when he saw all there was to be done.

'You going to the market tomorrow?'

'If the wind's dropped.'

'You can't sell stuff hanging on to a lamppost, gel.'

'Let's go to sleep.' Eve didn't want to talk any more. One bad thought seemed to give birth to another.

But all the same, she woke with a start in the night. Wondering what had disturbed her, she realized it was the silence. Pulling her shawl round her she went to the window. There was only the calm night outside and the bright stars twinkling above.

The gale was over.

All day, Eve's thoughts were of the cottage. She had been relieved to see its familiar outline in the dark this morning as she set off for work. Perhaps if she got home early tonight, she could sprinkle down a little of the disinfectant. But it was a chilling thought, as it would be dusk, the shadows producing any number of frights. It would be better if Joseph was with her, but he was an old man and it was still cold in the evenings. At least she had been able to give Peg the money for the rent each week. And although they were not living there, they were not in debt. When the fumigation had been done, they could move back and begin their lives again. She knew the boys and Peg were getting too comfortable at Joseph's house. And although he didn't complain, it must be an imposition to suddenly acquire a large family. He couldn't get on with his own life and although he didn't speak of it, she knew that he had one.

That morning the newspapers announced the gale

had claimed eleven lives as it had swept across Britain. Buildings had been demolished, vehicles turned over and the train service interrupted. Hard on the heels of the flood, once more the nation struggled to return to normal.

The city had been battered by its force, but it was business as usual for the market traders. Though some of the fruit, vegetables and flowers had been damaged, it was rich pickings for those who stood on the sides.

Trade was good as her customers were relieved to see blue skies. She sold all the contents of her first basket but didn't return for more as she wanted to get home and persuade Peg and the boys to come to the cottage.

But when she arrived in Isle Street, Samuel and Albert ran towards her. 'We ain't got no roof,' they cried, pulling her to the cottage. 'The wind blew it off.'

Eve stood with the boys in the backyard. The hole over Jimmy's room had become a yawning gap spreading up to the top rafters. It was a sad sight.

'What we gonna do?' asked Samuel disconsolately.

'We'll have to stay with Mr Petrovsky.' Albert looked pleased.

Eve's spirits sank. There seemed no end to the catastrophes befalling the cottage.

She looked down at the place where the watercress had once grown. There was now a thick brown sludge in place of the delightful green shoots. A black furry creature scuttled off from under a stone.

Eve jumped away.

Albert laughed but Eve found it hard to smile. It was as if the old stories were coming true and Father Thames really was punishing them. Were they really going to lose their home for good?

Eve forced the tears back. She didn't want the twins to see how upset she was.

Later that evening there was a knock at the door. Eve went to answer it.

'Hello.' It was Charlie Merritt.

Eve was shocked to see the tall figure on the doorstep. He wasn't in uniform, but wore a coat and scarf that hung loose around his neck. His dark hair was brushed neatly back, as though he had just combed it into place.

It was a moment before she collected her thoughts. 'What do you want?' She knew she sounded unfriendly. But Peg's warning was still ringing in her ears.

'Is it too late to come in?'

She frowned. 'Why?'

'I'd like to talk to you about your husband.'

Eve felt a shiver go through her. She hadn't expected him to say that. 'You haven't found another body?'

'No.' He smiled. 'But I have found something else and would like to discuss it with you.'

Eve slowly opened the door and he stepped in. 'The boys are in bed asleep.'

'Oh, I was looking forward to seeing them.'

'How did you find us?' she asked.

'I made enquiries with the Higgins.'

She opened the parlour door. Peg and Joseph were sitting by the fire.

Peg looked alarmed but Joseph stood up and extended his arm. 'It's good to see you again, young man.'

Charlie Merritt shook his hand and smiled at Peg. 'Evening,' he said politely.

But Peg looked suspicious. 'What do you want?'

'It's about Raj,' interrupted Eve, sitting down. 'Have a seat.'

He sat on the couch beside her. 'I've been following up enquiries.'

'What enquiries?'

His blue eyes met hers. 'First, could you tell me how long your late husband had been at sea?'

Eve nodded, but Peg interrupted. 'What's it got to do with you?'

'I'm trying to piece together what might have happened.'

'By asking a lot of questions?'

This time Eve spoke up. 'Raj went to sea when he was only thirteen. He was twenty-one when he died.'

'So his service was some eight years?'

Eve nodded.

'Would you say your husband was an experienced sailor?'

'Yes.'

'And not likely to miss his footing and fall overboard?'

'Are you suggesting he was pushed?' Eve felt her voice rise. It was a horrible thought.

'I'm keeping an open mind, Mrs Kumar. However, I did visit the Overseas Sailors' Home in West India Dock Road. It provides lodgings for seamen waiting for ships and educates the lascars on the unscrupulous men and women who prey on them in this country. My aim was to seek out any sailor that might have come into contact with either your husband or the *Star of Bengal* at the time of his death. I returned there on several occasions and last week I had a stroke of luck. I found a lascar who had served on the *Star* five years ago. He is an *agwala* by trade, a man who worked in the engine room.'

Eve sat up. 'But Raj was a cook in the purser's department.'

'Indeed. But he recalled the name of the head man who dealt with the galley crew. His name is Somar Singh. Unfortunately I could get no further information on his whereabouts. The lascar didn't speak much English and it was only with the help of one of the staff that I managed to get the information I did. However, I then proceeded to the lascar Transfer Office in Victoria Dock to make further enquiries and was told that all the lascar crews of the *Star* were transferred to her sister ship after she was taken out of commission. This vessel is known as the *Tarkay* and her next appearance in the port will be in April.'

'Do you think this Somar Singh will be on it?'

'I'm told it's likely, though the hiring of the crews in India is not always to be relied upon. Also a request has to be made to the ship's captain to speak to the man if he is on board. It can be done through official channels of course.'

Eve didn't know what to feel. She had tried to come to terms with the loss of Raj and she feared this investigation would stir up all the pain again.

'Why are you taking this trouble?' she asked.

Charlie smiled at her. 'It's all in the line of duty.'

'What is this about?' asked Joseph, speaking for the first time.

Eve knew she had to tell him the truth. It was only fair as she was living under his roof and enjoying his hospitality. 'Charlie is a policeman, Joseph.' She blushed as she glanced at the young constable.

'You ain't doing this out of the goodness of yer heart, son,' said Peg accusingly. 'What's the catch?'

Charlie just raised his shoulders slightly. 'It seems to me that there is more to be discovered about Mrs Kumar's husband's death.'

'Well, you are in the minority, son. Your high and mighty principles won't cut much ice with your superiors and neither will they with joe public. Don't you know this is Isle Street and we are the forgotten few?'

Eve intervened. 'Peg, I'd like to hear what else he's got to say.'

Joseph stood up. 'I think it is time to make tea. Will you help me, Peg?'

She went reluctantly. 'I need a fag anyway. The sight of the law always makes me nervous.'

'I'm sorry,' apologized Eve when they were alone.

'Don't worry. I'm growing a thick skin.'

'When are you going to take your barrow?'

He smiled. 'When you've finished with it.'

There was silence until they both spoke at once. 'How are you and the boys?' he asked eventually.

Eve shrugged. 'They're back at school and I've found work.'

'That's good news.'

Eve wanted to tell him all about it, but she didn't know if she could trust him. In the East End telling the police anything other than lies was taboo. Yet he only seemed interested, not nosey.

'I found a trader at Covent Garden to do business with.' She didn't say his name.

Once again there was silence as she sat uncomfortably, while he watched her patiently. She wished she hadn't said anything at all. But to her surprise, he said simply, 'Did the council send the fumigator?'

'No. They said we're on the list.'

'After the flood, everyone's on it.'

Eve was disappointed. 'I bought some disinfectant and was going to try to do it myself. But yesterday the wind blew off the slates, leaving a big hole in the roof. '

'That's not the end of the world. Roofs can be mended.' He smiled again but this time the warmth reached his eyes. 'Could you use an extra pair of hands this weekend? I've had a run of long duties but I've got Saturday and Sunday off. I could borrow me dad's ladder and nail the slates back.'

Eve sat there, once more thinking of Peg's warning.

He laughed at her expression. 'I promise not to tell anyone I'm a policeman. I hope it doesn't make any difference to you.'

She looked away. What did he mean by that?

Their conversation was interrupted as Joseph returned with the tea.

Charlie pulled up his collar and strode briskly along Westferry Road. He would walk back to Stepney and enjoy the fresh air even though it was freezing cold. He wanted to think over what had just taken place and try to sort out his feelings. He hadn't meant to tell her anything other than the facts. That they might be able to shed some light on her husband's death by interviewing this lascar. But then he had gone on to ask her personal questions and found himself becoming more involved. He could have stayed off the topic of the cottage and certainly not offered to nail the slates back on the roof. It wasn't that he couldn't, he'd had a fair bit of experience in that line, doing up his dad's shop and helping his twin brothers George and Joe on their houses. He could turn his hand to just about anything and it was true that he had this weekend off. But there was a match on Saturday afternoon. He couldn't miss that as they'd won their last one four–two. The team were still on a high and if he told Robbie he was helping out Eve, he'd get a right earful. He could protest all he liked about wanting justice and fairness and it was all in the line of duty. But was it?

As she had said, the case was closed. He'd had no real authority when he went to the Transfer Office to find out about this sailor. He'd more or less insinuated he was following up enquiries. They'd been only too helpful, mind. It wasn't often that an interest was taken in lascar seamen. The blokes he had spoken to could hardly speak English anyway.

Charlie passed the Queens and looked at the brightly lit posters of the forthcoming events. On Friday night the locals took their turn, enjoying a moment of glory as they followed in the footsteps of the great entertainers, Harry Champion, Sable Fern and Marie Lloyd. A few people were gathered outside the doors of the theatre. An old man was begging, his cap outstretched. Charlie took a sixpence from his pocket and dropped it into the worn cloth.

'Thank yer, m'lud,' said the old man grinning toothlessly. 'Gawd bless yer and may yer have many 'elfy offspring and they grow'd up as 'andsome as their dad.'

Charlie smiled as he walked on. Offspring, eh? Well, that was a thought. He'd not given much consideration to kids of his own. Growing up with twin brothers, older by ten years, their children had become his, nieces and nephews that seemed to come along each year without fail so that he often forgot which one was which. But he hoped he made a good uncle and loved

164

being with them, especially the boys who often came to the matches. He taught them how to bounce a ball on their toes and to dribble it and give a good header. Not to be afraid to attack. Yes, he'd plenty of experience with nippers. The thing was, they weren't his.

Perhaps that was why he'd taken such a shine to the Kumars. Being twins, he was familiar with their patter and both were good-looking boys, like their mother.

What had their father been like?

During his enquiries, Charlie had tried to put a picture of him together as he'd been taught whilst in training. Suss out your man and get to know him before nicking him. That way you saved a lot of time and trouble asking daft questions. As far as he'd gathered, lascars were industrious and loyal by character, hard workers and the last to cause trouble in a foreign country. If Raj Kumar's boys were anything to go by, their dad was a good all rounder.

As he entered the Commercial Road, he considered a drink with his mates. They would be putting the world to rights over a pint right now. But coppers' talk didn't interest him tonight.

He wanted to analyze his motives . . . he paused for a moment, then laughed to himself. Wasn't that a copper through and through? Perhaps the answer was he couldn't help himself from being a policeman when he smelt something fishy.

And what was nailing in a few slates for someone? The girl never asked for a favour and was going to put disinfectant down herself. He hadn't said, but that stuff wouldn't help. The rats would lap it up!

No, first thing in the morning, he was going to cycle past Poplar town hall and make an unofficial call.

And make sure the Kumars were moved to the top of the fumigation list.

Chapter Ten

'Clocking off early, then, gel?' Archie Fuller raised a bushy eyebrow. 'It ain't twelve yet.'

'Me roof is being mended today.'

'You going up the ladder an' all?'

Eve laughed as Archie helped her to stow her baskets on board the cart. 'I want to see if this person's turned up to do it.'

'You wanna watch out. There's a lot of wallahs out there that will rook you. And if you get someone that knows what he's about, it could be expensive. Me brother had his done and he had no change from a pony.'

'A pony?' Eve was shocked. 'I can't afford that.'

'Why don't you get the council to do it?'

'They don't do anything round our way.'

'Well, you'll have to give the roofer one of your pretty smiles and get him to do it on the cheap.' He laughed. 'See you on Monday then.'

Eve said goodbye and hailed herself a ride on one of the many carts leaving the market. After what Archie had told her, she was more suspicious of Charlie than ever. Twenty-five pounds was a fortune. Did mending roofs really cost that much? Perhaps Charlie Merritt had thought it over and decided against it.

There was a breath of spring in the air as they travelled home. The old horse's rhythmic plodding and the noise of the cart melted in to the Saturday morning hustle and bustle. There were buses, taxis and vans mixed in with the horse-drawn vehicles. The smell of horse manure and traffic fumes added to the underlying aromas of the docks and the thousands of smoking chimneys. In the Commercial Road they passed the pie and eel shops, the mobile coffee stalls and the thriving back street markets. She wondered if she might see the shop that belonged to Charlie's family. The name written on the side of the van was Merritt's Bakery and Provisions. But didn't he say it was just off the Commercial Road? That could be anywhere.

'I'll drop you off here,' shouted the costermonger over his shoulder as he pulled up the horse. 'I'm going straight on, down the East India Road.'

Eve handed him the bag of carrots she had brought for the horse. 'Thanks for the lift.'

'Ta, he'll have them for his supper.' He touched his cap and clicked his tongue, slapping the reins over the horse's rump. 'Get up there, gal,' he shouted as the cart rumbled off.

Eve always gave something in exchange for transport. Even if it was only small. It showed you appreciated the ride and guaranteed you a lift again. As she walked down the Westferry Road, she wondered if the young policeman had turned up. She didn't have long to wait to find out. Samuel and Albert rushed out to greet her. 'Charlie's mending our roof and we've been helping.'

Eve followed them as they jumped over the broken bricks of the wall and ran into the yard. Charlie Merritt was sitting high up on the roof.

He saluted her. 'Afternoon, Mrs Kumar.'

So, he had turned up after all! Eve saw all the neat rows of slates nailed back to the rafters.

'The bug man come too,' Samuel told her.

'The fumigator?' Eve asked, surprised he had visited them so soon.

'It don't half pen and ink.' Albert giggled.

'Has he sprayed inside the stove?'

The twins nodded. 'They ain't quite stone dead yet. Charlie told us to chuck 'em in one of Jimmy's paint pots.'

Eve shuddered. She wondered how long it would be before they knew the fumigation had been a success.

Inside the cottage, they trod carefully over the crunchy dying bodies. For the first time since the flood it smelt of something other than drains. The fumigation wasn't a pleasant smell but it was an improvement.

They went slowly up the stairs, knocking the dying bugs off the banister as they went. Jimmy's room was full of slates, dust and dirt. Eve looked at the chest in the corner. Was it locked? Had Charlie seen it? She immediately became suspicious again.

'I've got an old tarpaulin up here to cover the roof whilst it's being done,' called a voice from above. Charlie's head poked through the hole. 'It'll keep out the bad weather.'

Eve saw there was a lot of empty space to go.

'Don't worry, it won't take too long,' he assured her as he wiped his dirty forehead with the back of his arm. 'Should have it all done in a few weeks.'

'How much will it cost?'

'I can salvage a lot of the slates. They didn't break, just got blown off where they were loose. And I'll be able to replace the broken ones from a yard over East Ham where me brother works.'

'It's your time I was thinking of.'

He grinned. 'I'd better be getting on.'

Eve went into their own room and gazed up at the big hole in the roof protected by the tarpaulin.

'Charlie's coming again tomorrow,' Samuel told her.

'It's Sunday.'

Samuel grinned. 'He don't go to church or nothing like that, he only plays football.'

'You found out a lot in one morning.'

'Can we go and watch him?'

'No, of course not. We don't know him and he don't know us.'

'He said we're like George and Joe,' Albert told her.

'They're his twin brothers. Only they ain't kids like us, they're grow'd up and have got kids of their own.'

Eve felt they were getting too friendly with Charlie. She had insisted they tell no one he was a policeman.

'Charlie said he wouldn't mind but to ask you first,' said Albert, glancing slyly at his brother.

'Ask me what?'

'If we could go to watch him play football. We ain't never been to a proper match. We ain't even got a proper ball.'

'You haven't complained up till now.'

'Charlie said he might be able to get one for us.'

'The answer is still no.'

Eve vowed to have words with Charlie Merritt who seemed to have stirred up this unrest. Why had he filled their minds with grand ideas? Why was he mending the roof without asking for payment? And most of all, why did he want to further Raj's case? Like Peg said, it was suspicious.

Albert sulked at her refusal and Samuel turned away. Eve wondered what else Charlie had been saying behind her back. What questions had he had been asking? Was it to get information? She would have a word in his ear as soon as he came down that ladder.

'Now go home both of you.'

'Why can't we stay here?' They looked rebellious.

But one glance from Eve's flashing eyes had them obeying. When they were gone, Eve brushed the bugs off her bottles and personal effects. She would take them with her as she didn't want prying eyes to see what she had.

Eve's cheeks were flushed and not with the cold as she faced Charlie Merritt.

'It's not right for me not to pay you,' she told him as they stood in the bitter cold of the yard. 'For your time and for the new slates.'

'They won't be new, they're off old roofs. As for my time, I've got nothing more important to do with it at the moment.'

'We aren't a charity case.'

'We could do a trade if it makes you feel better. You could sort me out a decent bunch of flowers for me mum's birthday in March. There's nothing she likes better than a big vase of April showers.'

'Flowers aren't much.' Eve gripped her bag; the bottles inside felt heavy suddenly as if they were a reminder of her distrust and suspicion when he was being so nice.

He smiled. 'Is there anything else? If not, I'll pull the tarpaulin over the rest of the roof till tomorrow. I'm off to football now.'

'The boys told me.'

He stopped. 'I get the feeling you are upset about something.'

'My boys don't get many offers to go to football matches. And if they did I would expect that person who offered to ask me first.'

'I told them it wasn't up to me.' He shrugged his broad shoulders under his dirty white shirt and began to roll down his cuffs. 'It was just they saw me boots tied on the bike and told me they was mad keen on football. I said I had nephews, all little footballers in the making and that me brothers took 'em once in a while to a couple of the matches. When I saw the looks on their faces I said I'd be happy to take them too – with their mum's permission of course.'

Eve's mouth tightened. 'I'd rather you didn't.'

He frowned, his gaze intent of her face. 'Don't tell me this is all about me being a copper! Are you really that bothered what people would say?'

'You don't understand,' Eve answered coldly. 'You don't live round here. Samuel and Albert have been called names by the kids just because their skin ain't the same colour. I have to protect them as best I can, they don't have anyone else to do it.'

'Yes, but as boys, they'll need to fight their own battles. Standing up to bullies is the only way to prove yourself.'

Eve was annoyed. Like all policemen he thought he was right. How could he know what life was like for those who had grown up on the other side of the tracks? 'As for the football,' she added quickly, 'I don't want them to start something and be disappointed it can't be continued.'

He frowned. 'Who says it wouldn't be? Football is a good sport for any kid to follow.'

'I told them and I'm telling you, my answer is no.'

He stepped back and nodded. 'If that's what you want. Now, I'll pull over the tarpaulin and put the ladder away.'

Eve watched him climb back up the ladder and work quickly to secure the roof. Why was she feeling so upset? Was it because she didn't like someone telling her how to bring up her children? Or that he thought he knew best?

When the work was complete and the ladder put away, he walked over to his bicycle propped against the cottage wall. He wound his boots securely over the front and turned the handlebars towards her.

'I apologize for the trouble I seem to have caused you,' he said quietly. 'But I'd like you to know that being a copper is only my job, not all of my life. When I walk out the station door at night, I'm not P.C. Plod, but Charlie Merritt, an East Ender born and bred, just like you. I'm glad to say that your lads took me at face value and didn't think of me as the enemy. You've got great kids there, a real credit to you and I wanted to return their friendship. If we're talking honesty here, I'll come clean.' His blue eyes were penetrating as he spoke. 'One of the reasons I took an interest in your case was because of them. I felt the law owed them and you an explanation. But now I see it wasn't up to me to make that decision. I realize I'm just a copper to you and always will be, both on and off duty. The fact is I don't want to embarrass you or put your boys at risk of abuse. So perhaps we should call this the parting of the ways?'

Eve didn't answer. She hadn't expected that and didn't know what to say.

He nodded slowly. 'I'll take that as a yes, then.'

He pushed his bicycle over the crumbled wall and stopped. 'I'll come back for dad's stuff as soon as I can borrow the van. Say cheerio to the boys for me,' he called over his shoulder.

Eve watched him cycle off, aware of a sinking sensation inside her. Gazing up at the roof she realized that her pride had cost a lot. What would happen to the roof now? And what about the enquiries he was following? Would they stop?

A feeling of gloom descended as she made her way back to number seven. Charlie's words came back to haunt her. Even though she tried to tell herself this was for the best, his explanation that he had investigated Raj's death for their benefit made her feel ashamed. Apparently there was no ulterior motive for befriending them. All the suspicion was on her side and not on his.

That night, she and Peg were sitting in bed once more, talking in whispers. The room was full of smoke and Peg's roll-ups were mounting in the saucer. The boys had wanted to go to the cottage tomorrow to meet Charlie and Eve had told them he wasn't coming. Albert had refused to say his prayers.

'Don't worry about them, the boys'll soon get over

him. You can't have a copper telling you how to bring up your kids. They can tell you not to sell your bloody flowers on a street corner and to move on, all right, but one thing they can't do, is to interfere in family life. You done right, gel,' encouraged Peg as she inhaled deeply. 'As for the cottage roof, don't worry. I'll go up to the council next week and tell them that now they've done the bugs, they can nail the slates back on. When they've done that to my satisfaction, they'll get the rest of their rent.'

'I thought you'd paid it all,' Eve said in alarm.

'I ain't that daft. I'll give it to them when they deserve it. Till then I've put the rest away in me tin.'

Eve felt it was dangerous to challenge the system when your home depended upon it. She had heard of rent books being taken away if the arrears mounted. She felt Peg had acted unwisely. A lapse in the paying of the rent would put them all at risk. But she couldn't tell Peg how to do things.

'Wonder how old Joan and Harold are?' Peg said suddenly.

'We'll pay them back one day.'

'What for? They don't deserve it.'

'Well, they did put us up,' Eve said uncertainly. She still shivered when she thought of Harold.

'Yes, but look what happened,' said Peg, pulling the covers over and yawning. 'You don't have to like someone 'cos they're family and one day she'll find out the truth about her randy old man.'

Eve tried to put the thought of Harold out of her mind. 'Night, then.'

'Night, love.'

Eve snuggled down. She was asleep in seconds.

It was Sunday and the boys and Peg were asleep as Eve quietly got dressed. Downstairs she found Joseph making the tea.

'Ah, my dear, the brew is nearly ready.'

Eve sat at the table.

'You are looking pale, Eve. Did you sleep well?' He placed the china cups on the table. It was a habit he had formed since they'd come, using the best china rather than enamel mugs.

'I had things on me mind.'

'Can I help? Would you like to discuss them?' He sat beside her.

Eve nodded. Joseph was always easy to talk to. 'Yesterday, I was annoyed with Charlie,' she began.

'Oh? Was it over the mending of the roof?'

'Oh, no, I wish it was that straightforward.' Eve sighed. 'It was over the boys. He told them they could go to watch him play football and I refused.'

Joseph's silver eyebrows knitted. 'Why is this?'

'I don't want Charlie to start something he can't finish. They'd be really disappointed if that happened. But most of all I don't want them ridiculed by anyone when they find out Charlie is a copper.'

Joseph leaned on the table and pleated his fingers. 'Eve, this young man is a decent sort, yes?'

Eve nodded. 'I think so.'

'Have you any doubts?'

'No, not really.'

'You have nothing to hide.'

'I did think he might be after Jimmy.'

Joseph smiled. 'But Charlie's intentions are not to throw Jimmy in gaol.'

Eve smiled. 'No.' She began to tell him what Charlie had said about why he had followed up Raj's case. 'He said he thought we was owed an explanation, that he was fond of the boys.' Leaning her elbows on the table, she rested her chin in her hands. 'What upset me next was he told me my kids had to fight their own battles. He couldn't see I was only trying to protect them.'

Joseph stroked his chin thoughtfully. 'Perhaps it is your own tender heart you are protecting?'

'What?'

'You have become both mother and father to your sons and done a wonderful job,' Joseph assured her. 'But Charlie is right, sooner or later they will have to stand up for themselves.'

'I know. That's why I used to take them out selling with me on Fridays, even though Albert hated it. As young as they are it's good training for them. When they get older they'll realize why I made them do it.' She paused. 'I suppose I didn't like Charlie telling me what to do.'

'It may be something else that makes you uncomfortable.'

Eve glanced sharply at him. 'What's that?'

'Your actions in defence of Samuel and Albert are commendable. However, this young man is also taking you on a journey into the past with his investigations. Here you will be faced again with the problems that confronted you and your beloved Raj. None of us wish pain on ourselves, but perhaps in returning to old issues through your boys, the future will not be so frightening.'

'Joseph, it ain't the past I'm worried about, it's now.'

'I have learned that the same fears that beset us once,' he told her gently, 'will haunt us again tomorrow if we do not face them. I know this to be true, my dear as I fled Russia and owe my freedom to this country. But I do not practise who I really am, or wear my *kippa* or attend the synagogue. Instead I prefer to wait for the occasions when my *chevra* – my old friends – visit and we bathe in nostalgia of the homeland where, despite the persecution, our souls were free if not our bodies and I was once the true Joseph Petrovsky.'

'You mean you are not really being you?' Eve asked, trying to understand.

'I am not the man I would choose to be. I was a coward to leave, to leave my . . .' He stopped, his breath halting as he whispered, 'They died for what they believed in.'

'But you would have died too.'

'Sometimes I think it would have been better.'

'Don't say that.'

'It is only to you that I confide in the hope that Eve Kumar will always be the brave girl who I used to see walking hand in hand with her husband, unafraid of what people might think.'

Eve smiled. 'I had Raj then.'

Joseph nodded. 'If only love was a permanent state of affairs. There would be no wars or persecution. We would see the world through different eyes.'

'Thank you.'

'What for?'

'For telling me about the real Joseph.'

He smiled and patted her hand. 'Now drink your tea. I can hear the boys coming downstairs.'

The days passed and Charlie didn't show up again, and Eve knew that what she had said had driven him away. She hoped that Peg would get the council to come and finish the job. Meanwhile, all she could do was to clean the cottage each Sunday in preparation for their return. At the close of March Eve decided it was time to fill her baskets with flowers once more. Now she had saved enough money to buy from the cascades of flowers filling Covent Garden. Crocuses, violets, daisies, daffodils, roses and carnations to name but a few. The weather was kinder and lifted people's spirits as the warmer months approached.

Eve asked the Irish family if they would like to take

Archie's fruit and veg and the answer, as she had suspected, was a yes.

'I'll miss you, gel,' Archie told Eve on the last Friday of March as she prepared to leave. 'But you'll be back next winter. You won't get a better deal anywhere than from Archie Fuller.'

'I'll look forward to it.' Eve tossed back her long brown plait and lifted her new basket on her hip. She had invested in ones with strong handles, appropriate for flower-selling. 'Till then you'll have the Irish to look after you. I've given them me pitch just up the road and they're eager to make a few bob.'

'As long as they don't pinch me good stuff and are as honest as you, I'll see them all right. Where's your new pitch then?'

'Down Poplar. It's a long ride here of a morning and I want my boys to come out with me.'

'Who you gonna buy from?'

'I've struck a deal with Queenie Watts.' Eve gestured to the big flower stand in between two of the giant pillars. A large woman wearing an apron over her thick coat worked busily serving her customers. 'She's sending down flowers every morning on a costermonger's cart. They are the previous day's stock so Queenie won't have to dolly them up as fresh.'

'You're a bright lass, Eve Kumar. And you've chosen well in Queenie. No doubt you'll flog her stuff at a good profit just like you did with me fruit and veg.'

Eve was grateful to Archie for the start he had given

her back into business after the flood. But her heart didn't lie with fruit and veg. Flowers were her passion. Their colours and scents and the variety of people to whom she sold. If it was outside a hospital or theatre, a factory or place of business, or to a gent for his lady love, or a wake passing through to the cemetery where discretion was the essence of the purchase, each customer had different requirements. People's tastes were varied and she liked to see the pleasure in their eyes as they gazed into the whirlpools of colour. She wanted her boys to know the same satisfaction that she had. When they were older, they would have learned the business thoroughly, what to buy and what not. Perhaps they would hold a stand at market or rent a shop. It was her dream for them, a big dream and one she was determined to make come true.

'Take care of yourself, lass.'

'You too, Archie.'

'Call by when you're up here again.'

Eve caught a cart going towards Poplar feeling both excited and nervous. Had she made the right choice in selling close to home? Her mother and Peg had sold at Seven Dials, Drury Lane and Soho and these were still the most fashionable locations. But it was a long way up to the city. Albert already hated the walk to Aldgate and after what had happened on the night of the flood, Eve wanted to make the business more appealing to her sons.

As a stiff breeze blew down the street Eve took her

place under the middle arch of the famous theatre and music hall. The Queens didn't look imposing on the outside, it didn't have a grand set of steps to walk up like the West End theatres, but it was always busy, providing the general public with affordable entertainment. The best time for her to come would be Friday and Saturday nights when the theatre was always full, but she would experiment today and discover what business was to be done in the daylight hours. Arranging her bunches carefully Eve missed the little green heads of watercress that always enticed the punters. But it was a sunny day and the shoppers were out in force, so she hoped she could gain their attention without it. She had dressed with care for her first day of flower-selling and her calf-length black skirt and waist-hugging jacket with brightly coloured embroidery on the sleeves caused many heads to turn. After a good wash in Joseph's sink and a wring out through the mangle, the clothes had lost the smell of drains and the fumigation. Eve was proud of her mother's shawl tied lightly round her shoulders and the black hat with its ostrich feather that she now slipped on her head. Her appearance was important; along with the skill to present her flowers, she also had to sell herself. People liked to think they were buying from a genuine flower-seller. Not a hawker whose flowers and buttonholes went limp or died after only a few hours.

To her surprise, Eve was busy straight away and the morning flew by. One basket soon emptied and she stood the full one inside it. By four o'clock Eve had sold the last bunch of violets to a girl dressed in a white coat, turban and clogs who smelt of pickles.

She sighed in pleasure as she took the violets. 'These are for me mum, it's her birthday today.'

Eve knew the girls at the pickle factory worked hard for their meagre pay. In the course of the pickling process, the vinegar often coloured their skins a strange yellow. She felt lucky being out in the fresh air with roses in her cheeks. 'You can have them for tuppence,' she told the girl. 'As they're for your mum.'

Her customer was delighted. 'We're gonna have a knees-up tonight.'

Eve smiled, recalling another mother's birthday in March. Would Charlie Merritt's mother be celebrating too? Would she have a knees-up in the front room or would her family take her up West to wine and dine her?

As Eve gathered her empty baskets for the half mile walk home along the dock road, she remembered the hurt expression on Charlie's face when they had last spoken. She didn't know what she'd say to him if she ever saw him again, but then that seemed unlikely. His beat was in Stepney, though she had kept a lookout for his dad's van on her way to Covent Garden. The wheel-barrow and ladder had gone from the cottage. She knew Charlie must have collected them. Had he given the Kumar family any thought as he looked up at the tarpaulin on the roof? He hadn't taken it. The cover was the only thing that kept the rain out.

Eve came to Isle Street, relieved to see the welcoming sight of the cottage down in the dip. Flushed with success, she put the thought of Charlie from her mind, replacing it with the eager desire to return home. The mice, rats and bugs were still absent. Eve wanted to inhabit the cottage again before they did.

If the stuffed shirt from the council came round, he would see the work they had started and perhaps would be persuaded to complete the repairs.

Eve's steps quickened. The boys would be home from school and she couldn't wait to share her plans. If all went well, they would move after Easter, a lovely time of the year.

Chapter Eleven

Albert and Samuel sneezed and coughed their way into April. Eve administered her homemade remedy and a dose of Galloway's lung syrup, though it didn't make much difference. When Eve went to wake them on Easter Sunday morning, they didn't want to get out of bed.

'You can stay in bed,' Eve said and rubbed a dab of camphorated oil on their chests.

'Sister Mary said we've got to go to Mass today. It's a sin not to,' said Albert.

'We was going to be altar boys.' Samuel blinked watery eyes as the strong smell of the embrocation filled the room.

'You can't go with colds like that.'

'You'll have to write a note for us.'

'I'll tell her myself.'

'You don't need to.' Albert looked at his brother. 'She only wants a note.'

'I'll write one after the holiday then.'

After seeing to the boys, Eve went downstairs. 'Don't

look like we'll be moving to the cottage today,' she told Peg and Joseph as they sat down to breakfast in the kitchen. 'They've both got colds.'

'Poor little chics.'

'Sister Mary wanted them to be altar boys.'

'There's plenty of other kids to choose from,' shrugged Peg as she spooned out the porridge. 'And it don't really matter about moving, a couple of days won't make any difference.'

Joseph nodded. 'I'll make a strong borsch with plenty of onion to bring out their colds.'

Eve laughed. 'Don't spoil them or they'll never want to go back to school.'

'Can't blame 'em with that hard-faced cow as their teacher,' put in Peg as she lit the gas. 'I might be talking out of turn but nuns give me the willies. I pity them poor kids I really do.'

'Yes, but it's a good education at St Saviour's. One I would have liked if I'd had the chance.'

But Peg waved her hand dismissively. 'You had the best education, ducks, in the school of life. You may have only been twelve when you left school to help your mum sell flowers, but it ain't made no difference to the way you turned out.'

'I couldn't read or write properly,' Eve pointed out, recalling how hard it had been for her to fit learning in with helping her mother. There were always plenty of flowers, buttonholes and posies to be made but never enough time or books for her studies. 'At their age I was hardly at school because Mum needed me. She was always dodging the school inspector when he came round.'

Peg threw back her frizzy head and laughed. 'She had the luck of the Irish in more ways than one. How she managed to avoid him I'll never know. But maybe he didn't try hard enough to find her. She had a paddy on her that matched the fire in her eyes, just like you, ducks. She never suffered fools gladly.'

Eve smiled. 'And like you, she had to make a living and I was proud of her. When Dad was fighting in France, she didn't wear her heart on her sleeve. She told me that one day he'd come home, meanwhile we'd look after ourselves the best way we could.'

Peg nodded firmly. 'She was fair, your mum. Flower-selling was looked down on by some, as there are the girls who give us a bad name, trading at night and offering more than a posy or two to the gentlemen. But times were hard and Sarah never judged others. She just let 'em get on with their own business, whilst she minded hers. Which is more than I can say for them nuns.' She stood up and taking her tobacco tin from the windowsill, opened the back door. 'Anyway I'm going in the yard for a smoke.'

When Eve and Joseph were alone, he said quietly, 'Don't worry, you'll soon be going home.'

'Does it show on me face?'

'No, but I understand.'

'You've been very good to us.'

'Stay for as long as you like. My door is always open.'

Eve replied, 'I was going to say that ours will always be open for you too. The trouble is we ain't got a front door.'

They both laughed but Eve knew that Joseph meant what he said. Despite her plans having to be put aside yet again, it felt wonderful to have such a good friend.

A week later Eve lay in bed. A sweat was breaking over her body. Although the twins were well again, she had caught their cold. Once more her hopes for moving were dashed as Sunday came and went. Flushed with fever, she could find no energy to get up. It wasn't until two days later that she was able to struggle from bed and dress. The morning was cold and grey as she waited on Westferry Road for her delivery of flowers. It seemed beyond her to walk as far as the Queens or the Hippodrome cinema, so instead she stood outside the rope factory gates. Her legs felt weary and it was an effort to smile at her customers. But once more all her flowers sold, leaving just a few squashed heads at the bottom of her baskets.

When she got home, Peg was in the kitchen, making tea for the boys. 'We had a visit from the council today.'

'What, here?'

'No, I was at the cottage cleaning out a few things. This fella with a bowler hat walked in as bold as brass. He threatened to chuck us out.'

Eve closed her eyes and sat down quickly. 'I was afraid this would happen.'

'Said the rent wasn't paid.'

'You gave it to him, of course?'

'Well, five bob to keep him happy.'

'Five bob! But we had more than that.'

'Look, love, you may not have noticed but last week I bought the lads a few bits from market as their clothes was falling off them. Then I saw Joseph all right, gave him a few bob extra for all that borsch he cooked whilst you and the boys was ill. And then there's me baccy. I'll admit to the fact I've treated myself to a few Woodbines lately. I was going to put it all back when I started selling again.'

Eve knew that Peg's flower-selling days were long over. With her aches and pains she couldn't stand on street corners any more. Eve had seen the second-hand clothes that Peg had bought for the boys, some jumpers, shirts and trousers for school but hadn't expected them to cost a fortune. Was money, or the lack of it, the reason Peg wasn't eager to return to the cottage?

'Joseph will put us up a bit longer, gel, don't worry about the rent. We'll scrape it together somehow.'

'I just hope they don't put someone else in the cottage.'

Peg laughed. 'In my cottage? Just let 'em try! Now, I'll make us a nice cup of tea.'

Eve sighed. 'Are the boys home?'

'Not yet. They've gone up the park.'

'They should be doing their homework.'

'Oh, give them a break, gel. The nights are lighter now. And a bit of fresh air will do them good after being in school all day.'

Eve didn't want the twins going off after their lessons. She wanted them to do their homework first. They could play in the street after.

'Why don't you go in and sit by the fire? I'll bring in your tea.'

The effects of the cold were still with Eve because she gave in easily. Slowly she stood up and went to the front room. The warmth surrounded her as she sat down in the armchair. She looked into the tiny orange flames that lapped at the sides of the coke. As her eyes fluttered closed, she made up her mind to visit the town hall. She would give them the money she had saved, bringing them up to date with the rent. It wasn't that she didn't trust Peg, of course. But she trusted herself more. It was the last thing on her mind as she fell asleep.

It was the end of April before Eve could save up enough to pay the rent. The clerk at the town hall accepted the money without question but would not discuss the repairs to the cottage.

'Not this department,' was all he would say as he disappeared into his cubby-hole.

On the way home Eve decided to stop at St Saviour's and wait at the school gates. But the bell had already gone and most of the children had left.

A figure dressed in black robes swept across the playground. 'Mrs Kumar, I would like to speak to you.' Sister Mary crooked a finger. 'Please come inside.' Under the black frame of her habit and the white band that stretched across her forehead, she looked severe as she led Eve into her classroom. 'I've been waiting to see you about your sons' work.' She displayed their books on the desk. Eve could see splodges of ink and not a lot of writing.

'Albert in particular. He is a bright child, but won't make the effort.'

Eve frowned. Sister Mary was right, Albert tended to be lazy and his books showed that.

'As for Samuel, he tries harder and is good at arithmetic. But his English is not up to standard.'

Eve nodded. 'Is that all?'

'There are other things, but I won't go into them now. However, I must bring to your notice that Albert and Samuel are unable to receive communion. They say they have not attended confession for some while.'

'That's because on Saturday mornings, they help me with the flowers.'

'Is it really necessary?'

'Yes, Sister Mary, it is.'

'By missing confession they are not in a state of grace,' the nun objected, 'and ready to receive the body and blood of Our Lord. Now, do you want them to be good Catholics?'

'Yes, but—'

'Their spiritual welfare must come first.'

'I'll see they go to confession this week.'

'Also their Latin is poor. But then what more can be expected if they don't attend Mass on a regular basis?'

How long was this list going to be, Eve wondered impatiently. But before she could reply Sister Mary continued.

'But my main concern is that they are so often ill.'

'They only had colds,' said Eve. 'I wrote a note.'

Sister Mary narrowed her tiny eyes. 'I received one, but that was before they were absent again.'

Eve opened her mouth then shut it. She felt herself going red. 'I must have lost track.'

'Four days in all, Mrs Kumar.' Sister Mary pleated her fingers. 'And when I asked for confirmation in writing, Albert told me that you were too ill to write.'

Eve tried to look unsurprised. 'I caught their cold,' she said feebly.

Sister Mary's astute eyes didn't move from her face. 'No wonder their work is deteriorating. With such erratic attendance their work is bound to suffer.'

'It won't happen again.'

Sister Mary sat up stiffly in her chair. 'Samuel and Albert could be good scholars, Mrs Kumar, if they were given the support at home. The potential is there for them to excel at their work. And there are only places available at St Saviour's for those who wish to learn and – most importantly of all – to follow the church's teachings.'

'Yes, Sister Mary.' Eve was trying to digest everything she had said, but the news of the twins' absences had left her shocked.

'Our Sunday worship and daily Mass are the most important things in our lives.'

Eve nodded once more but she was hardly listening.

'That's all for now.'

Eve left the classroom, her mind in turmoil. She had felt about ten as Sister Mary had lectured her. Why had the boys been absent from school and told Sister Mary their mother was too ill to write a note?

Her anger mounted, both with the boys and herself as she hurried home. The boys for being deceitful and herself for allowing them to shirk their studies and miss school.

But when she got home Samuel and Albert were waiting for her with news of their own. 'We've seen Charlie, Mum,' Albert cried excitedly the moment she walked in.

'What?'

'We saw Charlie.'

'Where?'

'Up the park.'

'So that's where you've been?'

They nodded. 'Peg said we could. Charlie was there playing football. It was his day off and he was practising for a match.'

Eve wondered if the boys had been with him on the days they had been absent from school.

'He said to give you this.'

Eve took the crumpled paper from Albert. 'What is it?'

'Dunno. He said he'd had it in his pocket for a few days.'

Eve walked into the front room and sat down. She read the careful, upright handwriting.

Dear Mrs Kumar,
    The *Tarkay* docks at Tilbury in May, later than expected. Somar Singh may be on it, or not. Perhaps you will want this information, perhaps not, but I thought I'd write it anyway. Please let me know if I can be of help to you in the matter.
    Kind regards,
    Charlie.

Eve read it again.

'What does it say?' Albert asked as they stood beside her.

'It's the name of the man your dad might have known and the ship he sails on.'

'Is Charlie taking us to see him?'

Eve felt light-headed and strange. Even the matter of the truancy had taken second place to this. What was she to do with the information? Why hadn't Charlie come to see her instead of writing a note? Should she go and see him?

Joseph came in the door. 'Eve, are you all right?'

'Charlie's given us the name of a man that knew our dad,' explained Samuel.

'I see,' said Joseph sitting beside Eve on the couch. 'What are you going to do?'

'I don't know, Joseph.' Without Charlie's help to find the ship, there really wasn't much she could do.

'What else did Charlie say?' she asked the boys.

'Nothing. He was playing football with a mate. We was hoping they would let us play too, but Charlie didn't ask.' Albert looked glum. 'S'pose he didn't think you'd let us.'

'Is it with Charlie you've been on the days you didn't go to school?'

They both went red.

'I've just spoken to Sister Mary.'

Samuel and Albert looked at one another. Eve sat back in the chair. 'So, what have you got to say for yourselves?'

'We was going to tell you,' said Samuel, tears filling his eyes. 'But it wasn't Charlie we was with. Today is the first time we saw him.'

'So what did you do for four days?'

Albert shrugged. 'Just mucked about.'

Eve couldn't believe they had been so naughty. 'And why did you say I was too ill to write a note? That was a deliberate lie.'

'You was ill,' said Albert, 'but not as ill as we said.'

'That wasn't the truth, was it?'

'We didn't think it was a lie.'

'It was a lie for no reason.'

'But there was—' began Albert before Samuel nudged him.

'There was what?' Eve looked at them sternly.

They dropped their heads.

'Boys, please help your mother,' urged Joseph quietly. 'She is only trying to understand.'

Samuel wiped his eyes. 'We was afraid to go to school.'

'Afraid?' Eve frowned. 'Of Sister Mary?'

They shook their heads.

'Who then?'

'The other boys. They called us names.'

'What sort of names?'

'The ones like they called us before. Them rude ones.'

'Well, just as I told you before, you mustn't take any notice. They don't know what they're saying.'

Eve was furious. She looked at her precious sons and their lovely dark hair and skin as smooth as milky chocolate, and Charlie's words came back to her. Sooner or later the twins would have to fight their own battles. She couldn't protect them forever. But to her they were still little babies and she loved them so much.

That night after the boys had gone to bed, Eve and Peg sat with Joseph in the front room discussing what had happened.

'I don't reckon they deserve to be punished,' Peg said after Eve had told them what happened.

'I said they can't go up the park or play in the street.'

'Poor little buggers.'

'I had to do something. It won't be for long.'

'But it was those older kids' fault,' Peg protested. 'They wanted money from the twins. Even knocked them about when they didn't get it.'

'I'm going up the school tomorrow to complain to Sister Mary,' said Eve defiantly. Although she had punished her boys, in her heart she felt they didn't deserve it. They had been hiding from the bullies, that was all.

'I would think twice about that, my dear.' Joseph looked concerned.

'Why's that?'

'Because she has no control over those boys outside of school.'

'Samuel and Albert ain't big for their age. It's not fair, they can't fight back,' cried Eve.

'The kids to blame think our lads have got money from the flower-selling,' said Peg with a slow nod. 'So we know the cause of the trouble.'

'So what am I to do? Stop Samuel and Albert from coming with me to learn the trade? Why should my boys be threatened for doing something worthwhile?'

'It might be worth a try, just for a few weeks.' Peg looked at Joseph.

He raised his shoulders and held out his hands. 'It is for Eve to decide.'

'I could give it a try,' said Eve reluctantly. Then she smiled. 'They can go to confession instead.'

Peg laughed. 'They won't like that either.'

'Sister Mary is always saying they don't go enough.'

'Them kids is all innocence,' replied Peg with a sniff. 'Confession indeed! What they got to confess?'

Joseph chuckled. 'They are good boys. As they grow older they will grow strong and wise.'

But would they? Eve wondered anxiously. She was worried the name-calling had begun again. It wasn't surprising that Samuel and Albert didn't want to go to school.

That night Eve lay awake in the dark still worrying about the boys. Perhaps she should do what Sister Mary advised, make them concentrate on their school-work and be good Catholics. Though the flower-selling was important, their immediate welfare came first.

Then her thoughts turned to the note. Did she have enough courage to find the ship and speak to Somar Singh herself? Five years ago, she would have done anything to find out what had happened to Raj, but now she wasn't sure if that was what she wanted. Standing in the morgue and looking at that dead man had brought back all the unhappiness.

The next day Eve waited for Albert and Samuel at school. But it was raining and everyone sped through the gates, eager to get home. Eve searched the boys' faces, wondering which ones were the culprits.

Albert and Samuel trudged out alone. They didn't

look pleased to see her. The rain trickled down Albert's round face.

'Have you got your homework?'

They nodded. They knew they couldn't go to the park or play in the street and there was silence all the way home.

'Come on get dry,' said Peg when they walked in. 'You all look like drowned rats.'

Joseph was cooking in the kitchen. 'The borsch is nearly ready boys!'

When tea was over, they went into the front room. Eve inspected their books. 'Albert, you've got more crosses than ticks.'

He chewed the end of his pencil. 'I don't like the times tables.'

'Do you know them?'

They both looked at each other. 'No,' admitted Samuel.

Eve pulled back her shoulders. 'It's easy; if you learn them properly, it's like riding a bike. Once you do it properly you never forget again.'

Her sons looked unimpressed but Eve was determined that things were going to change. She was even going to send them to confession on Saturday instead of flower-selling.

Jimmy Jones put on his brakes so fast that he almost went over the top of the handlebars. 'Eve! What are you doing here?'

She stepped off the cobbles by the factory gates. 'Selling me flowers of course. Where have you been all this time, Jimmy?'

'With me mate at Shoreditch.'

'We've been worried about you.'

He stood his bike against the wall. 'Lovely flowers you got here. Are you selling on the island then?'

'Yes. I took a chance.'

'It's a long way from Aldgate and Seven Dials.'

'Yes, but closer to home. Jimmy, why have you stayed away?'

He looked embarrassed as he slipped off his cap. All his spiky brown hair stood on end. 'I changed me job.'

'You're not at the paint factory?'

'No, they rumbled me.'

Eve rolled her eyes. 'What did you do?'

'Nothing much. Just got hold of a few pots of paint from the flood and flogged them off cheap. Someone blew the whistle and I almost got me collar felt. But I was sacked instead.'

'Oh, Jimmy, you must be careful.'

He grinned. 'Anyway, I got a new job, down at the PLA. Running for some of the bosses.'

'Do you know much about the ships that are docked there?'

''Course. Why?'

'It's a long story.'

'I'm on me dinner hour. Do you fancy a 'apporth of chips?'

'I'll have to eat them here.' Eve glanced at the big factory gates. 'They'll all be coming out in a minute.' She dug in her money bag tied round her waist.

'Don't need that. I know where I can get them free.'

'I don't want you getting in trouble on my behalf. And I can afford it now.'

Jimmy's eyebrows rose. 'Blimey, who's coming up in the world then?'

Eve laughed and gave him the money. Jimmy pedalled furiously off to the fish shop. When he came back Eve decided to tell him all that happened with Charlie. She was going to confess that he was a policeman and was following Raj's case. If Jimmy knew some of the ships that were in, he might know of the *Tarkay*. She had the note in her pocket and brought it out ready to show Jimmy when he returned.

'I've seen the ship,' said Jimmy as he passed the note back to her. 'She's docked in the Pool.'

Eve's heart leapt. 'How would I get on board?'

'Don't know as you would. They're foreign.'

Eve served a customer with a pretty bunch of lavender.

'Don't let your chips get cold.' Jimmy was wolfing his.

Turning, Eve discreetly nibbled at the delicious hot food hidden behind one of her baskets. Although it was a warm May day, she hadn't eaten since early morning and the chips began to sustain her.

'You say Charlie is a copper?' Jimmy looked from side to side as though someone could overhear their conversation. 'Was he after me?'

''Course not.'

'What's he want with you, then?'

'He thinks more should have been done about Raj.'

Jimmy looked surprised. 'A copper with half a brain, eh? Do you think he's kosher?'

Eve nodded. 'But I sent him away.'

'Blimey, gel, why did you do that?'

Eve went red. 'Because of the boys. You know what people round here think of the law.'

'So what did the nippers say?'

She looked down. 'They liked him. He said he'd take them to a football match and I told him not to put ideas in their heads.'

Jimmy screwed up the oily newspaper. 'It don't seem to me that he'd get anything out of saying that if he was legit. If Charlie is just a good sort, p'raps you'd do well to keep in with him. '

'I never thought I'd hear you say that.'

'He seemed fine to me. Mucked in and didn't ask no questions. Thought he was all right meself.'

'I don't think he'll come round again.' Eve shook her head fiercely. 'Or he would have told me about the ship himself.'

Jimmy stepped back as a group of young women walked out of the factory gates. They wore overalls and turbans and crowded round Eve's basket. 'Could you save me some roses for when I clock off?' asked one, getting out her purse. 'And for me,' said another.

'You've got a nice little business here,' observed Jimmy as she dropped her takings into her bag hidden under the folds of her skirt.

'I hope so.'

'You deserve a bit of luck. What with the flood and having to put up at Bambury Buildings with Peg's two miserable dopes.' He shook his head slowly. 'I cycled by number three the other day and saw the tarpaulin. How long is it gonna stay up there?'

'Until the council finish the repair. Jimmy?'

'What?'

'Could you ask at the docks about Somar Singh?'

Jimmy hesitated. 'Dunno about that. Lascars keep themselves to themselves. Don't like mixing. Like long lines of ducks they are, all following each other.' He saw Eve's expression. 'Sorry, gel. No disrespect to your old man.'

Eve glanced away. Even Jimmy could say hurtful things in an unguarded moment.

'If I was you, I'd find that copper.'

'What? Go to the station?'

'Don't you know where he lives?'

'Only that his dad has a shop up the Commercial Road. And anyway, Jimmy, if I knew I wouldn't ask.'

Eve was determined not to ask Charlie for help. It was obvious he was not interested any more. She had her pride.

'Tell the boys and Peg I'll be seeing them soon,' said Jimmy shrugging. 'When are you moving back to number three?'

'Soon I hope.'

'I'll help you.'

'What about Sunday?' Eve said eagerly.

'Sunday it is.' Jimmy jumped on his bike. 'Do I get me room back an' all?'

''Course you do.'

Eve watched him cycle away, his feet going fast on the pedals. Would they really be back home on Sunday?

She didn't want to get up her hopes after being disappointed so many times before.

Chapter Twelve

At last it was moving day. It was a beautiful early May morning, soft and bright, like a true May day should be, Eve thought as she looked out of the window. She hoped Jimmy hadn't forgotten his promise to help and she wondered whether he had news of the grain ship and Somar Singh.

Eve dressed as the others slept. Downstairs she found Joseph, as usual, making tea. 'I'll miss our little chats,' she told him as they sat down at the table.

'Are you sure you want to go?' Joseph looked sad.

'It's time we did and we're only over the road.'

'Yes, that is true.'

'You can have your friends to stay now.'

'I think of you all as my friends. I am always here should you need a shoulder – is that the right expression?'

She laughed. 'Yes, and I've already leaned on it.'

'I'll cook something nice for tonight. Perhaps an *okroshka*, a good vegetable stew?'

'Sounds lovely.'

There was a knock on the door, and Eve jumped up to answer it. 'Jimmy, you're early.'

'Know what they say about the early bird.' He was all smiles as he stepped in.

'Where's your bike?'

'At the cottage. I had a quick shifty round. Blimey, it's in a bit of a state still.'

She smiled. 'Have you changed your mind about coming back?'

'Not on your nelly. There's five of us blokes in one room at my gaff up Shoreditch. Talk about plates of meat!'

Eve took his sleeve and drew him close. 'Jimmy, did you find out anything at the docks?'

'Yeah, listen.' He glanced over her shoulder and whispered, 'None of the crew would talk but I saw this poor sod – begging he was, close to the ship an' all. So I says to him, "Do you happen to know a lascar called Somar Singh, chum? Sailed on the *Tarkay*." He gave me the old vacant stare but I thought to meself, he's hungry and needs a few bob so I'll show him a tanner. "If you can help me, I'll give you this," I says and it works a miracle. The glint of silver causes an immediate under-standing of the old vernacular as he replies, "Sailortown, sahib, Singh in sailortown!"'

'But sailortown could be anywhere,' said Eve, dis-appointed, 'from here to Aldgate.'

'I know,' nodded Jimmy, putting up his hands. 'So, dropping the tanner in his turban, I then fishes in me pocket for another. His eyes are like organ stops then.'

'What happened?'

Jimmy puffed out his chest. 'Done the trick, it did, as I says, "Give me a nod mate if you mean Wapping" and I waits, then I says, "or Limehouse" – and still he don't move – "or Shadwell." And his head goes up and down like a flag on a pint of ale.'

Eve caught her breath. 'You sure he understood?'

'No doubt about it.'

'Did you get any more?'

'Word's out the *Tarkay* leaves soon, maybe in a week or so.'

'So Singh is still in Shadwell!'

'Yeah. But—' He looked at Eve uncertainly. 'You can't go there on your own, it's full of sharks and harpies.'

But Eve wasn't listening. She was already planning her route.

It was something she had to do.

That afternoon, the Higgins turned out in force to help with the move. Though there was no barrow, Duggie's hand cart was filled many times over and the front door was mended and nailed back. The walls were distempered and the quarry tiles washed till they shone. The closet was inspected for traces of life and Eve hung fresh pieces of newspaper from the nail.

'Can I go to the lav now?' asked Albert when she'd finished. 'Nothing's gonna come up and bite me bum is it?'

'No, it's safe.'

But when Albert was in there Samuel shouted out. 'Albert, I seen a rat.'

There was hollering from inside and Albert burst out. His pants were at half mast.

'It was only a joke,' Eve intervened as they began to fight. 'Now go and help Jimmy.'

The afternoon progressed with a lot of hard work but when Joseph arrived with a pan of *okroshka*, all activity stopped. They carried the table into the yard as there were too many to seat in the kitchen. A pitcher of ale appeared, glasses were filled and the hot stew filled each plate.

'For foreign grub that wasn't bad,' nodded Eric, smacking his lips.

'Very nice,' agreed Maude. 'I couldn't have done better meself.'

'Praise indeed,' smiled Joseph as second helpings were served.

Eve looked around at the happy gathering. Even though the cottage left much to be desired, she was so happy to be home. Inside, the stove was lit and no bugs had appeared. The beds were aired and a fire burned in Peg's room. The cottage would soon be warm and snug.

'Cheers!' shouted Duggie, raising his glass. 'Here's to the old gates of Rome!'

The men downed their beer as the sun set, shedding rays across the yard. Eve looked fondly at Joseph beside her.

'Don't know what we would have done without you,' she told him.

'*Kol tuv*,' murmured Joseph, patting her hand. 'I wish you all the best in your new life.'

Eve smiled. It was going to be a new life from now on. She was determined to make it so.

The following Friday, Eve was standing on the corner of Westferry Road. It was three o'clock in the afternoon, a sunny and windless day. She had sold all her flowers and had just put away her money bag under the folds of her skirt when a horse and cart rumbled by. The driver pulled on the reins. 'Eve, girl!'

She stepped into the road. 'Archie. What are you doing round here?'

'Got meself a perk.' He winked and nodded over his shoulder. The cart was piled high with sacks.

'What's in them?'

'Brown sugar, all split bags. Me mate, a stevedore, gave me the nod, said he'd show me where the sacks were if I could bag 'em up and get them out of the way sharpish. Got one more load tomorrow.'

'Ain't you worried about the dock coppers?'

'Nah, they can be bought. It's the blues and the whites you got to watch out for. They don't like nothing happening without their say so. But my pal stood on guard for me and I bunged him a drink.'

Eve knew that he was referring to the dock unions of which there were many. They kept an eagle eye on their members and were known by the colour of their membership cards, either blue or white.

He glanced at the empty baskets. 'Business good is it?'

'Yes, very.'

'Better be off, I'm going up the Ratcliffe Highway to shift this lot.'

'Would you take a passenger?'

He frowned. 'You going up there?'

'Got to see someone up there.'

'What, in sailortown?' He looked startled.

'No, the park,' she lied.

He shrugged. 'All right then, climb aboard and I'll take you as far as the park. Bung them baskets on the back.'

Eve did as he said and sat beside him; her heart was racing at the rash decision she had made, asking for a ride. But the *Tarkay* set sail soon. And now that Archie was going that way, it was too good an opportunity to miss. Anyway, it was too late now, she thought, as Archie clicked his tongue and the horse plodded off.

Archie reined in the horse. 'Whoa there, boy.' He turned to Eve. 'Do you want me to wait for you?'

'No thanks. Don't know how long I'll be.'

'Leave your baskets with me, then. I'll drop them off early in the morning.'

Eve nodded. 'Thanks, Archie.'

'Take care of yourself. Don't like it round this way much. See yer tomorrow.'

When the cart had gone, Eve hurried briskly along. She would make her enquiries swiftly as she didn't want to be here after dark.

Peg walked in to her front room, the room she had once thought she might never use again. It still didn't smell healthy, but it was clean. The stove in the kitchen and the fire in the grate had helped to dry out the cottage. But if the water had risen a few more inches, they'd still have been scraping the contents of the drains from the chimney!

The sound of the boys' voices drifted in from the street. They were having a rare old time. When she'd told them they could go out to play, their faces had been rays of sunshine.

She glanced at the mantel clock. Half past seven. It was unusual for Eve to be late. But perhaps she'd gone to the Queens after the factory gates. Made a few posies of what was left.

She smiled again as she watched from the window. Samuel kicked the ball, though it didn't go far. As flat as a pancake it was and well past its prime. Albert dug in his trousers for the liquorice sticks Peg had bought them. They squatted in the gutter, eating and laughing together. They were good-looking nippers, but a sitting target for those bullies at school. With the stigma of their dad being a lascar and dead into the bargain, they had had a lot to deal with.

Peg sighed thoughtfully. Would it be any different if Raj was still alive, she wondered. Could he have defended them? He'd been gentle and sensitive, but he hadn't been a fighter. He'd loved his wife and his boys and put money on the table for his family. They'd been content with the little they had. It was so unfair that he'd drowned.

Peg sat down on the chair by the grate. Expertly rolling a cigarette she inhaled with a satisfying gulp of smoke. She would give the boys another half hour then call them in. Eve would chew her off, but it was worth it.

Peg only realized she had dozed off when the pain woke her. The cigarette had fallen from her fingers to her thigh. She jumped up, brushing off the burning ash. There was a hole in her skirt.

'Bugger.' She picked up the dog end and threw it into the grate.

As she looked up, she saw it was eight o' clock. It was time to call the boys in, get them ready for prayers and bed.

Eve left the green lawns of the King Edward the Seventh Park behind her. It had been busy with people enjoying the late afternoon sun. Some strolled on the grass, others sat on benches while the children played, their laughter drifting on the breeze.

The twins had been a year old when she had last come here. The memory was bitter sweet. Samuel had been in Raj's arms and Albert straddled her hip; it had been a happy day. It was a journey they had made especially to see the new park, and many visitors had come to enjoy the new facilities. Though the area known as sailortown was close by, the park was a welcome diversion, providing new and luxurious green lawns, a few young trees and a promenade overlooking the river. Many of the older buildings had been knocked down for its construction. The park had replaced many unwholesome buildings and was now a place of beauty. But today Eve didn't linger here, instead she headed towards the meaner streets of Shadwell.

A glimpse of the river appeared on her left. In between her and the Thames wound the tiny lanes of boat-builders, sail-makers, riggers, coopers and ships' chandlers. She hurried on towards sailortown and the disreputable lodging houses and gaming institutions that were masked by grime-covered walls. That the dark side of life should run so closely to the wide open green spaces of the park was a surprise for Eve. She had never come as far south as this. Pushing her day's takings deeper into the folds of her skirt, she pulled her shawl around her and shivered.

Slowly the sun began to fade and Eve knew darkness would fall soon. She was beginning to think that it had been foolish of her to ask Archie for a ride. She shivered again in the cooling air.

Were there steps behind her? She turned round and saw nothing. Lights were going on in the houses, and sailors began to emerge. They walked in noisy groups, eager to find a tavern.

Eve kept her distance as they passed. Some shouted remarks and whistled, making her want to run back to the park and safety. She wasn't sure she had enough courage to go on.

Jimmy was trying to bear up under the verbal onslaught from Peg. He loved her like a mother, but sometimes her sharp tongue had him cringing. And tonight was one of those occasions. She hadn't listened to a word he had said, just torn him off a strip for being late, before he could offer a word in his defence.

'What have you been up to, Jimmy? Whose pockets have you been down? What fiddle have you been on?'

'Hold your apple sauces, Peg, let me get me breath.'

'What time do you call this to roll in?'

He laughed. 'It's only ten o'clock.'

'It feels like the middle of the night. You always disappear the minute you're needed. You're like bloody Houdini.'

'Peg, sit down. Take a breath and tell me what's wrong.'

'Where's me fags?'

'Your baccy's on the windowsill as usual.' He gave it to her. 'I'll put the kettle on whilst you light up.'

'Don't bother. I'm full to the eyeballs with tea. I've been here on me Darby and Joan, drinking one cup after another.'

He pushed her down gently on a chair. 'Now what's all this about?'

Peg ran her hands through her tangled grey hair. 'She ain't home, that's what's wrong.'

Jimmy frowned. 'You mean Eve?'

'The latest she ever come back from the Queens or the factories is eight.'

'But it's only ten.'

'Don't keep saying that. I can tell the bloody time.'

'What I mean is, it's not that late.'

'It is for Eve. I put the boys to bed meself.'

Jimmy pulled out a chair and sat down. He knew as well as Peg that Eve never missed their bed times. She said their prayers with them as regular as clockwork.

'I let them play out in the street tonight,' said Peg, staring into space. 'I knew their mother wouldn't like it. Not since Sister Mary's dressing down. They told me they'd done their homework and I didn't see why they shouldn't have a bit of fresh air. I was preparing meself for a bit of a showdown when she came home. Thing is, she never did.'

Jimmy didn't like the sound of this. Had it anything to do with what he had found out for her? But surely she wouldn't go to Shadwell on her own and at this time of night?

'Where can she be?' Peg's lips trembled around the thin cigarette.

'Have you been up to Joseph?'

'Yeah.'

'And the Higgins?'

'Them too.'

'They ain't seen her?'

'You know the answer to that.'

Jimmy tapped his dirty fingers on the table. 'She say anything to you about going somewhere?'

Peg rolled her anxious eyes. 'Do you think I'd be as worried as I am if she had? You silly sod, don't ask daft questions.'

'Right, I'll go and look for her.' He pulled on his cap and jumped up. 'I'll cycle up to Poplar and back again.'

'Take the Tilley on yer bike.'

He watched Peg turn up the wick of the Tilley and put a taper to it. Then giving her a peck on her cheek he hurried out to the yard. Placing the lamp carefully in his basket, he lifted the front wheel over the crumbled wall. As the dark night enveloped him, he tried to keep his fear in check. If Eve didn't turn up, there was only one place she was likely to be.

And he didn't want to think about that.

Eve stepped through the doors of the Drunken Sailor and the fumes enveloped her. The air was thick with tobacco smoke. Men were talking, drinking and laughing together.

Her arm was roughly taken. A tall man with a beard pulled her to him. 'On yer own are you? Come and sit on me lap.'

There was laughter from his friends as they jostled round.

'You're a flower-seller, ain't you?' He stared at her working clothes.

'What you got for sale, love? Come over here and show me.'

Eve managed to pull away. She pushed through the crowd to the bar where the landlord was serving.

'What do you want?' His dirty shirtsleeves were rolled across his tattooed arms.

'I'm looking for a man named Somar Singh.'

He frowned at her. 'Who wants to know?'

'My name is Eve Kumar.'

'And what would you want with a lascar?'

'You know he's a lascar?'

'The name suggests it, girl.'

'He's from the ship called the *Tarkay*. He sailed with my husband Raj on the *Star of Bengal* five years ago.'

'You was married to a lascar?'

Eve nodded and the big man rubbed his bearded jaw. 'It's dangerous to be a woman on your own in these parts. Ain't you got no one with you?'

'I only want to find this man.'

He took another look at her. Then calling for the barmaid, he nodded to the door at the side. 'Go through there.'

Eve made her way round, pushing past the men who gave her long looks. The landlord opened the door and nodded. She went in to a dark passage. The door slammed behind her.

Eve followed him, each step she took making her more uneasy.

Suddenly he turned sharply. 'A word of advice, girl. There's a few of 'em in this room, all enjoying the vices of sailortown. Any fool can see it's risky for a woman to enter. But see that door over there? It leads to the street. If I were you, I'd take it.'

Eve considered this, but shook her head.

'Better watch yerself, then. I've said all I can to deter you.'

'What does Somar Singh look like?'

'He's a big bugger, wears a jacket with brass buttons, like a flamin' admiral. Lords it a bit over the others. Now, at the risk of repeating meself, if I was you, girl, I'd turn round and go out that door, forget about lascars and go back to where you come from.'

'I can't do that.'

'Be it on your own head, then.' He left her, and Eve stood in the silence. She had found Somar Singh, but what would she say to him? The first question she would ask was if he had known Raj at the time of his death.

She tried to stop shaking. It wasn't too late to change her mind. The landlord had shown her the other door. But if she walked through it onto the street she might never find Singh again.

The air was thick with a pungent smell as Eve stepped

into the back room. All she could see were shapes both seated and lying on the floor. No one spoke.

Eve blinked, trying to adjust her eyes to the darkness. 'I'm looking for Somar Singh,' she stammered, suppressing a cough as the putrid smell surrounded her. 'My name is Eve . . . Eve Kumar. My husband was Raj Kumar. He sailed as cook on the *Star of Bengal* and was lost overboard five years ago.' She stopped. No one moved or broke the silence. 'If Somar Singh isn't here, then does anyone know where I can find him?'

Still silence prevailed.

Then everything happened at once. Bodies rushed past her and she stumbled back as arms and legs sped by.

When all was quiet again, one man remained. A row of brass buttons ran down his jacket.

Eve tried to regain her balance as she clutched at the wall. The whites of the man's eyes shone in the darkness.

He moved slowly towards her.

Then everything went black.

Jimmy had cycled so fast and so far, he had to stop to catch his breath. He knew by the town hall clock that it was past midnight, the big chimes making him realize how desperate the situation was. He had been cycling round Poplar and the island for two hours. He'd watched the crowds pour out of the Queens, going happily on their way after a good night's entertainment. Now there was no one around save a few drunks, singing their way back home and one or two carts that rumbled and creaked along the highway. A flash or two of a Tilley, an odd motor vehicle and definitely no women. Even the dock dollies were occupied on the waterfront and wouldn't come up this way.

What should he do now? Jimmy scratched his hot head under his cap then jumped back on his bike. He pedalled as fast as he could, his one hope that somewhere along the way, his and Eve's paths would cross. At the top of the hill, he stopped pedalling and freewheeled down the dip to number three Isle Street. The light was on downstairs, a softer glow from above. It meant the boys' Tilley was on, but downstairs Peg was still up.

He jumped off his bike and scraped the key string up through the letterbox. He didn't have to look far to know that Eve wasn't home.

'Did you find her?' Peg was standing at the kitchen door. She was puffing at her cigarette, her cheeks drawn.

Jimmy shook his head.

'Where did you look?'

'Poplar, the High Street and right down to Island Gardens. I even went up to Blackwall and Bambury Buildings.'

Peg stifled a cough. 'What was the good of that?'

'I was gonna ask Joan if she'd seen her.'

'You must be daft. What would Eve want with Joan?'

'I don't know. Thought I'd try.'

'You didn't knock on the door!'

'Didn't know the number, did I? But I remember you said it was on the top floor.'

'Did you go up?'

Jimmy sat down. He wasn't sure whether he should tell Peg what he'd found at Bambury Buildings, and anyway, he might be wrong. But in the end he said, 'Yes, I went up. Couldn't see no one and I wasn't going to knock at that time of night. But on the stairs there was a couple, all lovey dovey.'

Peg shook her head irritably. 'Get on with it, Jimmy. What's that got to do with Eve?'

'Dunno. But this bloke was all done up like a dog's dinner. He stood to attention when he saw me, but the woman just hung on to him. I asked did they know which was Mr and Mrs Slygo's, and the woman burst into laughter. She said, "You're staring him right in the face." 'Course I was a bit shocked as she wasn't Joan – at least, as I don't know her I could only guess. But this floos – this girl – wasn't no sister of yours.'

Peg dropped her cigarette. 'You mean it was Harold with another woman?'

Jimmy shrugged. 'Don't know him, do I? Only what you and Eve told me.'

'You can't miss Harold, he's short, fat and ugly.'

'That's him.'

'I don't believe it.'

'I could be wrong.'

'And she said, after you asked for him by name, that you was looking at him?'

Jimmy nodded.

'What did you do?'

'I buggered off. What else?'

For a while they sat there in silence. Then Peg dropped her head in her hands. 'I can't think about that now.'

''Course not.'

'Where can Eve be?'

'Did she say anything to you . . . about . . . about that Charlie Merritt?'

Peg's head shot up. She looked into Jimmy's eyes. 'What's he got to do with Eve?'

'Dunno. I was just wondering, that's all.'

'What's going on, Jimmy?'

Jimmy guessed that Eve hadn't said anything to Peg about the note. And then it dawned on him. Like a great big hammer banging on his head, the truth became clear. Eve had gone to look for Somar Singh.

Peg grabbed his arm. 'Jimmy, don't lie to me. What's up?'

Jimmy didn't want to betray Eve's confidence, but now he was certain that Eve had disappeared because of what he had done.

Chapter Thirteen

Eve felt stiff and sore. She was in a dark room. Was it the one at the pub? Had she fainted here? By the feel of the bump on her forehead, she had hit it as she fell.

Gradually she moved her arms and legs, groping in the darkness for something to hold on to: a table, a chair, a door. On all fours, she crawled around the black space. There was sawdust beneath her hands and she could smell the heavy tobacco scent. A piece of rough wood caught her palms. She tried to stand up, but a wave of sickness flowed over her. She sank down again, as her knees buckled beneath her. It was like being in a dark cave.

Eve called out for help. There was no answer. Each time she yelled she listened carefully for a reply. Was she locked in here? When she felt a little calmer, she would try to find the door.

Jimmy had finished telling Peg all about the note and what he had found out. Peg stared at him white-faced.

'Why didn't she tell me what she had in mind?' Peg said in a whisper.

'We don't know for sure she's gone to Shadwell.'

But Peg shook her head. 'She'd never stay out this late without a good reason.'

Jimmy stared down at his dirty cuffs. 'This is all my fault.'

'What do you mean?'

'I gave her the gen on Singh.'

'Yes, you did, son, but you didn't know this was going to happen. If anyone is to blame here it's me.'

Jimmy glanced up. 'Why's that?'

Peg's voice was troubled as she replied. 'Me and Eve ain't seen eye to eye lately. I let my feelings be known when I should have kept me trap shut.'

'About Charlie?'

'I didn't trust the bloke – well, he was a copper, it's me natural instinct to distrust them. And then she gave me the rent, poor cow, but I spent it and decided the council could sing for their supper as the roof wasn't done. Then when Sister Mary got on her high horse about the boys, I put me four penneth in again.'

'Yeah but that ain't nothin' to do with Singh.'

'She didn't want to tell me what was going on, though, did she?'

'She didn't tell me, either,' pointed out Jimmy, 'that she was off to Shadwell on her own. I said to her, she should get Charlie. He's a copper after all.'

Peg caught hold of his wrist. 'That's it. That's who we should ask.'

'What, Charlie?'

'You're right, he's a copper.'

But Jimmy pulled away. 'I ain't going to no station! They'd nick me for just stepping over the doorstep.'

'Then what do we do?'

He rubbed his chin. 'Wait a minute. Let me think.'

'There's no time for that,' cried Peg angrily. 'Gawd knows what's happened to her. Shadwell of all places! I've sold me flowers in some places and visited a few dives, but even I wouldn't go down sailortown at night.'

Jimmy stood up. 'I've just had an idea.'

'What?'

'Think back to the day when Charlie helped clear up the cottage.'

Peg nodded irritably. 'Get on with it, Jimmy.'

'Well, what did he come in? His old man's new runabout!' Jimmy gazed into Peg's uncomprehending eyes. 'And what was written on the side?'

'Christ, Jimmy, I don't know.'

'It was Merritt the Baker, something like that. Eve said the shop was somewhere off the Commercial Road.'

'That's a long bloody road.'

'Yeah, but a baker's shop! Now, some of 'em babble and brook till dawn. Have to have the stuff ready for their rounds men. If his dad's there, he'll put us right for Charlie.'

'What happens if you can't find it? What if . . .'

Jimmy slapped on his cap. 'Don't worry. The worst comes to the worst, I'll go to the law and that's a promise.'

'I'll keep you to that one, Jimmy.'

He gave her a peck on the cheek and left. He was going to cycle up to the Commercial Road faster than he had ever cycled anywhere in his life before.

Robbie Lawrence punched Charlie playfully on the arm as they finished their late shift. 'Do you fancy a snifter at my place?'

'It's a bit late,' said Charlie, buttoning up his donkey jacket. Robbie shared rooms with another copper, Johnny Puxley, a hardened drinker and it would be shop talk over the ale till the early hours. 'I'm all in.'

'It's Friday night, lad, you should be letting your hair down.'

'I'll take you up on a drink tomorrow night.'

Robbie snaked a hand through his blond waves. 'You certainly will. I've got a bit of a surprise for you.'

Charlie smiled. 'Oh yeah?'

'A foursome. Me and Venetia, you and Ven's chum.'

'A girl?'

'She's a cracker, Charlie.'

They strolled in and out of pockets of river mist, a soft breeze ruffling the leaves of the plane trees in the darkness. Charlie didn't object to working late when it was like this; he had time to gather his thoughts as he walked home. The last thing he fancied right now was lumbering himself up with a date. He wouldn't have minded a quick drink with Robbie. There wasn't much to do now the football season was over. Only a few games here and there, but tomorrow he had a free day and was going to help his old man in the shop.

'So, we're all set then? Say seven at my place?'

'I don't know, Robbie . . .'

'Hand on my heart, Bunty will knock your socks off.'

Bunty! The name alone made Charlie shiver. 'If there's four of us, we can hardly take Dad's van . . .'

'No need old son. We'll go in Johnny's motor.'

'He's letting you borrow it?'

'No, he's driving.'

Great, thought Charlie, racking his brains for an excuse, now Johnny was in the picture. Charlie liked a few ales, but he also appreciated decent company rather than drinking sprees. As for this Bunty, no doubt she would be plum in the mouth as Robbie's taste in women ran to more than he could afford, more than his salary paid. Venetia Harrington was a woman of substance according to the station grapevine and Charlie couldn't see himself enjoying the company of a Venetia mark two at any price.

'Rob, I'm saving for me own place, you know that.'

'The night's totally on me, chum.'

Charlie stopped and frowned at his friend. 'You can't afford this, Robbie. You're only on the same whack as me.'

Robbie leaned forward, his handsome face amused. 'I had a winner yesterday, a little filly with flying hooves. Trust me, Charlie, I can afford it all. Cocktails, dinner, a club and dancing the night away. And you don't have to fork out a penny.'

'I wouldn't have that,' Charlie refused abruptly. 'You know I'd pay my way.'

'You're on, my friend,' Robbie laughed, 'but I can promise you the expense will be worth it.' He nudged Charlie's arm sharply. 'Ah, here's Johnny now. You sure you don't don't fancy a nightcap?'

'No, thanks all the same.' Charlie glanced along the road to see bright headlights winking at them, illuminating the dark Stepney street. The big car drew up alongside them.

'Hey, you two, climb aboard.' Johnny Puxley's broad features, already blunted by hard living, were hidden under the brim of a trilby. As a detective, he was probably good at his job, thought Charlie as the exhaust fumes bottled out from the back of the motor, but as a man, Charlie was unimpressed with Robbie's new pal.

'I'll walk,' Charlie replied with a grim smile. 'It's a nice night for a stroll.'

Johnny shrugged, leaning his elbow out of the window. He lifted the trilby and gave a mocking smile. 'Still singing to the tune of the good and faithful copper on his beat, Charlie?'

Charlie's expression hardened. 'That's what I am, Johnny, a copper. And so are you.'

He didn't miss the coldness in Johnny's eyes as he felt Robbie slap him on the back. 'Seven on the dot,' Robbie shouted as he jumped in. 'Don't be late.'

Charlie stood on his own, his brow creased in concern. He was trying to separate his distaste for the driver of the car from his loyalty to Rob. How did Robbie afford his lifestyle? The new rooms he'd moved into up West with Johnny, a copper older but not a lot wiser, must cost a fortune. Had Robbie's penchant for the wrong sort of women surfaced again? Was Venetia a replacement for Diana Thomas, the married woman who had once almost ended Robbie's career?

Charlie walked on, deep in thought. The stars and moon were sitting high up in a flawless violet sky. The city was asleep and tomorrow promised to be a perfect day.

As he turned on to the Commercial Road, he realized it was only a short while ago that Robbie had warned him against Eve, calling her the wrong sort of woman and telling him not to confuse his high and mighty ideals with the way the law worked. Well, there was the pot calling the kettle black for you!

Charlie strolled slowly, enjoying the freedom and beauty of the uncluttered streets. He wondered if Eve had received his note, if the boys had given it to her. He'd taken a gamble on Eve reading it and coming to the station. He'd been on tenterhooks ever since, hoping she would walk through the door and ask for his help. But all he could assume from her silence was that she

231

really felt as strongly as she'd said. The fact that she thought he was bad news for her lads had cut him deep at the time, and still did.

Charlie sighed heavily as he considered his failed plan. He thought when the *Tarkay* had sailed in, Lady Luck was with him. Now he wished he hadn't given the note to Samuel and Albert and had mustered the courage to go to the cottage himself. At least he could have looked into her face and got the brush-off. He shouldn't take it personally, he knew that. The Force was not the most favoured amongst East Enders and the sooner he accepted that, the better off he'd be.

Still, on a night like this, as he gazed up at the moon, it was Eve Kumar and not a woman by the name of Bunty, who filled his thoughts.

Jimmy swiped the sweat from his eyes as he made a left turn from East India Dock Road into the narrow streets of Limehouse. Once or twice he was halted by a cart or barrow bouncing over the cobbles and the occasional motor vehicle. The breeze was full of summer's scents; the river and the tar and the taverns, the markets that would soon be opening and the food stalls, the barrows, the costers and his one big hope, the bakeries. Thank God it was a bakery. If you inhaled hard enough, you could find them blind. Though Peg was right, Commercial Road was a long one, the main thoroughfare from the docks to Aldgate and the gateway from the East to the city. All he had to do was find one little shop.

As he rounded a bend, he came upon a milk cart and asked for Merritt's.

The milkman held a large pitcher in his hands, full of fresh milk. 'Dunno it, lad. You say it's off the Commercial Road? Which end?'

Jimmy shrugged. 'Wish I knew mate.'

'You tried the station?'

Once more Jimmy had cold shivers at the mention of the law. He thanked the milkie and renewed his journey from Limehouse to Whitechapel. He'd cycled this way many times and flew past the headquarters of the Salvation Army and the many taverns overhanging the broad streets. On he went, skirting the locked gates of the metal industries, the foundries and sugar refineries and holding his breath at the fish curing plant. Emerging from the cheap lodgings for dockers were a few men and women either beginning their day or at the end of it. When he came to the intersection with the Commercial Road he pulled on his brakes.

Right or left? Now that was a poser. He wiped the sweat from his face with the back of his sleeve and cycled furiously to his left. It was the last stretch of the thoroughfare before Aldgate.

Peg wandered aimlessly. She kept going back into the front room to look at the clock. Then she lit another roll-up, went upstairs to glance at the kids. They were fast asleep.

'I'll wear those stairs through if I ain't careful,' she

told herself as she poked her head out of the front door and gazed up the hill. All was still, almost breathless. Perhaps there was a whisper of breeze in the plane tree at the top. She ventured out into the road and folded her arms, looking this way and that. If it wasn't for the lads she'd go off searching for Eve herself.

If Jimmy wasn't back in the morning, that's exactly what she'd do. Hadn't been near a bucket and pail in years and like Jimmy, hated the thought of breathing the same air as a bluebottle, specially one of them that stood like Lord Muck behind a desk. He'd look her up and down and have that smirk on his face that only coppers possessed. A flower-seller, he'd say – gone all night – what was unusual about that? He'd snigger to his 'oppo and they'd look at her as if she was no more than a dock dolly herself. Because who was going to believe that Eve Kumar, a mother of two kids, wasn't a tart but a decent sort, a girl who had never asked for the law's help in her life.

Peg sucked the last of the strength from her roll-up, cast it in the gutter and returned to the cottage. What was she going to tell the boys?

She sat down at the kitchen table and waited for dawn.

Charlie was striding along the embankment, his helmet square on his head, looking at the passers-by, a big smile stretched across his face. He was looking for someone, he wasn't sure who, but he'd know them when he saw them. Trouble was there was a brawl going on. He was reluctant to intervene, yet it was his job to do just that.

Or was it? Something was wrong. He looked down at his legs. Instead of boots, his feet were bare. One of his ankles had a manacle round it. Suddenly he heard laughing. He looked up to see Johnny Puxley standing outside the Tower of London. The jackdaws were flying around him and there was a woman dressed in royal attire and wearing a crown. A big red heart was painted on it.

The Queen of Hearts . . . now, how did she get there?

He couldn't run away, the ball and chain were too heavy. In the distance he heard the hooting of a ship and in the moat, a man was drowning. He knew in one part of his mind that he was dreaming but in the other, he was terrified. Johnny was going to throw him in too. And with the heavy weight on his leg he would drown alongside the sailor.

'Son, wake up.'

Charlie opened his eyes to see the flushed and flour-streaked face of his father under his floppy white baker's cap. 'Dad?'

'You all right, Charlie?'

'Yes . . . yes. I must've been dreaming.'

'You've got a visitor, son.'

Charlie took a minute to get his bearings. 'A visitor? What time is it?'

'Half three.'

'You still cooking?'

'No, we're all done now. Your mother and me are going for our kip now. Won't get more than a few hours as it's Saturday. You gonna lend us a hand in the shop?'

'Yeah, 'course.'

'Good lad. Now get downstairs and see what your chum wants. I'm off to me bed.'

Assuming it was Robbie, for it could only be him at this hour, Charlie threw off the covers hurriedly. What the devil did Robbie want? Had he been drinking until this hour and decided to play some sort of joke? If that was the case, he'd find out pretty soon that robbing a man of his well-earned kip would brook him no favours.

Charlie dragged on his trousers and shirt. With the disturbing memory of the dream still in his head, he hurried down the narrow flight of stairs that led to the bakery. As children, Charlie and his two brothers had enjoyed the diversity of the old building, playing tag, or hiding from one another in the warren of rooms above the bakery. From outside the row of shops seemed to be squashed together in a crooked line, but it had always been a happy home to them. They had helped out in the bakery, run errands and even pulled pies from the hot ovens and delivered them, still sizzling, to the local traders. Pounding down the wooden staircase, the unmistakable aroma of fresh bread engulfed him. He should be accustomed to it after all these years, but there was something about the smell that never failed to give him a sense of well-being. And by the time he reached the lower floor, his irritation at having been woken was already subsiding.

Charlie hurried past the little store room filled with provisions for the benefit of the local tradesmen, marketeers and rounds men. As he approached the counter, he saw the trays of freshly baked bread arranged on shelves, ready for the first purchasers of the day. The little shop at the front would be bustling, filled to capacity. As a family baker of long standing, his parents were well respected. Even the Jewish shopkeepers traded with them on occasion. His dad's bagels were beyond belief.

The light was on in the shop and Charlie blinked. He was surprised to see not Robbie, but Jimmy Jones, Eve's friend.

The boy was ashen faced and dripping sweat. 'I come on me bike, Charlie,' he said in a rush, 'been looking for you – didn't have no number or street. Only knew your dad's shop was off the Commercial Road.'

'Hey, take it easy lad. You look done in.'

'Charlie, I . . .'

'Here, get your breath. Come and sit down.' Charlie led him behind the counter and pulled out a stool. He brushed off the flour. The boy was out of breath and panting. 'Do you want a drink?'

'Yeah, wouldn't mind.'

Charlie ran cold water from the tap in the store room and handed Jimmy the enamel mug. He downed it in one.

'That better?'

He nodded.

'Now, take your time and tell me what's wrong.' Charlie was certain there was something amiss.

'It's . . . it's about the ship, the one that's docked in the Pool, the *Tarkay*.'

Charlie stiffened his back. 'What do you know about that?'

'Eve showed me your note.'

Charlie slowly pulled out another stool and sat down. 'Now why would she do that?'

Jimmy rubbed his wet lashes and blinked. 'I got this new job see. It's down at the PLA, running for the bosses. I gets about a bit, sees a lot of them lascars going and coming. So Eve shows me your note and asks me to find out something if I can. So I can't refuse, can I? Not Eve.'

Charlie felt a wave of apprehension. 'So what did you find out?'

'This beggar tells me Singh is in sailortown, Shadwell to be precise.'

Charlie swallowed hard. His mouth was going dry. This wasn't supposed to happen. If Eve had wanted help, why hadn't she come to him?

'Eve didn't come home last night,' Jimmy continued, his eyes full of fear. 'Peg and me, we don't know what to do. But I remembered the name on your dad's van and—'

'Are you saying Eve's gone to Shadwell?' Charlie felt sick to his stomach.

The boy nodded.

'Could she be anywhere else, with a neighbour, a friend?'

'We tried 'em all.'

'When did you last see her?'

Jimmy frowned. 'Friday morning it was, before she left for work. I was jumping on me bike and waved.'

'She didn't say she was going to Shadwell then?'

'No, doubt if she would. She knew I was against it. I told her to come after you.'

'Well, she didn't.'

'It was her pride, Charlie. I knew she wanted to.'

'She told you I was a copper?'

'Yeah. Don't make no difference to me though. I know you ain't like the rest. That's why I'm here.'

'You did right, lad.' Charlie rose to his feet, pushing his hand through his hair. He tried to clear his mind, think calmly. 'But I can't believe you'd leave it till now.'

'Didn't suss where she'd gone till last night. Wished I'd never told her about Singh.'

It came home to Charlie then that if he hadn't tried to contact Eve again, hadn't written to her of the *Tarkay*, she would be at home now, safe and sound.

'It's not your fault. I thought she would come to me.'

Charlie drew his hand over the back of his neck. He

tried to think what to do first. He was a policeman, for God's sake, he should know the ropes. Was that what he should do first? Go to the station and report her missing? Or should he search himself? He wanted to do everything at once. As he considered the options, a cold calm came over him. First he would get out his dad's van, drive with Jimmy to Shadwell, have a look round. If they could see nothing, find nothing, do nothing, then he'd go straight to the station and make a report.

As Charlie gathered his coat and his senses together, he was aware that dawn had broken. A soft light was making its way through the shop window. His parents would be rising in a couple of hours and he'd offered to help them.

He'd leave a short note, say that he'd borrowed the van and lock the shop behind him. He was lucky to have no duty this weekend. Though if he couldn't find Eve in the next hour or two, he'd be down at the station anyway, only this time not in his professional capacity but as a friend of the missing person.

'Where's Mum?' Samuel asked as he sat down at the kitchen table for his breakfast. 'She didn't say prayers with us last night.'

Peg waved her hand. 'You was asleep when she got in.'

'She said she was taking us to St Saviour's this morning.' Albert joined his brother at the table. 'We got to make our confession.'

Peg shrugged. 'It won't hurt you to go on your own. Now, eat your porridge.'

Albert pushed away his bowl. 'Don't want any.'

'It's not like you to refuse food.'

'I don't want another ticking off from Father Flynn.'

Samuel nodded. 'Or me.'

Peg would like to say a thing or two to that old misery Father Flynn. His hand shot out quicker than a lizard's tongue when he was holding the offertory plate, but ask him to give a word or two of comfort to his flock and you'd be more likely to get sackcloth and a bell thrown at you.

'He says he's going to learn us the catechism.' Samuel looked at his brother. 'We'll be in chapel all day. And it ain't even Sunday.'

Albert nodded. 'It ain't fair.'

'No, I don't reckon it is,' agreed Peg as she washed the dishes. She knew her tongue was getting the better of her but she couldn't have this. 'Look, your mother will be upset if you don't go to confession as she promised Sister Mary. But I tell you what, when the old bug – Father Flynn,' she corrected herself swiftly, 'has finished giving you the lecture, then you tell him you can't stop as you're gonna help me with the chores and if he wants to contest that, he can walk down to Isle Street and I'll tell him personally.'

Samuel and Albert giggled.

'He won't like it, but he knows better than to upset old Peg.' She dried her hands on the towel and pulled

241

open the table drawer. Inside it were the sweets she kept alongside her spare tin of tobacco. She gave the boys two long strips of liquorice. 'Don't eat them all at once and take a handkerchief to wipe yer lips.'

They dashed upstairs and she listened to the sound of their boots on the floorboards as they got themselves ready.

She had not had to explain their mum's absence thank goodness. If only Jimmy would hurry back and let her know what had happened.

''Bye Peg.' The boys ran out of the front door. She watched them play fight in the road and wondered if she should seize her chance now they had gone to look for their mother. But they wouldn't be long. She had given them the excuse to come home early and the thought of going to the police station was as repugnant now as it was last night.

She stood indecisively as a cart came down the hill. To Peg's surprise the big horse stopped a few yards away and a whiskery looking fellow jumped down. He pulled two baskets from the back.

Peg felt her blood run cold. They were Eve's.

Chapter Fourteen

'We'll try the waterfront now so keep your eyes peeled,' Charlie told Jimmy as they left the Commercial Road.

Jimmy suppressed a yawn as he pushed his face up to the window.

'Are you supposed to be at work this morning?'

'Yeah, the boss will have to run his own errands.'

Charlie felt a good deal of respect for this young lad. He was risking his job to find Eve.

'If Singh is on shore leave,' Charlie said quietly, 'he'll stay in lodgings. Perhaps with a woman, perhaps on his own.'

'We can't go knocking on every door.'

'No, but it's the doss houses we're interested in.'

'We'll have our work cut out,' Jimmy frowned. 'No one takes kindly to enquiries in sailortown.'

Charlie knew Jimmy had a point. Yet what other course of action could he take?

After a short drive, interrupted frequently by the early morning traders, their horses and carts and a few trams and buses, they arrived in the shabby streets of Shadwell. Here there was no movement from the near to derelict houses.

Charlie brought the van to a halt. Singh could be in any one of these stinking, truly shameful dwellings. Most of the doors were bolted by their hard-bitten landladies, pimps and prostitutes. Charlie had made a foray down this way in his training days. Even Sergeant Moody had not stayed long here to press the theft enquiry they were conducting.

Charlie got out of the van and narrowed his eyes at the silent street. The morning had a slight bite to it, and the silence was broken only by the distant river traffic and the cries of gulls overhead.

'You sure about this?' Jimmy asked nervously.

'Stay in the van if you want.'

'Don't be daft.' Jimmy pulled back his shoulders. 'What do you want me to do?'

'Go to the next road and knock. If you manage to get a response, ask for a room. Say your friend has told you there might be one going and you can pay a week's rent up front. That way you'll get their interest. Only then mention Singh is your friend. See if you get a result.'

'What kind of result?'

'You'll know when you get it.'

Charlie watched the boy walk off, his shoulders sloping under his dirty jacket. Had he done right in allowing the youngster to accompany him?

Charlie made his way to the first front door and knocked. There was no reply so he knocked again. He wasn't surprised when the window above him opened and a woman leaned out.

'What the bleeding hell do you want?'

'Do you take lodgers?' Charlie called up.

'Not at this time of the morning. Now bugger off.' The sash window came down with a crunch.

Charlie braced himself. He hoped that Jimmy would have better luck.

Eve felt herself being pulled up. The hands that were gripping her were rough and dug painfully into her arms. A light pierced her vision and she moaned as the daylight blinded her. Then suddenly she was blind again, but this time a cloth was pulled over her head. There were men shouting in an agitated way, but they weren't speaking English so Eve had no idea what they were saying.

Her wrists were bound and she was lifted and thrown like a sack of potatoes over a man's shoulder. He hurried along and she bounced up and down, driving the wind from her lungs. A moment later she was bundled onto a cart. She could feel the swaying and bumping over the cobbles, hear the horse's hooves clip-clopping.

Fear was paralyzing her. All she could do was lie there, her heart pounding in her ears.

There were voices again, close by. Couldn't anyone see her? Help her?

She tried to cry out, but the cloth smothered her cries. As fear overwhelmed her, a memory returned. She was at the Drunken Sailor. She was following the landlord along a dark passage. He was warning her to go away. Once more she was in that stinking room, amidst the smoke and the smell of many bodies. She saw the faces looking up at her and a tall man in the shadows. He began to walk towards her . . .

Eve screamed.

The cart had stopped and she was carried off.

Peg was sitting in her chair, staring at Archie Fuller.

'Sorry to give you such a fright, gel.' He passed the smelling salts back and forward under her nose. 'I only come to return Eve's baskets.'

Peg nodded. 'I dunno what came over me. S'pose it was seeing them and not her.'

'You took a bit of a turn.'

Peg grasped the bottle and took another sniff. She gave a half-hearted smile. 'So you're the Archie Fuller from Covent Garden?'

'And you must be Peg.'

'Yeah. Did she tell you about me?'

''Course she did. Didn't ever talk about nothing else. It was always you and her boys. And business, of course.'

Peg was just beginning to see Archie clearly. There had been two or three of him at one point. 'Look Archie, what was you telling me? Sit down a minute.'

'Can't stop long. I've got someone waiting for me with a job lot of sugar.'

'Did you say you gave Eve a ride yesterday?'

He nodded. 'She wanted to go to the King Edward Park at Shadwell.'

'Why was she going there?'

'Said she had someone to see.'

Peg leaned forward. 'Did she say who it was?'

'No.'

'Did she say anything else?'

'No, but the funny thing was when I looked back she was walking past the park towards the water. Gave me a bit of a turn to tell the truth as I'd expected her to go in the gates. As she didn't say who she was meeting and didn't want me to hang around I thought to meself she might have a — well, you know, a romantic interest, it being the park an' all.'

Peg sighed to herself. If only it was a love interest!

Archie sat back. 'So what's this all about then?'

'It's a long story, Archie. Eve ain't come home.'

'Well, maybe I was right then. She's got a fella.'

'Not to my knowledge she ain't.'

'Bet she don't tell you everything.' He smirked. 'She'll be back.'

'I hope so.'

'After all it's only one night. And a lovely gel like her, well she's got to have an admirer or two.' He winked.

Peg was about to contest the point when she thought better of it. She didn't know Archie well and he wouldn't understand. He seemed a nice enough bloke but he wasn't to know that Eve wasn't the sort to stay out all night and not say where she was.

'You all right on your own here?' he asked as he rose to his feet.

'Yes thanks, love. You get on.'

'It's been nice to meet you, Peg. Eve thinks the world of you and her kids. She's a good girl and a hard worker. Don't you fret now. She'll be home soon.'

Peg managed a smile.

'I'll see meself out.'

Once alone, she gazed at the empty baskets. Tears filled her eyes. If only Eve had talked to her more, taken her into her confidence. But lately they hadn't shared many chats. It wasn't like it used to be when the boys were younger. Now they were growing up, Eve seemed to have distanced herself. What was the saying? Out with the old and in with the new?

Peg put the bottle under her nose again. She coughed and sat there for some while thinking about what Archie had told her. Resting her head on the back of the chair she dozed.

The bottle was still in her hand when she heard a noise outside. Before she had time to get up from the chair, Jimmy rushed in.

'What is it son?'

'Is she back yet?'

'Does it look like it? What in God's name has happened to your face?'

Jimmy put his hand up. 'I got meself a shiner.'

'How?'

'I found Charlie at his dad's shop and we went in the van to Shadwell. We decided to knock on a few doors to ask about Singh. One bloke was about ten feet tall with a mush like the back of a bus. He took umbrage to me waking him up early and gave me a bit of a verbal. So I gave him one back.'

Peg sighed. 'That sounds like you.'

'Anyway, he clobbers me. I could smell last night's beer on his breath as he steps forward to hit me again. But then Charlie appears. He helps me up and tells me to go back to the van, but this big ox, he takes Charlie's shoulders with his great big Oliver Twists and is about to smash him too, when wallop! Charlie's knuckle is like greased lightning. The ox doubles up clutching his guts. He keels over and Charlie and me leg it sharpish back to the van.'

'Charlie clobbered someone because they hit you?' Peg asked in disbelief.

'Yeah, and it was a cracker.'

Peg took another sniff of the salts. 'Where's Charlie now?'

'Outside in the van. Says he's going straight up to the old constipation to tell 'em about Eve.'

Peg thought for a moment. 'He'd better hear what I have to say first.'

A moment or two later, Jimmy returned with Charlie. 'So you've had no success in finding Eve?' Peg demanded scathingly.

'I'm afraid not.'

'Jimmy tells me you're going up to the station.'

'Yes, to report her missing.'

'Will they send out a division to search for her?'

Charlie went red. 'No, not exactly a division . . .'

'How many then?'

He hesitated. 'They might not get on it right away as she's only been missing since yesterday.'

Peg huffed. 'So the answer is that no one is going to Shadwell on her behalf. Not today, or tomorrow. Well, they wouldn't, would they? She's only a flower-seller.'

Charlie looked uncomfortable. 'You don't have much confidence in the law, Mrs – er – Peg—'

'No I don't,' Peg agreed coldly. 'But I know rules have to be followed and it might as well be you that does it as me and Jim would rather walk hot coals than consort with the law. However, I do have a bit of information of me own. You'd better sit down.'

When she had their full attention, Peg related word for word what Archie had told her. 'So what do you think?'

'Is this Archie to be relied upon?' asked Charlie.

'Eve thought a lot of him. Gave her the chance to get back in business.'

'That's good enough for me,' Charlie nodded. 'If you've no objection to me delaying that report, I'll drive down to the park and retrace her footsteps. Perhaps someone saw her, or she spoke to someone – I'll do it whilst the trail is hot.'

'I'm coming too,' said Jimmy.

Charlie shook his head. 'No lad, you've done enough. Stay here with Peg and look after that eye.'

'Sorry, mate. I want to find Eve.'

'Go on, the pair of you,' said Peg, waving them off. 'Two is better than one.'

Peg watched them leave, then rested back, her brow drawn together into a frown. So Charlie Merritt was a bit of a dark horse, was he? But coppers were coppers the world over. Jimmy was young and impressionable. It would take more than a few lucky blows to a beer belly to impress Peg Riggs. Like finding Eve, for instance. And then she might take another view of the law altogether.

Charlie stood with Jimmy at the entrance to the park. He narrowed his eyes at the velvet green grass that flowed down to the walkway that provided a perfect panorama of the Thames. It was now midday and the children were playing on the green lawns, some of them sitting on the granite base which formed a garden seat and portrait of the late King Edward the Seventh. To them, it was just another king, a face that they would see in the pages of their history books. All they were interested in was playing their games, throwing their balls and enjoying the freedom that the park afforded. But to older East Enders who had never experienced the countryside, it was a little piece of heaven

A ball came bouncing towards them. Charlie couldn't

resist booting it back; he wasn't too old to remember what it was like to be their age, to believe you were going to be the world's best footballer. He'd had only one intention as an eight year old. He was going to play for Walthamstow Avenue, score goals and win medals. One day, the lord mayor of London would shake his hand and as captain, he would be the one to receive the cup, raise it above his head and bathe in the glory.

He'd believed in his dream right up till the moment he damaged his knee. Even then, he'd thought in time he'd get fit to play again. But it wasn't to be.

'Charlie?' Jimmy nudged his arm. 'I gotta thank you for what you did for me this morning.'

'What was that?'

'You clobbered that pudding on my behalf.'

'He was a darn sight bigger than you. And anyway, it was me that told you to go knocking on doors.'

'I did give him a bit of lip.' He grinned. 'I never seen a right hand land so quick as yours.'

'I did a bit of boxing at school.'

'Blimey, you done everything.'

Charlie smiled. 'You like football Jimmy?'

'Yeah, but I never played it. Didn't have the time for the outdoor life.'

'What, even as a kid?'

'You don't play games in an institution. You have to work for your supper. I was in the laundry, keeping the boilers going. Ran away when I was twelve. It was Peg that took me in and got me a job at the paint factory.'

'You've had it rough, Jimmy.' Charlie felt a sudden deep gratitude for his own privileged upbringing: a mother, father, twin brothers and a regular schooling.

'There's others 'as had it as rough.'

'Like Eve you mean?'

Jimmy nodded. 'It's a hard life being a flower-seller. And though her bloke was a decent sort, he was at sea most of the time. It was Eve that got all the flak with two little kids that looked a bit different.'

Charlie glanced at the street. 'So she walked along here, right? But didn't go into the park.'

'She went towards the river according to Archie. There's a lot of pubs down there. Three in this street alone. Do you reckon she went into one of them?'

'Fancy giving it a try?'

Jimmy nodded and pulled his cap down over his face. 'But this time I'm gonna let you do all the talking.'

Jimmy and Charlie searched all afternoon. They went in the pubs that were open and knocked on the back doors if they were closed. No one had seen Eve or knew the name of Singh.

When they entered the Drunken Sailor, the landlord was just opening for the evening's business. He gave them a furtive look.

Charlie leaned on the bar and looked around. There were two men drinking at the other end.

'You new around here?' the landlord asked.

Charlie nodded casually as Jimmy stood beside him.

253

'What's your poison, then?'

'An ale apiece,' said Charlie, digging into his pocket for the money.

'You're a young 'un ain't you?' He frowned at Jimmy.

Charlie laughed. 'Don't worry, he's older than he looks.'

'Ta very much,' said Jimmy indignantly.

Their drinks were served and as Charlie began to drink he saw the two men leave quickly.

The landlord smiled. He wiped his jaw with dirty fingers. 'I'm sorry to say that my customers don't take fast to strangers.'

'Why is that?'

'You're in Shadwell, chum, not Westminster.'

Charlie glanced at the floor, which was covered in filthy sawdust, then his gaze drifted around the room; the tables were sticky with spilled liquor, and although the mirror behind the bar proclaimed the finest ales, the cloudy glasses said otherwise. The opaque windows were streaked with smoke and the faded red wallpaper had long ago peeled from the grime-ridden walls.

'I'm looking for a young woman,' Charlie said quietly. 'Dark hair and small in stature. She may have come in here yesterday looking for someone. Her name is Eve Kumar.' Charlie looked into his eyes. This man knew something. 'The lascar seaman she was searching for is called Singh,' he persisted.

The landlord looked shifty. 'We don't get many women in here.'

'Then you'd remember her if you saw her.'

'Mebee.'

Charlie pushed his drink to one side. 'Listen, my friend, this girl has been gone for over twenty-four hours. She is now a missing person and I intend to discover what happened to her. Now, you either talk to me or the authorities.'

The landlord looked over Charlie's shoulder. 'All right, so what if I saw her?'

'So you did then?'

'She came in here, bold as brass. I told her she shouldn't have been doin' that.'

'What did she want?'

'The bloke you said . . . Singh.'

'So you know him?' Charlie felt a moment's elation. They had finally struck lucky.

The landlord wiped his mouth. 'I know of him and he ain't the sort any decent woman should be mixing with. He's a lascar and a right old handful to boot.'

The words fell on Charlie like a blow as the landlord continued.

'No woman with any sense walks into a pub looking for someone like she did. But I couldn't put her off. So I did her a favour and took her out back to where he was 'afore she was relieved of her money, or Gawd help her, somethin' far worse.'

Charlie couldn't keep the anger from his voice. 'You took her to Singh?'

'What else was I supposed to do? She was in me

tavern, refusing to go away. Listen, what would you have done, chum? Let her go round askin' others? So I took her aside and gave her a warnin'. It was all I could do.'

'What happened then?'

'It was like water off a duck's back. That girl was stubborn as the proverbial mule. I showed her the two doors and she took the one to the back room.'

'Did you accompany her?'

'I got a business to run, mate.'

'Did you see her again?'

'No, supposed she must've left by the side door.'

'And the lascars? What of them?'

The man shrugged. 'S'pose they went too. The room was empty at chuckin' out time. Stunk like a sewer an' all. It's them pipes they smoke, the dirty buggers.'

'Then why do you allow them in here?'

The landlord laughed. 'Would you turn away business just 'cos of the smell? Nah, not if you was me you wouldn't, nor any other poor bugger who tries to earn a living in this part of the East End.'

Charlie knew they were a step closer to finding Eve. But what had happened in that room?

'There is one thing,' said the landlord slowly, creasing his sweaty brow. 'It ain't gonna be much 'elp. But this character, Singh, is reputed to do a bit of business down on the foreshore.'

'Where exactly?' asked Charlie, feeling a flicker of hope.

'A place called Dead Man's Reach. And I can tell

you now that it ain't a place to go to by day, let alone night.'

Charlie's heart raced. What if Eve had gone there? He had to find out.

Eve could smell the river salt through the filthy cloth. She was near water, could hear its movement close by. They had argued, whoever it was that had brought her here. She didn't understand the language they spoke and when they shook her in a demanding way, she knew that they were trying to question her.

If only they had taken off the sack to let her breathe. Now they had left her in some place that felt wet and smelt of decomposed fish. She had tried to move a few minutes ago when she realized she was alone, but her foot had gone through what felt like rotten floorboards. She had fallen on her back, terrified to move again as the sound of the water grew closer. All she could do was lie still while endless, futile questions circled round her mind.

What time was it?

Where was she?

Who had brought her here? Was it the man with brass buttons, the one the landlord of the Drunken Sailor had said was Singh?

She had yelled until her throat was sore. If only she could get the cloth off her head. But her hands were tied behind her back. Why had they done this to her?

She gathered her strength and called out. There was

no response and she tried again. But she was alone, and without her hands or her sight she couldn't escape.

Charlie and Jimmy climbed out of the van and took the Tilley from the back. A weak light flickered over the wood strewn path down to Dead Man's Reach. Broken buildings littered the muddy foreshore. The stench of dead fish and rotting timber was everywhere.

As they picked their way down, Charlie's thoughts went back to the history lessons he'd had at school. The river was a constant source of trade and all his life he had lived near it, watching the boats go up and down and helping his dad to load the flour from McDougall's on to their cart and now into the van to transport to the bakery. The river was a lifeline, the longest road in the world it was called. But the foreshores were places that had a history all of their own. Long ago the men of war had anchored here to offload their contraband. Shadwell had been all marsh and waterways then, the perfect place for piracy and avoidance of the king's men.

Was Eve here? He shuddered at the prospect. This stinking and treacherous eastern boundary was not used now by the commercial boats. Only the smaller ones, a few fishermen and watermen. And at dead of night, the place should be deserted.

'It's deserted,' Jimmy said breathlessly, voicing his own thoughts. 'Do you reckon he was lying?'

'We couldn't take the chance.' Charlie stood still peering across the dark water, at the fleeting reflections of the south side of the river. 'It's the only link we have to Eve.'

'Why would they bring her here?' Jimmy asked. 'And what for?'

'I don't know,' said Charlie heavily as they stopped, peering into the darkness. 'Eve must have struck on something. If only she'd come to me first.'

'Yeah, well, if only I hadn't told her about that beggar.'

'We can't put back time, but—' Charlie froze. He turned to Jimmy. 'Did you hear that?'

'Thought it was a gull.'

Charlie listened again. There wasn't much breeze, so the noise was carrying from close by. 'Raise the lamp, Jimmy, there's something to our left.'

Jimmy held it high. 'What's that over there?'

Charlie moved forward. 'It looks like an old fisherman's hut.' They began to climb over the debris. There were no steps up to the jetty, just a mossy boulder.

'Give me your hand.' The lamp rocked as Charlie grabbed Jimmy and helped him up. The wooden planks of the jetty creaked under their feet and water swirled beneath.

'Stop!' Jimmy pointed. 'Look, the jetty's smashed.' He lowered the lamp. 'See? A blooming great hole.'

Charlie bent down to examine it. 'You're right. And freshly done too.'

'But why?'

'To prevent anyone going further,' replied Charlie as he removed his jacket and boots.

'Christ, Charlie, what're you doing?'

'If I fall in, I don't want my clobber on.'

'You ain't going to jump? This place ain't called Dead Man's Reach for nothing.'

'Just hold the lamp high.'

'But Charlie—'

He didn't wait to hear the rest. He knew that at the end of the jetty he would find something – or someone. If it was Singh, then a collar wouldn't be easy under these circumstances, but it wasn't impossible either. If it was Eve – and he couldn't bring himself to think of her as anything other than alive – then God willing, she was all right.

Chapter Fifteen

The wriggling she had done trying to loosen her bonds had caused the timbers to snap. Inch by loud inch the rotting wood broke under Eve's weight. As she fell her head hit something and ripped away the cloth. She could see the mossy struts of the jetty as she tumbled down.

The water was freezing. It crept over her body sucking at her clothes and pulling her into the weeds. Her feet were caught in them. She kicked out, holding her chin up for a last gasp of air.

Her heart seemed to stop as she slipped below the surface. Eve knew she was about to die. She couldn't swim without the use of her arms. Her last thoughts were of her sons; their faces, their smiles that seemed to be with her now in the eerie silence. There were regrets, all tumbling one after the other. She had wanted to see them grow up. She had so many hopes and dreams for them, had intended to make them all come true for her boys.

Why had she thrown her life away?

Her lungs felt as though they were going to burst. The taste of the filthy water filled her mouth. She struck out with her feet in a last effort to survive. But the water filled her boots, sucked her clothes and dragged her down. She remembered the stories of Old Father Thames. She would be lying alongside him soon.

The pain inside her chest increased. Her body arched, borne aloft in a strange lightness. And then Eve felt another presence. Was it the spirit of the river? Was this how it felt to drown?

It felt as if she was entering another world.

Charlie heard Eve's scream. As he raced to the hut and flung open the door, he could hear the water below. Without pause he took a deep breath and jumped. As he sank beneath the dark surface he was enveloped in freezing cold blackness. The weeds were thick and tangling as he kicked out. It would be a small miracle if he found her.

The cold sapped all his strength. He was a good swimmer, had swum the breadth of the river from Island Gardens to Greenwich when he was young once as a dare and many times after for pleasure. Even before he entered the Force, he was an accomplished swimmer. A copper had to be able to rescue a drowning man. During their training they had been put to the test one freezing cold morning at the open air baths. One loud blow on the whistle had them stripping off and diving in, swimming hell for leather for a marker. Robbie had never liked the exercise and somehow managed to avoid it. He said it was better to let some fool jump in first. Wait for a hero to arrive on the scene. And Robbie maintained there was always one who did.

But Charlie had never experienced these kind of conditions. Black water, the freezing cold and the shock to the body. He felt the tight restriction on his lungs. His supply of air was diminishing and he'd have to go up for another refuel if he couldn't find her. But that would mean he would almost surely have lost her.

Pulling hard with his arms he dived deeper. The water was even colder. He had about thirty seconds of air left he reckoned.

Maybe not even that.

Then his fingers touched something. It was floating, soft to the touch. He almost recoiled. He had found a body. It was clothed. Was it Eve? As his hands grasped the shoulders, he kicked out with his feet. His movement was impeded by the tangle of weeds. He tried not to think he was almost out of air.

If only he could reach the surface in time.

His lungs seemed to fill the entire space of his chest as he thrust both himself and the body upwards.

Somehow he broke the surface, rasping cold air down his throat. He pushed out, supporting the limp weight, but made a grim discovery, small hands that were bound at the base of the spine! Fortuitously the water had slackened the bonds. It was no great effort to slide them off and set the arms free. Then summoning the last of his strength, he struck out for shore. Was it Jimmy's light he could see? Or a vision? Were they being washed downstream – out into the estuary and towards the sea? In that moment he glimpsed the pale face on his shoulder. Eve's skin was washed to china whiteness in the light of the moon.

Peg was asleep by the fire when the sound of the key being drawn through the letterbox woke her.

She sat up, her eyes wide and staring. Everything came pouring back. Eve, Charlie and Jimmy. Where were they?

'Peg! Peg!' Jimmy burst in. His spiky brown hair was standing on end over his black eye.

Peg wondered if she was still dreaming. 'Christ, lad, what is it?'

'We've found her! We've found Eve!' he cried, running towards her. 'She fell in the old shake and shiver!'

Peg went ashen and reached out to steady herself.

'But Charlie saved her. You should have seen—'

Peg gulped in a breath. 'Slow down, lad. I can't take it all in.'

'Honest to God I thought she'd drowned, but he got her breathing again!'

'She nearly drowned?' Peg repeated feeling faint. She slumped back on the chair.

'Here, take a sniff of this.' He reached for the smelling salts.

'Just tell me this, is she all right?'

'It was touch and go. She must have swallowed half the river. Charlie's bringing her in. Said I should give yer a bit of warning.'

Peg pushed herself up. 'I'll put some water on and we'll get her in a hot bath.'

She stumbled to the kitchen, trying to think what to do first. Eve had nearly drowned. How had it happened? With shaking hands she filled the saucepans and put them on to boil. The tin bath was hung on a nail on the closet door. Peg didn't have enough strength to bring it in. Her bones felt weak with shock.

Slowly she lowered the pulley and took off the drying towels. When she returned, Charlie was laying Eve on the couch.

'Out of the way you two,' croaked Peg, pushing them back. 'Make yourselves useful and bring in the bath, then bugger off as I want to get these wet clothes off her.' She looked into Eve's ashen face. 'It's all right, ducks, you're safe now,' she whispered as she began to undo the buttons. But she didn't get far before Eve's hands reached out to hold her as the tears fell.

Eve felt as though she was drifting in and out of reality. She lay in bed under the warm covers still feeling cold even though the sunshine was streaming in the window. She couldn't stop thinking about those mossy green struts sticking up from the river bed as she fell between them and the strange feeling of otherworldliness before the water had rushed up from her lungs. It was as though she had been there, watching the scene as Charlie tried to make her breathe. She wanted to reach out and touch him, to tell him she was all right but then suddenly she was in Charlie's arms, feeling the cold, and the terror that she wouldn't see her boys again.

'How are you, love?' Peg came in with a tray. 'Look what Joseph's brought down for you.'

Eve eased herself up on the pillows as the bowl of steaming stew was placed before her. 'What day is it?'

'Monday.'

'I've lost track of time.'

'Seeing as you was nearly drowned, it's not surprising.'

Eve didn't have much of an appetite but she would try to eat to please Peg as she knew that her old friend was very concerned.

Peg sat on the end of the bed. 'I packed the boys off to school this morning although they didn't want to go. There might be a few visitors later as I kept everyone out till now, so's you could rest.'

'Do they know what happened?'

Peg laughed. 'You can't keep something like this a secret. Now finish that soup and then we'll see how you feel about getting up.'

'Peg?'

'What, ducks?'

'I'm sorry to have caused all this trouble.'

'You're back safe and that's what counts.'

'Peg, I lost me money bag.'

'Did them buggers take it?'

'I don't know. But it was all the day's takings.'

'Don't worry about that. You'll soon make it up.'

When Eve was alone she gazed round the room. Her eyes were hungry for things she thought she would never see again. The boys' bed that Joseph had given them, the shelves full of her bottles and the photograph of her parents. Why had she gone off alone to Shadwell? Instead of finding Charlie and asking for help she had sat on her high horse and gone her own way. Who was it that had tried to kill her? She remembered voices, a strange language and being roughly carried somewhere. But it was the river she remembered most, the water coming over her . . .

'Eve, Eve!'

Peg was shaking her.

'What . . . what happened?' Eve felt as though she had been in that dark river again.

'You must have dozed off, love.'

'Did the tray fall?'

'Yes, I heard the crash and came running up.'

Eve saw the broken bowl and soup over the floor. She burst into tears.

'Now, now, it's not the end of the world. You're still suffering from shock, so you go ahead and have a good bawl. You'll soon be back to normal.'

But Eve knew that it was going to be hard to feel normal again.

★

267

Later that morning Eve dressed. Her limbs felt stiff and sore but she was lucky to have only a few bumps and bruises to show for her recent experience.

'Sit in front of the fire, you're still cold,' Peg told her after she had walked round the house and into the yard to breathe in the fresh air.

The warmth went into her chilled bones as she sat in Peg's chair.

'I'll make a nice cup of tea.'

'Don't fuss, Peg, I'm all right.'

'Yes, but a cup of tea always helps.'

As she went out to the kitchen, Jimmy came in. 'So Sleeping Beauty has woke up?'

'Jimmy, I'm sorry.'

'For what?'

'For going off like that.'

He patted her shoulder and sat down. 'Yeah, well you did give us all a scare.'

'What's wrong with your eye?'

He told her all that had gone on since Friday night. How he had found Charlie and of their drive to Shadwell to look for her. 'So I knocks on a door and an ugly mush opens it,' grinned Jimmy. 'I took an instant dislike as he lands one on me.'

'Oh, Jimmy!'

'Then just as he was about to plant another, Charlie turns up and counter-attacks. Blimey, Eve, you should have seen him.'

Eve felt distressed that it was because of her.

'Anyway,' rushed on Jimmy, 'when we gets back, Peg tells us Archie's dropped you at the park. So me and Charlie goes off again. This time we strike lucky with the Drunken Sailor.'

Eve shivered at the memory. 'I saw these men in the back room. One of them was Singh. The landlord said he wore a jacket with brass buttons. But I must have fainted.'

'Then what?'

Eve's eyes filled with tears. 'They put a cloth over me head and tied my hands. I couldn't see who it was or where we was going. Jimmy, I thought it was curtains when I fell in the river.'

'If it wasn't for Charlie it might have been. He jumped in and I thought it was the last I'd see of the pair of you. Then all of a sudden he's pulling you out of the water onto the foreshore.'

Eve frowned, shaking her head in confusion. 'I can't remember. I thought I was looking over his shoulder.'

Jimmy laughed. 'No, gel, you must be a bit confused. You was lying on the mud not standing behind him.'

Eve didn't say anything. But she couldn't forget what she thought she had seen.

'And then Charlie done this artificial res-per-whatsit. Like pressing on yer chest and pulling your arms back.'

Peg brought in the tea and Jimmy began to tell it all over again. Eve sat with her own thoughts. Something mysterious had happened that night. She didn't understand what, but she knew that she owed her life to Charlie.

'Peg said you fell in the river.' Albert sat at her feet and Samuel on the arm of the chair when they arrived back from school. 'Did you see Old Father Thames?'

'No, 'course not. Now tell me what you did today.'

'Sister Mary gave us a star for our catechism,' said Samuel, wrinkling his nose. 'And for going to confession on Saturday.'

'I'm very proud of you. What about those rough boys?'

'Didn't see 'em today,' replied Albert. 'It was Charlie that saved you, wasn't it?'

Eve smiled. 'Yes it was.'

'Jimmy told us he done a rescue. A good one an' all.'

'It was a very good one,' Eve agreed.

'He come round yesterday with Jimmy's bike but we was at Mass.'

'You'll see him another time.'

Peg came in with a tray of yet more tea. 'Well now, all of us together for once. Jimmy you're early. Did you get the push again?'

'Yeah, but it don't matter as I'll soon get something else.'

Eve sat up in alarm. 'Was it because of me?'

''Course not.'

But Eve wasn't sure she believed him. Once again the tears pricked.

As she blew her nose there was another knock at the door. Joseph entered carrying a large pot. '*Refuah sheleimah*, dear Eve. A full and peaceful healing,' he said lowering the pot so that Eve could smell the delicious aroma. 'Eat this broth and your recovery will be assured.'

Everyone was being so kind. But for some reason their actions only made her feel more responsible for the worry she had put them through.

It was early on Monday morning when Charlie walked into the station. As he pushed open the door, Sergeant Moody stepped out from behind the desk.

'Constable Merritt, take these files into the office and sort them out,' he boomed. 'I want every one labelled in nice big black capitals and filed in alphabetical order.'

'Yes, Sarge, but I er . . . wondered if I could speak to you first on a personal matter.'

'A *what*?'

'Something happened at the weekend and—' Charlie began but was cut short.

'Run away from 'ome have you?' demanded his superior. 'Your mother gone and packed your sandwiches in a street map, has she?'

Charlie knew his superior was of the old school, believing that at twenty-seven, a bloke should be married with a wife and kids of his own, not still enjoying a single life.

'And where's your uniform?'

'I've only just arrived, Sarge. I came early to ask—'

271

'It's Sergeant Moody to you and don't you forget it,' he was interrupted again. 'And remember it could be this week or the next or gawd knows when, but the top brass will be looking over our shoulder like vultures, even hanging from the bloody ceiling in order to show us how to do our own jobs. In other words how to catch criminals. So, lad, I don't want a laughing stock made of my patch. The super would hang me out to dry without a second's thought if it meant a choice between his job and mine, so don't pass wind or pick your nose without looking behind you first.'

Charlie's spirits sank. He had forgotten that Scotland Yard's special Mobile Patrol, formed only about eight or nine years before, was taking a special interest in the East End and Moody had been treading on hot coals ever since. Now nicknamed the Flying Squad because of their quick appearances on the scenes of armed robberies and professional crime, the elite group of police officers was held in both esteem and fear by the lower ranked officers. Charlie sighed inwardly, realizing it was completely the wrong time to talk about what had happened at the weekend.

'Well?' Sergeant Moody demanded, his thick eyebrows colliding. 'What are you waiting for? A flamin' knight-hood?'

'No, Sergeant Moody.'

'Get off with you then. And remember: I want this station running like clockwork.'

Charlie made his way down the passage to the

changing rooms. Now what was he to do? Yesterday he'd tried to see Eve, but had been sent packing by Peg. He had hoped to discover more of what had happened to her in order to decide what to do. Without her consent and cooperation, he couldn't officially take things further.

Charlie rubbed his chin thoughtfully as he opened his locker. In talking to Moody first he had hoped to gain his superior's understanding if not his sympathy. No chance of that now. With the Flying Squad at his heels, Moody would work to the book. He would demand an explanation as to why an officer had continued with enquiries into a closed case. Charlie knew this was a serious breach of the rules.

As he put on his uniform, the memory of Eve's deathly pale face kept coming to mind. Whoever had left her in that death-trap of a hut, had to be found and prosecuted. A few seconds more under water and she would have been beyond his help. He would never forget the desperation he had felt as he'd tried to get her breathing again. And the wave of relief when she finally did.

Why had they done that to her? Had someone over-heard her conversation with the landlord? Was there another more sinister motive connected to Singh?

There were voices along the corridor. Robbie strolled into the changing room with another P.C. 'Hello there, you old reprobate,' he called coming over to slap Charlie on the back. 'Where were you on Saturday night?'

Charlie looked blank. 'What?'

'We had an arrangement, remember?'

Charlie rolled his eyes. 'Sorry, mate, I forgot.'

'The girl was very upset. She was looking forward to meeting you.'

Charlie was about to explain what had happened when he thought better of it. The last discussion they had had about Eve hadn't gone down too well.

'She's some looker too. If I wasn't seeing Venetia, I'd fancy her myself.' Robbie smirked as he opened his locker.

Charlie shrugged as he pulled on his jacket. 'I'm sure Johnny stepped into the breach.'

'He did indeed. Good man, Johnny. Knows how to enjoy himself.'

Charlie wasn't going to take the bait. He wasn't at all disappointed to have missed out on an evening that would have ended in having to excuse himself early. Now that the football was over for the summer, Robbie seemed hell bent on living life in the fast lane again. His social life was now wine, women and gambling to excessive degrees. After the Diana Thomas affair, Charlie would have thought his friend had more sense, especially as he'd had the nerve to warn him off Eve.

'Where were you, then?' Robbie asked, seemingly unwilling to let the subject drop.

'Nowhere special.'

'Come on, man of mystery, own up.'

'Certainly not at the Ritz,' Charlie evaded. 'I wasn't born with a silver spoon in me mouth.'

'Nor was I, but what the hell! Women only go for looks and what you tell them, not for details on your birth certificate.' Robbie grinned.

'Did you see Moody on your way in?' Charlie asked quickly.

Robbie shrugged disinterestedly. 'I don't know what all the fuss is about. If you ask me the Flying Squad is nothing more than a glamorized bunch of cowboys.'

'You don't mean that, surely?'

Robbie returned a mirthless grin. 'Oh, pardon me, I forgot, we're still supposed to believe in heroics, aren't we?'

'Not necessarily,' said Charlie, feeling foolish. 'But the Squad have achieved very impressive results.'

Robbie looked serious. 'So you really do believe they're better than you or me?'

'Not better perhaps, just quicker.'

'I can see stars in your eyes, laddo,' his friend mocked. 'I suppose if that's all you want to do with your time – swan around nicking easy targets . . .' Robbie began combing his blond hair in the mirror above the wash-basin.

Once more Charlie refrained from speaking his mind. It was a bit rich, he thought, insulting the Flying Squad like that. Robbie's attitude seemed to be close to cynical now. Was his friend losing interest in his work again?

As Robbie returned to the subject of Venetia Harrington and the various clubs they had trawled through on Saturday night, Charlie realized that he could no longer really talk to his one time pal. Robbie had other things on his mind these days.

And it certainly wasn't his job.

Eve was beginning to feel more like her old self by Wednesday. The apple cider infusions that she drank each day and the crushed lavender heads that she rubbed into her joints were working. She wanted to forget about Shadwell and get on with her life.

But when Archie called round that afternoon, Peg was quick to tell him what had happened.

He shook his head in disbelief. 'And I thought you was having a romantic interlude!'

'Knew she wasn't,' muttered Peg as they sat in the kitchen.

'I'd have looked for you too, gel, if I'd known.' He scratched the stubble on his big chin. 'Come to think of it, I should 'ave turned the cart round when I saw you walk past the park.'

'Wouldn't have made any difference,' said Peg, glancing at Eve. 'Like a dog with a bone she is when she wants something.'

'Don't I know it,' Archie agreed. 'Good thing an' all as she got herself back into business whereas many would've given up.'

'Archie,' Eve interrupted, 'would you ask Queenie to send me some stock?'

'You going back to work then?'

'She ain't this week,' said Peg, flattening her palms

on the table. 'She's just back from the brink of death.'

'On Monday p'raps?' ventured Archie, giving Eve a sly wink. 'I'll tell Queenie to sort you out a nice bit of stock.'

'Archie, I lost me money bag.'

'Did those sods take it?'

'I don't know. But how will I pay Queenie for the stock?'

'Queenie'll be all right. I'll have a word in her ear. You flog the first lot and pay her after.'

'Thanks, Archie.'

He wiped his mouth on his sleeve. 'I'd better go now as I left the Irish running me stall. They're doin' well an' all.'

Eve thought of the outside world, how everything was going on as usual. When would she feel her old self again?

At the door, Archie put his arm round her. 'Come on, give us a smile.'

'I should be working.'

'You'll be there soon enough.' He grinned at Peg. 'You stay on your feet too, gel. Don't want to pick you up off the floor again.'

'What's this about you on the floor?' Eve asked when he'd gone.

'I had one of me turns, that's all. But a sniff of the salts did the trick.'

Eve felt guilty again. She had caused a lot of worry to her nearest and dearest. Is that why she hadn't heard from Charlie? Did he, too, think she had been irresponsible?

Eve was up early on Friday morning. Standing at the kitchen window, she found herself staring into space. She was once again trapped below the surface of the water, the eerie sound of silence all around her. What had happened then? Her chest had felt as though it was being crushed by a great weight. She had known what it was like to drown. Then suddenly she was transported to the land. She was looking over Charlie's shoulder at herself, lying on the ground. When she told Jimmy this, it sounded far fetched, but it was true. What had happened in those minutes before Charlie brought her back to life?

Suddenly a movement caught her eye. Eve came back to the moment with a jolt.

A pair of feet were protruding from the closet.

Her heart raced, she hadn't known anyone was there.

Slowly she opened the back door. A rush of warm May air flowed in. The early morning sun shone on the piles of broken slates. A ship's hooter sounded in the distance.

Eve stepped cautiously forward and stopped at the sound of loud snoring. 'Hello?' she called warily.

Was it a tramp? It was a woman's legs with a nasty cut on one of her ankles.

'Hello?' Eve said once again, creeping forward.

The figure stirred. A face surrounded by tangled grey hair rose towards her.

'Joan?' Eve gasped. She couldn't believe it was Peg's sister.

'Who the 'ell are you?'

'It's me, Eve.'

'What you doing round 'ere again?'

Eve bent down beside her. 'This isn't Bambury Buildings, Joan, it's Isle Street.'

Joan's head wobbled. 'Don't talk daft.'

'I'm not. You're in our lav.'

'Where's that cow of a sister of mine then?'

'She's indoors. I'll get her.'

As Eve stood up, Joan fell back and began to snore again.

Chapter Sixteen

Peg was in the front room, folding her mattress behind the couch where it was kept during the day.

'Peg, you'd better come with me.'

'I'm packing me bed away.'

'Leave it for now.'

Peg turned, a cigarette dangling from her lips. 'Blimey O'Reilly you sound as if—' She stopped when she saw Eve's expression. 'What's up?'

'I think you'd better come and see.'

They went out to the yard and Eve pointed to the closet.

'Is that someone in there?' Peg demanded. 'In our lav, in our backyard? Bloody cheek!'

Eve nodded. 'Before you say any more go and see who it is.'

Peg went over. She stepped back, her hand to her mouth. 'It can't be!'

'It is.'

'What's she doing here?' Peg's face was filled with suspicion.

'I don't know. She must have come round in the night.'

'Look at the state of her. She's got no stockings on and what's she done to her ankle? It looks nasty.'

'She must have hurt herself.'

Peg went closer. 'I hardly recognize me own sister and, blimey, don't she pen and ink!'

The twins joined them, wearing only their pants, yawning and rubbing the sleep from their eyes. 'What's going on? Who's that in there?' They tried to look in but Eve dragged them back.

'Pooh!' Samuel held his nose.

Albert giggled. 'Smells like the drains again.'

Peg nodded. 'She don't look very healthy, does she boys? I reckon your Aunty Joan has been on a bit of a bender.'

'But why would she come here?' Eve said. 'I would have thought this was the last place in the world she'd want to visit.'

'Not in her right mind she wouldn't,' agreed Peg. 'There's only one answer and that is she's got nowhere else to go.'

'What do you mean?'

'Didn't tell you this,' whispered Peg, 'but Joan's old man has got himself another woman. Jimmy went over to Bambury Buildings when you was missing.

He caught Harold and her on the apples and pears.'

'How did Jimmy know it was Harold?' asked Eve disbelievingly.

'It was Harold's ugly mug all right.'

'Where was Joan?'

'Dunno. Jimmy didn't wait to find out. Had more important things on his mind.'

'So you think it might be Harold's philandering that put her in this state?'

'I ain't taking no sides,' said Peg harshly. 'I tried to warn her years ago but she wouldn't take no notice. Accused me of leadin' him on, like she did you.'

'Even so, we can't leave her here,' Eve said and turned to the two boys. 'Run up to Jimmy and wake him. Tell him we need his help.'

When they were gone, Eve made a last attempt to rouse Joan, but all she got was snoring.

Samuel and Albert were sitting at the kitchen table after they had finished their tea. They had been at school all day and had bolted their food, eager to find out what had happened to their aunt.

'Is Aunty Joan gonna live with us?' they wanted to know.

'Yes, until she's better,' Eve told them as she cleared away the dirty dishes.

'What's wrong with her?' asked Samuel. 'Has she had a row with Uncle Harold?'

'I don't know,' replied Eve. 'And you mustn't ask.'

'Has she got a bad leg? Will it fall off?' Albert was eager to know the gory details.

'No, 'course not.'

'She ain't gonna sleep with us, is she?'

Eve smiled as she made them rinse their sticky hands after eating the jam roly-poly she had cooked for tea. 'Aunty Joan will share Peg's mattress. So don't go banging about or she'll think a herd of elephants lives upstairs.'

The boys burst out laughing.

'As you've been very good you can go out to play. But remember, I don't want you going down to the river.' She had become very nervous about them playing near water.

'Can we go to Joseph's?'

'Yes, but don't get in his way. And don't stay late as you've got to be up early for confession.'

They sped off. Eve sighed. She seemed to be full of 'do's and don'ts' these days. Was it because of what had happened at Shadwell that she was so anxious?

Just then Jimmy rode in on his bike and let it fall down by the wall. He pulled off his cap as he came in the kitchen. 'How's the patient?'

Eve cut him a slice of roly-poly. 'She's in the front room with Peg. Now, sit down and eat this whilst it's warm.'

Eve sat beside Jimmy. 'Did you find a job?'

'No. I went up as far as Aldgate, asked at the markets, but work is short everywhere.'

'Oh dear.' She felt responsible as she guessed he had lost his position at the PLA because of her.

'There's always tomorrow,' he grinned, licking his lips.

Just then Peg appeared, her cheeks flushed and her hair all over the place. 'You look like you've been eight rounds with Jack Dempsey,' Jimmy laughed.

Peg took her tobacco tin from the windowsill and flopped down on a chair. 'You're not far off the mark, my lad. She's got the delirium tremens, wanting her flamin' gin and it took all me willpower not to give her a right-hander.'

Eve smiled. 'I never thought we'd manage to get her in the bath.'

Peg laughed. 'She fought us tooth and nail, didn't she?' It had taken the best part of the day to wash and disinfect her and the air had turned blue as Joan and Peg had battled.

'Don't know why I'm laughing,' cackled Peg, drawing deeply on her roll-up. 'I've got to sleep with her tonight.'

'You can sleep with me, there's plenty of room in me bed,' said Eve.

'No, she might run off. Or break something. Or set the house on fire.'

'Do you think she would?' asked Jimmy, looking alarmed.

Peg and Eve both nodded, keeping straight faces.

'I think I'll lock me door tonight,' said Jimmy taking his dish to the sink. 'In case she tries to get in.'

Peg and Eve burst into laughter.

'It ain't funny really,' chuckled Peg, 'the poor old girl don't know if she's coming or going.'

'I can give her something to help,' said Eve.

'Tell her it's a drop of the old Lincoln's Inn,' said Jimmy and everyone laughed again.

'Do you want me to cycle over to Bambury Buildings?' offered Jimmy as he put away his clean dish and spoon.

'Someone should tell Harold,' Eve nodded.

'Yeah, but he won't care,' Peg retorted, stubbing out her cigarette in the saucer and immediately rolling another. 'We'd better see what she says when she's sober.'

They were considering the prospect of a sober Joan when there was a knock at the door.

'Now who's that?' demanded Peg, frowning. 'I wonder if it could be Harold?'

Jimmy went to answer it.

Eve and Peg listened to the quiet murmurings. And Eve's heart jumped fiercely as Charlie walked into the kitchen.

Charlie smiled at the three faces staring up at him. He was glad to see Eve looking better, but he didn't want to get in the way. 'Hope I haven't called at an inconvenient time.'

Peg laughed. 'What's one of those when they're at home?'

'I could call back later.'

'No, sit down,' Eve said quickly, 'I'm glad you've come.'

Peg crooked a finger at Jimmy. 'Look sharpish, son. Let's leave these two alone. S'pect they have a lot to talk about.'

Jimmy put on his cap. 'I'm going on the hunt again.'

'What for?' Charlie asked.

'Lost me job, didn't I.'

'I'm sorry to hear that.'

'Don't matter, me old plate.' He grinned and shot out the back door.

'If you hear a shemozzle from the other room, ignore it,' said Peg as she left.

'What was that all about?' Charlie asked Eve.

'We found Joan outside this morning. She was worse the wear for drink. We gave her a bath, but she's got a dreadful temper. We don't know how long she's been away or what's happened between her and Harold. Jimmy saw him with another woman.'

Charlie didn't say that he wasn't surprised. He thought Harold Slygo was a devious man that day he had come into the station to ask about Eve. The Kumar case was not open to discussion and Charlie had been quick to tell him so.

'How are you feeling now?' he asked.

'Better, thanks.'

Charlie felt an angry knot in his stomach. She looked so fragile and pale. Who would want to harm her? He felt protective. 'I hope you're getting some rest.'

'I'm not going back to work till Monday. Charlie, Jimmy told me what you did. How you jumped in and pulled me out. I wouldn't be sitting here now if it wasn't for you.'

'Can you remember who did it to you?'

'No, I was blindfolded. It came off when I dropped to the water.'

'Did they threaten you or take anything?'

'I lost me money bag, but I don't know if they took it. It could have come off when I fell.'

'Eve, the police will want to speak to you—' he stopped as she shook her head.

'Charlie, I can't do that.'

'Don't you want those men brought to book?'

'I've already caused a lot of worry and I've got Samuel and Albert to consider. If anything happened to me . . .'

'Nothing is going to happen to you,' Charlie said fiercely. 'I can promise you that. Eve, you may have been robbed and were left to die. Don't you want to see justice done?'

'You say that because you're a policeman.'

He shook his head. 'I'm thinking of you.'

She looked away. 'In that case, I hope you'll under-stand.'

The awkward silence deepened. Suddenly Charlie found himself blurting, 'Eve, would you like to come for a drive?' His heart thumped as she hesitated.

'When?'

'This Sunday? Dad doesn't need the van in the

morning and we could go up to Hyde Park. The boys can sit in the back if they don't mind looking out the back windows.'

'They go to Mass on Sunday.'

'Oh.' He felt disappointed. Was she refusing because she thought he would try to talk her out of her decision? 'Another time perhaps?'

She smiled. 'But I'd like to come.'

He sat forward. 'You would?' He couldn't believe it.

Just then there was a scream from the front room and a loud bang. Charlie jumped to his feet as two women sped into the kitchen. One of them was dressed in a nightgown and he recognized her as Joan Slygo.

'Good evening,' he said politely.

'It might be to you,' she cried her eyes looking wildly about her, 'but it ain't to me. They won't let me go down the pub.'

'They're not open yet, I'm afraid, Mrs Slygo,' he replied and received a wink from Peg who grabbed hold of her sister and pulled her along the passage.

Charlie smiled at Eve. 'See you on Sunday, then.'

'I'll walk out with you.'

In the yard, Charlie glanced up at the tarpaulin. It had turned a muddy brown and was sagging in the middle. 'So they haven't completed the roof.'

'No.' Eve looked up at him and smiled. 'I was rude to the man who was doing it before and he left.'

Once more they laughed together. Charlie had a strange feeling in the pit of his stomach. 'The offer's still on from that same man,' he said quietly as a wave of hot colour sped up from his neck. 'Take care of yourself, Eve.'

Quickly he made his way round the side of the cottage before she had time to change her mind about Sunday. As he drove off, his heart was hammering. He should be concerned that he wasn't doing his professional best to persuade her to follow the lines of the law. But all that had been put to one side when finally he'd found the nerve to ask her to go out.

He laughed aloud as he drove. He'd never felt like this in his life before. Eve was different to any other woman he'd ever known. And this time, he wasn't going to let anyone talk him out of getting to know her. And that included Eve herself.

Eve had butterflies when she went to bed on Saturday night and they were still there on Sunday morning. She was seeing Charlie today. At breakfast, the boys had been reluctant to go to Mass and miss his visit. But she'd told a white lie and said it was only in order to give more information on what had happened to her.

As the day was bright and sunny she wore a green dress that had been all the fashion several years ago. She had bought it second hand as usual from the market. It was the soft shade of green that had attracted Eve. When the boys had gone, she looked in the mirror to study the effect. Her brown hair hung in waves around her shoulders, freed from its plait. As the mirror only reflected half of her, she hoped the dress had still kept its attractive shape.

'Eve, your bloke's here,' cried Peg from below.

Eve hurried down. 'Peg, don't call him that.'

'Well, what else do I call him?'

Joan appeared wearing Peg's plaid dressing gown. She was quieter this morning, chastened by the exhausting experience of the fight that had taken place between the sisters the day before. Eve had listened gloomily to the recriminations that had come fast and furious. The old grudges, resentments and accusations pouring forth.

'You sure you'll both be all right?' Eve glanced at them uncertainly. Would they kill each other in her absence?

''Course,' nodded Peg glancing at Joan who folded her arms over her chest.

'Got to be, haven't you?'

'The boys will be back after Mass,' Eve told them as she slid her bag over her shoulder. 'Tell them I won't be long.'

'You enjoy yerself,' said Peg. 'You ain't missing nothin' here.'

Eve could hear the quarrel start the moment she left. Charlie smiled and opened the van door as she walked towards him, and Eve saw the look of admiration in his deep blue eyes. Despite the racket back in the house, she really did feel like Cinderella climbing into her golden coach.

★

The whirlwind tour of the city left Eve with a sense of wonder. She wasn't used to sitting on a comfortable leather seat, being chauffeured through the motorized traffic. She was more used to standing on the corners with her baskets watching it all go by. She also felt very feminine in her dress, rather than wearing her traditional flower-selling garb of black skirt, shawl and feathered hat. Though she was proud of her trade, the flower-seller was slowly becoming a figure of the past. London life was changing and single flower-sellers were scarce, their pitches replaced by stands and run by families like the industrious Irish. While the Italians had put their mark firmly on the coffee houses, restaurants and delicatessens, laundries and modern barber shops of Soho. Although Eve was pleased to see that Harrods in the Brompton Road with its distinctive terracotta fascia was still displaying wonderful new fashions in its windows, flanked by the ever stalwart jewellers with their dazzling arrays of merchandise.

As Charlie drove through the streets, Eve leaned forward to see the smartly dressed men alighting from sleek black cars that pulled into the kerb beside the exclusive gentlemen's clubs. These were the types that often bought a buttonhole from her if they had a lady on their arm. Or perhaps a spray of lavender, winking at her discreetly as they walked away.

At Hyde Park, Charlie parked the van in a side road and they strolled on the green to Rotten Row, where the Sunday horseriders slowly passed by. These were followed by well-groomed horses pulling elegant carriages and guided by top-hatted drivers.

Eve smiled as they leaned together on the railings. 'Is this where you usually come of a Sunday?' she asked Charlie. He was dressed in Oxford bags and a tweed jacket that hid his broad chest and wide shoulders. He looked very handsome. Why was she noticing so much about him today? Was it because she no longer regarded him as just a policeman?

'No, as a matter of fact I'm more likely to be found at Regent's Park, at the carthorse meetings.'

'You prefer carthorses to these animals?'

'I do have a fondness for older horses,' he admitted. 'Dad used to take me to Regent's Park as a kid as we had a cart before the van. It was a smart one too, with a painted running board with our name on it, and Dad sometimes let me drive it. Our carthorse got old though and finally went to the old carthorse home in the sky. Dad decided on a van then, easier for his rounds and the stable was converted to a garage.'

'Your dad must have missed the horse.'

'Yes, but times change.'

'Is that when you learned to drive?'

'Yes, my brothers and me. Even Mum had a go, but gave up when she reversed into a wall.' He laughed again, his blue eyes twinkling. 'The last time I came here was with a friend.'

'Oh.' Eve wondered who the lady was but didn't ask.

'There was a band playing,' Charlie mused as yet

another sleek brown horse trotted by with its well-dressed rider. 'We sat over there and listened for a while.'

'Does she like horses as well?'

'What makes you think it was a she?' He turned and leaned on the rail, gazing into her eyes.

Eve felt embarrassed. 'Don't all young men of your age have young ladies?'

He laughed. 'I was with a mate from the Force. His passion is horses, though it's not actually for riding them.'

Eve was pleased it wasn't a girl.

He didn't seem interested in telling her more about his friend or talking about his work. Eve was relieved as she didn't want to talk about something that might remind her of Shadwell.

The sun shone down through the trees to where they were standing, and Eve breathed in hoof-turned earth. The park was very green and leafy and all around people were having a good time.

'The boys would have liked this,' she mused.

'Do they always go to church on Sundays?'

'Their teacher, Sister Mary, says their religious education is important.'

'Do you think that too?'

'St Saviour's is a good school and I don't want them to get behind.'

'Perhaps one Sunday you could make an exception?'

She laughed. 'We wouldn't be having this conversation if they were with us. It would be, "Charlie, what's this?"

and "Charlie, what's that?" and you'd be dragged all over the place and never given a minute to think.'

'I'm quite used to that. I've got plenty of nieces and nephews.'

'Yes, the boys told me.'

He smiled. 'I'd like you to meet them one day.'

Eve blushed.

He took her hand and placed it over his arm. 'Let's walk. And since you've warned me that after today, I'm not very likely to have your undivided attention, you can tell me more about yourself, and if you're interested, I'll tell you about me.'

As they walked, Eve told him about her childhood and he listened attentively to her description of her flower-selling days with her Irish-born mother. She went on to explain how her father had died from yellow fever and her mother soon after. When she spoke about Raj and the wonderful husband and father he had been, she felt a little uneasy. Here she was walking with another man, her hand on his arm, enjoying the sweetness of life that Raj had been robbed of.

But when she had finished, he, in turn, told her of his early years as the youngest son of a shopkeeper. When he described his parents, his twin brothers George and Joe and his nieces and nephews his voice was filled with tenderness. But she was surprised at his cool tone when he spoke of his job and Sergeant Moody, the policeman she had met at Bambury Buildings. Then there was Charlie's friend Robbie Lawrence, who had come here before with Charlie. Eve was eager to hear more about him but Charlie returned to his love of football and the family bakery.

As the morning drew to a close, they returned to the van. Eve enjoyed the sunny ride back to the island, happy that not one word had been spoken about Shadwell.

That experience felt more and more like a dream and she didn't want to think about it now. And neither, it appeared, did Charlie.

Chapter Seventeen

When Eve went to work early on Monday morning she wondered when her flowers would arrive. She stood on the corner of Westferry Road, watching each cart go by.

It was a cloudy day, but as Eve waited her mind drifted back to the day before, bringing a rush of heat to her skin. When they had got back to the cottage, Samuel and Albert were waiting eagerly to see Charlie. To her surprise he produced a brand new football from the back of the van. The twins' eyes had come out on stalks. He'd taken them in the van to Island Gardens and they had spent an hour playing football before he had dropped them back. Their cheeks had been bursting with colour.

Eve was smiling at the memory as a horse and cart pulled up. The toothless driver dressed in a long leather coat and cap let down the back of the cart. 'These for you, ducks?' He nodded to the bunches of flowers, sprays and posies.

'Did Queenie send them?'

'Yeah.'

Eve was delighted with the stock. 'Will you be delivering tomorrow?'

'Yeah, should be.'

And with that he slapped the horse's rump with the reins and the cart rumbled off. Eve hardly had time to inspect her stock before her first customers arrived. They were the two girls from the pickle factory on their way to work. 'Save them roses for me,' said one of the girls getting out her purse and paying. 'I'll pick them up on me dinner hour.'

Eve sold well throughout the morning. Some of her customers had missed her and others told her that even the Cox Street and Chrisp Street markets couldn't beat her prices. Eve was flushed with success. It was only at tea time that a fearful thought came into her mind. It was at this time of day that Archie had given her that fateful ride to the King Edward Park.

Her last bunch of chrysanthemums sold to an elderly lady going to the cemetery. As Eve prepared to leave, she thought again about the wonderful morning she had shared with Charlie. 'Can I call round next Sunday?' he had asked.

And the boys, of course, had answered for her.

The following Sunday, the last in May, Eve allowed the boys to miss Mass. She knew Sister Mary would have something to say about it, but she had promised them a special treat. Instead of going to Mass, Charlie was taking them to the city.

As Eve predicted, the boys kept Charlie busy with questions and seized any opportunity to play football. The parks provided plenty of space and the weather kept warm and dry. As Charlie didn't have to return the van early, they stayed out all day, ending with a picnic at Regent's Park.

When Charlie was breathless from all the exercise he sat down beside Eve on the grass. With his open-necked white shirt and cream flannels he looked very young and athletic. The sun was drifting down behind the leafy trees, but its rays still crept over the green grass, making lacy shadows on the lawns. The laughter from Samuel and Albert and two other boys they had palled up with to play football, drifted over to where they sat. Eve poured a glass of lemonade and handed it to Charlie.

He gulped it back quickly after which he ate several of the thinly cut cheese sandwiches she had prepared. Giving a deep sigh of satisfaction, he turned on his side. 'How are things at home?'

She smiled. 'Joan has given Peg a new lease of life. It was all aches and pains before and now she's like a two year old trying to keep up with Joan and her attempts to get out to the pub.'

'And Harold hasn't called?'

'No. I don't think he will.' She looked into Charlie's

eyes. 'Charlie, did he really have the nerve to come to the station and ask about me?'

'Yes, but I told him I wasn't at liberty to discuss your case.'

'You've never said.'

'I didn't know if you knew and thought it was better forgotten.'

'Do you know why we left there?'

'No, was it something to do with him?'

Eve nodded. 'Joan wouldn't believe me when I said what he did.'

Charlie sat upright. 'What did he do?'

Eve blushed. 'I had to use me knee.'

'What? The——!' He stopped abruptly as she put up her hand.

'Oh, don't worry, he didn't do nothing but there was no question about us staying on at Bambury Buildings after that. And later, Peg told me the same thing happened to her many years ago, which caused the family rift. But now Joan isn't drinking, Peg is worried she'll go back to kick Harold's other woman out.'

'Would she really try that?'

'I don't know.' Eve paused. 'Is there anything she could do to get her out in a peaceful way?'

'It's a domestic situation,' Charlie replied thoughtfully, rubbing his chin. 'It rather depends on whether Joan and Harold make it up.'

'Yes, I s'pose so.'

'If he won't let her back then I think she would have to get herself legally represented.'

'I can't see Joan doing that.'

'It might all blow over,' Charlie said reassuringly. 'You shouldn't be worrying about Joan. After all she is an adult and has to make her own choices.'

Eve gazed into the fading sun. 'Don't know how long she'll lay off the booze though.'

Charlie nodded. 'It's a difficult situation.'

Eve laughed. 'That's putting it nicely. We seem to have a lot of family skeletons in our cupboard.'

Charlie grinned. 'Every family has those.'

Eve made a face. 'Not in yours. From what you've told me, your family sounds really nice and decent.' She looked under her lashes. 'Just like you.'

He grinned. 'So you think I'm decent, eh? Suppose I have another side to my character that I haven't revealed yet?'

Eve giggled. 'That would be the policeman side I suppose.'

He made a mock grimace. 'It might be.'

'I think I like the policeman Charlie too.'

'Do you?'

She nodded.

'Well, since we seem to be friends, I wonder if you'd like to meet Mum and Dad?'

Eve almost jumped. 'What?'

'They'd like to meet you.'

Eve shook her head. 'Charlie, I don't think so.'

'Why?' He sat closer. 'I've met your family.'

'It's different.'

'Is it? Tell me why.'

'Because . . . because . . .' she stumbled over putting her doubts into words. 'I'm not what they'd expect. I was married and have children . . .' She didn't add 'and live in Isle Street' to the list although she was thinking it.

'What difference does that make?' Charlie took her hand. 'I'm on duty next weekend but the Sunday after I'm off. I know the boys go to church in the morning, so would you all come to tea?'

Eve was stunned into silence. The fact that he was holding her hand startled her so much she wasn't aware of the twins staring down at them, giggling as Charlie quickly withdrew it.

When Sunday came, Charlie arrived at half past three on the dot.

'Charlie's here!' cried the twins who had been looking out of the window for the past hour. Eve had made them wear clean white shirts and ties, their Sunday best jackets and trousers, all brushed and rag cleaned for the occasion. The darns in their long grey socks were disguised and their boots were shined until any blemish was hidden. Only the sound of the many metal Blakeys in the soles gave a clue as to their age.

Eve had made a visit to the market on Friday. She

planned to wear a navy skirt and white blouse and had bought a dark green wrap-over jacket with a side clasp to complement it. She had replaced missing buttons and turned the faded collar, adding a petersham braid to relieve the severity. She wanted to look smart as it was a Sunday visit, but most of all, she didn't want to let Charlie down. Therefore the addition of a hat was equally necessary. It came in the form of another second-hand purchase: a rust-coloured cloche with an upturned brim that shaped Eve's face and accentuated the shining pleat of her thick brown hair.

As Samuel and Albert ran out of the door to greet Charlie, Eve hurried downstairs. Peg, Joan and Jimmy waited in the hall. 'You look nice, gel,' said Peg. 'All done up like a dog's dinner.'

'I wouldn't have chosen that colour for a titfer,' snapped Joan. 'Looks like you've been standing out in the rain.'

'You'll like it at the bakery,' said Jimmy quickly trying to cover Joan's insult. 'Good luck, gel.' He gave her a wink as she said goodbye.

'We'll come out to see you off,' said Peg, but Eve shook her head.

'I don't want to keep Charlie waiting.'

'I wouldn't mind a nice crusty loaf if you think about it,' called Peg after her as she hurried out.

'Or a fruit cake with icing,' cried Joan. 'Don't like it soggy though.'

Charlie was helping the boys in the back of the van

as Eve stood on the pavement praying that Joan and Peg wouldn't follow. Then from the top of the hill there was a loud whistle. Eve looked up to see four silhouettes all waving: Maude and Eric and two of their sons.

Charlie returned a salute as he opened the van door. 'Quite a send-off.'

'I didn't know they knew,' said Eve as she glanced back at the house. 'Peg must have told them.'

'You look very nice, Eve,' Charlie said as he courteously helped her in. Eve wasn't sure about the 'nice'. Charlie was wearing perfectly creased grey flannels, a well-cut navy jacket and plain tie. Painfully remembering what Peg had said about looking like a dog's dinner, Eve wished she could go back in and put on her green dress as her jacket felt shabby and the hat rather odd. But it was too late now. She pulled back her shoulders and gritted her teeth.

The boys waved to Peg and Joan from the back window as they drove off. When Charlie turned into Westferry Road, Jimmy pedalled furiously past. He yelled out something and made the boys laugh. When he took the right fork to Poplar, Eve breathed a sigh of relief. She didn't want an escort all the way to the bakery.

It was hard to keep her composure as the boys began to play noisily about in the back.

'Sit still,' she told them abruptly. 'Charlie won't be able to drive if you do that.'

They burst into laughter once more. Charlie gave

her a big smile that reassured and frightened her all at once.

Charlie was standing with his twin brothers, Joe and George, in the corner of the upstairs front room. His mother always referred to it as the living room, since when they were young, all the living was done in here, the warmest, largest, most comfortable room of the five upper rooms over the shop. He was looking into Joe's cherubic face, but not listening to a word his brother was saying. He was aware of the women on the other side of the room; his sisters-in-law, fair-haired Pamela and brunette Eileen, who were talking to his mother and Eve. Charlie knew that Eve had been so nervous about meeting his family that she kept her coat on until a few moments ago, when his mother had managed to persuade her out of it. Of the three younger women, Eve was the smallest, but was by far the most attractive. To Charlie, who was finding it difficult to keep his eyes off her, her well-proportioned figure, straight back and full bosom were the epitome of femininity. His sisters-in-law were large girls, big-boned and strong looking. One or other of them was usually pregnant as Pamela was now. Joe often joked that his wife wasn't just eating for two but for all of England as well.

Every now and then, Charlie would drag his attention back to Joe or George and it was now George who was leading the discussion. His twin brothers were thirty-five, eight years older than himself, but like Samuel and Albert, quite different in looks. George had light brown hair and a serious expression and was considerably taller at six foot two than Joe at a modest five ten. Charlie was in the middle, just tipping six foot, but they all shared one thing in common, the piercing blue gaze of their father, Edwin. Their mother's eyes were a soft grey, a shade lighter than her still abundant grey hair that she kept coiled in a bun at the nape of her neck.

Charlie was relieved to see that his mother was sitting next to Eve. His sisters-in-law were salt of the earth but wore the trousers in the family. Not that either of his brothers would admit as much, but with ten offspring between them, they had willingly handed over the domestic reins to their wives. Not long ago all his nieces and nephews, four girls and six boys, and Samuel and Albert had been ushered down to the backyard behind the garage to play. Here there was a large net strung up, a boxful of bats and balls and skipping ropes for the benefit of the small visitors, so that when the families visited, the boys and girls had something to occupy them.

Suddenly Joe tapped his arm. 'You listening, brov?'

Charlie stared at his two brothers and father who reclined in the big armchair drinking from a tankard. The two younger men were perched on stools and Charlie was leaning against the mantel. He was positioned perfectly to watch Eve and the women over by the window.

'What's that?' Charlie responded, frowning.

'Why, Dixie Dean of course!' clarified Joe, good humouredly. 'It was the legend's sixtieth league goal this year. Surely you read about it?'

'Yeah, of course,' nodded Charlie, taking a long gulp of his ale.

'Not bad, eh?' continued George. 'No wonder Everton are the champions.'

'Walthamstow Avenue will be there one day,' grinned Charlie glancing back at Eve. The women's conversation, as far as he could hear, was all about kids and babies, thank God. It was a fairly safe subject, and although he knew that Eve was a working woman, his brothers had selected wives from middle-class families who hadn't been brought up to continue a career after marriage. He wondered if and when the focus of attention would get round to Eve. Feeling the need to support her, he made his excuses and went over.

His mother looked up at him as he joined the group and smiled. He'd arrived just as Eileen asked Eve where she lived. Eve duly answered and Charlie felt for her as he saw the surprised expressions on both Eileen and Pamela's faces.

'The Isle of Dogs?' repeated Pamela, frowning at Charlie. 'You mean the dock area?'

Eve nodded and to Charlie's dismay answered forthrightly, 'Our cottage backs on to the dry docks.'

'Oh, how interesting.' Eileen knitted her brow. 'So what do you—'

'I think it's time we ate,' broke in his mother diplomatically. 'Pamela we don't want you on your feet too much today, so why don't you sit by the fire and toast the marshmallows? Eileen, I've set out the food in the kitchen. If you'd like to help me make tea? And Charlie, why don't you and Eve go down to the shop and bring up the bridge rolls that your father made this morning?'

Charlie took Eve's arm. 'This way, young lady. We have our instructions.' He grinned back at his mother who was already propelling her daughters-in-law in the opposite direction.

It was quiet at the top of the stairs that led down to the bakery, away from the noise of the living room. Charlie stopped on the landing, turning to look at Eve. She was pale and in the silence, he said gently, 'Mum didn't say she was putting on a family do. I honestly thought it was only going to be us.'

'Would you have asked me if you'd known all your family would be here?' she asked hesitantly as she pushed back a lock of brown hair that had fallen over one cheek.

'Of course I would. But I know Pam and Eileen can sometimes be a bit, well, overpowering.'

She looked up at him, flushed now. 'They're very pleasant.'

'You must take my sisters-in-law with a pinch of salt. Once you get to know them you'll like them.'

'Charlie, how much have you told your mum and dad about me?'

'What is it you think they should know?'

'That's not an answer.'

'Eve, what's wrong?'

'You could find yourself a nice girl to introduce to your family, without any kids and who comes from somewhere like Blackheath, like Pamela does.'

'I don't want a girl from Blackheath, and I certainly don't want anyone like Pamela. Eve, I want to be with you.' He couldn't stop himself from reaching out and taking her in his arms. He felt her stiffen, then relax as he pulled her close. Before he knew what was happening he found himself kissing her.

When she pushed him away he said hoarsely, 'I'm sorry. I shouldn't have done that.'

'The children might come up.'

'We'd hear them open the back door. Eve—' He went to take hold of her again, but she stepped back against the landing wall.

'No, Charlie – no!'

'Have I offended you?'

She put her hand up to her cheek. 'It's just that . . . that . . . I haven't kissed a man in a long while. In fact I've only ever kissed one and that was Raj.'

'Eve, I understand. But I was watching you in there and felt protective.'

'Charlie, you're a good man—'

'Don't say any more,' he broke in, placing a finger to her lips. 'I can hear a "but" coming on. Just give me – us – a chance. Please.'

Just then, the noise of the yard door crashing open made Charlie jump back. A long line of children ran up the stairs.

'Is the grub up, Uncle Charlie?'

'Is it time for tea?'

'We're hungry!'

'Has Grandma got lemonade?'

Finally Samuel and Albert came rushing up. Charlie tousled their heads as they too flew past. He saw that Eve was watching them uneasily until Samuel stopped at the top of the staircase and looked back. 'I don't half like it 'ere, Mum. They got a big net out in the yard and we played football.'

Charlie watched Eve smile as Samuel disappeared into the living room.

Charlie smiled too. 'You see, your boys aren't having any difficulty in making friends,' he told her softly.

'Them all seem like nice kids.'

'They are.'

Eve gazed up at him and once more he had to fight the desire to take her in his arms. She looked like a frightened deer, ready to bolt at the least unexpected movement. He knew that this was a difficult experience for her and his heart went out to her. But he hoped and prayed that she would agree to see him again. And the next time he took her out with the two boys, he was going to make sure it was just by themselves.

He tilted his head towards the bakery. 'Now, let's go

down and get the bridge rolls, and by the time we return Mum will have the kids all washed and spruced up ready for tea.'

He waited for her to pass him, aware of her every movement, the delicate, upright posture of her small body, her beautiful skin and lustrous hair and her wide, almost innocent marmalade-coloured eyes. Yet he knew that inside her was a strong and determined spirit. He had never met anyone like Eve before.

He doubted he ever would again.

That evening, when the twins were asleep, Eve knelt at Joan's feet in the front room. Her leg was supported by a stool, her stocking pulled down and the ankle wound revealed.

'Don't press too hard, it hurts.' Joan made a face as she gripped the arm of the chair.

'It's much better than it was.' Eve smoothed the reddened skin with another application of puréed carrot and roasted onion.

'Don't reckon vegetables can cure me.'

'It's an old remedy, Joan. I've used it meself and on the boys.' Eve waited as the vegetable poultice used as antiseptic took effect.

'I ain't a flamin' 'orse.'

'Sit back and be quiet you daft 'aporth,' ordered Peg who entered the room with a small bowl of warm water. Placing it beside Eve, she folded her arms and gazed down at her sister. 'You should be grateful Eve got you walking again. Three weeks ago you couldn't 'obble let alone gad about as you do now.'

'What's in the bottle?'

After cleaning off the poultice, Eve unscrewed the top. 'A remedy I made meself.'

'What's in it?'

'Amongst other things, a herb called thyme. It grows wild and prevents infections.'

'There's only weeds round here, ain't there? Are you trying to polish me off?'

'No, 'course not. I'd use something else on you if I wanted to do that.' Eve laughed as she cleared away her things. 'Now, do you both want some cocoa?'

'That'd be nice,' said Peg as she sat down by her sister.

'Ain't we got something with a bite to it?' asked Joan.

'No,' answered Peg sharply. 'We ain't letting you go back on the booze whilst you're under this roof. And don't pull a boat race! Think yourself lucky you ain't got a bad back no more, nor a dodgy ankle and you ain't 'omeless.'

'No, instead I'm forced to share that rotten old mattress with you and your snoring.'

'You're lucky to have somewhere to kip!'

'Don't start you two,' said Eve.

Peg smiled. 'Go on, love, get the cocoa. And when you come back you can tell us all about what it was like at Charlie's.'

Eve stood in the kitchen, listening to the echoes of the argument in the front room. Their quarrelling didn't seem to irritate her so much tonight. Her mind was full of what had happened today and Charlie's kiss. When she'd pulled away, her heart had been beating a tattoo inside her chest. She knew he was embarrassed by his actions and they had only parted just in time before the children ran up the stairs. What if they'd seen them and told their mothers? A slight smile played on her lips as she thought of Pamela and Eileen's reaction.

'What did yer 'ave to eat?' Joan asked immediately as Eve returned with the mugs of cocoa. 'Was they a stingy lot?'

'No, quite the opposite.' Eve was happy to tell them about the bakery food as she sat down by the window. 'There was everything you can think of. Cup cakes, Dundee cake, small sandwiches without crusts with finely sliced cucumber. And Mrs Merritt opened a box of buttered Brazils and Turkish Delight, whilst the kids had toasted marshmallows.'

'Cor blimey, what a feast,' sighed Peg, slurping her drink. 'Did they give you anything to bring 'ome?'

'No, and it wasn't expected.'

'Some of them Brazils wouldn't go amiss.' Joan narrowed her small eyes. 'Ain't had nothing like that since Harold's old girl died.'

Eve took the opportunity to change the subject. 'Did Mrs Slygo like sweets then?'

Joan sniffed loudly. 'Used to sit in front of me with

a bag of 'em. Put 'em in her mouth all slow like, licking her lips and crunching loudly without ever offering me one. It was torture, just to watch her. And so when she had her kip of an afternoon, I used to pinch one. When I cleared her room I found more sugared almonds and crème de menthe in her chest than she had pairs of drawers.'

'Why didn't she share her sweets?' asked Eve.

''Cos she was tight, that's why. Wouldn't give anyone the droppings off her nose let alone something of value. All that stuff in the room you slept in, it was her world, her beloved possessions that she thought was worth a bob or two. Including that flamin' animal fur. She used to sit in the chair strokin' it around her neck.'

'She never!' exclaimed Peg.

'You've no idea what I had to put up with. I looked after her like me own mother before she died. And never got a word of thanks. Nor a penny, neither, not even a farthing.'

At this, Eve remembered what she had long promised herself to do. She went out and got her purse. When she returned she dropped five shillings into Joan's lap.

'What's that for?' screeched Peg, glaring at the money.

'It's what we owe Joan for our keep when we stayed with her.'

Peg looked disapproving, but Joan picked up the shiny coins and spat on each one. 'Thanks, gel. But I did it out the goodness of me heart.'

Eve kept a straight face and went out to the kitchen

to wash the mugs. But at the sink she allowed herself to smile. What a day it had been! There was Mrs Merritt, Pamela and Eileen, all speaking the King's English, drinking Lyon's best tea out of bone china cups and eating with little fingers crooked. And then there was her and Peg and Joan, drinking cocoa from chipped enamel mugs, the air blue with Cockney and stories that could make the hair on your neck stand on end.

The two worlds couldn't be further apart. How long would it be before Pam or Eileen discovered she was a flower-seller? Did Dulcie and Edwin Merritt know? No one had enquired about her dead husband, they had been brought up too well to ask outright on the first time of meeting. Samuel and Albert's darker skin indicated their bloodline, despite their accents being pure Cockney. How would the family react when they knew Raj was a lascar seaman?

Eve recalled the moment they had all gathered in the living room and the adults and children had played charades. Samuel and Albert were very good at pretending to be Laurel and Hardy whose black and white films they loved. The other children had fallen about laughing at their antics. But Eve had watched Pam and Eileen's faces. Their expressions were a mixture of curiosity and confusion. And when Charlie had slipped his hand around her waist, Eve had felt Pam and Eileen's eyes on them. Had Charlie done that deliberately?

Eve stared into space as she washed up the mugs. Charlie had asked if he could come to complete the roof repair. She had agreed but was still uncertain. Not because he was a policeman, because now she didn't care that he was. But she was worried she could never fit in with his family, and she would hate it if Charlie felt ashamed of her.

Charlie sat down and stared at the pile of paperwork on Sergeant Moody's desk. He was sure it had grown over the past month. He had waded through the case histories, checking, labelling and filing each one in the big wooden cabinet. It was, he thought, ironic, that the Yard was visiting the likes of Limehouse, Ratcliffe, Stepney, Mile End, Bethnal Green, Whitechapel, St Katherine's and Spitalfields' stations in an undercover operation, when every nick knew well in advance when the Met boys were turning up. Did the criminals also know?

Once more he thought about his career. The notion that one day, as a police officer, he would be able to be part of a system that he held in such high esteem had always been something he'd aspired to. As a youngster he had worn the pages thin of his *Strand* magazines, reading over and over again Conan Doyle's adventures of Sherlock Holmes. His love for a good game of football had only been rivalled by his fascination for the practice of investigation. And now what was he doing? Sitting behind a desk, envying the excitement that he could plainly hear outside. The Yard boys were discussing the day's agenda. He could hear the engines of the Flying Squad vehicles.

He returned his attention, with difficulty, to the papers in front of him: the torn and thumb-marked files full of loose papers all browned at the edges; photographs of villainous faces, mostly men and a few women; prostitutes and convicted thieves, even murderers; and descriptions of appearance with crossings out by the hundreds, embroidered by tea spills.

Charlie laboured on, though there was little light relief until he discovered another sighting of Jack the Ripper. He'd found at least ten over the last week. Witnesses testifying that they had seen a tall, cloaked figure in the alleyways of the East End, the top hat and medical bag being the most consistent details. The Whitechapel Murders, as they were known, still drew the public's imagination over thirty years on and Charlie was amused at some of the eyewitness statements he read of this mysterious figure still stalking his prey. Luckily most of the murders that were now committed were not in the gruesome category of the Ripper. It was the myth that had been perpetuated to this day.

Charlie reached down to the pencil drawer and lifted out his mug of strong tea. He'd made it and brought it in here before anyone had arrived. He took a slow sip, enjoying the refreshment when his hand froze in mid-air.

His eyes went over the heading on the sheet of paper he was holding. He read it again. Then he continued to read until he got to the bottom of the page.

A page that was by no means twenty or thirty years old.

He slowly placed the mug on the desk. His breath stilled as his eyes flew over the page. When he came to the last paragraph, he put it down and looked for the next page. He searched through the nearest files and the next and next and found none. Then once more he returned his attention to the heading. He read again the unmistakable words, 'No Action to be Taken by the Port of London Authority, in respect of the case of the male body recovered from Limehouse Reach on the 9th January 1928 and identified as a lascar by a ship's officer on 18th January 1928. Cause of death a blow to the head possibly the result of a fall from a ship, concussion and drowning.'

Eve was finished for the day having sold all her stock. It was a beautiful June afternoon and the weather had been kind to her all week. Queenie had continued with the deliveries and now Eve returned a third of her profits to Queenie to pay for the next day's delivery. It was an arrangement that worked well and the flowers were always fresh and colourful. Eve knew that both Archie and Queenie had a soft spot for her. Although they were hard-headed business people, they liked to look after their own. Which they now considered Eve to be.

'Can I give you a hand, Miss?'

Eve was bending over to place one empty basket inside the other. 'Charlie!' Her heart turned over as she saw first the black shiny boots, then long, uniformed legs and finally Charlie's wide, handsome smile.

'Are you packing up?'

'Yes, I've sold out.'

'Can I help with those baskets?'

'I haven't got far to go. A woman down the road lets me leave them in her backyard.'

'I'll put them on me handlebars.' He lifted them on the bicycle. 'These aren't light. How do you manage to carry them when they're full?'

'I don't have to now, as they sell so quickly.'

He balanced the baskets with one hand and as they walked down the road, the sun glinted on the badge of his helmet and the strap underneath made Eve think of the guards outside Buckingham Palace.

'What do you do in bad weather?'

'Find somewhere to shelter.'

'It's a tough job for a woman.'

She smiled. 'It's better than most. I'm me own boss and I don't have to answer to anyone, like you do.'

He laughed. 'That's true. But what about running a shop?'

'A shop? I can't see me behind a counter. And anyway, there ain't none round here.'

Eve stopped at a terraced house, the last one of the block. Charlie lifted the baskets and accompanied her round to the side entrance. When the baskets were stowed under a sack in the yard, they continued on their way.

'Are you on duty?' she asked as the carts and vehicles clattered by on their way to the docks.

'Yes. However, this is the first day I've been out of the office. The Flying Squad is investigating crime in the East End and Sergeant Moody wants the paperwork up to scratch.'

'The Flying Squad? What's that?'

'A team of officers trained for special duty. They've been named the Flying Squad because with their motor vehicles they can get to the scene of the crime very quickly.'

'That sounds exciting,' said Eve. 'Like something you might want to do.'

'Yes, but I'd need to go up in the ranks first.'

Eve frowned. 'So why are you down this way?'

'I've come to see a pretty girl that sells flowers.'

Eve blushed and laughed all at once. 'Don't forget, you're on duty.'

His expression suddenly changed. 'Eve, I've been thinking about your husband.'

Eve stopped, her heart jumping. 'About Raj?'

He nodded, pushing the brim of his helmet up. 'As I said, I've been doing the paperwork and by chance found a letter from the Lascar Transfer Office. It named the body we saw at the morgue as Dilip Bal. It said the cause of death for him was a blow to the head, possibly suffered as the result of a fall from the ship. There is to be no further investigation.'

'Like Raj?'

'Yes, and although it pains me to admit it, I feel the port authorities are simply avoiding responsibility.' He paused. 'Are you all right?'

'I think so.'

'Come on, I'll walk you home.'

They walked in silence, each with their own thoughts. When they got to Isle Street, Eve stopped and turned to him. 'Has the *Tarkay* sailed?'

'Yes, she put to sea just after . . .' he gave an uncomfortable shrug. 'What happened to you at Shadwell.' He gently touched her arm. 'Listen, I'm working this weekend, but I've two days off next week. I'll come over and mend the roof if you've no objection to a copper in your backyard?' He laughed, his blue eyes full of humour.

'You can stay to dinner if you want.'

'That would be nice.'

Eve watched him jump on his bike and cycle off, waving to her as he pedalled hard up the hill.

His news had brought back her fears. It was like a shadow that wouldn't go away. Would she do better to face them instead of blocking them out? Added to this she felt a deep sense of guilt. She felt disloyal in starting her life again whilst Raj had lost his so young. Should she try to put her fear behind her and find out the truth?

When she got home Eve drew up the key and let herself in. Joan and Peg were going hammer and tongs, their voices reassuring and familiar.

Some things never changed.

Chapter Eighteen

The summer wore on and Charlie mended the roof. By late August the tarpaulin was gone and lines of slates were nailed neatly in to place. Eve looked forward to Charlie's visits as did Samuel and Albert. After coming down from the roof he would take them to the park to play football or to the open air baths for a swim.

One glorious Sunday, Charlie took them all to the bakery for tea again. This time the wooden tables and benches were arranged in the large, paved area behind the garage. The space was surrounded by high, red brick walls and covered in beautiful flowering vines. Tea was brought out on trays – freshly baked bread, cakes and buns from the bakery – and a delicious smell rose in the air. Only Eileen and her children joined them, as Pamela was near to her time. It was a much happier experience for Eve, as the talk was of the forthcoming event. A birth that was going to be celebrated with as much eagerness as Pamela's four boys. She wanted a girl now and hopes were high she would produce one.

Eve was delighted when, on the first Saturday in September, the last before returning to school, Charlie took them to the zoo. As they walked through the big gates, they could hear all the animal noises. The lion's roar, chatter from the monkeys and the high pitched whistles from the aviaries. The boys laughed as the giraffes with their long, prickly tongues tried to eat their ice creams. The pygmy hippopotamus wallowed in the mud and splashed the onlookers. A tiger cub followed its mother into the shade and lay at her side. The air was full of excitement as they went into the warmth of the reptile house. Snakes of all shapes and sizes slid through the moist, exotic grasses and under damp boulders. A horned toad sat casually on the back of a tortoise. An Indian rhinoceros called Felix waded into the water and submerged, spilling water in every direction. Eve watched the wonder on the boys' faces. They had never seen these animals before except in picture books. A day at the zoo was a luxury and one they could never afford. But Charlie had insisted that Eve wasn't to pay for a thing.

Charlie and the two boys waited patiently for the camel rides. The slow moving animal finally arrived. The keeper helped Albert onto the saddle tied over its humpty back, whilst Samuel sat in the curve of its strong neck.

Eve waved as the animal was led off. Her sons had never been near such a big animal before, let alone ridden one.

'Charlie, will they be all right?' Eve stared after them as the keeper led the camel down the path.

''Course they will.'

'It don't look very safe to me.'

'Stop worrying. They're very competent young lads. Did they tell you how good they are now at swimming?'

'Not really. They know I'm afraid of the water.'

Charlie put a gentle hand on her shoulder. 'That's perfectly natural after what you went through. Now, come on, let's sit down while we wait.' He led her to a wooden seat close by and they sat down. It was an Indian summer, the papers had said and Eve had worn a light cotton dress in a shade of blue that was not dissimilar, she noticed, to Charlie's eyes. It was the colour that had attracted her to it on the second-hand clothes stall in the market. It had been a snip at sixpence and with a little alteration to the hem fitted her perfectly. She had set her brown hair loose from its plait and the curls softened her face. Charlie's eyes hadn't left her for very long that day.

'When they return we'll go for tea,' he said and Eve smiled gratefully.

'Charlie, it's been such a lovely day. The boys have never been anywhere like this. The zoo is somewhere I always wanted to take them, but I've only ever sold flowers outside it.'

'I'm glad it was with me you came. I'd be jealous if it was anyone else.'

She searched his face. Was he joking? 'How long do you think they'll be away?' she said craning her neck, unable to look in his eyes.

Charlie chuckled. 'Well, if the camel don't take off at a gallop, then soon, I expect.'

'It couldn't could it?' Eve was alarmed.

He put his hand over hers. ''Course not. I'm only joking.' He looked into her eyes with such an intense expression that she shivered.

'Are you cold?'

'No, someone was treading over me grave.' She blushed at her real thoughts.

'Eve, this has been a good summer for me too.'

'Has it?' She felt his fingers tighten. It was only a small movement, but her body reacted at once. Why did he make her feel this way? After the kiss at the bakery, he had never attempted to kiss her again. Perhaps it was because the boys were always around.

'Eve,' he said quietly, 'would you come out with me again? I mean, one evening?'

She felt hot and a little dizzy. 'Where to?'

'I thought we could go to the pictures, then have something to eat after.'

'Charlie—'

'If it's the boys you're worried about, we could take them too. But it would be a bit late.'

She saw the camel plodding slowly back up the path. The boys were now confidently waving from their perches.

Eve waved back but as she stood up, Charlie caught

her arm, raising a questioning eyebrow. She smiled then, unable to resist the look in his eyes which searched for an affirmative answer. 'Ask me again in a month's time. It's me birthday then.'

'A month is a long time to wait. But I will.'

Eve stepped towards the keeper, her cheeks flushed as the boys came running towards them.

Eve's summer flowers were more popular than ever. Sometimes she sold out by midday. Other days she arranged with Queenie's driver to sell from Aldgate where there were many visitors, business people and office workers. On these occasions she took the boys to help her since they had little to do in the holidays. But over the weeks Eve felt that even Samuel seemed to be losing interest despite the sixpence she gave them at the end of each working day.

When it was time for them to go back to school, there weren't the usual moans and groans. On the appointed day in September, Eve accompanied them to school. She wanted to make certain the boys that had frightened them before didn't start their old tricks again.

But when Eve bent down to kiss them goodbye, they turned shyly away. 'Mum, we ain't babies any more,' said Albert, to Eve's surprise.

'It was just a kiss.'

'We're eight now,' said Samuel, smiling nervously. 'We don't want to look cissies.'

'You're not cissies.' Eve stared at her sons wistfully. They seemed to have grown up over the holidays. Samuel had filled out and Albert had lost his puppy fat. 'Now, stay away from those boys, won't you?'

Samuel and Albert looked at one another. Eve knew they didn't need words, as twins they could read each other's minds. This morning was the first time she felt a bit on the outside.

'Bye Mum,' they called and she watched them line up before a nun, who was blowing the whistle loudly.

When they had disappeared under the Victorian gable of St Saviour's, Eve hurried to meet Percy, Queenie's driver. She had told him she would be late today as she was taking the boys to school. He was waiting for her as she hurried up Westferry Road.

'Nice day, innit?' he mumbled as, dressed in his long leather coat and cap, he unloaded her flowers and helped Eve to arrange them in her baskets. Almost before he had finished the first customer arrived. Eve enjoyed a busy morning, but it didn't stop her thinking about her sons, and feeling slightly hurt that they didn't want her to embarrass them or be seen to be kissed by their mother.

The following Sunday morning Eve woke to hear a noise downstairs. It was early and Peg and Joan were always the last to rise on a Sunday. Quietly getting out of bed and putting on her dressing gown, Eve went out to the landing. All she could hear was the gentle breathing of the sleeping twins and the mews of the gulls outside. Even their cries were distant, the new slates on the roof being a barrier to exterior noise.

Hearing nothing, Eve went back to the bedroom, and in the privacy of her small quarter behind the curtain, washed in the bowl on the chest of drawers. After plaiting her hair, she put on her warmer clothes. It was chilly in the mornings now as autumn arrived. Soon they would light a fire. Her customers would want holly, red berries and mistletoe for Christmas. Could she ask Queenie to provide her with stock? Would Percy agree to continue in the same way? It had only been a temporary arrangement for the summer. She had thought a lot about the shop Charlie had suggested. But shop work had never interested her, and she wasn't sure whether it would pay the rent.

Eve was still giving the subject some thought as she went downstairs. To her surprise the front door was open. Had Jimmy come in late? He was now working as an errand boy in the city and the hours were so long that they hardly saw him from week to week. Eve looked outside. It was a fine September morning. Quietly closing the door she went back along the hall. Peg's door was also open. Maybe one of them had gone out to the lav.

Hearing nothing, Eve went into the kitchen. She looked through the window and onto the yard. A fine mist was lifting from the dry docks behind. The closet door was closed.

As Eve put the kettle on the hob to boil, she waited

for the appearance of Joan or Peg. By the time she had made the tea, the yard and house were still quiet.

Eve put a cosy over the teapot and went out the back door. 'Joan, Peg, are you in there?' she called.

No reply came.

She pushed the closet door open. It was empty.

Returning to the kitchen she hurried into the hall. Putting her head round the open door, Eve gazed down on the makeshift bed. The mattress as usual was draped from the couch to the two wooden chairs that formed a base. The quilted eiderdown was pushed back. There was an empty space next to Peg, who lay asleep.

Where was Joan? She went out to the yard once more and into the street. There was no one.

Eve ran back inside. 'Wake up, Peg,' she said, shaking the limp arm.

Peg slowly opened her eyes. Without her false teeth in she was all gums. Her frizzy grey hair trembled as she moved. 'Hello, ducks, what—' She saw the vacant side of the bed. 'Where's Joan?'

'She's not in the lav. Or outside.'

'Oh gawd!' Peg pushed the eiderdown off.

'Did you hear her get up?' Eve asked as Peg pulled on her dressing gown.

''Course I didn't. Or she'd still be here.'

'I heard a noise early this morning.'

'What sort of noise?'

'It was a bang but not very loud. It must have been the front door.'

'Her clothes have gone,' Peg said pointing to the chair. 'Or some of 'em have.'

'That means she got dressed and—' Eve didn't finish as there was a tap at the door.

She hurried into the hall and opened it. 'Joseph!'

'I am sorry to wake you so early.'

'I was up. We can't find Joan.'

'That is why I am here. I saw her this morning.'

'Where?' Peg demanded over Eve's shoulder.

'I was in my front room and looked out of the window. Your sister went by. I was not dressed or washed at the time or I should have come sooner. I know she does not venture out alone.'

'I never let her out of me sight,' said Peg anxiously. 'Only when I close me eyes. I've often thought about tying her to the bedstead and I would if I had one.'

'What time was this?' asked Eve.

'It could be an hour ago.'

'Oh blimey,' shrieked Peg, 'she's bolted.'

Eve opened the door. 'Come in, Joseph.'

They were standing in the hall, discussing what to do, when Jimmy came down the stairs in his underpants. 'What's all the racket about?' he asked, scratching his skinny chest.

'Joan's gone.' Eve was trying to think what to do first.

'You looked in the lav?'

Everyone nodded. 'We had a tiff last night over her clothes,' confessed Peg. 'Said she was fed up wearing my old togs. She wanted to go back to Bambury Buildings to get her own. But I said that Harold's probably chucked 'em out by now. She threw a tantrum and plonked herself in the armchair with a face like a poker. I made up the bed and told her to get her arse in it. She wouldn't move. So I thought, bugger it, I'm too tired to argue. She'll come to bed when she's ready.'

'So she could have gone back to Bambury Buildings?' Eve asked.

'Yeah. S'pose so.'

'She must have been thinking about it all night,' said Eve.

'She's been a bit funny lately,' nodded Peg. 'Fidgety and talking all about Harold. She ain't done that whilst the drink's been wearing off. Now he must be on her mind.'

They all looked at one another. Eve knew that if Joan had gone to Blackwall, it wasn't for her clothes, but to confront the woman that Harold had taken up with.

Dressed for the first time that autumn in coats and hats, Eve and Peg made their way to Blackwall. It was a long walk, the best part of an hour and Peg's rheumatics were playing up.

'I'll give her a piece of me mind when I find her,' said Peg as they went through the quiet streets. There were only one or two people up, good Christians going to worship. Eve hoped that Jimmy would make certain the boys went to Mass. They had wanted to come with them to find their Aunty Joan, but Eve had refused. She didn't know what or who they would find at Bambury Buildings.

'When did she start talking about Harold?' Eve asked.

'It was when she found a photograph in me drawers. I caught her one day, looking through them, the nosey cow. It was a picture of me and her as kids, with our two brothers and Mum. Dad wasn't around, but then he never was. It was me older brother that brought us up really. Mum died when I was about eight and Joan six. She was a good woman and a bloody good flower-seller. But what good did that do her? Benny was about fifteen, kept us all together till he went into the army and then we was turned out on the streets. That's why I always felt sorry for Jimmy. Knew meself what it was like not to have no home.'

'When did Joan meet Harold?'

'He was a bit of a charmer, though he don't look it now. And me sister was a good looker. Whilst I sold me flowers, she got a job up the Strand, in an office. We was sharing rooms at Seven Dials, a real pig sty with a load of brasses. Harold worked in the same office as Joan, she told him a story about being orphaned, didn't have no one or nothing and he married her. A year or two later, Harold was up to his old tricks. Tried it on with me and the rest is history.'

'So Joan ain't been with another man?'

'Not to my knowledge. The silly cow. If that'd been

me, I'd have fleeced Harold for every penny and enjoyed meself into the bargain.'

'Did Harold always live at Blackwall with his mother?'

Peg nodded. 'That's what he wanted Joan for. A nurse-maid. Whilst he enjoyed himself. The old girl was a real tyrant too.'

'Poor Joan.'

'She should have ditched him years ago. She wouldn't listen to me.'

'She must have loved him.'

'Don't know about that.' Peg caught her breath, clinging to Eve's arm. 'Can tell the weather's changing. Me back's playing me up something rotten.'

'Let's walk slower.'

They moved off again at a slower pace. Which only served to increase the tension as they made their way to Bambury Buildings.

Eve recalled the day they had first come to Bambury Buildings at the beginning of the year in the company of the young Salvationist Clara Wilkins. It was Joan who had opened the door to them after their climb up the dirty stone steps that led to the cold and soulless balcony outside the Slygos' rooms. Joan had been well dressed in a green suit and wearing make-up, with her hair dyed red. But Eve had been able to tell they were sisters, even though Peg took no trouble at all with her appearance. As they went slowly up the steps, Eve remembered the cold greeting that had awaited them. If it hadn't been for Harold, Joan would have turned them away. But Eve had soon learned that Harold had a motive for his actions.

'What shall we do if he says she ain't there?' said Peg, stopping on the cold and draughty stairs, her head tilted to one side. Eve could hear the sounds of the residents of Bambury Buildings waking up. The smell of the lavatories was overpowering.

'Don't know,' said Eve.

'Can't hear a ruckus,' whispered Peg, pulling her coat tighter round her. 'And you couldn't miss Joan's old Hobson's choice.'

'She might be inside.'

Peg grimaced. 'Yeah, strangling the floosie.'

'She might just have wanted her clothes,' said Eve doubtfully as they continued to ascend the stairs.

On the fourth floor they looked along the balcony. It hadn't improved, thought Eve as she stared at the peeling railings and dirty brown doors with small opaque glass windows. Two small children came out of the lavatory at the end. The door banged, followed by a dreadful smell.

'Brace yerself, gel,' said Peg, raising her fist.

The knock echoed around the tenement. Eve waited with baited breath. Expecting to see Harold, Eve was shocked when a woman opened the door.

'Where is he?' demanded Peg rudely, staring belligerently into the crudely made-up face under dyed yellow hair.

'Who are you?'

'None of yer business,' snapped Peg. 'Now are you gonna get him or do I have to push me way in.'

'He ain't here, so push off.' The woman folded her arms.

Peg thrust the woman against the wall and marched in, going from room to room, calling for Joan. ''Ere, what's all this about?' called the woman after her.

'Peg's looking for her sister,' said Eve trying not to inhale the unhygienic smell that came off the woman. At least when Joan was here, she kept herself and the place clean.

'She won't find her here,' sniffed the woman, untroubled by the noise that Peg was creating as she searched the rooms.

'Have you seen her?'

'Huh!' the woman scoffed. ''Course we seen her. She was hammering on the door at first light. 'Arry had to get out of bed, to see to it. Reckon she's off her trolley, looked as though she should be locked up.'

'It's not Joan that needs locking up,' answered Eve angrily. 'It's you that don't belong here.'

'Don't make me laugh. He booted her out.'

Overhearing, Peg pulled her roughly by the shoulder. 'You won't be here long, dearie, you'll be out on your arse just as soon as he's tired of you. Now tell us what happened.'

The woman looked startled. 'All right, all right, but let go of me.' She brushed her shoulder. 'She barged her way in and got a right eyeful. Saw him and me enjoying a bit of slap and tickle.' There was a look of satisfaction in her eyes.

Eve reached out to stop Peg from grabbing the woman by the neck. 'Calm down, Peg. She's not here. Let's look somewhere else.'

There were shouts from along the landing.

'Shut up you noisy cows! This is Sunday morning!'

Eve pulled Peg onto the balcony.

As they stood there, the woman shouted, 'He was going to take her down the Sally Army. That's where they keep all the elephants' trunks, ain't it?' The door slammed.

Once more there were loud protests. A man stood on the balcony in his trousers, bare-chested. He shook his fist at them. 'We've had enough to put up with this morning. Shut your gobs once and for all or I'll come up there and shut 'em for you.'

'Don't worry, we ain't stopping,' cried Peg angrily as Eve hurried her down the steps.

When they were outside, Eve caught Peg's arm. 'What if he did take her to the Salvation Army?'

'She wouldn't have gone willingly,' said Peg shakily. 'He must have cut up rough.'

'We'd better try there.'

As they made their way to Poplar High Street, Eve couldn't help thinking that Harold Slygo was a man to be given a wide berth and that Joan was better off without him.

★

To Eve's relief, the first face she saw at the Salvation Army Mission Hall belonged to Clara Wilkins. She was wearing her bonnet and full uniform as she stood at the door.

'Mrs Kumar, isn't it?'

'Yes and you're Clara.'

'Did you get back to your cottage?'

Eve smiled. 'Yes, thanks.'

Peg stepped forward. 'Have you seen me sister?'

Clara looked puzzled. 'The lady from Bambury Buildings?'

'Yeah.'

Clara shook her head. 'No, but I've only just come on duty.'

Eve glanced quickly at Peg. 'Mrs Slygo hasn't been very well,' said Eve diplomatically. 'She's staying with us. But today she went off and someone said she might be here.'

Without asking more, Clara nodded. 'Come in and we can look.'

Eve and Peg walked into the big hall where two rows of beds were placed to the left and right leaving an aisle down the middle. Men and women dressed in dirty, patched clothing were sitting on the beds or on wooden chairs. The air was pungent with tobacco smoke and the aroma of vegetable soup.

'We've just served up a hot meal in the canteen,' said Clara as they walked slowly down the aisle to a chorus of coughs, sniffs and breaking wind.

Eve followed Clara to a bed at the end where the occupant was asleep under a grey blanket. Clara lifted the cover and shook her head. Turning to Eve, she whispered, 'An elderly woman beset by the demon drink.'

Eve was about to walk away when she stopped. Clara had only seen Joan when she looked smart and wore make-up. Would she recognize her now if she saw her?

'Would you mind if I had a look?' asked Eve as Peg came to join them.

Clara stepped back and Eve went to the bed. She lifted the cover. A strong wave of alcohol fumes wafted up. It was so overwhelming that Eve had to turn away. But she had seen enough. Returning to Peg and Clara, she nodded. 'It's Joan.'

Clara looked shocked.

'As I said, Joan hasn't been well. Do you have any idea who brought her here?'

Clara shook her head.

Peg went over and also looked under the cover. She sat down on the side of the bed, her head bowed. Eve knew she would be trying to stop the tears.

'Clara, we want to take her with us.'

Clara looked doubtful. 'I could get her some soup to sustain her. Wait here and I'll see what I can do.'

When Clara had gone, Eve went to stand at the bedside. 'I hope we can get her to walk.'

Peg nodded as she blinked red rimmed eyes. 'Something 'ot in her stomach will help.'

'It's only a small setback.'

'That bloody Harold. I bet he gave her the booze. She would never have come here of her own accord.' Peg shook her sister. 'Wake up, Joan.'

'Go away!'

'You're coming with us.'

Joan pulled the blanket over her head just as Clara arrived with the soup. 'Mrs Slygo, you must eat this.'

There was no reply. Peg stood up and took off her coat. Determinedly she rolled up her cardigan sleeves. 'We could do it the easy way, Joan, but you ain't getting the better of me.' She took hold of Joan's shoulders and forced her to sit up. Joan's bleary eyes bulged in her ashen face.

'Now drink this, or I'll tip it down yer throat meself.'

Very soon the bowl was empty.

'Right, gel, whether you like it or not, you're in for a spot of fresh air. Now let's get you on your feet.'

'But it's a long way,' protested Clara as they helped Joan up the aisle.

'We'll be all right,' Eve shouted over her shoulder, determined to attempt the long walk home.

They were half way home when Joan refused to walk another step. She slumped down on the cobbles, her dress stained from where she had been unable to control herself.

'Just look at the state of you!' cried Peg, close to tears.

Passers-by were staring at them. Eve knew that although she wouldn't admit it, Peg was embarrassed.

'I don't need yer help, you interfering old cow.'

'What are you going to do, sit there all afternoon?' screeched Peg at the end of her tether. 'At this very moment, I could willingly put me hands round yer neck and squeeze.'

Joan suddenly began to cry. It was a soft moaning, not the loud wail that Eve was accustomed to. All the dramatics seemed to have left her and she looked a broken woman.

Suddenly a horn sounded and Eve looked round to see a van pulling up. It was Charlie's van, but it wasn't Charlie who jumped out. It was George. For a moment Eve wished that the earth would open up and she could fall into it.

Eve and Peg followed George as he assisted Joan into the front room. He wouldn't allow either Peg or herself to help, other than to close the van doors behind him. When they were inside, he lowered her to the couch, pulling a cushion behind her head. 'There you are, my dear, you'll feel better soon.'

Peg quickly wiped a tear from her cheek. 'God bless you, son.'

'I hope so,' grinned George, giving her a big smile. 'I can do with all the blessings I can get.'

'I don't know what we'd have done if you hadn't passed by.'

'Do you want me to get the doc?'

'No,' said Eve quickly, 'she just needs a good rest.'

Peg pulled a cover over Joan who had fallen asleep again exhausted by her efforts.

'Come into the kitchen and I'll make you a cup of tea,' said Eve.

'Oh, don't trouble on my behalf.'

'It's no trouble.'

George followed Eve into the kitchen. 'You've got a nice, cosy place here, Eve.'

She smiled as he sat down. 'We've had a lot done to it after the flood.'

'Charlie said you had to move out,' nodded George, smoothing back his dark hair which, Eve noticed, wasn't quite as dark as Charlie's. He was also very tall, and when he sat down, Eve stood only a little higher. His lean face was softened by gentle brown eyebrows above clear blue eyes.

'Did he tell you that it was him that rescued us in the boat?'

'Really?' George smiled. 'Charlie don't talk much about his work. Don't know why, as he was very keen once, but these days it seems to have taken a back seat. However, he talks a lot about Samuel and Albert and how keen they are on football.' He looked round. 'Ain't they about today?'

'I expect Jimmy, our lodger, has taken them up to the park.'

'Charlie says they could play well one day.'

'Does he?' Eve was surprised George knew so much. 'Charlie has been very good to them.'

'They're twins, aren't they? Like me and Joe. And like us, look chalk and cheese. Was they the same at birth?'

'No, Albert was the biggest and the first to be delivered.'

George was nodding. 'Yeah, that's what happened to us. Mum says as the biggest I took up more space inside her and jumped the queue to get out.'

Eve looked into George's smiling gaze and laughed with him. She liked this easy going man very much. They seemed to have a lot in common.

'Did Charlie tell you our sister-in-law Pam has just had her fifth?'

'No, when?

'Two days ago.'

'I haven't seen Charlie this week. Was it a girl?'

'Yes, and you know how much Pam and Joe wanted one as they've got all boys.'

Eve placed the tea in front of him and sat down. 'Did the birth go well?'

'Yes, I hear the baby weighs almost ten pounds and is going to be called after her gran, Dulcie. I'm just off over to see them now. Pam and Joe live in Blackheath so I have to cross the river. Which is why I was passing your way today.'

'We would have been in trouble if you hadn't turned up,' Eve admitted. 'You see Joan is Peg's sister and she lives at Blackwall. But her husband . . .' she hesitated, reluctant to share this with George whom she didn't know well, but she felt he would understand, '. . . he took up with another woman.'

'Oh, poor soul.'

'So she came to live with us.'

George sipped his tea thoughtfully. 'So what happened today to get her so upset?'

'This morning she got up early before we were awake and went back to where she lived. We think it was because she wanted to – well, see this other woman. She's been thinking about Harold and I wouldn't be surprised if she didn't want to give him a piece of her mind.'

'It's a wonder she didn't want to knock his block off.'

Eve smiled. George was easy to talk to. 'Harold must have got her drunk and took her to the Sally Army.'

'The scoundrel!'

Eve nodded. 'We couldn't leave her there.'

George beamed her a smile. 'Now is there anything else I can do for you?'

Eve was touched at his kindness. 'Tell Pam I send me regards to her and the baby.'

He finished his tea and stood up. 'Well, I'm sorry to have missed the nippers.'

'They'll be sorry to have missed you too.'

She walked out with him. Eve couldn't hear Peg or Joan and hoped that the closed door of the front room meant that Joan was still sleeping and not being throttled by Peg.

'Now, if ever you need a ride and Charlie ain't about,' said George as he stood on the pavement, 'Joe and me or even me dad will help you out. Didn't like to see you in distress today.' He smiled and jumped in the van, waving from the window as he drove off.

Eve breathed a deep sigh as the peaceful Sunday afternoon settled round her. George Merritt was as nice a person as his brother, Charlie. He could have driven by today, but he'd stopped to help. Eve hadn't spoken much to him before and had thought he might be a bit stand-offish, but she knew now that he was quite the opposite

She had been embarrassed at the scene that she, Peg and Joan had presented on the pavement, but George had done everything to set her at ease, and had carried Joan in his big arms, laying her in the back of the van without commenting on the appearance or smell of her. Eve wondered, though, whether he had really meant it when he had offered to help whenever Charlie was absent. She hoped so.

Chapter Nineteen

C harlie took Eve's arm and guided her through the sea of furs, satins and silk-covered female forms that crowded the entrance to the Diamond Club just off Piccadilly. He hadn't been here before, as the club was newly opened, but there was a buzz about it at work. He strongly suspected it was the Yard boys who had put the word about, as most of the beat coppers couldn't afford the West End prices. But Charlie had wanted to do something special for Eve's birthday and without her knowledge he had made arrangements for the night's entertainment. Though her birthday was the following day, the Saturday evening meant that they would be able to dine and dance and drink to the accompaniment of the singers and dancers.

Charlie glanced down at Eve as they walked into the reception lobby where a hat girl stood behind a small counter. He put his arm around Eve's shoulders and politely offered to take her scarf. He couldn't see a more attractive woman in the room, despite the obvious affluence. Eve had swept her lovely dark hair up and curved a glossy wave over the side of her head. Since she was small, the style became her, as did the heels of her shoes that brought her another few inches higher. The sleek amber dress that she wore with slim cut straps that, despite their delicacy, seemed almost too heavy for her bone china skin, outshone every other woman around them. Her lovely eyes, always so expressive and wide, were a perfect match to the colour of her gown. They sparkled, their golden glints and dark purple flecks quite stunning. He couldn't believe that he was finally alone with her.

He gave their things to the attendant for safe keeping and received a ticket in exchange. He'd borrowed George's evening suit as he hadn't one of his own. George was a couple of inches taller, but the trousers fitted. The jacket was roomy, but quite well fitting. George had suggested the outfit when Charlie had told him they were going to the West End for Eve's birthday. It was then that Charlie had realized that Eve had made a big impression on his brother. As Charlie tried on the suit, George had told him about the day he'd given Eve, Joan and Peg a lift back to Isle Street. George and Eve had got on like a house on fire. This had reassured Charlie no end, as he'd had no real feedback from the family. He knew that his mother had been charmed by Samuel and Albert. But very little else had been said about the sudden blossoming of their son's love life.

Charlie smiled to himself. Love life indeed! He'd not

had much of one in the past few years. He'd had a few girls but nothing serious. He'd never wanted much more on a Saturday or Sunday than to play football. He adored his nieces and nephews, and was happy enough to share in their family life, without feeling the need for children of his own.

'Is my hair all right?'

Charlie came quickly back to the present. He was looking into Eve's beautiful face, but he had been thinking about his love life. 'Yes . . . yes, it's lovely.'

'Only you're smiling and staring at me.'

'Was I? Sorry. I was just thinking that it's a bit of a crush out here. Shall we go inside? Here take my arm.'

They made their way through the bow ties and glittering frocks to the big silver and gold doors where a girl in a very short skirt and pill box hat was taking the tickets. As Charlie had his tucked in his top pocket, he whipped them out and presented them.

'Good evening, sir, madam,' the girl smiled. 'Please go in and turn to your right. Table fifteen is up on the balcony, as you're having supper.'

Charlie smiled and led the way into the softly lit room with lights shining up onto the stage. The musical instruments were already there in front of a geometrically designed backdrop. The glass and chromium tables were decorated with ashtrays and fan shaped vases with a rose in each one. They ascended the stairs and together with the other diners, took their place above the rest of the room. There was music playing in the background that he recognized as the new craze from America, jazz.

Charlie pulled out the leather dining chair and Eve took her place at the table. He ordered two cocktails from the waiter and asked Eve if she would like to smoke.

'No thanks, Charlie.'

'Are you comfortable?'

'Very.'

Charlie noted that the women around them were conspicuously well heeled. With expensive clothes and jewellery, the affluence was obvious. But Eve had a breathtaking natural beauty that outshone them all. Her straight back and feminine figure caused many men to take quick glances in her direction. He felt jealous and proud all at once.

She whispered, 'This is a lovely place, Charlie. Do you think I'm dressed up enough?'

'Of course you are.'

The waiter brought the drinks. 'What do you think of it?' he asked as they sipped the fizzy liquid with cherries on sticks. He wasn't a cocktails man, but thought it was the appropriate thing to drink as everyone else was too.

'It's very nice.'

'Should I have got something else?'

To his dismay, she began laughing. 'Charlie, everything is wonderful.'

He wanted to please her and yet he felt a bit out of his depth. This was the place to come these days, but in all honesty he'd prefer to be in the park, sitting on a green lawn, enjoying a picnic with the boys or playing football. It was as he caught himself thinking this that he realized how much his life had changed. How much his thoughts had changed. His career, his dreams, his existence seemed to have moved on their axes since he'd met Eve.

'Charlie?'

He was doing it again, staring at her. 'Sorry, I was wondering what you were thinking . . . I mean, I didn't give you a choice about coming here.'

Her reply was soft amongst the high pitched and sometimes affected loud voices. 'It was a wonderful surprise. When you came round yesterday to tell me I couldn't believe it.'

'I thought you was going to say no.'

'Only because I wasn't sure if Peg could look after the boys. She has a lot on her hands with looking after Joan. But she seems to be better now after what happened.'

'Is Joan drinking?'

'No, just as long as we keep an eye on her.'

'That must be difficult all the time.'

'We're used to it now. Even the boys follow her around. And when Jimmy's here, he takes her up to Joseph's for a cup of tea to give Peg a break.'

'Do you think you'll ever be able to trust her to go out on her own?'

'Don't know. But we live in hope.' Eve laughed.

'I've great respect for Peg,' said Charlie quietly. 'Although we didn't hit it off at first.'

'It was only because of what you are, not who you are.'

He chuckled. 'A copper's lot is not a happy one, someone once said and I'm beginning to believe it.'

'You know it doesn't matter to us now, Charlie.'

He nodded, but wondered just how being a policeman and perhaps achieving his aim to become a detective would seem to everyone then. His brothers were always teasing him about how they would have to behave themselves when he became a detective. But after meeting up with the Flying Squad, he admired the men who were a breed on their own. He had overheard some of the officers talking. Some of the most dangerous work was what they called pavement ambush, often tackling armed robbers at the scene of a crime. This had left Charlie wondering if he was capable of such heroic action, and whether that was the sort of career he really wanted.

A loud drum roll caused him to turn his thoughts back to the moment. For the next hour they enjoyed the entertainment from the musicians, singers and dancers. During a break when the lights went up, the waiters came round with the menus. Charlie and Eve chose their supper for the evening from a selection of fish and meat and any amount of salads. Those who hadn't been allocated a dining table adjourned to the bar next door where drinks and snacks were being

served. Both he and Eve chose the house recommen-
dation: a salmon in sauce, followed by something called
petits fours glacés. He also ordered wine, but was
concerned when Eve wrinkled her nose at the taste.

'Don't you like it?'

'I just ain't never had it before, Charlie.'

'It is a special occasion. Happy birthday, Eve.'

'I feel like a queen,' she laughed.

Charlie put down his glass and, feeling mellow and
less nervous, he said, 'I had a dream once, a few months
ago. It was a bit muddled, but you was in it.'

'You never said.'

'I didn't think of it till now. There was this queen at
the Tower of London. She was the Queen of Hearts
and she looked like you.' He watched her look away.
Why had he told her that? He was thinking what a
fool he was, when she said quietly, 'I had a dream too.
But not like a real dream. It was that night . . . that
night at Shadwell.'

He waited as she seemed to search for words. 'I don't
know if it was a dream. But I saw you, Charlie. You
was on the foreshore . . . and I was there too. Only you
was bending over me. I wanted to tap you on the
shoulder and tell you I was all right.' She looked at him.
'Only I wasn't, was I?'

Charlie shivered. That dream he'd had was about
drowning and it was only a few hours later that Eve
had almost drowned. Now she was telling him that she
too had had a similar experience. But did people dream

when they were actually drowning? He remembered that moment under water, when he'd felt her hands bound and her small body limp and floating, he'd thought that he was too late. It was the most harrowing experience of his life. Now when he gazed at her, all he wanted to do was protect her and yet he didn't know if there was room for him in her life.

He took her hand. 'Do you believe that dreams can tell us something or even predict the future?'

Eve frowned. 'I don't know.'

Charlie smiled. 'Well, it ended up with us here tonight.'

'Yes, and it's wonderful.'

When the band began to play again and scantily clad dancers filed on to the floor, everyone began clapping which meant that Charlie had to let go of her hand. He forced his attention on the show, but he wished that tender moment could have gone on for much longer.

Tonight Eve had lost all her fears about going into a place like the Diamond Club. Since she had only ever sold flowers outside them, she had been in trepidation when Charlie surprised her yesterday with the tickets. She'd had no idea what she could wear, she only had her green jacket. But all those concerns had been put aside as Peg and Joan had encouraged her to go up to Aldgate to look in the shops. But the new fashions had been far too expensive, and anyway the current rage was the cape effect with knee-length skirts, dropped waist and flutes and frills that Eve thought didn't suit her small stature. She hadn't wasted any time in returning to Cox Street market on the island where she had found just the thing she was looking for. A simple evening frock with a long matching scarf that was transparent enough to see her dress underneath. Although one of the dainty straps was broken, the loose golden bodice was easy to repair. Even Samuel and Albert had commented on how good it looked. Peg and Joan had agreed.

Now, on the small floor in Charlie's arms, she could hardly believe she was dancing. It was a slow dance and amongst the other couples, it didn't seem to matter about the steps. Charlie was a marvellous partner, guiding her gently around and holding her tightly. The Charleston that they had just finished had been fun. It had left them breathless, and the wine had helped melt away her worries about dancing. Everyone at the club was having a good time, flinging their arms and legs about, enjoying the music and the wonderful band.

Charlie put his mouth close to her ear. 'Are you having a good time?'

'Wonderful.' She had never enjoyed herself so much. Never been to a place like this. The chrome and glass furnishings, the glassy black lacquered wood and the silver and gold wallpaper under the geometrical shaped lights were like those she had only seen when she and Raj had gone to the films.

At the fleeting memory of Raj, she felt guilty about being here, as Charlie's arms held her against his chest. She wondered what Raj would think of his wife with another man. She hoped he'd be happy for her. They had had so little time together to find happiness.

If it was love she had felt for Raj, what did she feel for Charlie? He had seen her as the Queen of Hearts. And she had watched him as he'd tried to revive her. They had been close in another world. It was a connection she felt with him. But Raj had been her dear husband, the boys' father. Eve gave a little sigh. Her life had changed, and if her life had changed, could her feelings also change?'

'Eve?'

She lifted her face as Charlie spoke.

'I'd like to think we could . . . well, we could think of ourselves, as not only good friends, but—'

Charlie stopped and Eve saw a sudden wariness in his eyes. She followed their direction. A figure was beside them. She looked up into a startlingly handsome face, with dark eyes that were keenly assessing her. The young man's blond hair was thick and well styled and the woman he was dancing with was young, slim and dressed in one of the fashions Eve had seen in the shop windows; a sleek silver dress with a fluted cape that shone under the lights. Around her short dark hair she wore a band of silver. Her dangling earrings were shining like little stars.

'So this is where you get to, you rogue!'

Charlie glanced quickly at Eve. 'Eve, this is my friend Robbie Lawrence.'

Eve smiled.

'I'm very, very pleased to meet you.' He took her hand and lifted it slowly to his lips at the same time looking into her eyes. She felt embarrassed.

She quickly withdrew her hand, but the man still continued to gaze at her.

'I can understand now why you ditched Bunty for this young beauty.'

Eve glanced at Charlie. Who was Bunty?

'Robbie, come along.' The pretty girl was turning away, pulling at his sleeve.

'Hold on Ven, this is quite an occasion. Charlie, please introduce me.'

Eve sensed that Charlie didn't want to say who she was. Was he embarrassed to be seen with her?

'This is Eve,' he said abruptly.

'Eve . . . Eve . . . ah, the temptress from the Garden of Eden. How fascinating.'

'Don't keep Venetia waiting,' Charlie said nodding to the girl who now had her hands on her slim hips.

'Won't you join us?' Robbie replied with a smooth smile. 'Johnny and his girl are over there. Let's make an evening of it, shall we, Charlie old man?'

Eve was startled when Charlie immediately refused. 'No, we're just going.'

'Are you? Yet you looked as though you were enjoying yourselves.' The tall blond man once again gazed into her eyes. For some reason Eve found herself not liking his attention and turned away.

'Perhaps another time?' he murmured.

Charlie took Eve's arm and saying an abrupt good-night to the couple, he led her off the floor. The music had returned to the ever popular jazz and as they arrived at their table, Eve saw that the pair they had just been talking to were now with another man and woman. She noted that Charlie had also seen them and without saying more, he handed Eve her bag and took her out. Returning his ticket to the attendant, he helped her with her scarf and after collecting his coat, they walked out into the cool night air.

It was only when they were in the van that Charlie apologized for their abrupt departure. 'I'm sorry we had to leave early.'

'Had to? I thought Robbie was a friend.'

'He is,' he replied, not taking his eyes from the road. 'But I'm afraid the crowd he's mixing with aren't a sound influence.'

'They just looked as though they were having a good time.'

After a long pause he said, 'Yes, probably. Now, it's just half past eleven. Will Peg be expecting you back?'

Aware of his reluctance to discuss it, Eve merely shrugged. 'Peg told me not worry about time. The boys will be fast asleep and now Joan is on the mend, they'll probably spend the evening playing cards.'

'In that case, if there's no hurry . . .' He took his eyes

briefly from the road. 'What do you say to a late night coffee? Somewhere along the Embankment.'

'I'd like that.' Eve stared out at the glittering evening and the lights of the city as they flashed past. Although she hadn't wanted to leave the club, she realized that Charlie must have had his reasons for doing so. And she hadn't liked Robbie Lawrence very much anyway. His gaze had been very forward, like the men she sold flowers to outside their clubs, when they tried to flirt and if possible engage further services. But she was curious about this Bunty. If she had been anything like Robbie's companion, she would be beautiful and sophisticated. So why had Charlie chosen her instead?

The October night was fine, if chilly, as they strolled down the Embankment. The lights from the city reflected in the water, dazzling Eve as she gazed down into the rippling Thames. Blackfriars Bridge seemed to twinkle against the sky as did Westminster Bridge. The Houses of Parliament and Big Ben towered above the streets, a glorious spectacle of light. The avenues of trees were also silhouetted against the darkness and the smell of coffee lingered enticingly in the air. The late night coffee stand was a blaze of light as Charlie took off his coat and slipped it round her shoulders.

'Can I get you something to eat?'

Eve smiled. 'Just coffee, thanks.'

When the drinks were poured they sat on a bench close by. Eve wondered if Charlie was going to refer to Robbie and the other man called Johnny. But instead he loosened the bow tie at his neck, finally removing it altogether. Eve thought how handsome he had looked this evening, his tall, lean frame and thick, dark head of hair quite distinctive from the other men, many of whom looked well off. Robbie had been very handsome too, but in a way that said that he knew he was good looking. Charlie had an understated quality about him. Eve remembered how her mother had said that the eyes were the mirror of the soul. And Charlie had very soulful eyes.

'It's a pity we had to bump into Robbie tonight,' Charlie said suddenly as he sipped his coffee. 'I apologize if he seemed a bit forward. He'd had a few drinks and by the looks of it was going on for more.'

Eve shrugged. 'It didn't matter to me. But who is Johnny? Is that the person you said wasn't sound company.'

He nodded. 'As a matter of fact, yes. Johnny Puxley is another policeman.'

'Don't you like him?'

'Let's just say we don't see eye to eye.'

'Oh, I thought it might be that he was with Bunty.'

'Bunty?' He frowned at her.

'The girl Robbie said you threw over for me.' Eve blushed. She knew she was being inquisitive.

Charlie laughed. 'Believe me when I say I've never met her. It was a foursome arranged by Robbie that I never turned up for. It was on the night that you went missing.'

'Then it was me who spoiled Robbie's plans and disappointed your young lady.'

'I told you, I've never met her.'

Eve looked up at the night sky, studded with twinkling stars. She was thinking how pleased she felt that Charlie didn't have a girlfriend. But did it matter that much to her? It was nothing to do with her what Charlie did with his friends, although Robbie really didn't seem like Charlie's type at all – or Bunty. She wondered if that was jealousy on her part? If so, it was silly, as at this very moment Charlie was sitting beside her, with his coat around her shoulders and the city buzz all around them on a breathtaking autumn night. 'Thank you so much for my birthday present,' Eve said softly. 'I'll never forget it.' She giggled. 'Wait till I tell everyone tomorrow that I had a cocktail and wine and salmon in a sauce with those delicious afters. The boys will make me tell it over again and Peg and Joan will ask questions all day.' She paused, glancing at him uncertainly. 'Would you like to come round tomorrow? We're having a small party for friends and neighbours.'

'I'd like that. But I've a match tomorrow. I'll try to come afterwards.'

'That would be nice.'

His gaze didn't quite meet hers. 'We're playing at the King Edward Park in Shadwell of all places.'

Eve felt cold as he said it.

'I would have asked the boys to come along if it had been anywhere else.' He paused. 'And whilst we're on the subject, I went to the PLA to find out when the *Tarkay* is next in. According to their records it will be just after Christmas.'

'Oh.' She smiled up at him. 'Charlie, that's a long way off and I don't—'

'Eve,' Charlie interrupted gently, 'once there was no doubt in your mind that you wanted to discover what happened to Raj. It was because of your strong desire to know the truth that you tried to find Singh. Of course, your experience at Shadwell must have terrified you, but without resolving the question of what happened to Raj and setting his memory to rest, can there be a future for us?'

Eve sat up straight. 'A future for us?'

'I would like there to be one.'

She tried to free her hand, but he held on. 'Eve I am beginning to feel I am fighting a losing battle. I can't compete with a memory as great as Raj's. What's more, an unresolved memory. Don't you think you must make peace with the past? And the only way I can help you to do that, is to discover the truth about his death.'

She looked down. She had no words to say to Charlie, for in her heart she knew he was right. She couldn't help feeling disloyal when Charlie was close.

Was it because she felt that one day, Raj would walk back into their lives again?

It was late when Eve crept in.

'We're still up!' cried Peg as Eve was about to tiptoe upstairs.

'You shouldn't have waited up for me,' she told them when she opened the front room door. Eve thought how they looked like sisters with their turbans and the same small, close eyes staring at her above the bedclothes that were spread over the mattress.

'Tell us all about it.'

Eve told them about the club and the supper and dancing, but left out Robbie and his friends. Neither did she mention the coffee on the Embankment. She had a lot on her mind when she finally went upstairs. Charlie had seemed distant when he'd brought her home.

As she lay in the dark and listened to her sons' soft breathing, his words came rushing back. Was she keeping him at arm's length because she couldn't forget Raj?

Though nearly drowning had frightened her, something else had happened that night at Shadwell. She had watched Charlie bending over her, trying to revive her. As though she had stood in a place between life and death, just waiting . . .

'Mum?' a little voice whispered.

Eve sat up in bed. The sweat was pouring off her. Had she been dreaming?

She threw off the covers and drew the curtain. Samuel was sitting up in bed.

'Did I wake you?' she asked in concern.

'No. Was it nice where you went?'

She put her arms round him. 'I'll tell you all about it in the morning.'

'Aunty Joan and Peg told us stories. We was late to bed and didn't say our prayers. Will we have to tell Father Flynn in confession?'

'No, that's not a sin.'

'Sister Mary says it is.'

'Sister Mary doesn't know everything.'

He snuggled close. 'Are we still having a party?'

'Of course we are.'

'Is Charlie coming?'

'I don't know. He has to play football.'

'I wish we could go.'

'Another time perhaps.' She kissed his forehead. 'Now, it's late and we mustn't wake Albert.' She gently tucked him under the clothes.

Eve drew the curtain and climbed into bed.

As always she thought of Raj and wondered what life would have been like had he lived.

Chapter Twenty

Eve studied the table in the kitchen, laden with good things to eat. Everyone had brought something. Two large plates of handmade pies from Maude and a chocolate covered sponge. A large bowl of steaming borsch from Joseph and a plate of buttered rolls. A big jelly wobbled in a dish beside a large square cake covered in white icing that Joan and Peg had baked. Archie and Queenie had brought her fruit and vegetables in a basket tied up with a large red ribbon. Percy produced a bottle of ginger beer and a large bunch of green grapes from under his long coat. She had placed these by the apples and oranges that were called clementines, only ever seen in this house on Christmas Day. A vase of Queenie's red roses stood in a milk jug on the windowsill, their ruby heads surrounded by shiny green leaves.

'Enjoying yer party?' Peg asked as she came into the kitchen. Eve saw that she had tied back her grey bush of hair especially for the occasion. She was wearing a skirt and jumper that had no holes or stain marks.

'Thanks, Peg. Twenty-seven feels a bit old.'

'Wait till you get to my age. You're just a spring chicken.'

Eve frowned. 'Where's Joan?'

'In the front room with everyone else. I've told Maude and Jimmy that she ain't allowed to drink.'

Eve laughed. 'We've only got lemonade or ginger beer.'

'Yes, but Eric's put bottles of ale in the yard. Knowing Peg she can smell it a mile off.'

Eve knew that Peg was even more suspicious after what happened at the Sally Army. Joan knew it and used it to torment her.

'Don't trust her, see?' said Peg in a whisper. 'Reckon she'd still end up in the boozer given half the chance. Not that it matters ter me if she drinks herself to death. But I don't want old randy 'Arry to have the satisfaction of hearing he broke us up.'

Peg went to the sink and busied herself with the dishes. But Eve knew that Peg wouldn't admit to the fact that she cared deeply for her sister. Through tantrums, delirium tremens and arguments she had been at Joan's side.

Eve went to the front room and clapped her hands. 'Food's ready. Help yourselves.' Everyone made a dash for the kitchen. Joseph stood by his bowl like a sentry and Eve gave him a spoon to help everyone to a portion. As the noise of the gathering mounted, Eve glanced at the clock hoping that Charlie would come.

When the candle on the cake was alight, everyone sang 'Happy Birthday'. Eric and his sons and Jimmy boomed out the verses whilst the children tried to blow out the candle. Joan was gulping a large glass of ginger beer, a generous allowance from Peg. Queenie began to sing a chorus of a popular song called 'Ain't She Sweet?' and Archie accompanied her with a set of spoons, slapping them on his thigh. Percy began to dance in his long coat, his toothless smile wide under his cap.

Eve felt very happy. It had been a wonderful birthday. But it would have been even better if Charlie had been there.

Charlie was cycling to the recreation ground at the King Edward Park in Shadwell. He was playing in a match that had been arranged with the Trafalgar Road boilermakers and found it slightly unnerving to be back in the area he'd last visited when looking for Eve. Then it had been a warm May day and the kids had been running about on the green grass enjoying the sunshine. Today it was a brisk October Sunday and the plane trees were almost leafless, their branches like spears piercing the blue sky. The supporters of the two clubs were beginning to arrive, well wrapped up in warm coats and scarves.

He was looking forward to thrashing the opposition, and being able to tell Samuel and Albert and his nephews and nieces that his team had won. Charlie steered the bike towards the pavilion and stood it outside in the stand. Throwing his kit bag over his shoulder, he leapt the wide wooden steps, eager to join his team. Despite both sides being squeezed like sardines in the changing room, there was a friendly buzz inside. Dave Wilkins, the police team's trainer and general factotum, was giving a pep talk. Robbie, though, didn't appear to be listening. He was deep in conversation with his opposite number.

'No fraternizing before the match,' Charlie laughed, causing the other player to walk off.

'What?' Robbie looked flustered.

'It was just a joke.'

Quickly Robbie regained his composure. Slapping Charlie on the back, he murmured, 'Didn't think you'd make it today, old boy.'

'Why's that?' Charlie hung his kit on the peg and began to change.

'Thought you'd be too caught up with your pretty lady.'

'We went to the Embankment for coffee and I returned Eve at a decent hour.'

Robbie laughed. 'Oh, is that all? Well, you missed all the fun as Johnny got us into a rather daring little club in Soho. Dropped the girls off early then played a few hands of poker.'

Charlie was once again relieved to have escaped Robbie's idea of fun.

Dave Wilkins appeared beside them. 'Now lads, are you two ready to give these boilermakers a run for their money?'

'We certainly are,' said Robbie, pulling on his shirt and threading his long fingers through his blond hair.

'Don't forget, same formation as last season.'

'Sure, Dave,' Charlie nodded eagerly, 'just leave it to us.'

'I'm counting on you now.'

When their boots were tied and everyone was ready, Charlie followed Robbie to the pitch. He felt a thrill of expectancy in the pit of his stomach as he warmed up.

The first ten minutes of play were exhilarating. Charlie smashed a pass across to Robbie and the ball was in the back of the net in an eye blink. But twenty minutes later, the going was slower. Robbie's footwork seemed to be sluggish, whilst Charlie worked hard to pass the ball. At half time, Dave told them all to stop being lazy buggers, but the second half began with a score from the boilermakers. Ignoring the sinking sensation in his stomach, Charlie began to run until his lungs ached, trying to be everywhere at once. Suddenly he saw his opportunity and took possession of the ball, he sent it across but Robbie drifted into sight too late and the ball disappeared into the crowd. A disappointed cry came from the police team's supporters.

The ref looked at his watch. Charlie seized his last opportunity. The ball landed at his feet and he began to dribble it, the adrenaline pumping through his veins. In and out he went, from left to right; this goal had his name written all over it. Suddenly his legs were brought from under him, and the wind was knocked out of him. A splinter of agonizing pain shot through his knee. Lying there for a moment, with the smell of the turf in his nose, he closed his eyes, praying that no damage had been done. When he tried to move his leg, the pain was still there and he groaned aloud. As his teammates formed a group round him, he knew it was all over.

'Bad luck, old son,' said Robbie as the ref came over to see what had happened. 'Anyway there's only a minute or two more.'

Charlie knew it was bad luck indeed. The tackle had been a vicious one. And he had been so close to scoring.

The next thing he knew he was being helped into the pavilion by Dave Wilkins.

'I'll get some cold water to take the swelling down,' he said and moments later returned with a bucket. Sponging Charlie's knee, he frowned. 'Can you bend it?'

Charlie tentatively tried and winced. 'Yes, I'll live.'

'You've had trouble with your knee before?'

'It put me out of professional football.'

Dave shrugged. 'Don't feel too badly. Every player has an Achilles heel.'

Charlie laughed. 'It's me knee, Dave.'

'Look, I'll be back in a minute. Keep sponging.'

Left alone, Charlie made a few tentative steps forward. He could hear a sudden cheer from the Trafalgar Road supporters. They had won.

Hobbling back to his kit he managed to towel himself off and dress. Lacing his shoes was difficult, but he managed.

'How's the knee?' Dave asked as the team trooped in, all with long faces.

'It'll be all right.'

'Don't think you've done any permanent damage. Good try, son, if you'd pulled it off we might have won.'

Charlie was annoyed with himself for not anticipating the tackle though it had come from behind. The ref hadn't penalized anyone. He was also annoyed with Robbie as he was parading around the changing room with a big smile, brushing off the fact they'd been spectacularly defeated.

'You won't be doing any cycling today.' Dave nodded to the bike stand. 'I'll put your bike in the cupboard. It'll be safe enough here for a couple of days until you're ready to collect it. Your pal will give you a lift in his car. Saw him roll up in a damn great monster.'

Charlie looked at Robbie who grinned. 'Now, Dave, don't insult my new beauty.'

Before Charlie could speak, Robbie picked up their kit and threw the two bags over his shoulder. 'Come along then, Charlie boy, I know a nice little place on the other side of town. We can stop for a quick one. That knee of yours needs a liquid soothing.'

Charlie hobbled out of the pavilion, gritting his teeth against the pain.

When they got to the road he stopped at the large

motor car parked there. 'That belongs to Johnny Puxley, doesn't it?'

'Not any more. I won it off him last night. I was bloody lucky too, as I lost serious money before Lady Luck shone down on me.'

'You won his car?'

Robbie laughed as he opened the door. 'Come on, jump in, or rather, lower yourself gently.' As Robbie took his place at the wheel, he smiled. 'Don't you ever feel like retiring that two-wheeled toy of yours and sporting out on a motor?'

Charlie frowned. 'What, on a copper's wage?'

'Things might be arranged.'

Charlie wondered if he'd heard right. 'And what's that supposed to mean?'

Robbie looked briefly at him. 'We'll have a chat later.'

Charlie was still puzzling over this when he caught a heart-sinking glance of the Drunken Sailor. 'Stop a minute!'

Robbie put his foot hard on the brake. He peered out of the window. 'You can't want to drink here!'

Charlie narrowed his eyes at the saloon doors which were thrown wide open. A decent looking middle-aged woman was sweeping the steps. He wound down the window as the car stopped. 'Are you open for business?'

'We're always open for business, sweetheart.'

'Are you the landlady?'

'That's me, Elsie 'Oskins. That there is me husband,

Ted.' She nodded to a small man inside the pub who was washing the tables.

Charlie frowned. 'I haven't seen you here before.'

'That's because we've just taken over. What a dump it was an' all.'

Charlie nodded. 'Yes I know.'

'You drink here?'

'I did once.'

'Well, I think you'll enjoy a more comfortable tipple this time round.'

Charlie turned to Robbie. 'I'll take you up on that drink now.'

'A bit of a dump isn't it?' Robbie looked doubtful.

It was Charlie's turn to smile. 'Afraid of getting your flannels dirty?' Charlie struggled with the door and gingerly lowered his foot to the ground. The pain in his knee gave him a jolt but he managed to hobble his way inside.

'So when was you here last?' asked Ted Hoskins as he poured a frothy ale for Charlie and a whisky for Robbie.

'When the *Tarkay* was last in.' Charlie watched for a reaction but the man showed none. Unlike the previous landlord, he was well dressed, with a waistcoat and a hairstyle and moustache that reminded Charlie of a friendly barber.

'A boat is it?'

'Yes, do you know of her?'

'Don't know anything yet, mate, as we've only been

here since August. We're building up the business after the fire.'

Charlie sat up on the stool. 'What fire?'

'The one in the back room.'

'What happened?'

'There was a lot of lascars that used to smoke in there. The police reckoned it was them that started it on their 'ubble-bubble pipes. And the landlord died trying to put it out.'

'Died?' Charlie repeated in astonishment.

'Yeah, poor bugger. Fried alive he was. Must've been an 'orrible death.'

Charlie had heard nothing of this nor read anything in the papers and he said as much to Ted.

'This is Shadwell, chum,' Ted replied dourly. 'It's all foreigners round 'ere, ain't it? The coppers don't want to waste their time on investigatin'. And the landlord didn't 'ave no family. This place has been runnin' on a wing and a prayer for the last few years. But me wife and meself, well, we reckon we can do somethin' with it. We was south of the river before in Deptford, as rough as wot this is, and we turned our gaff into a nice little earner.' He pushed the two drinks towards Charlie. 'Anyway, enjoy yer tipples, friend, and I 'ope you'll both come again as you're the sort of customer me and the missus is lookin' for.' He took his cloth and walked over to serve another customer.

'What was all that about?' asked Robbie, who had, until now, been silent.

'You wouldn't believe me if I told you.'

'Wouldn't I?' Robbie pushed his empty glass forward. 'I'm all ears.'

Charlie hesitated but finally called Elsie who quickly refilled the tumbler. Charlie paid her, then rather uncertainly began to tell the tale of the *Tarkay* and Eve's visit to the Drunken Sailor to look for Singh.

By the time he had finished, his friend was looking surprised. 'You're telling me the girl you were with last night is the flower-seller you took to the morgue?'

Charlie didn't much care for Robbie's tone. 'Eve Kumar, yes.'

'And she tried to look for this Singh fellow and then was attacked and nearly drowned? Sounds rather far-fetched to me.'

'I told you it was hard to believe.'

Robbie slung the last of his whisky to the back of his throat. 'I believe you, of course, but if she's cooled off about the whole thing, aren't you wasting your time?'

'Perhaps.'

'And, anyway, you are making assumptions.'

'Two sailors from the *Star of Bengal* have died in mysterious circumstances. Singh is the connection to the Drunken Sailor. Now the landlord is dead.'

Robbie shook his head with a wry smile. 'Charlie, you're turning into quite the little detective.'

'The *Tarkay* returns after Christmas,' Charlie said in a low voice. 'Singh could be on it.'

At this, Robbie chuckled. 'Old man, why don't you

just settle for a little fun in life? I'm sure you could have any amount with your flower-seller.'

Charlie felt insulted. He was seeing Robbie in a very different light these days and he wished he hadn't confided in him.

Robbie swayed on the stool as he looked into Charlie's eyes. 'If I was you, I'd have another crack at Bunty. Her family is very well heeled. I understand they have a great old pile in Scotland somewhere.'

'Well, thank God I'm not you, Robbie.' Charlie stood up.

'Oh, come on, Charlie boy, stop being such a prig.'

'Robbie, I think you've had enough to drink.'

Robbie threw back his head, laughing. 'Let's have one more for the road!'

Charlie looked round at the watching faces. 'Come on, Robbie,' he said quietly, 'remember you're a copper.'

His friend gave a snort. 'Sorry, old man, but that is a bit of a joke.'

'What do you mean?' Again Charlie was puzzled.

'I could tell you a thing or two about coppers. There are some rotten apples in the barrel and—'

'Robbie, shut up.' Charlie gripped his friend's arm and almost dragged him out. Outside in the fresh air, Charlie took a deep breath, trying to ignore the pain in his knee as he pushed Robbie into the passenger seat.

'What the hell—' Robbie began as Charlie clumsily climbed in and started the car.

'You're in no fit state to drive, Robbie.'

'I'm actually still on a roll from last night.'

'No wonder you were talking drivel.'

Charlie watched Robbie's face darken. He stared morosely out of the window as they drove back to the bakery. It wasn't an easy drive as his knee was throbbing and each time he changed gear and depressed the pedal, a knife went into his muscle.

But he still felt a certain responsibility for his friend. He would take him to the bakery and feed him some decent food. After which he could sleep his hangover off on the couch.

As Charlie drove he couldn't help thinking that it was Johnny Puxley who had a hand in all this changed behaviour. He had generated a cynicism in Robbie that hadn't been there a few years back. And it had finally led to a rift between himself and Robbie. It was only the football that still held them together. And unlike Robbie, Charlie continued to believe in the British justice system, no matter if there were a few rotten apples in the barrel, as Robbie had been so keen to enlighten him.

But what concerned Charlie most was his discovery today of the death of the landlord. It struck him that a fire could be a way of silencing someone who knew too much.

Just as someone had tried to silence Eve.

When business for the day was over, Eve was in time to meet the boys from school. She was surprised when

Sister Mary came to the gate and singled her out from the waiting parents. 'Sister Superior would like to speak to you,' she said sternly.

Aware of the looks cast at her as she followed the nun, Eve became apprehensive. The feeling deepened as she entered the refectory, a long, austere room used by the Sisters as a common room for staff and parent meetings. Eve found herself standing in front of Sister Superior and Father Flynn.

'Your sons, Mrs Kumar, have today disgraced themselves,' said Sister Superior coldly. 'Father Flynn has sent them to chapel to pray for their sins.'

'But what did they do?' Eve demanded, unable to believe such a thing.

'They attacked another boy—' broke in Sister Mary, only to be silenced by the raised hand of Sister Superior.

'We cannot tolerate violence at St Saviour's,' she said eyeing the priest. 'Repetition of prayer will concentrate their minds. Don't you agree, Father?'

'Oh, yes, indeed. Indeed.' Father Flynn knitted his fingers over his portly stomach, his port wine nose flaring.

'Violence?' repeated Eve, staring from one to the other of them. 'My boys aren't bullies.'

'I'm afraid you're wrong,' replied the nun. 'They set upon a child, bruising his face. They are fortunate only to have incurred a spiritual punishment rather than a physical one.'

'They don't deserve to be punished at all.'

'Mrs Kumar, surely you can see that they do? Don't you want something better for your sons than growing up to be street brawlers?'

Eve couldn't believe what she was hearing. Did the nun mean that she would cane them? But it was never Albert or Samuel who attacked anyone. It had always been the other way round. And since the time of the truancy they had been to confession regularly and observed all the school's strict rules.

Eve braced her shoulders. 'I want to hear what Samuel and Albert have to say.'

Sister Superior straightened her back in silent refusal. 'They are saying their penance.'

Eve refused to be browbeaten, she knew the nun didn't like her and she spoke up immediately. 'They can say their penance later – if it's deserved. Now, shall I make my own way down to the chapel?' She stepped towards the door. But the tall, thin woman was there before her, peering angrily from the folds of her white wimple.

Eve's heart was pounding as she followed the swish of the black hem down the highly polished corridor. What could the twins possibly have done to deserve this? They were not violent children. If they had been in a fight it was because they were defending themselves.

At the chapel, Sister Superior took out a large key and turned it in the big black lock. With alarm, Eve realized that this was why she hadn't wanted her to come on her own.

'Do you always lock it when children are in there?' Eve asked.

Sister Superior ignored her and walked in. 'Samuel and Albert, your mother is here.'

Eve shivered in the freezing cold chapel. Two little figures knelt in front of the altar. They stood up, lost under the high vaulted ceilings. She could see Albert was holding back the tears. Samuel's black hair had fallen over his eyes.

'Please hurry and come here,' shouted Sister Superior, 'as Father Flynn is very busy today. He has to say Mass at half past six.'

'I'd like to be on my own with them,' Eve said.

'Mrs Kumar—' the nun began but Eve wouldn't be moved.

'The sooner I hear their side of the story the sooner Father will be free to say Mass.'

Sister Superior glared at her, but left eventually, closing the heavy door after her. Immediately the boys ran into Eve's arms. Albert burst into tears. Samuel's chin wobbled.

'Now, don't cry, or you won't be able to tell me what happened,' she said, sitting them down in a pew. 'Sister Superior said you attacked another boy.'

They looked down.

Eve was shocked. 'So you hit him?'

Samuel nodded as he fingered the graze on his cheek. 'Him and his mates was saying bad things. And Charlie said we had to stand up to them or else they'd do it again.'

'What did they say?'

'It was things about Dad. We know they ain't true.'

'Like what?' Eve pressed.

Samuel sniffed. 'They said he was a black devil and went to hell.'

Eve looked into their little faces. What right had these ignorant boys to say such things? It was disgraceful. How was she to protect them from such a painful experience?

'You know that's a very bad thing to say?'

They nodded.

'Those boys are ignorant. They don't know any better. But you do and I'm proud of you both.'

Samuel wiped his nose with his cuff. A tear slipped down Albert's cheek. Eve hugged them to her. They had been brave and stood up for their dad. She took their hands. 'Now, I want you to wait here whilst I talk to Sister Superior.'

'Do we have to pray?'

'No, it's those boys that need to pray, not you.'

Eve strode out to the refectory. Her cheeks were red with anger.

'Did they own up?' Sister Superior demanded as she walked in.

'Do you know why Samuel and Albert hit that boy?' Eve asked.

'There is no excuse for what they did.'

Eve's eyes flashed. 'It was because they had things said to them about their father. Things that I don't want to repeat as they are so bad and should never be said to anyone whatever religion or colour they are. It was only natural for Samuel and Albert to retaliate.'

'Please keep your voice down.' Sister Superior didn't want anyone outside to hear.

But Eve ignored her. 'Why should my sons be punished when it was those other boys? It's you, Sister Superior, who is responsible for what happened today. You've failed to teach the children to love each other. It's you who should be praying for forgiveness, not my boys.'

Eve knew her temper had got the better of her but there was no answer from the nun. Eve turned and walked out.

Taking a deep breath as she walked along the cold, shiny corridor she wondered what more those boys had said. No matter what the Sister Superior said, Samuel and Albert had done what Charlie had told them to do and she was proud of them.

'Mum! Mum!' They flung themselves at her.

'Come on, let's go home.'

'We didn't do nothin' wrong.'

'I know that.'

'Do we have to confess it tomorrow?'

'No, you can have a lie-in instead.'

They jumped up and down. 'Can we go down to the park and play?'

Eve nodded. Why had the nuns blamed her boys for

what had happened? Was it because Samuel and Albert's father was a lascar? Or was it because their mother was a flower-seller? Perhaps it was both.

Chapter Twenty-One

During the weeks that followed an icy tension almost as bitter as the weather settled between Eve and Sister Superior. The nuns were at their busiest time of the year with the preparation of school nativity plays, end of term reports and a stream of services in the chapel which the children and parents were required to attend. Since the confrontation with Sister Superior, Sister Mary and Father Flynn, there had been no further communication but each time Eve stood at the gate to wait for the boys or went into St Saviour's and sat in a pew, Sister Superior's glances were not ones of warmth. Eve knew she had challenged the establishment. The one good thing to come out of it was that the twins had not suffered any more bad treatment from the bullies of the school. Eve asked Samuel and Albert frequently if they were set upon or called names, or treated with disrespect, but as much to her delight as Samuel and Albert's surprise, it seemed the teachers had been more vigilant than they had been before.

Despite this vigilance, neither Samuel nor Albert was

chosen for shepherds, wise men or Joseph for the nativity play, although in Eve's opinion their appearance was much more suited to those characters than the blond angelic-looking boys that were cast. On a cold Wednesday afternoon, the last before Christmas, Eve left her pitch early to attend the class version of the birth of Jesus in Bethlehem. She had enjoyed the hour-long production, but had only caught a brief glance of her sons as they filed to the back of the stage to sing the selection of carols. When the festivities were over and it was time to go, she passed Sister Superior in the aisle. Eve stopped.

'Happy Christmas, Sister Superior.'

A brief nod was followed by a tight-lipped, 'And a holy one to you, Mrs Kumar.'

Eve didn't lower her gaze as the thin faced woman looked into her eyes. It wasn't the time, Eve knew, for resentment, so she smiled. This was received with an embarrassed twitch, which Eve took to be a favourable response.

Several women then surrounded the nun. Eve made her way to the backstage changing room where the children were noisily preparing to leave. Albert and Samuel appeared, pushing paper hats, books and shoe bags into her arms. They were full of excitement as they walked out into the easterly wind that had persisted since November. Heads down against the chill and aware of the darkening skies, Eve hurried them through the crowded playground and set off for home. Paper chains scurried in the gutter and a touch of ice nipped at their noses and fingers making their cheeks rosy. Suddenly a bicycle came flying round the corner.

'Charlie!' the twins cried, jumping in his path as he brought the bicycle to a halt.

Breathlessly, he ruffled the twins' hair. 'So what have you two been up to lately?'

'We sung carols in the nativity play.'

He chuckled. 'Hope you sung the one about shepherds washing their socks at night. That's my favourite.'

The boys giggled.

Eve looked into Charlie's blue eyes twinkling under the rim of his helmet. She was aware of the other women casting glances in their direction. The children too were stopping to stare at Charlie. A policeman talking at length in a friendly fashion to members of the public was a rare sight.

'I didn't reckon the whole school would be turning out,' he grinned. 'I chose my moment, didn't I?'

Eve smiled. 'What are you doing round this way?'

'I went past your pitch and guessed you'd come to meet the lads.'

'How is your knee?' Eve asked, for when Charlie had come at the weekend to take the boys to the park he had been limping.

'I can kick twice as good now.'

'Can we go to the park today?' Albert said hopefully.

'Albert, you know Charlie's dad's not been well,' Eve interrupted. 'And Charlie's got to help in the bakery.'

But Charlie just shrugged. 'Dad's feeling better now,

but have you ever seen a policeman in his helmet playing football?'

Everyone laughed and Charlie looked at Eve. 'But I'll walk you all back and there might be a cuppa at the end of it, if I ask your mother nicely.'

'You can see our Christmas tree,' said Albert eagerly. 'We ain't never had one before. Archie brought it on his cart and we're gonna make decorations for it ternight.' Without waiting for Charlie to reply they ran ahead, pushing and shoving each other playfully.

'Did everything turn out all right at school?' Charlie asked as he accompanied Eve along the street. 'The lads told me they'd been in a spot of bother with another boy but didn't say what it was. It's been on me mind ever since as I encouraged them to stand up for them-selves.'

Eve pulled her coat round her against the cold. 'It was the name calling again, only Samuel and Albert got the blame. These boys said that Raj was a black devil and had gone to hell.'

'What!' Charlie stopped the bike, his exclamation loud.

Eve looked round. She was glad there weren't many people about now. 'The boys were very upset.'

'Of course! What did this head nun have to say about it?'

'Sister Superior gave Samuel and Albert a punish-ment because they hit the culprit. When I got to school they were in the chapel saying penance.'

'What's a penance?' Charlie asked in alarm.

'It's prayers said repeatedly for having committed a sin.'

'What rubbish!' he exclaimed, astounded. 'It's quite obvious that those other boys were at fault. Did you tell the nun so?'

'Yes,' Eve said patiently, 'but this ain't the first time, Charlie. The kids hear the grown-ups say something, then repeat it. Because of the colour of the boys' skin, they are easy targets.'

Eve heard Charlie comment under his breath. 'I'd like a word with that nun,' he growled. 'Doesn't she understand that it's her job to stop the playground rot? More important than the supposed religion they teach.'

They walked on in silence and Eve knew that Charlie was angry. When they came to the top of the hill and looked down on Isle Street, he paused for a moment. 'Eve, Mum and Dad would like you and the boys to join us for Christmas dinner on Sunday, the twenty-third. Would you be able to come? If so, I'll pick you up in the van at about three.'

'Is it a family celebration?'

'Yes, as Christmas Day I'm on duty and Joe who works for the electricity company is working too. George hasn't got to work but this year they are going to Eileen's parents in Bromley as they spent the day with Mum and Dad last year. So Sunday is the Merritts' designated Christmas Day.'

Eve knew that Charlie meant well, but what would

his family think of her and the boys accompanying him on such a special day?

The twins began to run noisily up the hill and quickly Eve nodded. 'All right,' she agreed, her cheeks flushed. 'But I won't tell the boys until the day before in case you change your mind.'

He laughed. 'I won't be doing that.'

Eve felt happy as they all walked down the hill to the cottage, although she was a little apprehensive about joining the family gathering, but Charlie had been very persuasive. And perhaps it would be a good opportunity to get to know the rest of the family better.

Three-month-old Dulcie, Pamela's baby, was as blonde and blue eyed as her mother, and as different from her four brown-haired brothers in looks as it was possible to be. Eve was sitting in the arm chair holding Dulcie in the crook of her arm, whilst Pam was pinning ginger-bread men on the Christmas tree. She could hear a lot of laughter coming from the children who sat round the fire playing charades. But Dulcie's four brothers had tired of the game and were staring at Eve cradling their sister. Eve had memorized their names and ages. Daniel was the oldest at twelve, James and William were seven and eight and Oliver was five.

Daniel was a mirror image of his father Joe, moon-faced and with serious brown eyebrows. He was the tallest of the boys, but not as tall as his two girl cousins, Emily at thirteen and Lucy, twelve. These were George and Eileen's two oldest daughters and, as their grand-mother said, they looked like thin streaks of lightning.

Though all the boys, including Samuel and Albert, had gone into the yard earlier to play football, it was now close to dinner time. Eve glanced down at the subject of the boys' scrutiny. Their baby sister was dressed entirely in pink, with a wisp of blonde hair turned into a kiss-curl on the top of her head. She gurgled content-edly in Eve's arms.

'Did you have a good game of football?' Eve asked and all the boys nodded at once.

'I got a grazed knee, but Granny washed it,' said William, holding up his leg for her to see. 'It hurt a lot.'

'You're a very brave boy,' said Eve, giving him a big grin.

'Uncle Charlie's got a badder knee than you,' pointed out James, looking down his nose at his brother.

'Yes, but I can't walk on mine. See?' William limped back and forth.

Eve smiled. 'It will soon get better I'm sure.'

William beamed at her but Oliver was staring at her curiously. 'Is Uncle Charlie going to be Samuel and Albert's new dad?'

The three older boys immediately turned on their young brother. 'You mustn't ask that, Olly.'

'Why not?'

''Cos it's rude.'

'But Mummy asked Daddy it.'

Eve felt her face go scarlet. 'Samuel and Albert had a daddy once,' she said gently to Oliver. 'But he died.'

'Does that mean they can't have another one?' Oliver persisted.

As Eve was thinking how to reply, Lucy came sprinting over. Pushing her plaits back over her shoulders, she smiled at Eve. 'Samuel and Albert are very clever. Samuel was the horse and Albert was Tom Mix. We all guessed it when Albert threw his lasso. Come on now, boys, it's your turn before dinner.'

Eve was grateful for Lucy's arrival as she hadn't known what to say to Oliver. Had Pam and Joe been talking about her? Eve's thoughts were brought back to the present when Dulcie began to cry. Her big eyes were like glistening blue pearls set in her heart-shaped face. Her grip on Eve's little finger tightened as her lips quivered into a small cry. Rising carefully to her feet, Eve walked over to the Christmas tree. Pam was still tying on the gingerbread men, one for each child this evening.

Eve knew that Eileen was helping Mrs Merritt in the big kitchen where the smell of roasting turkey was creeping out and filling all the other rooms. The men were talking at the big bay window overlooking the street below. Although Mr Merritt had been poorly, he was now feeling more like his old self and sat on the window seat smoking his pipe.

Eve caught Charlie's eye and he grinned. She returned his smile a little shyly as Pam turned to face her. 'Thanks,

Eve,' she said as Dulcie let out a scream. 'I think she must be hungry.'

Eve reluctantly handed over the baby. 'I don't want to let her go.'

Pam laughed as she took the child in her arms. 'She's delicious enough to eat, isn't she? I'll take her into Charlie's bedroom and feed her. She'll want her nappy changed too.'

'Can I help?' Eve asked.

'Dulcie keeps the nappies in the scullery. You could bring one for me and a bowl of water so that I can wash her.'

Eve nodded and watched Pam walk away, her tall figure skirting the large and noisy circle of boys and girls, taking the exit that led down to the bedrooms.

In the kitchen, Eve found Eileen and Mrs Merritt preparing the meal.

'Oh, Eve, I'm sorry to leave you,' apologized Mrs Merritt. 'I hope Charlie's been taking good care of you.'

'I've been holding Dulcie.'

Eileen smiled as she lifted the turkey from the oven and placed it on the top of the stove. 'She's gorgeous, isn't she?'

'Don't start getting broody, Eileen,' chuckled Mrs Merritt as she set the glasses on the long, well-scrubbed family table, decorated with holly and candles. 'You've a football team as it is.'

'Yes, but every team needs reserves,' said Eileen, winking at Eve.

The women laughed and Eve looked around for the nappies. 'Pam said she'd like to change Dulcie and give her a wash.'

'Yes, of course.' Charlie's mother gathered the required things and placed them on a tray. 'There you are, Eve. And tell Pam that as soon as Dulcie is settled we'll eat.'

Eve carried the tray along to Charlie's bedroom which she had been shown earlier as all the coats had been piled on his bed. The room was full of books and personal effects. The brown wood furniture was well polished and the carpet felt luxurious under Eve's feet, muting the noise, unlike the bare boards of the cottage which echoed noisily. The smell of polish hung in the air and the tall window was decorated by a curved velvet valance, where two long curtains fell beneath, tied back with thick cords.

Pam was sitting in a large upholstered chair, the baby at her breast. 'I couldn't wait to change her,' she said. 'She is always so hungry.'

Eve placed the tray on the dressing table, next to Charlie's pens, pencils and writing books, beside a huge tome that Eve noted was about policing.

'Why don't you push the coats over on Charlie's bed and sit and talk to me?' Pam said as she adjusted the baby's position.

Eve did as she was bidden, feeling the comfortable give of the springs under her weight. The deep blue cover was old but as Eve touched it, she felt something of Charlie run through her fingertips.

'Eve, would you think it forward of me if I asked you what happened to your husband?' Pam asked after a while.

Eve looked into Pam's healthy face, her blonde hair falling softly around it, her matronly figure and wide shoulders the epitome of motherhood. Was this a chance to get to know her better?

'He was a cook on board a ship and died whilst at sea,' she explained after a while.

'Through illness?' Pam asked, her voice full of concern.

'No, we think he may have fallen overboard. Raj was taken on in India, as part of the lascar crew and the British authorities didn't make many enquiries. So all we can do is guess at what happened.' Eve hesitated wondering if she should go on, but Pam seemed genuinely interested.

'Can Charlie help?' Pam asked before Eve spoke. 'He is, after all, a policeman.'

Eve smiled. 'Charlie was with me when they found a body in the river and I went to the morgue to look at it.'

Pam gasped. 'The morgue!'

'It wasn't Raj as he had been dead five years, but Sergeant Moody said the case was still open.'

'What a dreadful experience,' Pam sighed.

'Charlie stayed with me. He was very kind.'

'Now I know why Charlie spoke so highly of you,' Pam said softly. 'I would simply go to pieces if I lost

Joe and had to look at a dead man that might be my husband.' She was silent for a moment as she eased the baby's head from her breast. A dribble of milk dripped down Dulcie's chin. Pam wiped it carefully with a handkerchief then did up the buttons of her dress.

'You have two lovely boys, Eve.'

'Yes,' Eve replied proudly.

'Charlie is very fond of them.'

Eve remembered what Oliver had said about what he'd overheard from his parents. 'They're fond of him too . . .' She paused.

Pam just smiled, then lay the sleeping baby in the crib. 'Now, it's time for dinner. Let's go and join the family.'

Pam slipped an arm through Eve's as they left the room. They were still walking in this fashion when they entered the kitchen and joined the others for Christmas dinner.

Charlie found himself once more pursuing his own enquiries. He was standing in a Port of London Authority office, waiting patiently for the clerical worker to return with information on the *Tarkay*'s arrival. It didn't help that it was Christmas Eve, since all the staff were anticipating an early departure and the sight of a uniformed officer meant work for someone. When Charlie had visited before, a young woman had been able to help him. But that young lady was not in evidence and he was feeling doubtful whether he would discover when and where the *Tarkay* would berth.

The room was stacked high with books and ledgers and a thick, papery smell filled the air. Two or three other clerks were hurriedly sifting through their work and glancing at their watches.

To Charlie's immense relief, the male clerk returned. But the relief was short-lived as the pinch-faced and bespectacled older man shook his head. 'The *Tarkay* was due to dock the day after tomorrow. But we are told she has been delayed.'

'Delayed?' Charlie frowned.

'This could be due to any amount of reasons,' the clerk said dismissively. 'Not sufficient crew, bad weather, a storm somewhere – especially if the voyage takes in Cape Horn through the Straits of Magellan. Never know what weather they hit round there.'

'When will you know?' Charlie persevered.

'When the vessel's owners enlighten us further.'

'When will that be? I mean, could it still be before the New Year do you think?'

The man slid off his spectacles and frowned at Charlie. 'Constable, I only work in this office; I don't have a crystal ball.'

Charlie smiled. 'I'm sorry, it's just that this is important.'

The clerk gave him another stern look. 'Can you tell me why it's so important?'

Charlie sighed softly. 'It's a long story, but we are trying to trace a member of the crew.'

'British or Indian?'

Charlie frowned. 'A lascar, a man named Somar Singh.'

'And you are certain he's on board? These crews change quickly, you know.'

Charlie frowned. 'I can't be entirely certain he's on the *Tarkay.*'

The clerk pushed his spectacles further up on his nose. 'Have you consulted the British Consul or Customs Office?'

Charlie shrugged. He knew that without Sergeant Moody's authority he couldn't do such a thing.

The clerk peered at him. 'The masters of each ship must notify the Customs Office of all lascars taken on at the commencement of a voyage.'

'But what if Singh was taken on in India, not here for the return journey?'

'Then the Indian authorities would hold that information.'

Charlie thanked the man and left the office. He had no way of securing this information, not without help from his superior. He cringed to think of what Sergeant Moody would say if he knew of all Charlie's exploits in an effort to get at the truth about Raj Kumar's death. No, it was just a question now of patience and waiting for the *Tarkay* to dock.

Outside in the cold air, the Christmas spirit abounded. People were preparing for the celebrations. Charlie felt the exertion of his late shift suddenly kick in. Though he was tired, the morning air was sweet and crisp. He was looking forward to changing from his uniform into his vest and cotton trousers to help his father with the last of the bread that would stand cooling in the shop for the local tradesmen. Thank heaven his dad was recovering from his chill now. But he'd had a few worries of late. The big oven in the bakery wasn't behaving itself and business had suffered in the Depression. Not as badly as some, but with the relentless upkeep of the bakery and shop, it had been a strain.

Charlie hopped on his bike, intending to enjoy an easy ride from the station, casting a smile to anyone who looked likely to return it. His thoughts as usual turned to Eve; it had been a wonderful Sunday celebration with Eve at his side. She seemed to have taken to Pam and Dulcie especially. Samuel and Albert had got on well with all his nieces and nephews and his parents had been charmed by the beautiful holly studded with red berries and the fragile stems of mistletoe that Eve had brought with her.

After dinner as they sat round singing carols, he'd felt the warmth of the open fire as it reflected on their faces. Eve sat beside him on the couch in the big family room full of the people he most cared about in all the world. He'd been grateful that his family had welcomed Eve in the way they had.

He'd driven Eve and the boys back to the cottage that evening, wondering if he'd ever get the chance to take her in his arms and tell her how much he thought of her. But Peg and Joan had been waiting, eager to hear their news. Another two hours had been spent in the company of Eve's family and time had flown. How touched he had been when Samuel and Albert had given him his present from under the tree. The scarf and gloves were perfect for winter. He had something rather special of his own to give to them too. A leather football to replace the well-worn one that he had previously given them. This one was top notch quality from one of the big city stores. He'd purchased it at the same time as he'd bought a shawl for Eve, not as colourful as her flower-selling shawl, but it was a good quality wool, and very warm. He'd given Peg a wallet of her favourite tobacco and for Joan he'd got what was now her favourite tipple, a large stoneware bottle of ginger beer. After singing a few carols and eating mince pies for supper, it had been time to leave. Once again, a private moment with Eve had escaped him, but as he drove home he knew that he couldn't have wished for a better Christmas.

Charlie was deep in thought as he turned onto the Commercial Road. Had he done right in not telling Eve of the fire at the Drunken Sailor? But again, there didn't seem to be the right time before Christmas. And what good would it have done? Perhaps in the new year they could sit down on their own and quietly discuss things.

What would the new year hold for them? He hoped for good health for his dad and continued employment for George and Joe. For himself and Eve and the boys, he hoped for a fresh start. For now it was clear that he couldn't think of his future without them.

But did the memories of her husband burn so brightly that the light could never be extinguished?

It was this that spurred him on in searching for the answers to Raj Kumar's death.

Eve and the boys walked to St Saviour's for Midnight Mass. The night was cold and clear and though it was late, both pupils and parents filled the chapel to its last inch. After the carol service, the Christmas Mass began. Soon the air was full of incense, strengthened by the whiffs of the alcohol that had been consumed during the evening. The babies and younger children were sleepily squashed in the pews, hushed into silence as Father Flynn began his oratory.

Eve sat with Samuel and Albert watching their class-mates, the altar boys, as they served the Mass. Their black floor-length cassocks and white surplices were complemented perfectly by the golden vestments draped over the altar. Though her sons now knew the Latin Mass word-perfect, they had not been chosen to assist Father Flynn. Eve knew that Sister Mary and Sister Superior hadn't found it in their hearts to forgive her for her outburst. But as the service continued, Eve comforted herself with the thought that Raj would have been proud to see his sons as they sat straight-backed in the hard wooden pews, reciting the Latin responses.

Raj had been a good Catholic, this was what he would have wanted for his boys.

When the Mass was over, they filed out into the night and hurried home for the excitement of Christmas Day. Eve had bought large ripe oranges and big red apples, two brown bags full of liquorice and a pennyworth each of barley twists to put in the boys' stockings. Under the tree there were small presents from Joan, Peg and Jimmy. It was going to be a wonderful day.

On Boxing Day the Higgins asked them all to tea. There were cold meats, pickles and bubble and squeak that they ate to their hearts' content. The Higgins' cottage was full to the brim with family, and dirty-faced, squabbling children ran up and down the stairs playing hide and seek. The out of tune piano was in use all day as Maude played a never-ending series of music hall tunes. Joseph had been invited, but he had declined. Eve knew that he had visitors of his own, a young couple who had travelled from Russia to start a new life in this country and to whom Joseph was affording hospitality.

Jimmy brought his friend from Shoreditch, another errand boy, with whom he had stayed during the flood. And together with Samuel and Albert and some of the Higgins' grandchildren they went to the park with Charlie's new football. Enjoying the peace, the grown-ups were left to entertain themselves for an hour.

When it grew dark, the visitors began to leave. As Eve, Peg, Joan, Jimmy and the boys walked down the hill to number three, they were singing carols. Behind them, Joseph's lights shone out, reflecting the silhouette of a tall ship at the dock walls. The darkening sky still held a little light blue magic and the rigging and furled sails looked like a picture postcard. Eve inhaled the tarry salt and oily scents that rose up from the quiet river. There was no water traffic to speak of and the docks were still.

She could hardly believe that a year ago, there had been such a violent storm that shook the whole nation. This same peaceful river had risen up and leapt over its banks to flood the city's capital. Just like the stories she had always repeated to the boys, Old Father Thames seemed to have lifted his weed-covered spirit from the riverbed and tossed his watery vengeance at the people of London.

It was cold as they entered the cottage, but Eve quickly made up a fire in the front room whilst the boys went upstairs to put on their cut-down coms. Peg busied herself in the kitchen, stoking the stove and squeezing out the last of the heat.

Eve stared into the flames and thought of Charlie. Had it been a blessing in disguise when they were trapped upstairs in the cottage by six feet of foul water? It was then, almost a year ago, that she had first met Charlie. Since then, with his help, she had searched for the truth about Raj and had only been saved from drowning by the very man who had rescued her from the flood. She had also been 'outside of herself', as she had now come to think of the experience on that murky night on the foreshore when she had watched Charlie trying to revive her.

Eve sat on the chair in her coat, mesmerized by the scarlet flames licking at the chimney from the piece of wood she had placed on top of the cold embers. The fire had caught and was burning brightly.

It was as if that was what had happened to her. When she met Charlie, small sparks of happiness began to land on her grieving heart and bring it back to life.

Yet she still thought of Raj and wondered when and how he had departed this earth. Had he sunk below the waves as she had and struggled for his life? Or had something else happened? And why? If only she could set her mind at rest . . .

As Eve tucked the boys into bed that night, she saw Raj in their innocent faces. They had lit a candle for Raj after Midnight Mass and a warm feeling had come over her, as though his presence was close by.

Was he trying to tell her something? Was he reluctant to leave his family until all was well?

Could another person ever love their two boys as Raj had loved them?

'Mum, when's Charlie coming round?' Samuel yawned as she sat on the foot of their bed.

'In the new year, I expect.'

Albert stuck his nose over the cover. 'Duggie said he ain't seen such a good football as what Charlie bought us.'

'Yes, it's a very good one.'

'Charlie said we could go to a match,' said Samuel yawning again. 'With Willie and James and Olly. We can all squeeze in the van, just about.'

'But what if it's on Saturday morning?' Albert said in alarm. 'Father Flynn'll get cross if we don't go to confession.'

Albert's question hung in the air but it wasn't long before he spoke, his dark eyes studying her face. 'Mum, do you think Charlie is nice?'

'Of course I do,' said Eve as both boys giggled.

'But nice, like you thought Dad was nice?'

'What's this all about?' Eve ruffled their hair and pulled up the covers.

'He thinks you're nice.'

Eve blushed. 'How do you know that?'

'He told George and Lucy heard and she told Emily and Emily told Daniel. And then Daniel told us.'

Eve laughed. 'You children are worse than the adults. Now come on, let's say our prayers.'

When they had yawned their way through their prayers, she bent to kiss their heads. 'Goodnight and God Bless, see you in the morning, by God's good grace, Amen.'

Later that night before Eve climbed into bed, she

gazed out of the window. The lamplight reflected the ruins of the cottage across the road and, beyond, the dazzle of the sky was breathtaking. A million stars glowed above the city. In six days time it would be 1929, and she wondered what the new year would bring.

Chapter Twenty-Two

It was New Year's Day and Joseph Petrovsky watched the young couple walk away from his house and disappear down the hill. He had provided them with food and drink for their long journey to the north where they hoped to find work and a new life. Though he had bidden them a cheery farewell, he was uncertain of their future. They were seeking freedom and had come to England to escape their problems. But they would not find it an easy path, Joseph thought as he went back inside to the warmth of his fire. However, they were in love and had survived an outrageous persecution and that strength of character would see them through.

He had given shelter to many such aspirants, as he quietly went about his life's work, which was to provide shelter and encouragement when his countrymen fled from the persecution. Though England's streets were not paved with gold and most of them were cold and empty places to be at this time of year, the tales of hardship in the old country were abominable to Joseph's ears. The peasants forced into communes and the kulaks destroyed, whilst each unique spirit was broken for the good of all. In one form or another, the tyranny had come down through the ages. The young man and his wife who had poured out their hearts to him over Christmas had escaped this imprisonment in their search for freedom.

He sat quietly for a while, a gentle satisfaction filling him that once again he had been able to provide a safe house for the needy, but life in England was not an easy one either. Those who sought his help were often starving, tired and frightened when they came secretly to his door. He provided a brief rest for them, but that was all. Until he drew his last breath, he would serve them. It was his destiny and he thanked God he had the means in this old house; though he and Gilda had not been blessed with earthly children, he could aid these infants of the political storm.

Suddenly a knock came on the door and shaking his head from his drowsy state, he went to answer it. Eve, her young man and the two boys stood on the doorstep.

Eve stepped forward to kiss his cheek. 'Happy New Year, Joseph.'

'And a happy New Year to you too. Come in, come in.'

'Only if your visitors have gone.'

'Yes, yes, I'm quite alone.'

They stepped into the hall and he led them into the front room where he took their coats and scarves.

Afterwards he fed them hot toast from the end of a fork and made fresh tea in the samovar. Whilst they were talking he gave the boys permission to climb on the shed and swing from the tall ship's bowsprit. Then, smiling at Eve, he asked if they had enjoyed a good Christmas. After a while the conversation turned to the events of the past year, the wonderful discovery of a germ-killing mould by Professor Alexander Fleming, the health of the king which had taken a turn for the worse in November, the Equal Franchise Act that the Commons had passed giving the vote to women, and the outstanding triumph of Amelia Earhart as she crossed the Atlantic in her small plane. But it was not long before they were recalling last year at this time when the skies had darkened and the ice and snow that had covered the country in a bitter winter had thawed suddenly in the Cotswolds and turned the River Thames into a turbulent enemy.

'I never thought we'd get back into the cottage again,' Eve said as she sipped the hot tea. 'And we wouldn't if it wasn't for my friends and neighbours and Charlie of course.'

Joseph could see by his guests' exchanged glances that these two young people, like those he had just seen off from his front door, were beginning the year with fresh dreams. Those two little boys, he thought as he listened to Eve and Charlie speaking, would benefit from the flood in ways that no one could have imagined. He felt that life had been very good to him, allowing him to see such expansion. In Russia, his own dreams had been crushed, but other younger, brighter and more courageous souls would take over the work when his was done.

'Joseph, are you feeling all right?' Eve touched his hand.

He smiled as he blinked at them. 'Just a little tired, that's all.'

'We must go.' Charlie shook his hand and Eve put her arms around him.

'I wanted to thank you for giving us a home when we didn't have one.'

'You were most welcome.'

'Joseph, if there is anything me and Charlie can do . . .'

He smiled and nodded slowly as it seemed that a prayer might have been answered. 'One day, my dears, I may call on you.'

When they went to the yard, Samuel and Albert were sitting high on the tall ship's bowsprit. They swung their booted feet and waved mittened hands, their breath white in the winter's cold.

'A wonderful picture,' nodded Joseph in satisfaction.

'A happy New Year,' said Eve fondly beside him as Charlie went to get them down.

Joseph nodded slowly. Nature had played its part in his life and in the young woman's. He was satisfied now.

When the family had departed, he went inside and drew a large leather pouch from the dresser drawer.

The soft material brought back memories of Gilda's long fingers and her gentle touch and the many love letters they had exchanged, the most precious of which he kept in here. He opened the pouch and began to speak softly to the woman he had left behind so long ago, but who had never missed a day in his thoughts.

It was Monday the seventh of January and the first day back at school for Samuel and Albert. The morning was bright but cold and breezy with an easterly nip. Eve walked with them to St Saviour's and watched them as they met their friends in the playground. They seemed to have grown taller over the Christmas holidays and they were more like one another now than they had ever been, with Raj's stunning good looks and his natural elegance. Today a young girl that she hadn't seen before, with parchment-coloured skin and almond-shaped eyes, haloed by long straight black hair, joined them. Her smaller companion, who Eve took to be her brother, was also almond eyed and his hair was a luxurious black. Other children surrounded them and laughter erupted. Eve smiled. They were obviously new pupils and it seemed that Albert and Samuel had taken them under their wing.

Eve left St Saviour's and hurried to the house on Westferry Road where she collected her baskets and waited for her first delivery of the morning. She was an hour late, but had arranged the time with Percy and very soon the old man and his horse and cart came along.

''Appy New Year to yer, gel,' he said, as he unloaded the stock sent by Queenie and Eve arranged it in her baskets. 'You'll do the bee's knees terday.'

Eve nodded. Last week trade had been unusually quiet. But now everyone had turned the corner into the new year and she felt confident that interest would resume. Despite the cold weather, people still wanted a posy or two to cheer them up in hospital or to take to a loved one's grave, or a buttonhole for a jacket lapel or a sprig of heather for luck.

Once more, Eve's two regular customers, the girls from the factory, asked her to set aside posies, new year's gifts for their mothers. The talk that morning was of the events of the seventh of January last year, when the island's residents had woken to see the streets submerged in water. Eve felt a deep sense of well-being, as she discussed the ups and downs of the flood. They had come through a natural disaster and her business was better than ever. By eleven o'clock most of one basket had disappeared and Eve arranged the remainder attractively, so that by early afternoon, she was ready to go. She was about to take the basket on her hip when a figure passed by on the other side of the road. The man was swathed in scarves and a cap so she couldn't see his face. Since she knew most of the people who passed this way, Eve smiled at the stranger. He paused briefly, his hands stuck down in the pockets of a long, grey coat.

By the time she had raised the basket and adjusted the money bag under her coat, he had vanished.

Eve gave no more thought to the figure until she caught sight of him again after stowing away the baskets. He was walking behind her, though it wasn't his footsteps she'd heard, but an instinct that told her someone was there.

When she arrived at Isle Street, she turned back. There was nothing, just a horse and cart passing and a few pedestrians.

Eve hurried down the hill. Had he wanted flowers and saw that she had none? But why didn't he ask? There was something about him that seemed familiar. But when she got indoors, Eve soon forgot about the stranger as Joan was standing in the passage, a bowl of steaming water in her hands as the antiseptic smell of friar's balsam filled the air.

'I 'ope you don't mind me going upstairs for one of your pick-me-ups, gel. I had to do somethin' as the smellin' salts wasn't working.'

'Is it Peg?' Eve asked in alarm.

'No, we got a visitor.' She jerked her head to the front room. 'Peg's in there with 'im.'

Eve went in to find Peg sitting beside Joseph on the couch. The old man's collar was loosened, his head back on a cushion. His face was grey and he was breathing with difficulty.

'Joseph, are you ill?'

413

Peg looked up at Eve. 'He was trying to get up that flamin' slope. Saw him out the window with 'is shopping basket, taking one step forward and two back against the wind.'

'Ladies, please, I'm just a little . . . out of breath.'

'Here,' said Joan, placing the bowl on his lap and taking his bony hands to place round it. 'Hold on to that and breathe in. It'll either kill or cure you, ducks.'

For a moment all four of them were engulfed in the cloud of Eve's strong balsam. Joseph coughed as he inhaled and Eve could hear his wheezy chest. 'You should wrap up at this time of year,' she told him gently. 'And going out was unnecessary. I could have done your shopping. I told you to call on me if there was anything I could do.'

He nodded. 'I don't want to be a burden.'

'Joseph, you're never that.'

'Come on Joan,' said Peg, pulling her sister with her, 'we'll make ourselves useful and brew a nice cup of rosie.'

When they were gone Eve took off her coat and sat down. The old man didn't look at all well. She smiled. 'I think you've been doing too much running after all them visitors.'

He gave her a weak grin. 'I thought a walk would do me good. I must go now.'

'What for?' Eve chuckled. 'Unless you've got more visitors to look after?'

'No, the house is quite empty now.' He sighed softly

and looked into Eve's gaze. 'How can I refuse my kinsmen? I know I'm getting old but they come to me for help. They are desperate, my dear.'

'Is it that bad in Russia?' Eve asked curiously.

'The new regimes are terrifying. Terrifying! The revolution in which our Czar died only bred a new kind of monster. His name is Stalin.' He stopped, struggling to get his breath as his agitation grew. 'Those young people were threatened with the labour camps, an abomination to humanity! They refused to work in the mines under intolerable conditions. There is no freedom to choose, you see, just the good of the state.'

Eve gently pressed him back against the cushions. 'There now, don't upset yourself. I'm sure you did all you could to help them and now you must try to take care of yourself. Lay back and try a little nap.'

He nodded, submitting to her pressure as his eyes grew tired and weary. A minute later, he was asleep.

Eve stood up and went out, quietly closing the door behind her. In the kitchen Joan and Peg were sitting at the table, smoking their roll-ups. The kettle was boiling and Eve turned it off.

'Don't think Joseph will want one.'

'Is he kipping?'

'Yes.'

Joan looked at Eve. 'If you ask me an old pot and pan like him shouldn't be running around after people.'

Eve sat down with them. 'He won't stop.'

'Who are they?'

'It's to do with what's happening in Russia,' Eve tried to explain. 'They come to find freedom as they have to work so hard in places like these terrible mines.'

Peg sat back and laughed. 'Work in the mines?' she repeated incredulously. 'What casual standing on the dock stones wouldn't give his right arm to work in a mine, no matter how terrible it is? You just ask them blokes that scrape infected hides off the floors of the skin holds with the stink of anthrax in their noses! Would these foreigners volunteer to work in such a way? Any docker will tell you that you don't have no freedom if yer belly's hungry and your wife and kids are starving.'

As Eve was considering this, there was a knock on the door. Hurrying to open it, Eve was shocked to see Charlie and beside him, Sergeant Moody.

'Mrs Kumar,' Sergeant Moody boomed. 'We have the pleasure of meeting again.' His voice was filled with sarcasm.

'What do you want?'

'Another body has been found in the river.'

Eve went weak at the knees. 'But it can't be my husband if that's what you think.'

Sergeant Moody's face grew very red under his helmet. 'Please get your coat and come with us.'

Eve looked at Charlie in confusion. He went to step forward but the sergeant put out his arm. 'Stay where you are, Merritt. And leave this to me.'

Eve felt very frightened. What did Charlie want to say? And why did she have to see another dead body?

Eve didn't want to look at another dead man. The memory of Dilip Bal was still clear in her mind as he'd lain on that cold hard slab of a table, all the life gone from him.

'Please step forward.' This time it wasn't Charlie who was beside her in the freezing cold mortuary, it was Sergeant Moody. Charlie had been dismissed and instructed to stay outside.

The terrible smell that she remembered so clearly was making her feel sick. The room was bereft of any comfort, not even a chair to sit on. There was only the table with a cover over it and an attendant standing behind.

Eve moved slowly forward, pulling her coat collar up to her chin as though she could hide under it.

'Ready,' said Sergeant Moody and the man pulled back the sheet. Eve closed her eyes. Perhaps she could pretend she had looked. But when her arm was shaken she was forced to open them.

The gasp that came from her throat was like a cry. She put her hand to her mouth.

'Do you know him?'

Eve nodded.

'Is it your husband?'

Eve could only shake her head. She turned and Sergeant Moody opened the door for her as she stumbled out. In the corridor Charlie rushed forward. 'Eve!'

'That will do, Merritt!' Sergeant Moody ordered but Charlie ignored him as he helped Eve to a chair.

'It's all right,' said Charlie quietly, 'it's over now.'

'I said that is enough, P.C. Merritt. Bring Mrs Kumar to the car immediately. She has made an identification.'

Charlie helped her to her feet again. He supported her as they walked along the corridor. Tears filled her eyes as she looked into his concerned face.

Outside, they stopped at the car. Quickly Charlie said, 'Who is it Eve?'

As the car engine growled, she managed to whisper, 'It was Singh, Charlie. Somar Singh.'

Charlie was seething. Sergeant Moody had been cross-questioning Eve for the past two hours and wouldn't hear of him being present. She had been allowed a drink of water, but nothing since then. It was now dark outside and as his superior's voice broke into his thoughts, Charlie pulled back his shoulders.

'Step in, Merritt.' Sergeant Moody's order was abrupt.

Charlie walked into the small, cluttered office and saw Eve sitting on the chair, her face ashen. He wanted to put his arms round her and tell Moody to leave her alone.

The older policeman sat down and studied a large sheet of paper that was lying on the desk in front of him.

Charlie stood with his hands behind his back. 'Can I get Mrs Kumar a cup of tea?' he asked quietly.

Moody's head shot up. 'There'll be time enough for tea when I've got this statement down on paper. Now,' he said as he settled himself in his chair, 'my first question is to you, P.C. Merritt. After all I've heard from Mrs Kumar, I understand that you have been following up a case that I had officially closed in February of last year. What's more, you have deliberately withheld information. Now that, son, is an abuse of the trust and confidence put in you as a member of His Majesty's police force.'

Eve stood up and, to Charlie's horror, burst out, 'It was me that didn't want him to tell you. It's got nothing to do with Charlie!'

Charlie reached out and gently sat her down. 'Eve, don't upset yourself—'

'She has every reason to be upset,' interrupted the police sergeant angrily. 'And so have you, son. You do realize, I suppose, that your decision to investigate a case that I personally closed might cost you your job?'

Charlie's whole body tightened. 'No, Sarge, I was only trying to—'

'And all this was going on whilst we had the Yard boys here,' roared Moody, jumping to his feet. 'Just think what they would have made of it, if they knew you were consorting . . . assisting and abetting . . .' He didn't seem to be able to throw enough at Charlie as his lips quivered and his eyes bulged. 'Running around Shadwell like a blue-arsed fly—'

'I did nothing of the sort,' Charlie retaliated only to

draw a look of fury from the other's face. 'I only did what my conscience told me to do. If you remember, I tried to tackle you about a personal matter at the time, but you waved it aside.'

'What bloody rubbish!' Moody stalked round the desk and dug a finger into Charlie's chest. 'You are a loose cannon, Merritt, and the Force can't be doing with coppers going it alone. You've got yourself into a right mess here, and with this body being found today and what I've heard from this . . . this *lady*,' he glanced contemptuously at Eve, 'you don't deserve the uniform you are standing up in. Take the law into your own hands would you? Who do you think you are, flamin' Sherlock Holmes?'

This comment irked Charlie. He was trying to control his temper, but when Moody continued to stab his chest and insinuate that he had struck up a liaison with a woman of dubious character, Charlie retaliated.

'That's uncalled for,' he retorted. 'Mrs Kumar deserves the same respect as any other member of the public. She has been through a great deal and was brave enough to try to discover the facts surrounding her husband's death—'

But Charlie's indignant words were cut short as Sergeant Moody bawled fiercely into his face. 'You're dismissed, Merritt. From this moment on you can leave all the investigations to those who know best. I'm suspending you from duty until I make me mind up what to do with you. And you'd better start praying that I don't decide to take this to the Super and spill the beans.'

Charlie wiped the spit that had come from Moody's trembling lips from his cheek. He glanced down at Eve and wondered for a second if he should grab her and haul her away with him. It's what his heart was yearning to do, but his head was saying something else. He knew that no good came of any action done or word said in anger and Moody was taking him to the limits of his endurance. He no longer cared for himself. His first concern was for Eve and it would only make things worse for her if he interfered. He tried to give her a swift glance of reassurance, then turned on his heel and with shoulders pulled back left Moody's office.

As he walked past the desk, a new recruit turned to look at him, a fresh-faced copper, just like he had been two years ago. Enthusiasm and eagerness shone out of his eyes as he watched Charlie stride down the corridor.

But if he had been addressed, Charlie couldn't have brought himself to reply. He was trying to contain his anger, resentment and dislike of Moody as he pushed open the doors of the changing rooms with furious force.

Robbie was standing at the washbasin and looked up sharply. 'Charlie, what the blazes . . .'

Charlie began to strip off his jacket. His fingers were shaking and the colour that had left his face whilst standing in the office now swept to his cheeks in a hot wave.

Drying his face with a small hand towel, Robbie sauntered over. 'I heard Moody bawling as I came in. What was that all about?'

Charlie sat heavily down on the bench. 'He's got Eve in there. She had to look at another body today. It's Singh, the lascar I told you about.'

'Christ!' Robbie exclaimed. 'What do you make of that?'

'I don't know. But Moody dragged it all out of her, everything, including the Shadwell business. He tore me off a strip saying I had no right to take the law into my own hands. He was furious it happened at the time when the Flying Squad were here, insinuating it would have looked bad for him. But what got my goat was when he accused Eve of being . . . being a . . .' He shook his head, running a hand through his thick, dark hair. 'It was inexcusable, the slant he put on Eve and me.'

Robbie folded up his jacket and shrugged. 'You don't want to take it too seriously. If I know Moody, the Yard thing is what upset him most. He would lick the soles of their boots if they told him to and yet he'll never get a promotion, not in a million years. He's a glorified clerk, an ignoramus.'

Charlie gave a grunt. 'Well, that ignoramus has just suspended me.'

'What? He can't do that. He hasn't got the authority.'

'Robbie, I'm beginning to feel like I don't give a damn. I don't care for myself but what he said about Eve . . . it was just so bloody unfair.'

Robbie sat down beside him. 'So you're beginning to wake up are you?'

Charlie shook his head. 'Wake up to what?'

'Come on, you need a drink.'

'I'm going to wait for Eve.'

'It won't look good for her, you know, hanging around. And anyway, Moody will send her back by car as it's still parked at the front. The new boy, Moody's little protégé, is eager to drive.'

Charlie thought about this. He wanted to be with Eve but knew Robbie was probably right.

'All right,' he agreed without conviction.

'Good man,' said Robbie as he folded his uniform into a locker. A few minutes later they exited the station through the rear door and walked across the car park to the street. Charlie felt as though he was letting Eve down. What was happening in there? What was Moody saying to her?

Several streets away, Robbie unlocked his car. 'Don't like to park this little beauty right under Moody's nose,' he told Charlie as they climbed in. 'The old bastard would think I'd been up to no good.' He laughed and winked at Charlie. 'Which, in a manner of speaking, is true.'

Charlie's thoughts were still with Eve and what she might be suffering under Moody's verbal assault when he realized what Robbie had said.

It was only when they were standing in a hotel bar off the Strand half an hour later, that Charlie began to understand how slow off the mark he had been.

Chapter Twenty-Three

Eve walked into the warmth of the front room to find Peg and Joan asleep in their chairs. Peg had her mouth open and her arms folded across her chest. Joan was snoring softly, her face lost under her hair, which was now entirely grey like Peg's.

She looked at the clock on the mantel. It was half past eight. She was exhausted from all the questioning. Neither had she eaten, though the young officer who had driven her home had made her a cup of tea at the station.

Leaving the room quietly, she went upstairs. Samuel and Albert were fast asleep too; their first day back at school had tired them. Eve kissed their soft hair. They looked so peaceful with the covers tucked up to their chins.

She made her way down to the kitchen and thought about Joseph as she put on the kettle. Had Peg and Joan walked him back to the cottage?

Making a strong cup of tea Eve sat at the table. Her hands were still shaking as she lifted the cup. She still couldn't believe what she'd seen: the lifeless body of

Somar Singh. He had walked towards her in the back room of the Drunken Sailor with that menacing look on his face. She had had no doubt it was him, especially as he had still been wearing the jacket with the row of brass buttons running down the front.

Sergeant Moody had told her they had recovered the body from the Thames that morning, but it was not as bloated as Dilip Bal's. Standing in that mortuary room she had felt as though she was in the middle of a recurring nightmare. She had longed for Charlie to be by her side, but Sergeant Moody had kept them separated. Over and over again she had repeated her answers, telling him all she knew. She hadn't wanted to say that Charlie had helped her, but in explaining how she knew Somar Singh, she had to reveal her journey to Shadwell and the events that had taken place after.

Eve leaned forward, dropping her head in her hands. She was so tired she couldn't think straight. All these deaths . . . how were they connected to Raj?

She longed to talk to Charlie, but she had no idea where he was or when she was likely to see him again. Had Sergeant Moody really suspended him? He hadn't done anything wrong. He had tried to help her and in doing so had incurred this punishment.

Eve wiped a tear away.

What was she to do now?

Charlie was still drinking his beer when Robbie ordered his third whisky at the bar. The clever lighting in the hotel, the gold and black décor and glass tables gave a sophisticated glow to the big, well-furnished room. Charlie would have preferred not to have gone as far as the Strand, but Robbie seemed intent on visiting this watering hole. He had greeted the uniformed man outside with a smile and was addressed as Mr Lawrence.

Charlie sat quietly with his thoughts as Robbie continued to talk to people he knew. They were all very well dressed and occasionally Charlie caught the cut-glass accent of a tall man in his late fifties to whom Robbie was particularly attentive. Beside him there was a blonde woman wearing a fur stole, smoking a ciga-rette in a long holder.

'Friends of yours?' asked Charlie as Robbie finally took the chair beside him.

'Harry Burnett,' said Robbie easily. 'Heard of him?'

Charlie shrugged and shook his head.

'Retired from the Force. Moved out to Essex last year. She's his . . . well . . . you might say, companion. But then, Harry has plenty of those.'

'You seem to know a lot of people.'

Robbie grinned. 'I make it my job to know them. And for them to know me.'

'Are they friends of Johnny too?'

Robbie slid the whisky over his tongue, narrowing his eyes. 'Yes, I suppose you could say we're all on nodding terms.'

Charlie looked again at the man and back to his friend. 'What's going on, Robbie?'

'I thought you'd never ask.' Robbie smiled and leaned forward, his good looks seeming, to Charlie, to be a little less smooth: his eyes had a furtive look and his fingers shook a little as they held the tumbler.

Charlie tilted his head. 'I suppose I've tried not to see what I don't want to see.'

Robbie chuckled. 'Bury your head in the sand, so to speak? Not a bad idea, but you have to be selective. Best to bury it and be paid for it.'

'You're on the take, aren't you?' Charlie said, watching Robbie's face as it lost its candour. 'You and Johnny. These people and the crowd you mix with, it's all for a reason. The car, the clothes, the women, the gambling and the drinking—'

'I'm simply making the job pay,' Robbie replied smoothly. 'You won't hear me complaining or whingeing, I just make the very best of what I have. And look where being straight has got you, Charlie. You said yourself tonight that Moody's attitude was bloody unfair. And all you did was a good turn and not a penny to show for your trouble, except a copper's wage packet. Now, can you look me in the eye and tell me that's what life is all about?'

Charlie gazed into his friend's shifty eyes. 'No, I couldn't tell you that. But I don't believe you've got it perfect either.'

'How do you know? Give it a try and see what it's like. Meet a few of my friends, socialize. I told you once that it was who you knew not what, remember?'

Charlie smiled. 'Yes, I do. But I wasn't ready then to believe my friend was bent.'

Robbie didn't bat an eyelid. 'Think on this Charlie, I'm still sitting here with a job whilst yours is in jeopardy.'

Charlie had to agree with Robbie on that. If Moody went higher and took it to the Super, there was a chance he could be dismissed.

'Come on, have a chat with my friend. Lighten up and enjoy yourself.'

'What is it you're up to?' Charlie asked. 'Protection? Prostitution? Pimping? Or has it a classier touch? Are Venetia Harrington and Bunty all part of the game?'

Robbie sat back slowly, dislike filling his face. 'I don't care for your tone, Charlie. I am, after all, trying to help.'

Charlie stood up. 'I don't need that kind of help.' He began to turn away when Robbie caught his arm.

'You know, you're a fool, chum.'

Charlie could think of no answer. Instead he shook off the tight grip and strode out.

It was raining as he stood on the pavement and listened to the swish of tyres on the wet streets. Then, with the roar of London's nightlife in his ears, he turned up his collar and hunched his shoulders, and set about the long walk to Stepney.

The next morning, Tuesday, Eve woke the boys early. 'I'm sorry I didn't see you last night.'

They sat up in bed. 'Peg said you was at the police station.'

'Yes, to help with their enquiries.' She wasn't going to say she'd been at the morgue again.

'Was Charlie there?'

She nodded. 'He was on duty.'

'Did he drive you in the police car again?'

'No, another young policeman did.' She chose her words carefully, as she didn't want to alarm them.

Albert yawned. 'Is it time to go to school yet?'

'No, it's early. You can lay in bed for another half hour. Don't forget to put on your hats and scarves for school, it's cold outside.' She pulled the covers over them. 'Did Peg and Aunty Joan say how Joseph is?'

They nodded. 'We went up to see him. He's better now.'

'Good.' She smiled. 'Tell Peg and Joan I'll see them later.'

All morning Eve thought about what had happened the day before. She wanted to talk it over with Charlie, but what had happened to him after he had been dismissed? When the young constable was ordered to drive her home, she'd looked out for him, but he was nowhere to be seen.

'Me mum liked those flowers I bought yesterday,' said a familiar voice and Eve turned to see the two girls from the factory. Like her they wore their heavy coats, but their white turbans and clogs were already stained from the vinegar they used in the pickling process. 'Have you got a cheap buttonhole for me brother? Don't want anything special but it's his birthday t'morra.'

Eve smiled. 'You can have one for sixpence.'

She was just about to bend down and pick a small red rose twirled in dark green leaves and twisted in paper when she saw a figure on the other side of the road. It was the same man she had seen before in a cap and long coat. Eve felt her pulse race as he stood there. This time there was no mistaking that he was watching her.

The girl pulled a sixpence from her pocket but as she had gloves on, it fell into one of the baskets. By the time Eve had searched for it and found it at the bottom, the figure had disappeared.

'Thanks, he'll be made up with that.' The two girls walked off, laughing and shouting goodbye. Eve wasn't listening. She was looking up and down the street. But he had disappeared.

It was late in the afternoon when a van drew into the kerb. Eve rushed forward and looked in the open window. 'Charlie, are you all right?' She was relieved to see him, but he looked tired and unshaven.

'Yes. Have you much left to sell?' he asked as he got out of the van and came round to stand beside her.

'Just a few bunches, that's all.'

'Let's go somewhere and talk. I'll put your baskets in the back and we'll drop them off.'

Once the baskets were deposited at the house in Westferry Road, Charlie drove them away from the island and up to Mile End. He parked outside a small café.

Once inside they sat at a window table, where they could see the busy trade flowing by: heavily laden horses and carts, bulging market barrows and warmly dressed pedestrians making their way either to the Bow Road or Whitechapel. The lorries, vans and buses that passed were hampered by the big carthorses that slowed down the stream of traffic as their dung was shovelled into a sack by an enterprising young street urchin.

Eve sat watching the movement while Charlie brought her a steaming mug of tea from the counter. The wooden table was grimy with the pease pudding, mash and jellied eels that had been served during the day, while the windows were steamed from the hot breath of the customers. But it was cosy and quiet and added to the reviving drink, Charlie bought them hot buttered buns that were toasted so perfectly they looked almost too good to eat.

Eve undid the buttons of her coat as did Charlie and for a few moments they savoured the warmth of the café. There was only one other table taken and other than the hissing from the big, steaming kettle and the clatter from the kitchen at the back, it was peaceful.

'I felt powerless to help you yesterday,' he said quietly as they drank. 'What more did Moody want when I'd gone?'

'He just asked the same questions over and over again

as if he was trying to trip me up. I'd told him the truth, but look what happened. He blamed you.'

'Some of it was deserved,' Charlie muttered, 'but not when he insulted you.'

'You shouldn't have got yourself suspended, Charlie. Not for me.'

'He was out of order, Eve.'

'Charlie, it doesn't matter now.'

'But it does. However will we close the gap between the public and the Force if that kind of attitude continues?'

Eve smiled, touched at the sentiment. 'Now you know why East Enders don't care for authority and why, when we first met, I didn't trust the law. I'm a flower-seller, Charlie and I dared to marry a lascar. Me and Raj . . . we knew what we'd done when we got married. It wasn't easy then and it ain't easy now. But none of it is your fault, so please don't get into any more trouble.'

'Eve, are you sure the dead man was Singh?'

'I couldn't forget a face like that. And he had brass buttons down his jacket.'

'So Singh is dead,' Charlie murmured pensively. 'And he goes to his grave with his secrets.'

Eve looked into Charlie's concerned face. 'If he was found yesterday, the *Tarkay* must be in.'

'No, it's been delayed.'

'How do you know that?'

'I went to the shipping offices before Christmas to find out when it would arrive. And there's something

433

else. I found out that there was a fire at the Drunken Sailor. The landlord died trying to put it out.'

'He's dead?' Eve exclaimed in alarm.

Charlie nodded. 'Now there are four unexplained deaths: your husband's, Dilip Bal's, Somar Singh's and the landlord. And other than your husband's, they occurred here in the East End.'

'Charlie, what does all this mean?'

'It means that Singh, who we were convinced was responsible for attacking you, has been silenced. If his death wasn't an accident, I believe that someone, somewhere, is behind the deaths of two lascars and your husband.'

'But why would anyone want to kill Raj? He was just an ordinary sailor, and never got into no trouble; his job meant the world to him. Even when we got married, he didn't take no time off as he couldn't be sure of a passage back on another ship. It was three months before I saw him again.'

'But Eve, someone tried to kill you too. And why would anyone want to do that? It can only be because you walked into that tavern and said who you were, Raj Kumar's wife.'

Eve frowned, trying to reason out her thoughts. 'Charlie, I've been thinking. I can't believe the men who blindfolded and tied me were really bad. I didn't understand what they said, but I knew they was arguing. Think about it, if they wanted to kill me they could have just thrown me in the water.'

Charlie agreed. 'That thought crossed my mind too. It was as if they were carrying out someone else's orders and got cold feet at the last moment.' He took her hand and squeezed it. 'Eve, I don't want you to be on your own.'

'What?' She laughed. 'Why?'

'Surely you can take a few days off? They will do a post-mortem on Singh to discover how he died. For my peace of mind, stay with Joan and Peg until then.'

Eve sat up. 'Sergeant Moody said you wasn't to do any more investigating—'

'Moody said a lot of things,' Charlie nodded, an icy tone to his voice. 'But I doubt if he'll lift a finger to help us. Eve, promise me you'll do as I ask?'

Eve knew Charlie was worried, so she reluctantly agreed. 'I'll tell Percy to let Queenie know that I don't want no more flowers this week.'

'Thanks, Eve.'

'What are you going to do now?'

'I'm going to revisit the place where I began my enquiries, the Overseas Sailors' Home on West India Dock Road. That's where I found the lascar who told me about Somar Singh.'

'Don't do anything dangerous.'

He grinned, looking into her eyes. 'So you really do care?'

Eve smiled sadly. 'If you hadn't met me, you might be driving one of them big police cars by now. You might be like you always wanted to be, a proper detective.'

'There's plenty of time for all that. Now, eat up and I'll take you home.'

As they drove, Eve reflected on her promise. She had agreed to do as Charlie asked, but she couldn't lose business for long. Her customers would go elsewhere. And besides, what could happen to her standing on the corner of Westferry Road with the world and his wife passing by?

But that night when Eve told Peg and Joan what had happened they were in full agreement with Charlie.

'You don't want to worry about the money,' Peg said immediately. 'Jimmy's paying his rent on Friday. We can manage on that.'

'It will only be for a few days,' said Eve feeling guilty already.

'Fancy that jumped-up old sod of a copper keeping you in the nick all that time,' Peg exclaimed angrily as she puffed on her roll-up. 'You would think you was a criminal.'

'He should try going after someone like my old man!' Joan exclaimed. 'Where was the law when he kicked me out and got a sour-faced old cow to replace me?'

'They ain't interested in Harold, Joan,' Peg said with a dismissive wave. 'He's a randy old sod but he's not Jack the Ripper.'

The conversation continued in the same vein until Eve went to bed. It was then she remembered the man in a long coat and cap. Had he really been watching her or was it a figment of her imagination? After all,

Somar Singh was dead and a dead man couldn't harm her.

Eve thought of the questions that Sergeant Moody had asked over and over again. But at the end of the interrogation he had not seemed to suspect anything underhand. His opinion was that it had been foolhardy of her to go into the Drunken Sailor on her own and she had brought trouble on her own head, and that she had been robbed by the men who had later dumped her at the jetty.

Could that be all there was to it? Was Charlie trying too hard to be the perfect policeman?

The next day Eve told Percy that she wouldn't be working for the next few days.

'You wanna watch it, gel, you might get some young whippersnapper steal yer pitch now you've worked it up.'

'It won't be for long.'

Percy jumped up on his cart. 'S'pose yer knows what yer doing.'

Eve watched him clatter noisily back the way he had come. She was beginning to wish she hadn't made her promise to Charlie. There were no strangers about, no one to alarm her.

When business was over, she looked up and down the road but other than a steady stream of horses and carts and a few motor vehicles making their way to the docks, there was nothing unusual. At the top of Isle

Street, she met Maude Higgins who was shouting at three very small and disobedient children.

'Just taking our Stanley's kids up the park,' Maude said breathlessly as she yanked one back from the road by his collar. 'The beak sent him down last week for six months.'

'Oh dear,' said Eve in concern.

'He'll do it standing on his head,' Maude shrugged. 'It ain't as if he's never coming back like our Tommy. He's only on his 'olidays.'

Nothing seemed to worry Maude much after the loss of Tommy and she took her sons' frequent absences in her stride. 'By the way, I saw Joseph this morning and he looked a bit peaky.'

Eve nodded. 'He couldn't get up the hill the other day.'

'Carryin' a bag he was. Looks like a stick, he's got so thin.'

'I'll go and see him tomorrow.'

'You're back early, ducks,' Maude frowned.

'Thought I'd take a few days off,' Eve said as she rubbed her hands together in the cold. 'It's bitter on the pitch.'

'You're not wrong there,' agreed Maude, 'it's parky enough to freeze the drip on yer nose. Oh, well, better get on. Come here, you little sod, or Gran will clip yer ear.' She waved goodbye, still yelling orders despite the racket the children were making.

When Eve got in the boys were home. Peg had made tea and they wanted to go to the park.

'Be back before dark,' Eve told them. 'Put on your coats and caps, it's cold outside.'

They were dressed in no time at all, leaving Eve alone with her thoughts. Tomorrow she would call on Joseph and offer to do his shopping. After all, she had the entire day to please herself!

The next day Eve knocked twice on Joseph's front door but received no reply. Crossing the road she saw Maude and her grandchildren. Maude was trying to whiten her doorstep as the kids jumped over it.

'Want to get this done before the rain starts,' said Maude shooing off the tiny children. 'You won't find Joseph in. I tried earlier and got no reply.'

'He must have gone out early again.'

'Must have.'

'Do you think he's all right?'

'I looked through the chink in the curtain. Couldn't see nothing untoward.'

'I'll send the boys up after school.'

'They can come in if they like and have tea with these nippers. Play out in the yard till dark.'

Eve smiled and left Maude to finish her step, but she was concerned. It was not like Joseph to be gone like this.

Eve filled the day with cleaning, washing and ironing. Joan and Peg went shopping and she had the house to herself. She felt at a loose end. So this was what it was like not to work?

At half past three she left for school. The boys were full of mischief when she met them, laughing about Sister Mary whose wimple had been stained by a big bird that had flown over the playground. When they arrived home, Eve told them to call on Joseph.

'Then go to Maude's. She asked you to tea with her grandchildren.'

The boys looked disappointed. They felt too grown up to play with small children, but they went all the same.

Ten minutes later, the twins, Maude and her three grandchildren stood on Eve's doorstep. They all looked very worried.

'Joseph ain't in,' said Maude anxiously. 'I don't like the look of it, Eve.'

Quickly Eve put on her coat and was soon joined by Peg and Joan. The little group marched up the hill and stood at Joseph's front door. They knocked and tapped on the window but could get no reply.

'Is his key hanging down?' suggested Maude.

Peg slid her hand through the letter box. 'There ain't nothing, not even the string.'

'We can climb over the back wall,' said Samuel. 'There's dustbins round there you can stand on. We use 'em when we climb up to the bowsprit.'

A minute later they were standing at the rear, waiting for the boys to try the back door.

'It ain't open,' they shouted over the wall.

'Try the window,' Eve shouted back. 'It's never closed properly.'

She could hear the boys lifting the sash. Once again they all hurried round to the front of the cottage and waited.

Samuel and Albert let them in and when the search of the house was complete, they stood in the kitchen.

'His bed's made but it don't look like it's been slept in. Cold as ice it is in his room,' said Maude.

'And look at that stove,' nodded Peg. 'It's as clean as a whistle. It ain't been used lately.'

Eve nodded slowly, then saw the samovar on the dresser. The internal pipe was dismantled and the metal bottom and tap looked gleaming as if newly polished. 'He's taken apart the samovar, Peg, and cleaned it. As if . . . as if—'

But she was cut short as Peg grabbed her arm. 'And look, hanging from the tap is the front door key.'

'Did he take it off the string deliberate like?' pondered Maude.

'P'raps the nail fell off.'

They went out to inspect the letter box. But the nail above it was in place. 'Shall we hang it up again?' said Eve. 'It can't do any harm. And I expect he just forgot.'

Everyone nodded and the key was returned to where it always hung.

'If I didn't know better,' said Maude, frowning at the clean grate in the front room, 'I'd say he's gorn away. And he had a bit of a spring clean before he went.'

'But he don't go away – ever,' pointed out Peg as they studied the tidy room.

'The larder's bare,' shouted Samuel and Albert from the kitchen.

Everyone went to have a look. 'What? No vegetables' for 'is borsch?' said Maude disbelievingly.

'P'raps he's gone to the market,' suggested Joan. 'Get 'imself a few nice spuds and beets.'

'It's a bloody long shopping trip if he did,' remarked Peg, and they all nodded in agreement once more.

They stared at the empty shelves and Eve knew they were all thinking the same thought. Why hadn't Joseph told them where he was going?

Chapter Twenty-Four

Charlie stood at the door of the Overseas Sailors' Home, staring into the large interior chamber. Unlike the busy halls of the Salvation Army with its noisy and ill-mannered destitutes, this retreat housed a surprisingly quiet and well-ordered number of human beings. He had thought on his first visit here that he was unlikely to discover anyone who had known Raj Kumar, for there were so many Asiatic, African and South Sea Island sailors.

As most of the sailors had fallen on hard times and spoke only fragments of English it was no wonder, thought Charlie, that they carried a certain detached look on their faces. He knew from what he had learned before that these good-natured seamen often fell victim to thieves who robbed them of their small purses and left them destitute on the London streets. This big, airy, substantial building with its natural order was their only refuge. And the sailors who ended up here – Charlie understood – once removed from the city's temptations, reverted to their natural quiet demeanour.

Charlie studied the dark faces, the downcast eyes under the colourful tarbooshes and turbans that alternated with the dull and uniform English peaked caps, and wondered if they were missing the warmth of their native shores. He imagined many had families and children to maintain and yet they were stranded here.

Watching them move around in their unresisting manner, his heart went out to them. It must be dreadful to end up here in a bitterly cold winter, without a return passage. He knew, however, that despite the discomfort and abuse these men were subjected to, the number of lascars employed by British trading vessels was increasing every year. It seemed the country's ships could not run without them. And equally important to the lascars was the work provided on these shipping lines. When one lascar failed to take a contract, another swiftly grasped it. And yet Raj Kumar had been an exception; he had not only faithfully served his employers but he had chosen to marry and live in a land that regarded him as an alien.

Charlie wondered once more what sort of young man he had been. Obedient and conscientious without doubt. Charlie had learned from his investigations that many lascars were trained to endure 160 degrees of heat in a stokehold, if they were contracted on such a voyage as a Red Sea trip. Others were forced to freeze as they maintained the exteriors of the vessels that sailed on winter passages through storms and gales. Raj Kumar had worked his way up through the lascar ranks and become a cook in the purser's department. Not only would he have mixed with his fellow lascars, but with the British crew too. He spoke English – and by all accounts rather well.

So what had led to his death, this respected man who was neither threatened by the elements nor the unbearable heat of an engine room? Who were his friends? How had his employers regarded his marriage and efforts to settle in the docklands of England?

Eve's words sprang to his mind. 'I dared to marry a lascar. Me and Raj . . . we knew what we'd done but it wasn't easy . . .'

Charlie shook his head slightly, as if it to clear his thoughts, and found himself staring at a small group of men seated at a table. He walked over and joined them.

'My name is Charlie Merritt,' he began quietly, not knowing if they understood him. 'I'm looking for anyone who knew a man by the name of Raj Kumar.' This time he didn't add that he was a policeman. He knew now that it could count against him and that it was sheer luck that he'd happened upon the lascar who'd told him about Singh.

The four faces stared at him in silence. Each with that curious expression of detachment.

'If not Raj Kumar,' he continued, enunciating each word, 'then Dilip Bal. Both men served on the *Star of Bengal*.'

It was several moments before two of the seated

sailors rose quietly to their feet. Almost bowing, they lowered their heads and moved silently away.

Charlie looked at the two remaining lascars; one wore an ordinary peaked cap and boiler suit, the other the loose, native costume of an Oriental seaman. It was cold inside the big room, but he had made no attempt to dress warmly. His eyes stared into Charlie's and Charlie was certain that when he said the next three words, there was, for the first time, a fleeting flicker of recognition.

'Or Somar Singh,' he murmured, 'who also served on the *Star* and, later, the *Tarkay*.'

Once again there was no response and soon he found himself sitting alone at the table, the air of quiet around him deepening to a disturbing silence.

The four women stood on the pavement outside Joseph's house. Eve had sent the twins and younger children into Maude's yard to play whilst they decided what to do.

'But what *can* we do?' posed Maude, pulling her collar up to her double chins. ''Cept worry!'

'He wasn't in the peak of health,' nodded Peg, shivering in the cold wind.

'Has he got any relations?' asked Joan, tying her scarf tighter under her chin.

'None that I know of.' Eve thought of the two young people that had had stayed with him recently. But they hadn't been relations, and all she knew about them was that they'd gone up north.

'Do you think Charlie could help?' asked Maude.

They all looked at Eve. She hadn't told them he had been suspended. 'I don't know.'

'You don't think he took ill somewhere?' suggested Joan.

'Don't forget, the larder was empty. Like someone deliberately going away,' Maude pointed out.

Peg shrugged. 'There's nothing more we can do tonight.'

'He might be back soon,' said Joan hopefully. 'Give us all a nice surprise.'

They all nodded. But Eve had a heavy weight in her stomach. It was as if he'd left the house clean and tidy for a reason. But what kind of reason could it be? He had lived in the cottage ever since she could remember. He didn't take holidays or go away; he was a home-bird.

'Better get in for me old man's tea,' said Maude.

'Send the boys back when you've had enough of them,' called Eve as she watched Maude hurry across the road. It was dusk and the chill night was settling in. Could an old man like Joseph really stay out in this weather?

The three women walked down the hill very slowly. But the more they suggested this or that, the more it seemed a puzzle. Eve decided that tomorrow she would go to the hospital. And she would ask Jimmy to call at Charlie's and tell him that Joseph had disappeared.

★

On Friday, after Eve sent the boys to school, she tried knocking again on Joseph's door. There was no reply.

'I used the key and took a gander early this morning,' shouted Maude, dragging on her coat as she hurried across the road. 'It just don't make no sense.'

'I think I'll make enquiries at the hospital.'

'If you wait till Eric or Duggie comes in, I can leave the kids with them and come with you.'

But Eve shook her head. 'No, it won't take me long if I leave now.'

'Well, wrap up warm, love. And I hope to gawd you don't find 'im. Not in 'ospital anyway.'

Maude needn't have worried, Eve reflected as she left the hospital and returned to the island. All her enquiries had been fruitless. The hospital hadn't had anyone brought in of that name or description. She went to the market at Cox Street as she knew that Joseph shopped there. But once more she was met with the same answer. No one had seen Joseph Petrovsky. The next place to enquire would be at the police station. Had Jimmy remembered to call on Charlie?

As Peg and Joan were out and the boys at school, Eve decided she would go to Joseph's house. Perhaps there was some indication as to where he might have gone that they had overlooked previously.

Putting on her coat again, she made her way up the hill. Should she ask Maude to help her? But she was probably busy with the children. Eve drew up the string and let herself in. The house was very cold and already beginning to smell strongly of damp. Joseph always had a fire burning but the empty grate was lifeless now. As Eve walked through the rooms, she shivered. The cottage was an empty shell without Joseph. She missed the delicious smells that always came from the kitchen.

Upstairs she looked in the big wardrobe in Joseph's bedroom. She couldn't tell if any clothes had been taken as she only ever saw Joseph in the same clothes: heavy trousers, a shirt and waistcoat and jacket. There were just a few things hanging inside. A large pair of boots were tucked neatly at the bottom, but Joseph's big coat was missing. There seemed to be no cap, gloves or scarf either. Had he been wearing them on the day Maude saw him?

Eve pulled out a drawer beside the bed. It contained just a few papers and not very much else. A bill from the coal merchant and another from the shoe mender.

Eve gazed round the room that she and the boys had occupied when they had lived here. It brought back many happy memories of a very kind man who took them under his wing.

'Where are you, Joseph?' Eve asked aloud and sighing heavily she made her way downstairs to the kitchen. Everything was in its place, neat and tidy. Maude was right, it was as though Joseph had decided to go away and cleaned the cottage before leaving.

Just then, Eve heard the front door creak. 'Maude, I'm in the kitchen,' she called, bending down to open the drawer in the kitchen table. This time she saw it was full of papers.

'Maude – I'm just searching for anything that might help us find out—' she began only to feel the words freeze in her throat as she looked up.

A man in an overcoat and cap was standing there. The same man who had been watching her on Westferry Road . . .

Charlie had his head stuck in the big black interior of the oven at the bakery. He hadn't got a clue what had gone wrong, but it wasn't heating up enough to bake the bread properly inside. His dad had been complaining about it for weeks, months probably. But they all knew that if they had to have it repaired it would cost an arm and a leg.

'Look at this, Charlie,' said his father prodding him in the ribs. 'My customers are beginning to complain Soft as a baby's bum inside and yet it's baked to perfection outside.'

Charlie pulled his head out of the oven, hitting it as he did so and cursing under his breath.

'What was that, son?'

'Dad, I think we've got to face it; this oven has had its chips.'

'But we've had it for years, before you were born.'

'Then it's about time it was retired. Look, let's give it ten minutes to cool down and then I'll have a closer inspection.'

Charlie sat down with his father in the small room kept for groceries. The two wooden chairs were just in view of the shop where either the tinkle of the bell or a customer's call could be heard.

Edwin Merritt removed his floury baker's hat and stood it on a shelf, then rubbed his eyes with his doughy fingers. Charlie knew his father's health had been suffering, what with the chill last year and the pressures of the business, but since he'd been suspended he'd seen firsthand that it was getting too much for the old boy. His mother who helped out in the shop was now spending more time with Pam and the baby and it didn't take a genius to see that neither of them were getting any younger.

'Dad, have you ever thought about selling the business?' Charlie knew this question wouldn't be welcome. His dad would go on till he dropped unless the family took an interest. And as soon as he'd said it, Charlie knew he'd let himself in for a challenging answer.

'Like to take it on, would you son?' Edwin said, laughing half-heartedly.

'Dad, with the best will in the world I'm not—'

'You're not a baker. Yes, I know. Nor is George, or Joe, to my regret. But lad, from what you've told your mother and me about this . . . this misunderstanding at the station, wouldn't it be worth your while to give it some thought?'

'I don't intend to be suspended for ever, Dad.'

'No of course not, the truth will out as they say. But

this business is a sound one. It just needs a bit of young blood. Folks always need their bellies filled and the markets won't ever stop selling. They need an early opening bakery that's cheap, close to their stalls and good quality. Merritt's is all three. Now, me and your mother have a bit tucked away for a rainy day. It's yours if you want it to plough back in the business. A new oven, do the shop and bakery up a bit and you're living above the job so it won't cost you nothing, not a penny. You could make this into a tasty little earner, set you up for life.'

'But, Dad, I'm a copper. And although I'm single, one day I want to wed.'

'Of course you will, son,' said his father with a gentle smile, leaning forward to pat his knee, 'and what better place than here to sire any amount of offspring? There's your brothers' room, big enough to fit in four strapping sons, and the spare room, nice for a daughter or two. And then, well, Mother and me won't be around for ever. You could be very comfortable by the time you get to my age. And I forgot to mention the best thing of all: you'd be your own boss. Now there's nothing in life that could taste more sweet when you're young, as having things run the way you want them to run.' He raised a bushy grey eyebrow. 'You'd never have to doff your cap to Moody or his like again.'

Charlie smiled at his father. 'Dad, you know what to say to drive home a point.'

'It's only common sense, son.'

Charlie sighed, 'I s'pose so.'

Edwin rested back on his chair and nodded. 'This business was made for you, Charlie. You know it inside out.'

Charlie laughed. 'One thing you've forgotten, Dad, and that is I can't boil an egg for meself let alone make forty loaves a day and God knows how many pastries.'

Edwin grinned. 'You'll learn it all in a month or two. After all, you'll have the best teacher.'

Charlie felt the heavy weight of family responsibility on his shoulders yet again. It grew heavier every time he faced reality. What had happened to his dreams of being a professional footballer or a Scotland Yard detective? Gazing into his father's hopeful, flour-flecked face, he recalled all the years he'd grown up here, watching the two people he loved most become slaves to the interminable hours, the heat and the monotony with never a minute to call their own even when the shop sign was turned to 'Closed'. Someone always wanted bread. Even on Sundays there were deliveries. As he'd grown, stubbornly holding tight to his dreams, he'd tried to help as much as he could, pretending he didn't feel guilty. But now the inevitability of the situation was upon him. Charlie Merritt, youngest son of Dulcie and Edwin Merritt, unattached, in good health and, at this moment, temporarily unemployed, heading towards a crown indeed, but one made of dough.

'Think it over, lad.' His father's voice brought him back to the present. 'Might be what happened at the station is a blessing in disguise . . .' Charlie didn't hear the rest as the shop door bell tinkled and a voice shouted out.

'Charlie! Charlie! It's me Jimmy!'

As Charlie jumped to his feet and rushed to the shop, he felt a slight alarm. 'Jimmy, what's up?' he asked as he saw the boy's flushed face.

'I tried to get here earlier,' Jimmy gasped breathlessly. 'But I had too many errands to run for me gaffer. I come 'cos Eve asked me to call by. She can't find old Joseph anywhere.'

Charlie sighed in relief. 'Lord almighty, Jimmy, I thought you'd brought bad news again.'

Jimmy shrugged. 'Well, it ain't good, is it? Not in this weather an' all.'

'What do you mean when you say he's missing?' Charlie asked, grateful that it was not to do with Eve, though he was well aware of how much she thought of the old man.

'Just gorn.' Jimmy lifted his arms. 'Like a puff o' smoke. Left the cottage all tickety-boo and disappeared.'

'But there must be a rational explanation.'

'If you can find one, I reckon Eve'd like to know it. She's even gone up the hospital today to see if he's there.'

'The hospital?' Charlie repeated anxiously. 'She's not gone alone?'

'Yeah, s'far as I know.'

'Jimmy, I told her to stay with Peg.'

Once more the young lad shrugged. 'Dunno nothin' about that, Charlie. Why?'

There was a moment when Charlie couldn't get his brain to work fast enough. Was he overreacting in worrying about Eve? Yet, something wasn't right.

Suddenly he was rolling down his sleeves and grabbing his jacket from the peg in the store cupboard. 'Dad, I'll look at the oven later,' he said to his father. 'Can I use the van?'

Edwin shrugged lightly. 'We've got no more deliveries today, lad.'

'Thanks, Dad.'

The older man frowned in puzzlement as he watched his son tear out of the bakery door followed closely by his young friend.

'Who . . . who are you?' Eve stammered. 'What do you want?'

The big figure moved closer. She could only see his eyes. His mouth was covered by a long woollen scarf and the cap was pulled down hard over his forehead. But she had a feeling, an instinct. Something about him was familiar.

Trembling with fear, Eve stepped back. She wanted to run, but he was blocking her path. Even if she got out into the yard, there was the high wall to climb over. The only escape was the front door.

'Don't . . . don't come any closer or I'll scream.' Eve regretted the threat immediately. Why had she said that? His spine straightened as he pulled himself upright and she heard the growl of his laughter.

'You want to know who I am?' The voice was rough and low. Somewhere in the back of her mind she knew who this man was.

'I . . . I . . .' Eve felt the fear take over. Her arms and hands were tingling with it. She shuffled another step back until she reached the dresser.

'Recognize me now, girl?' He began to unwind the scarf. Slowly he peeled it from his mouth. Tipping the cap upward, his face became clear.

Eve stared at the face she would never forget, the bearded features and narrowed eyes of the landlord of the Drunken Sailor, the face she had seen so many times in her nightmares since that night at Shadwell. 'But you . . . you're supposed to be dead,' she croaked.

He laughed, a sharp coarse sound that was no laugh but a hiss of contempt. 'I am dead. As far as the law goes, I was burned to a cinder. Unrecognizable I was, a lump of charred meat, a bag of burned bones.'

Eve grasped the dresser. 'Who . . . who was it that they found?'

The big man shrugged, a leer on his thin lips. 'Who cares? Some lascar I took in 'afore I set the fire.'

'You *set* it?'

'Went up in minutes, quicker than I planned. Should've took the whole place down by rights. Would have done too if some of them locals hadn't seen the blaze. I watched 'em, see. From the alley close by. Chucking their buckets of water and the fire engine comin'. I had ter stay and see if the job was done right.'

'But . . . but why?'

'Now the girl wants to know why!' He took a step forward, sliding the scarf into his hands. 'Questions, questions, little miss nosey, ain't you? Well, I see no harm now in tellin' you, girl, as soon that pretty mouth of yours will be closed permanent and Jack the Lad here will be smoking his best pipe as he watches your funeral.'

Eve felt the strength drain from her legs. He was going to kill her. She watched, mesmerized, as he slid the scarf through his thick, dirty fingers. He was going to strangle her. She edged sideways, knocking a cup from the dresser as she did so. Her only hope was to get round the table. But he seemed to read her mind and laughed.

'Don't waste your time, girl. I promise you it will be quick if you don't fight me.'

'I . . . I've done nothing to you—' Eve began.

'Nothin'! Nothin'?' he repeated fiercely, lowering his head and raising his shoulders as he came towards her. 'Do you call blabbing yer mouth off nothing? Shouting out for Singh, insisting you wanted to go into that room. I gave you a chance, not once, but twice, to change yer mind. But oh no, just more questions . . . a woman on her own . . . enough to arouse suspicion . . . but a lippy chit of a girl . . . this Eve . . . Eve Kumar . . . darin' to set foot on me territory and bring the law after her . . . darin' to ruin me business that took me ten long years to get running and payin' . . . '

As Eve took another step, he fell on her. She struggled

457

against his weight, but his hands clutched her hair and pulled back her head. He stared into her eyes and growled, pinning her arms against him as she tried to lash out.

'You done for me, girl, do you know that?' he roared, his body trembling with anger as he held her against him. 'You ruined me and now you're gonna pay.'

'But how . . . how could I ruin you?' Eve whispered hoarsely as he jerked back her head.

'By nosin' around, that's how. By finding them lascars, that no one else knew or cared about. Dregs they was, deserved what they got, each and every one of 'em. I did decent folks a favour gettin' rid of 'em, selling 'em off cheap an' all to the rich and lusty . . .'

'You *sold* them?' Eve gasped, but they were the last words she spoke as he pinned her with the weight of his body and they fell against the dresser. She struggled as the crash of china mingled with her own terrified screams. But the scarf was soon around her neck and growing tighter.

She felt her breath stop as she searched his eyes. Eyes that were wild and full of hate. Her fingers reached up to his face, tearing at his beard.

Choking, Eve gasped for breath. Then suddenly her fingers stroked the cold metal of the samovar. Could she reach it? She managed to lever herself another inch. Grasping the big, round base she hurled it, closing her eyes as she did so.

★

Charlie and Jimmy hurried from the hospital and jumped in the van. At least they had discovered from the nursing attendant that Eve had called earlier in the day in her search for Joseph. But since there was no record of the old man being there, she had left again.

'Where's the fire?' Jimmy joked, bracing himself as the vehicle jumped forward. 'What's the hurry?'

'I can't explain it all now,' Charlie barked. He knew he was driving too fast, but he felt there wasn't a moment to lose. Why hadn't Eve listened to him? Ever since Singh had been found, he'd known something wasn't right. He had been certain that Singh was responsible for what happened to Eve at Shadwell. But why? This was the missing piece of the puzzle. If only he knew what Singh's motives were!

'Watch out!' Jimmy's warning came too late as Charlie swerved to avoid a car. The bonnet of the van clipped its wing and caused Charlie to fight with the steering wheel. Before he knew what had happened, the van was mounting the pavement. He had a moment of terror when a lamp-post whizzed past his right wing, but he managed to avert disaster. Dragging the wheel hard left Charlie heard the wheels skid noisily as the van span once and then twice in almost painful succession, missing the oncoming traffic by inches as he fought for control. From the corner of his eye he saw Jimmy cover his face and Charlie's own arm swung out automatically to protect him. He heard someone cry out, a car horn blare loudly and then, to his sickening dismay, the loud crunch of metal.

Charlie stared through the shattered windscreen. He saw the houses, the roofs, the walls, the windows and the chimneys, all of which seemed to be spinning. Then someone opened the door and pulled him out.

Charlie gazed up at his rescuer as he sat on the ground. 'Wh . . . what happened?' he asked dazedly.

'I'm afraid we had a small collision. You were heading rather fast into Westferry Road.'

'Did I . . . are you hurt?'

The young man smiled under his trilby. 'No, it was just a touch. My car is over there,' he nodded over his shoulder. 'And all in one piece. But I'm sorry to say you've made rather a mess of your own.'

Charlie stared at his dad's van and groaned. What an idiot he was! He'd crashed his dad's van! There was steam coming from the bonnet that had engaged a brick wall with some force. Suddenly he remembered why he'd been driving so recklessly.

'I had to get somewhere . . .' he began and then frowned. 'Jimmy — where's Jimmy?'

'He's here,' the calm voice assured him.

Charlie saw Jimmy's face come into focus and closed his eyes in relief. 'Thank God.'

'That was a close one, Charlie,' Jimmy said in shaky tones. 'It was lucky this fella here swerved to avoid us.'

Charlie nodded. 'I'm sorry. I was driving too fast.'

Jimmy and the man helped him to his feet, dusting the dirt from his shoulders.

Charlie gulped air into his throat as he looked around

him. A crowd was gathering, staring at the van and the remains of the wall.

'This is gonna take a bit of explaining to the coppers,' said Jimmy, pulling off his cap and wiping his forehead. 'They'll be here any minute, Charlie.'

At this, Charlie nodded. Wiping the dust and dirt from his eyes, he put his hand on the shoulder of the young man. 'I'm sorry friend. Really I am. But you see, I was heading for Isle Street—'

'Isle Street?' The young man's dark eyes flashed. 'Not too far away. What say I drive you there in my motor?'

'But after what I've done—' Charlie began only to stop mid-sentence as a firm hand went under his elbow and guided him across the road towards the large black car. 'It's terribly decent of you to do this,' Charlie murmured bewilderedly as he climbed in to the back seat, followed by Jimmy.

'Not at all, Mr Merritt,' said the young man as he climbed in beside Charlie.

'How . . . how do you know my name?' Charlie asked with baited breath as he watched his escort reach inside his coat and bring out a small wallet.

'Perhaps I had better introduce myself,' was the calm, unruffled reply. 'I am Detective Inspector Mathew Fleet, working as part of the Metropolitan Division of the Central CID, better known as the Flying Squad.'

Eve was still clutching the samovar to her chest when Peg, Joan and Maude rushed in.

She was staring down at the man lying on Joseph's kitchen floor. The man she had just hit over the head while fighting for her life.

'Eve! Eve!'

'Here, who's that?' Peg and Joan shrieked together.

'My God, it's a burglar!'

'She's caught a thief!'

'What's he doing on the floor?'

Eve slumped down on a chair. 'He . . . he . . .' The words seemed to be stuck in her throat.

'It's all right love, we're with you, now.' Peg waved the smelling salts under her nose.

'Oh, Peg, he just walked in, as bold as brass. I thought it was Maude.'

'What did he want? Who is he?'

'He's the landlord of the Drunken Sailor,' Eve croaked as she stared at him.

'But I thought you told us he died in a fire,' said Peg in confusion.

'He told me it wasn't him. It was someone else instead, an innocent victim.' She touched the scarf that still hung round her neck. 'He tried to strangle me, Peg.'

Joan gasped as Maude took the scarf from Eve's shoulders. 'Oh, you poor love, your neck is all red!'

'He was tying the scarf tighter and tighter. Then somehow I got hold of the samovar . . .' She shuddered as she closed her eyes to try to block out the memory.

Peg knelt down by the body. 'He's a bloody ugly customer. But he's still breathing.'

Eve put her hand to her mouth. 'He . . . he blamed me for ruining his business.'

'What did he mean by that?'

Eve gulped as she clung to the samovar. 'He said he sold lascars to the rich. Human beings that wouldn't ever be missed because they are all dregs . . .' Eve burst into tears.

'There, there, lass.' Peg pulled her close, sliding her hand gently over Eve's untidy hair. 'It's all over now. He ain't gonna harm you again.'

They all looked down at the body. 'How did he know you were here at Joseph's?' Maude asked.

'He's been watching me,' Eve whispered. 'I didn't know who it was but he seemed familiar. He must have followed me back here today. Charlie told me to be careful, but I forgot.'

They all stared down at the unconscious man. A few seconds more, Eve reflected . . . if it hadn't been for Joseph's samovar, she would have been lying there instead.

Glancing down at the heavy metal urn she was still cradling to her chest, Eve saw the top had fallen off. Inside the cavity was a sheet of paper. With trembling hands, she slid it out.

Was this the answer to Joseph's disappearance?

Chapter Twenty-Five

Joseph's once cold front room was now warm and the fire burned brightly in the grate. Charlie sat beside Eve on the couch, his hand over hers as she recounted all that had happened since the landlord of the Drunken Sailor had walked into the house and attempted to kill her. The rest of the detective's team had arrived in Isle Street and taken away the man responsible not only for attempting to kill Eve but for other crimes in the East End that stretched back many years.

'But who is he?' asked Eve as she looked at the tall, dark-headed police officer who sat opposite in the big arm chair. 'Why would he want to kill me?'

'The man who attacked you today, Mrs Kumar,' explained Detective Inspector Mathew Fleet, 'is known to us by a number of names. Walter Donovan, Maurice Owen, Jack the Lad Bannister, all aliases. His real identity is Alfred Rattigan, known to us as a tout, thief, smuggler and slave trader.'

'Slave trader!' Charlie repeated on a gasp.

Eve nodded. 'Charlie, that's what he told me. He said he found lascars . . . that they deserved what they got . . .'

The detective shifted his position in the chair. 'Rattigan would befriend seamen in distress, then expose them to the excess and addictions that you saw for yourself, Mrs Kumar, in that back room of the tavern. Once his victims were under his control, he would market them to the wealthy, to be used in debauchery and for the entertainment of the upper classes. We have even discovered these unfortunates begging, imprisoned by circuses and brothels and other places.' The young man paused briefly, raising his shoulders. 'You see, the slave trade is quite sickening and most of the Oriental seamen who fall on hard times in our ports have no wealthy relatives to follow up their disappearances. They are like lambs to the slaughter once they become involved with people like Rattigan.'

'Is that what happened to Dilip Bal?' Eve asked in quiet tones.

'We can only conjecture that he had become a liability and was . . . disposed of.'

'And Singh?' Charlie said abruptly.

'Oh no,' replied the detective, his dark eyes hardening. 'Singh was a different kettle of fish. He wasn't killed because he was vulnerable. He was murdered because he knew too much about Rattigan. Singh was a *serang*, a native boatswain. These men have almost autocratic power over their charges. Now, some *serangs* are honourable and look after their crew, but some bad apples are corrupt, as was Singh. He would first gain a man's confidence by arranging a working passage, promising him the means to support his family. But on the next trip, he would extract *dustoorie* or payment from his wages until finally he bled him dry. It was then, when the man was desperate, he would take him to Rattigan to serve his final purpose.'

Charlie shook his head slowly. 'So Eve became a danger too, after what she saw at Shadwell?'

'From what you have told us,' the policeman nodded, 'something must have gone wrong on that jetty. Perhaps those men were disturbed or maybe they just took fright.'

'They were arguing,' Eve nodded. 'As if they couldn't make up their mind what to do with me.'

'And perhaps that is the truth of it,' agreed the detective. 'But had not Constable Merritt appeared on the scene soon after, I'm afraid the outcome would have been very much as Rattigan had planned.'

Charlie squeezed Eve's hand as he felt a shiver go through her. 'But if you knew about Rattigan,' Charlie asked their companion, 'why didn't you arrest him?'

'We knew he had moved to London from the north,' continued the Flying Squad officer, 'but we had lost track of him for some time. It was only when we received Sergeant Moody's request to have you formally suspended from duty that our enquiries began to mature. Even last year, during our more intensive investigations into East End crime, we had no real evidence to support the facts. The lascars disappeared, they were invisible to us and with no communication between us and the Indian authorities, our enquiries were inconclusive.'

'If only I had made Moody listen to me,' Charlie said on a distressed sigh.

'If only you had,' agreed the detective.

Charlie looked down. 'I thought it was enough to follow my own instincts.'

Detective Inspector Fleet laughed lightly and Charlie glanced up. He deserved to be mocked, but it was a deep humiliation.

'Instincts are what we all work on,' said the policeman, still smiling. 'And you were going in the right direction. Had we not followed you to the Overseas Sailors' Home and discovered all we needed to know about Singh, then we wouldn't have put a case together as solidly as we have now.'

'You followed me?' Charlie repeated.

'It is our job to work undercover.'

'But . . . but I couldn't get anyone to talk to me there!' Charlie protested. 'It seemed like a wall of silence.'

'And perhaps it was,' nodded the policeman. 'But after you left, we brought those four men in for questioning at the Yard. They were quite innocent of course, but terrified. Each of them revealed the truth about Singh and how, beginning on the *Star of Bengal* and later on the *Tarkay*, they and men like them poured all their wages into Singh's pockets and slowly these same men began to disappear. Singh had become a figure of terror to any lascar. There will be very few who mourn his passing.'

Charlie frowned as he sat forward. 'And Eve . . . Eve's husband . . .'

Detective Inspector Fleet nodded slowly, his dark eyes travelling to Eve. 'There is no evidence to show that your husband was involved with either Singh or Rattigan, Mrs Kumar. Marriage to a British citizen and his work in the purser's department where he would be under the jurisdiction of the officers and not a *serang*, would set him apart. It is the low-caste sweepers, the agwalas, paniwallahs and khalassies who become the victims of men like Singh and Rattigan.'

'So . . . so my Raj . . . he wasn't . . .' Eve began tremulously.

The tall, dark man smiled gently. 'I think it is fair to say that your husband perished in unfortunate circumstances, an accident perhaps, a fall from the ship – and we can find no evidence at all to suggest that his life was taken.'

Charlie felt Eve slump back beside him. She gave a tight sob, dropping her head forward. He needed more than anything to comfort her and was grateful when the detective rose and went out of the room. 'Eve, I'm so dreadfully sorry.' He took her in his arms and held her to him.

'I'd been thinking such terrible things,' she whispered into his shoulder. 'That someone killed him.'

'No, it was an accident, Eve.'

'Do you believe that?' She looked up into his face and he brushed a tear from her cheek with his thumb.

He nodded and, kissing the damp spot, he whispered, 'Raj was a good man, a fine man. I believe what the detective says. And you must too.'

He felt a little shudder go through him as he held her. In the silence of Joseph's front room, he came closer to praying than he had been in a long time. He asked that now Raj Kumar's soul could rest in peace. And that when all this was over, he and the woman he held against his heart could make a future together.

Chapter Twenty-Six

It was Sunday 14th April 1929 and Eve sat alone on one of the two wooden chairs propped side by side in the backyard of number three Isle Street. Her face was lifted to the pale sunshine and her feet were tucked neatly at the base of the newly repaired wall that Charlie had just completed whilst waiting for Samuel and Albert to return from Mass.

The wall now stood a good four feet high and had returned a pleasant intimacy to the cottage that had been missing ever since the Great Flood of last year.

Not that there had been much peace here a few moments ago, Eve reflected, for as Charlie had tapped the last brick into place with his trowel, the boys had returned from St Saviour's with only one thing on their mind: to pack their shorts, tops, long socks and boots into their shoe bags for the afternoon match. It was a friendly between the Millwall Under Elevens and Cubitt Town's Primaries. Samuel and Albert were members of the first team and this was to be their third outing since January. Charlie was their coach and trainer and had spent every spare moment with his new protégés.

A smile touched Eve's lips as she thought of her sons' noisy, exuberant delight, equalled only by Charlie's own unstoppable energy. In a whirlwind of enthusiasm they had left to conquer the world. Well, at least a small playing field of it, Eve thought fondly.

How fortunate they were to have Charlie for a friend. And not just a friend – Eve knew that Charlie meant more to them all than this. But even though the events of the last year had meant that now she could start a new life, still she was reluctant to commit herself.

The letter in Eve's hand fluttered gently. She gazed down at the single sheet that had never been very far from her person since that day in January. It was Joseph's own personal goodbye and she had never tired of reading it.

Eve, forgive this old man for leaving without a farewell. But I am ailing now and it will not be long before my time on this earth is complete. This country has a special place in my affections but now I return to join Gilda and those loved ones who sleep on Russian soil. I leave you a parting gift. The top of the samovar was given to me by my visitors and now I give it to you, my dear. Redeem its value and it will provide a generous sum for your future. *Shalom*!
Your grateful friend and neighbour,
Joseph

Just then Eve heard Joan and Peg's voices. As usual they were enjoying a disagreement, shouting above the clatter of pots and pans. Dinner was being prepared in the kitchen, ready for Charlie and the boys when they returned home. As Eve listened, her mind went back to the day that had changed her life. When Alfred Rattigan had followed her to Joseph's cottage and she had stared into the eyes of a killer. Her hand went up to her throat automatically and she felt a chill despite the warm sun. If the samovar hadn't been on the dresser, if she hadn't managed to defend herself . . .

Eve shuddered, trying to put the memory behind her. Rattigan was in custody awaiting trial for the heinous crimes he had committed against the unsuspecting lascars of London's docklands. Detective Inspector Fleet had assured them that Rattigan would never see the light of day again. But still Eve shivered at the memories.

Folding the letter, Eve tucked it into her pocket and turned her thoughts towards all the good that had come out of that day. She had discovered the note from Joseph, and though she missed him dearly, she understood his decision to return to Russia and die on his native soil. But her shock had been great at his parting gift. The heavy metal top of the samovar that looked like brass, was in fact, gold.

''Ere, gel, look at this!' Peg came running from the kitchen, followed closely by Joan. The two women were dressed in aprons and turbans and a lighted roll-up hung from the corner of Peg's mouth.

Eve sat up. 'What is it?'

Peg pushed a newspaper into her hands. 'It's Friday's rag. Old Reg Barnes at the market wrapped the beef up in it. Look!'

Eve frowned at the crumpled newspaper.

'It's about Harold!' exclaimed Joan, jabbing it with her finger. 'See, it's my old man!'

The three women stared at the bloodstained sheet that Eve held out. 'Charged with lascivious behaviour—' Eve began, to be stopped mid-sentence by Joan.

'What's las . . . las . . .'

'It's being a dirty old man, that's what!' chuckled Peg, pulling the paper close. 'He got caught with his trousers down, up Aldgate, in one of them dock dollies' gaffs. See? It says he was in . . . im . . . impor—'

'Importuning,' read Eve. 'That means it was more than once.'

'The dirty old sod!'

'I always knew it,' cackled Peg, sucking hard on her roll-up. 'And to think me own sister believed I was lying when I tried to warn her!'

Joan put her hands on her hips. 'Don't start all that again.'

'It says here that Harold Slygo is of no fixed abode,' read Eve slowly. 'So he ain't at Bambury Buildings any more!'

'He must've been kicked out.' Joan gave a little sob. 'All me lovely stuff was there an' all.'

'It wasn't your lovely stuff,' pointed out Peg sharply. 'It was your mother-in-law's.'

'Same thing, as it was me that polished it.'

Peg almost choked on her cigarette. 'You never done a day's polishing in yer life, you lazy cow!'

Eve put the paper down. 'Shush, you two. Just think, Joan, Harold didn't get off scot free after all.'

Joan smiled, nodding in satisfaction as she tucked a wisp of grey hair into her turban.

Peg sat down on the wooden chair beside Eve. She took the newspaper and folded it in two. 'Well, ladies, I reckon we'll keep this as a souvenir.'

'Could frame it even.' Joan folded her arms over her chest and looked slyly at her sister. 'It'd be nice to raise a glass to British justice.'

Peg and Eve looked up quickly. 'British justice me foot,' muttered Peg. 'You ain't going on the juice again, Joan. Not in this house you ain't.'

'Didn't say I was, did I?'

'Well, go and make a cuppa, then. And bring out me baccy when you come.'

'The trouble with you, Peg,' muttered Joan as she turned and walked back to the kitchen, 'is that you don't know 'ow to enjoy yerself.'

Eve and Peg laughed softly as they glanced at each other. Then Peg put her hand on Eve's wrist. 'You all right, gel?'

'Yes, thanks.'

'Queer the way life turns out, ain't it? It was only fifteen months ago that this backyard was a lake.'

'And all the lavs overflowed.' They laughed together.

Peg sighed. 'Then this 'andsome young copper comes along and rescues us . . .'

Eve nodded slowly. 'And who would have believed what happened after that?'

Peg glanced at Eve. 'Has he popped the question yet?'

Eve laughed. 'Peg, I ain't getting married.'

'But you're selling yer flowers in his shop!'

'That's a business arrangement between me and Mr Merritt. It ain't nothing to do with Charlie and me.'

Peg spluttered disbelievingly. 'When you're rich you won't wanna live in Isle Street.'

Eve smiled affectionately. 'I'll never be rich, Peg, but I'd like to think we'll be comfortable. Nothing changes the fact that you and Joan and Jimmy are the closest to family that me and the boys will ever have.'

'Yeah, we'll always be that, Eve. But times change. You've got Samuel and Albert to think of. They need a bit of space like what the Merritts have got at the bakery.'

'Don't forget I've changed the name now,' Eve gently reminded her friend, 'to Eve's Flowers.'

'I know, ducks. And I'm proud of you. As Sarah would be proud of her daughter – and yer dad too.'

'I wish they were alive to see it. Never thought I'd own a shop, Peg. I always thought it was me destiny to sell on the streets. But to tell you the truth I knew in my heart it wasn't enough for the boys. I couldn't admit that Sister Superior might be right, that my sons deserved something better.'

'Don't you take no notice of her,' spluttered Peg, almost choking on her words. 'You've done a fine job with your lads. They'll grow up to appreciate what you've taught them, more than all that chanting and praying will do. They've learned to stand on their own feet and use their brains. In a few years' time they'll be 'elping you or maybe they'll be pushing pens in an office, or even bashing a ball round on a football pitch. But I can tell you this, whatever they do, they'll be successful at it, just like their mum.'

Eve put her arms around Peg and hugged her. 'I feel so lucky.'

'Yer, we all need a bit of luck in life.'

'If it hadn't been for that old oven packing up and Mr Merritt wanting to sell and me being able to buy the lease on the shop with Joseph's gift . . . then I s'pose I'd still be selling from me pitch.'

'As I said, times change. And you come a long way gel, since Rattigan.'

Eve shivered at the mention of his name. 'Peg?'

'Yes, ducks?'

'Charlie is a good man don't you think?'

'He's a good'un all right.'

'I never said, but I saw him once, in a kind of vision. Like I was standing outside of meself, just watching.

He saved me life, Peg, and it's something I'll never forget.'

'A vision you say?' Peg coughed and slapped her chest with her hand. 'You sure you're feeling all right?'

Eve laughed. 'I know it sounds daft.'

'So what's stopping you from getting hitched? You'd have a nice place to live above the bakery. It'd do fine for a family. Them nuns at St Saviour's would soon change their tune if they knew you was living in such a posh place.'

Eve smiled wistfully. 'Nowhere could ever be like Isle Street. I can still see Raj walking down the hill, see his long legs in them cotton trousers, see the smile on his face when he saw us . . .'

'Ducks, I don't like all this talk about visions and . . . and ghosts. It ain't healthy. You're young yet, you ain't supposed to cling to the past.'

'Is that what I'm doing?'

The two women looked at each other. Peg gave a sigh and nodded. 'You'll work it out, wait and see.'

Eve looked around her and all that comprised her life. Thanks to Joseph's gift, which she fully intended to redeem from 'Uncle' when she made enough profit at the shop, her life had taken on a new meaning. She hoped that her sons could learn a decent trade and perhaps Peg was right when she said whatever they did they would be successful.

Eve thought with gratitude of Mr Merritt's shop that was now hers, where she had begun to build up a thriving business. There was nothing she enjoyed more than opening the door in the morning and planning the array of flowers that would soon fill it. Her customers had followed her from the streets and brought new interest. The local traders elbowed each other for her stock. Queenie was sending down Archie each morning on a regular basis and sometimes even twice. When Eve turned the sign to 'Closed', the shop still smelt sweetly of her distinctive blooms.

The arrangement had been satisfactory to everyone. Charlie and his brothers had been relieved to see their parents retire. George and Joe had even helped Charlie to redecorate the shop and Dulcie, Edwin, Pam and Eileen, with the children and baby Dulcie, had often come down from the upper rooms to admire the blaze of glorious colours that now replaced the floury shelves of the bakery.

Eve sighed softly, bringing her thoughts back to number three Isle Street. She owed Charlie so much. She was grateful to him. But was Peg right? Did a small corner inside her still belong to Raj? Was it fair to deny Charlie all of her heart?

'Oh, Raj,' she sighed, 'help me, tell me what to do!'

Eve breathed in the soft April sunshine as her eyes fell on the muddy brown soil at the end of the yard by the dock wall. It was all that remained of her patch of cress. It was cracked and parched from the winter's cold, but today there was something . . . a sparkle . . . a glint . . . a thread of moisture.

She stood up and went over. At her feet, a bubble of water escaped the ground. Eve bent down. Stroking her fingers in the cold, clear water, she saw a green shoot.

Her breath stopped. The stream had started again. And in its thrust one stout little emerald treasure grew.

A tear of joy slipped down her cheek. Was this her answer from Raj? Like the cress, her first love had slipped away but was not forgotten. Was a new love now free to grow?

Epilogue

Tuesday 9th July 1929

Charlie gazed down on the narrow street below and his heart gave a small twist. This was it, then, the day when his parents would go to live with Joe and Pam in Blackheath. The plan had been mooted last year when the old man had looked so tired and caught that chill. But until the stroke two months ago, when he'd lost his speech and movement in one arm, Joe and Pam's suggestion hadn't really been taken seriously. But his brother had a big, rambling house and Pam was eager to have her in-laws safe with the family. And as in-laws went, Charlie reflected proudly, his mum and dad were just about the best. They adored their grandchildren especially the star of the show, little Dulcie.

He frowned as he saw the two strong figures of George and Joe lift the big couch into the removals van. This was the last real piece of furniture to be loaded before the journey to the auction house. There were just a few bits and pieces remaining, like his mother's sewing box and his father's leather bag crammed with his books. Although Charlie had insisted they could leave all their furniture since it wouldn't be required by Pam and Joe who had a well-furnished home, they had refused, quietly maintaining that much of what they had kept over the years was purely sentimental value. The only things remaining were the beds and wardrobes, and the big kitchen table and chairs. The rooms now looked spacious, freed of their clutter, but he was missing the warmth and untidiness that had characterized his childhood.

With their sleeves rolled up and their arm muscles bulging, Joe and George made his watching parents look suddenly frail. This move certainly wasn't before time. With Joseph's gift, Eve had bought the lease of the shop. His parents had no money worries now, and there was no threat in a future living in comfort and security with their son and his wife.

A smile slowly formed on Charlie's lips as he watched a trim figure join his parents. To him, Eve was everything he admired in a woman and more. Her fierce independence was what had first attracted him, but now it also alarmed him. Would she ever consent to be his wife?

His eyes lingered on her figure: her straight back and the intimate tilt of her dark head that she always gave when close to his mother. They had become firm friends and Charlie knew that Dulcie's earnest wish was to have Eve for a daughter-in-law. But even as Charlie watched

Eve lay the bouquet of red roses in his mother's arms, he knew in his heart that the woman he loved was still out of reach.

Charlie dug his hands in his pockets and looked around him. He'd be rattling around in this place for months to come, no doubt. But he had several ideas; redecoration for a start, doing away with the old Victorian embellishments. He wanted to shed light into the rooms, to lift their spirits, but he was no interior decorator.

Charlie turned away from the window and made his way towards the bedroom he had occupied since infancy. As he walked in he smelt the nostalgia of his youth, this place where he'd forged his dreams and aspirations. His books and magazines were lined on the shelves, each one containing the adventures and thrills that, as a boy, he believed really could happen. Beside these was a photo of him and Robbie as police recruits. He hadn't been able to put away the picture, even though Robbie had disappeared to the other side of the world. He had been a friend, a sharer in his dreams for a while, but for Robbie the dream had turned sour. Detective Inspector Fleet had told him that Robbie had been fortunate to escape an investigation. And Charlie had kept all he knew to himself. For wasn't the old saying, 'But for the grace of God and there go I'?

He might well have gone the same way if he hadn't met Eve. Or would he? Charlie wondered as he stared again into Robbie's smiling face. Was his own character solid enough to have withstood the temptations that Robbie had introduced him to? He hoped so. He still had ideals, something that Robbie had grown to scorn. For if a man had no ideals in life, what then?

A pair of his old football boots stood on the shelf below, pristine clean now, though the leather was cracked and the laces cut down. A team photograph stood beside it, this time of sepia faces of eleven-year-old boys smiling in their striped jerseys, arms folded over proud chests and the captain, himself, carrying the cup. He wasn't much older than Samuel and Albert then. Next season, they too would stand in front of the camera. He had great hopes for his Millwall Under Elevens . . .

Suddenly Charlie's eye caught the flash of polished buttons and he turned to stare at the navy blue driver's uniform that he had collected from the Yard last night.

He'd still not absorbed the fact that his six months' driving training at Central CID was now over. It was even more of a mystery to Charlie that the whole thing had started from the time Moody had suspended him and drawn Fleet's interest. Charlie felt his cheeks flush with pride as he recalled their interview at the Yard.

'How would you like to join us?' Fleet had asked him as they sat in the detective's small office. 'We need good men like you to serve with the Squad.'

'But sir, I'm suspended!'

'We've taken care of all that,' replied Fleet, waving aside the issue. 'Sergeant Moody has been informed of your transfer to headquarters. That is, of course, if you're up for the job, Charlie.'

Charlie had stared in bewilderment as Fleet had continued.

'You have the makings of a damn good Flying Squad detective. You followed your instincts in the Kumar case, determinedly pursued your quarry and collected information. And most importantly, Charlie, you drive and drive amazingly well. Speed is of the essence in the prevention of armed robbery and related professional crime.'

Charlie had been so shocked by this, that Fleet had taken his silence for reluctance. A grin had come on the detective's face as he added in a conspiratorial tone, 'And I can let you into a little secret. This year the Squad is to be allowed forty handpicked officers in total, of which you will be one. We shall be known as C1 Branch. This is a remarkable achievement in a short time since it was only a decade ago that we started off with Detective Chief Inspector Wensley's twelve inexperienced recruits.'

It was then, Charlie reflected as his heart leapt yet again at the memory of the conversation, that all his dreams of adventure and honour had been fulfilled. Everything he had ever imagined and desired. All brought about by a twist of fate: the Great Flood and his rescue of a woman he was to fall deeply in love with and their efforts to seek the truth of the past.

As he looked at the uniform, he knew that he was

the luckiest man in the world. Yet, without Eve and the boys in his life, what would this mean to him?

Just then, a hand touched his shoulder. He turned, slightly startled as he came swiftly out of his thoughts.

'Charlie, your parents are just leaving.'

He smiled, his heart doing yet another flip at the beauty of this woman. Her deep brown hair swept up behind her head in a style that added elegance rather than age to her years. The soft grey business suit that had replaced the shawl and traditional dress of the street flower-seller. Her startling amber eyes, as they smiled up at him.

'I only wish I had a motor to drive them over to Blackheath in,' he complained. 'If I hadn't wrecked the van . . .'

'You'll get another one soon.' She took his face in her hands. 'Charlie, I'm so proud of you. Detective Constable Merritt of the Flying Squad.'

He laughed in embarrassment. 'Not a detective yet. It's only an honorary title. I've a long way to go before I'm plain clothes.'

'Honorary or not, you're our hero.'

'Eve, perhaps this isn't the right time to ask—'

'Charlie, let's go down and say goodbye.' She looked up into his eyes and just at that very moment when he felt that there would never ever be the right time to tell her how much he loved her and just how much he wanted to take care of her and the boys, she drew his head down and placed her mouth to his. He held her so tightly against him that he felt he might break every bone in her body. And then, as the passion coursed through him and his heart melted, she breathed soft words in his ear.

'And then I'm closing the shop for an hour. After all,' she murmured, raising her mouth to his again, 'I'm a shopkeeper now and I've got to take me perks where I can find them.'

At this they began to laugh, laugh so desperately and deliciously that Charlie knew beyond a shadow of doubt that he would always have this woman beside him as they stepped into their long-dreamed of future.

**POCKET
BOOKS**

Don't miss Carol Rivers'
other gripping sagas, all set in
London's East End.

These **Pocket Books** titles are available from
your local bookshop or can be ordered direct
from the publisher.